PENGUIN TWENTIETH-CENTURY CLASSICS

MITTEE

Daphne Rooke was born in Boksburg, Transvaal, of an English father and Afrikaans mother. Her grandfather was Siegfried Maré, founder of Pietersburg, and her uncle was Leon Maré, Afrikaans short story writer. Her mother was a writer and journalist, and 'a marvellous storyteller'. Her father died during the First World War, and Daphne Rooke grew up in Durban and Zululand.

During the 1930s she began work on a novel about Zululand but it was not until 1946 that it was published under the title of *A Grove of Fever Trees*. She married an Australian, Irvin Rooke, and lived in Australia, visiting New Zealand and India after the Second World War. In the 1950s she returned to South Africa after writing *Mittee*, which became a bestseller. Some years and several novels later, she returned to Australia where she lived for many years, continuing to write on turbulent South African themes. She now lives with her daughter and grandchildren in Britain.

MITTEE

DAPHNE ROOKE

AFTERWORD BY J. M. COETZEE

PENGUIN BOOKS

To my Mother

PENGUIN BOOKS

Published by the Penguin Group
Penguin Books Ltd, 27 Wrights Lane, London W8 5TZ, England
Penguin Books USA Inc., 375 Hudson Street, New York, New York 10014, USA
Penguin Books Australia Ltd, Ringwood, Victoria, Australia
Penguin Books Canada Ltd, 2801 John Street, Markham, Ontario, Canada L3R 1B4
Penguin Books (NZ) Ltd, 182–190 Wairau Road, Auckland 10, New Zealand

Penguin Books Ltd, Registered Offices: Harmondsworth, Middlesex, England

First published by Victor Gollancz Ltd. 1951
Published in paperback by Chameleon Press, South Africa 1987
Published in Penguin Books 1991
1 3 5 7 9 10 8 6 4 2

Printed in England by Clays Ltd, St Ives plc
Set in 10/10½ Monophoto Bembo

CONTENTS

CHAPTER I

We are happy in our hut on the mountaintop for here we call no man Baas and Fanie hunts with a rifle like a white man. When he needs cartridges he goes to the trader in the valley, who, Outlander and robber that he is, will deal with him secretly. Always Fanie brings something back for me; print for a dress or some wool to crochet into quilts for the winter; or a new kettle. We have cattle and chickens and a dog.

But sometimes when we can see the gorge and the cross on a clear day we remember those we loved when we were young.

Often Mittee called me Sister or Dear Selina when we were alone. She was a sparkling girl, perhaps too fine in build for the taste of some; but so graceful as to be like manna in the desert to the young men of the Wolkbergen, for their mothers and aunties and grandmas were either fat or shrivelled up. It was seldom that you saw a young girl there because so many men wanted wives that the girls were married off as soon as decency permitted.

We lived then in another part of the Wolkbergen, to the south where the mountains are less forbidding. Our home was really near Plessisburg but Mittee had come to that isolated place to teach. She found it dull there but she did not complain because she thought she was growing rich with the ivory and skins the farmers paid her for teaching their children. Even when she was in church listening to the minister's prayers, she told me, she dreamed of the beautiful house in which we should live one day and of the fine clothes we should wear. I was to have new dresses of my own and not her cast-off clothing; as well as a dozen aprons and doeks, some of these to be silk and the aprons all to have an edging of lace. 'Just imagine the pleasure of tying a silk doek round your head,' Mittee would say. As it was, she contented herself with print dresses for the most part, though she always put an extra ruffle round the neck or puffed the sleeves full so that she looked different from the other girls; while I patched up the old things that she gave me and many a Jacob's coat I wore, all brilliant with many colours.

We had been on the Wolkbergen for two years, travelling from farm to farm, sometimes staying two months, sometimes three or four. The last farm where Mittee taught was the Coesters' and here we were happier than anywhere else for Mittee had a room to herself, whereas at the other farms she had had to share, at times with as many as six children. There was no furniture in the room except a big bed, a chair and boxes covered with faded print, but everything was spotless.

We sat there during the hot afternoons when school was over. Mittee would sit in the chair, with her arms behind her head, the sleeve of her dress falling back to show the white and delicate skin that sun had never touched. She told me about the wonders she had read of in books and what the great world beyond the Transvaal was like. Sometimes we would crochet, trying to copy Mrs Coester's wonderful patterns, but neither of us was good at crochet work then and we made up some strange patterns, believe me. Our work always seemed to get grubby so that we were ashamed to show it even when the patterns worked out right. Often Mittee reckoned up how much money she would have when we returned to Plessisburg; perhaps with the ivory and skins, four hundred pounds. Mittee's grandfather had left her a farm outside Plessisburg and the land was worked by Gouws and his sons, bywoners and distant relatives of Grandpa Van Brandenberg. Poor Gouws, he was a hard-working man but he had been a bywoner all his life because he was so unlucky in everything that he did. Mittee drew an income from the farm as well as from her teaching. She counted every penny avariciously for she had made a wonderful plan to visit Pretoria before she married Paul and there buy a trousseau that would make the girls of Plessisburg faint with envy. I was to go with her and so often did we talk about it that it seemed we had already made the journey. We would go to Pretoria in the New Year because she could not put Paul off much longer. He had been waiting for her for three years.

Christmas was drawing near and we would be leaving the Wolkbergen for good. Mittee had brought her own waggons with her and these stood ready loaded by the end of November. That was the year 1890. I remember because Mittee gave me a Bible when I had learned to read properly and she wrote the date in it. I still have it, with Mittee's writing on the front page, 'To a most excellent pupil from her teacher', and the date. The airs she put on.

The weather was sultry on the afternoon before we started for Plessisburg. We were doing nothing because the heavy air made even of talking a slow affair and there was no hope of crocheting with our hands so sweaty. Mittee was in a bad temper because she had quarrelled with Mrs Coester. She detested Mrs Coester's youngest son Kosie, a spoilt and lazy child, but she had hidden her feelings right up to this last day on account of staying in the woman's house. Kosie was a fat child who wore trousers that had grown too small for his brother. They were always too long for him, revealing only an inch of flesh above his veldschoens. It was when he recited that Mittee really grew angry with him. Not only did he say the wrong words, but he bent his knees outwards in time to the verse, his arms hanging slack at his sides.

'Sheep, my little sheep . . .' he had begun but Mittee let him get no further.

'How many times have I told you not to bend your knees like that and still you do it,' she shouted, and seizing him by the shoulders shook him until his teeth rattled.

Poor Kosie screamed from astonishment and Mrs Coester, hearing his noise, rushed into the schoolroom.

'What was Kosie doing?' she asked in anguish at seeing her youngest and best-loved attacked.

Mittee could not explain. You cannot say to a loving mother that a fat boy in trousers too long for him is a sight to make you lose control of yourself; that he was innocently reciting 'Sheep, my little sheep' when you fell upon him. Instead she burst into tears of temper and shut up the school. Sitting in her room, she was bored and I did not dare to say boo or baa for fear she should take it out on me.

When the sun grew milder, she tied on her bonnet and we went into the yard. The Coester boys were at the end of the yard, getting into practice for the sports on Dingaan's Day, some wrestling and others throwing skeis. The Coesters used the skeis from the oxen's yokes as the Voortrekkers had done when they played jukskei, but in Plessisburg some of the men had special skeis which they kept for the game, bars of polished teak that gave elegance to their throwing.

'Come and judge who is best, Mittee,' one of the boys called out, but she turned her nose up at him.

She held out a crust of bread that she had saved for the little blue monkey that was chained to a pole, with a strip of cowhide about his middle. The monkey slid down the pole and snatched the bread from her fingers. Far from being grateful, he pulled a face at her, threatening her with his jerking body. Then he climbed to his house at the top of the pole and sat on the platform, turning his small, tragic face to the mountains. He flung the bread to the ground to show his contempt for us, lifted his arm and scratched underneath it. Whatever it was that he found there, he ate it. All the while he darted sidelong glances at us but try as you would you could not catch his eye for a second.

Jacob Coester, who fancied Mittee, left his brothers and stood close to her. From his huge body came such a smell of sweat, brought out by the wrestling, that Mittee had to move away from him. It was of no use. He edged up to her again.

'Give us a little kiss, Mit.'

He was only teasing but Mittee was in no mood for such nonsense. Seeing the temper flare into her face, I nudged her as a warning not to swear at him. She did not swear, but when he put his arm about her she shook her head and body violently like a dog shedding water from his coat; and then kicked Jacob in the shin.

He laughed with the roar of a bull. 'I'll show you for that.'

Three of his brothers came to watch the fun and to hold Mittee while he climbed up after the monkey. This was an old game of the Coester boys with Mittee, usually on Sunday afternoons when the place was devoutly quiet and she dared make no noise. They forced her to sit on a log and then put the monkey on her lap. She sat still for he was a spiteful thing when he became excited and the boys, breathing hard with the restraint that they put on their laughter, kissed her until her pale face became red and the unwilling dimples broke her smooth cheeks.

'Look out, here's Ma,' cried Jacob suddenly.

He grabbed the monkey from Mittee, snapping its chain to the cowhide. Mrs Coester, who stood in the doorway with her hands on her hips, shouted at them, 'I'll tell your father on you. Teasing the girl's life out of her. Go and find the girls, Mittee. They're up at the waterfall. It's cool there.'

Mittee was relieved to find Mrs Coester friendly again and waved enthusiastically. 'I'm going to, Auntie. I was just watching the monkey for a few minutes when the boys started on me.'

'I'll tell their father,' Mrs Coester promised, 'but what's the use? Coester is a tease himself and the apple doesn't fall far from the tree.'

Mittee flounced past the sheepish boys and took the narrow path that led to the waterfall. A mischievous Kaffir had tied the grass in a loop across the path in the hope of tripping somebody up and Mittee, gathering her skirts, bounded over it with the agility of a little duiker. We climbed up to the grassy ledge and sat beside Rita and Lisbet, who were playing fivestones and arguing over the game with the bitter intensity that only young girls can bring to a matter of small importance. Mittee began to weave a chain from the long grass that grew fatly in the loam edging the pool, while I went to wash my hands under the little waterfall that enchanted this place. It was a ghostly waterfall that floated over a high krantz, its force spent before it swirled into the mossy pool and ran shining through a crevice to fall like vapour over the rocks far below.

Mittee sang:

Tonight the girls are sowing corn,
sowing corn, sowing corn,
Tonight the girls are sowing corn . . .

'Harmonize, Selina.'

I joined my shrill voice to hers:

My beloved hangs on the bush,
My beloved hangs on the bush,
My beloved hangs on the bitter berry-bush.

We sang sadly, though we did not know what sadness was. The sun went down and shadows hung on the mountain, so thick you felt you could cut a dress from them. Mittee went back to the house with the girls but I stayed beside the waterfall, for always this is the precious time for me when the horizon shines like water and the night wind goes through the grass. Then, grand prayers flowed through my soul and God bent towards me.

That evening I was sorry I had stayed alone for when the others had gone a few minutes I felt hands pressed over my eyes. A voice that I knew only too well said, 'Guess who?'

'Jansie. And let me go because my nonnie needs me.'

He slid his hands from my eyes to my breasts. I pushed him away and sprang up to face him. He was a big coloured man with a face marked by smallpox; a man whose body and limbs were covered with thick, coarse hair. On his chest the hair was as close as a mat and he was so proud of it that he often laid my cheek against it or stroked it himself. His features were coarse and I hated him though I could not always keep away from him because he was the only coloured man in the district without a wife.

He smiled at me. When he smiled I was inclined to forget how cruel he was when he got a chance.

'When everybody is in bed tonight, creep away here, Selina. I'll wait for you.'

'No.'

'There will be more for you if you lie by me than if you sleep on the floor next to your nonnie's bed all night,' he taunted.

'Hi. Fancy talking to a decent girl like that. I'm going now or else I'll get into trouble from my nonnie.'

He let me go but he followed just behind me, every now and again pulling one of my curls out straight or biting my neck. Every time he touched me he hurt me, even when he was trying to be playful.

The candles were already lit and Mrs Coester was calling the people to the evening meal. It was the rule that the servants stand at the door when grace was said. I always liked prayers at the Coesters' house, especially the grace when Coester tenderly took his wife's hand and prayed loudly for blessing on the food. The only unpleasant part was having to stand next to Jansie who constantly nudged me though his face wore the docile expression with which he masked his real nature from the white people.

When the prayers were over, Jansie and I took our plates from the kitchen table. Mrs Coester always gave us the same food as her family ate because we were not Kaffirs and this was more than you got in some of the other houses where they made no difference between black and coloured. We ate our food outside, sitting on a bench, and I always shared mine with Jansie's hunting dog. He purposely kept it half starved so that it would be keen. Jansie was angry with the dog that evening because it had made off with a guinea fowl that he had brought down with his sling. Greedy Jansie. He tried to snatch for himself the pieces of meat that I gave to the dog. He was a big animal called Wagter, all black except for a white patch over his eyes that gave him a comical and lovable look. Such eyes he had. When you looked into them it seemed that here was an imprisoned soul. He enjoyed the pieces of meat from my hand though he was not as hungry as usual because of the guinea fowl.

'He deserves to die,' said Jansie. 'I would have given you a nice picnic tonight down by the stream if he hadn't stolen my guinea fowl.'

'Ag, what can you expect when the thing's always half dead with hunger.'

As soon as I had washed the plates and put them away, Jansie grabbed my arm, pulling me out of the kitchen.

'Come for a little walk down to the stream,' he whispered. 'I won't hurt you, I promise you.'

'Let go. I'm quite anxious to come for a walk in the cool. As long as we are away only for half an hour or so.'

Even then he held my arm, afraid that I would give him the slip. The dog followed us. He was big enough to walk with his head under my hand. When I stopped to pat him and rub his ears, Jansie jerked me.

'Leave the dog alone. You're spoiling him.'

Still I did not take warning. Sitting on the grass beside Jansie, I nursed the dog's head in my arms and spoke to him in baby-talk.

Jansie said, 'I think you would rather have that dog than me, you stupid thing.'

I thought he was joking. 'Of course. But Wagter really is a good dog, Jansie. So tame with those he knows but let a stranger set foot on the yard . . .'

'He's a thief,' shouted Jansie.

He kicked the dog flying. It bared its teeth as it lay flattened in the grass and oh, how I wished it would bite Jansie. I would sit there no longer with him. Before he could stop me I had jumped up and was running across the veld back to the house. As I ran I heard him laugh. Then the dog yelped. I ran back to the stream.

Jansie was killing Wagter. I hate to think even now of Jansie's strong legs from which the muscles sprang when he jumped as though they had a separate life of their own. He beat the dog with a stick and then he jumped on it until it was dead. I tried to stop him but I might as well have faced a lion. He grabbed me by the throat and I thought he was going to kill me too.

His chest was rising and falling with the harsh gusts of his breath. 'If you tell anyone I'll do the same to you. The very same thing.'

'Hi. Oh God, let me go.'

'If anybody finds out, I'll jump on you until you're pulp. It was your fault for teasing me.'

'Heavenly Father, deliver me, save me.'

'He won't save you from me if you tell. I'll leave you on the mountainside for the vultures to feed on.'

'Ag, no.'

Now his voice became soft, more horrible than his snarl. 'But if you don't tell, I won't hurt you.'

'I won't tell, Jansie, I won't tell.'

He let me go then. I ran back to the house by the shortest way, through the long grass and not caring whether I trod on a snake, for to be bitten by a mamba would be better than to be grabbed by Jansie and stamped to death. I looked back, to see him hump the dog across his shoulders and spring across the stream on his way to the top of the mountain, there to leave it for the vultures to pick. One word wrong from me and I would be lying next to the dog, a skeleton not much bigger than his.

Mrs Coester was in her kitchen, bustling about in search of any speck of dirt that the Kaffir girl might have left, and at the sight of me rushing in from the darkness she stepped back, spilling candle fat in a shimmering streak down her skirt.

'Heaven, Selina, you gave me a fright. What's the matter? Have you seen a ghost or what?'

'Jansie,' I sobbed. 'It was Jansie.'

I would have told her there and then but Kosie called out to her and she hurried from the kitchen, throwing advice to me over her broad shoulder.

'Don't be upset by the boys. All girls have to put up with it, Selina, probably he meant no harm. I'll get the baas to speak to him in the morning, all the same.'

'No, please, missis, don't say anything,' I implored, running into the passage after her. Already I saw Jansie dragging me to a lonely spot and jumping, jumping.

Mrs Coester said impatiently, 'Girls and their silly ways. It makes no difference what the colour, they go into hysterics for nothing. The only thing to do is to marry them off and that stops it . . .' Her voice trailed off into a grumbling sound as she went into Kosie's room.

Mittee was already in bed, reading laboriously from an English poetry book. She put her finger between the pages and looked at me sternly for interrupting her. I sank to the floor, shuddering.

'Hi God, Mittee.'

'You're sick, I can see it. I'll give you a dose of leaves to purge you.'

'No. I don't need anything like that. I was going to tell you about something terrible that happened to me tonight.' A low whistle sounded outside. I wrung my hands. 'That's Jansie.'

He had not gone all the way up the mountain but come back quickly to find out if I had told on him. I felt sick now but I did not dare to go outside, with him waiting there like a hyena after a weak calf. I fought against the waves of sickness until Mittee bounded from her bed and pushed my head out of the window. She was just in time.

She gave me water to drink and then a tablespoonful of mixture for the stomach, with a taste so vile that you were blinded after swallowing it. She unrolled my bedding herself; undressed me with the powerful but gentle hands of a born nurse; sponged me with vinegar and water. All the while she nagged about the rubbish she supposed I had eaten.

I thought I would be able to tell her about Jansie the next day when we were travelling. The pace on this first day was leisurely and the waggon was so peaceful that my fears of the night before weakened.

'Mittee, I want to tell you something about Jansie.'

'I know he fancies you, Selina,' she said impatiently. 'He's got round me for a job on the farm, he's not going back to the Wolkbergen after Christmas. Coester talked it over with me this morning before we left . . .'

'Mittee, don't have Jansie on the farm,' I cried, beginning to tremble.

'Heaven, what's the matter with you?'

'Last night he nearly frightened me to death.'

'Well then, I'll tell Coester when we outspan. He'll give him a good hiding and that will teach him a lesson. What did he do, Selina?' She leaned forward, her eyes bright with interest.

I could not tell her. Jansie, as though the devil had warned him that we were talking about him, suddenly appeared behind our waggon. His face and bearing were meek before Mittee but that only made him seem more dangerous to me.

'It was nothing, nonnie,' I said dully.

'Don't think your affairs are important to me, Selina,' said Mittee. 'It would be foolish for me to mix myself up in coloured people's affairs.'

That made me sulky and I answered her Yes and No when she spoke until she gave it up, taking out a book to read. I thought, I won't tell her anything about Jansie and if he cuts her throat it will serve her right for being such a cat.

Mrs Coester, thinking that Mittee must get lonely travelling by herself, had transferred her feather mattress to our waggon. Within an hour she was sound asleep on the mattress, soothed by the unaccustomed quiet.

'My God, how that old woman snores,' Mittee whispered. 'It is because she is so fat.'

'One day you will be old and fat, Mittee, and the dear God will take vengeance on you for using his name in vain,' I said.

'Don't you dare to preach to me, Selina; the very idea. And how many times must I tell you to call me Nonnie Mittee? What will people think of a coloured girl calling me Mittee?'

'If I call you Nonnie anything it will be Nonnie Maria which is your proper baptized name although you are so ashamed of it.'

Colour spread thinly over Mittee's pale face. 'You shall not call me Maria. You cheeky girl, I shall send you away one of these days, straight to Auntie Lena's. And see how you will like living in a house without windows. But I shall not argue with you, Selina, I have to remember my dignity now that we are going back to the town.'

She pushed me with her foot, her shoe grazing my sleeve and shooting away to come to rest on Mrs Coester's bosom. The good lady had taken off her corsets and they lay, neatly rolled up, on top of the tin of rusks. Her breasts, without anything to prop them up, rolled and wobbled so much that in her sleep she folded her arms under them to keep them still. She sat up now, rubbing the spot where Mittee's foot had touched her.

'Heaven, what was that?' she cried, and shook her head to dash away the large beads of sweat that clung to the coarse, pink skin of her temples.

'I'm sorry, Auntie Marta, it was my foot, it flew out in some strange manner from underneath me. I'm very sorry I woke Auntie up.'

'It is dangerous,' grumbled Mrs Coester. 'If a person was to get a knob there . . .'

She folded her arms again and fell almost immediately into a doze. Mittee allowed the twinkle in her eyes to grow into a smile. With every word that she spoke the shadows of dimples came into her cheeks but when she smiled they became two little hollows into which you could have poured water. Man, when Mittee smiled. Somehow she seemed to lift your heart up and up, like Wimpie Maritz did when he played folk tunes on his violin; not the dances, they made your body tingle and your feet tap as if you wanted to offer yourself to a man. The folk tunes that he played were gay but they held sadness, too, like the veld does just as that last light fades away and listening, you became all spirit and the wickedness of the body left you.

To keep Mittee smiling, I said, 'Nonnie, tell me about that time you went to the Governor's ball. I've forgotten.'

'Would you really like to hear, Selina?' She put her arm across my shoulders. 'Well, I suppose you would, it must seem wonderful to a girl like you who has never been out of the Transvaal. When I am married, Selina, and I travel to the Cape, I shall take you with me and your eyes will pop out at the grandness of everything. We Transvaal Boers are very simple, Selina, but in Capetown they do things in style, especially the English. There nearly everybody lives as grandly as the magistrate. In fact, more grandly. The women have at least five summer dresses each, good ones, and my Aunt Margarita had six, and that wasn't her whole wardrobe for she had left some of her dresses at her house in Pretoria. When she took me with her to the Governor's ball, she lent me her canary-coloured satin ball gown.' This was untrue and absurd, for when Mittee was in the Cape, she was no more than fourteen and I do not think that her aunt would have been such a fool as to put her into a ball gown. Really, I do not think that Mittee ever went near the ball, even to watch, but that she heard about it from her guardian and had built up this tale to beguile the hours. 'Naturally, with my dark hair and light skin, the yellow proved a great success and we drove to the ball in a carriage drawn by two beautiful white horses . . .'

'But last time you said it was a scotch-cart.'

'Don't be ridiculous! A scotch-cart! I probably said that to make you understand better. It was a carriage. When we got to the Castle there was a red plush carpet laid out from the carriage step to the very entrance hall and my aunt, who had told me to call her Margarita that evening . . .'

Mittee's hushed voice merged with the shuffle of the oxen's hoofs as they passed over the road with the sound of slippered feet. A jangling chain hit against the pole; a child's threadlike laughter spun through the air.

We had come a hundred miles from the Wolkbergen, at first only the two waggons that belonged to Mittee, this one in which we rode and the other behind stacked high with tusks, karosses and biltong; and accompanied by two of the Coesters' waggons. Now there were twenty waggons strung out along the newly made road that led to Plessisburg, driven by farmers on their way to keep the Christmas festival in the town.

Plessisburg now lay only a day's journey away, less than that really for we would break camp at sun-up the next morning and march through without resting the oxen. Only another hour's travelling and we would outspan for the night. Jansie would come and speak to me.

'. . . and then the Governor came up to me and bowing said, Miss Van Brandenberg, excuse me for this dance . . . Selina, you damned creature, you're not listening to a word I'm saying.'

'Don't swear like that. To think you teach the innocent little children. It's a disgrace and you should be reported to the minister. Anyhow, I don't believe it. I don't believe the Governor asked you to dance or that you wore a yellow dress of your auntie's.'

'I did.'

Mittee's hands flew into my hair. With each tug she brought forth a shrill cry from me. Mrs Coester sat up, rubbing her eyes.

'Mittee Van Brandenberg, let go of that girl. You little cat. Here, come and sit at the back with me, Selina.' She pulled me on to her feather mattress, an unheard-of honour for me but I was smothered in the heat that rose from it and from her body. She panted, 'Merciful Father, when will this journey end? Mittee, where does the sun stand now?'

'It's turned well to the west, it will be outspan in about half an hour, Aunt Marta,' consoled Mittee who now sat up straight with her black-mittened hands folded in her lap.

Mrs Coester groaned. 'Ag, I'll never get to Plessisburg. I'm rubbed raw with chafe from the sweat. Man, it pours off me.' She parted her legs and mumbling, 'Don't look, you two,' tenderly sprinkled cornflour on her thighs and then between her breasts.

Mittee looked directly at me. I tried to avoid her gaze but my neck and jaws ached with the effort of forcing back my laughter. Mittee twiddled her fingers to make me look at her again. This time her lips stretched flatly across her teeth and I fell howling with laughter into the feather mattress.

'Father of Pity,' exhorted Mrs Coester, 'help me with such madness. Get out of this immediately, you pest, I can't stand it any more.'

I crawled to the edge of the waggon and dropped to the road, still shaking with laughter. Mittee sat with her back to me, primness in the set of her shoulders. Hypocrite, I said fiercely, all the laughter gone from me as I plodded through the stinging dust.

It was not long before Coester called 'Outspan!' The voorloper, his black little face anxious because he was new to his job, dashed to the heads of the leading oxen and drew them off into the veld. The pace quickened through the long line of waggons as the cry of 'Outspan, outspan' floated from driver to driver. Kosie, sitting up beside his father, shouted, 'Outspan' and his nurse, who walked beside the waggon, clasped her hands and bent her knees in ecstasy at his cleverness. 'Aaeee,' she screamed.

The thornveld took on a homely air of bustle once the laager was formed. Men went off into the veld with their rifles so that they could shoot before the light faded; women set their servants to making fires, and filling pots and kettles. Young mothers, white and black, suckled their babies; girls, with arms entwined, wandered about in twos and threes while the younger children leapt and yelled, exuberant after the monotony of travelling.

Mittee nodded to me and we went into the veld together, a good distance from the laager. We squatted down, sheltering modestly each behind an ant heap, Mittee singing all the while an English song that she had learned in the Cape. The words sounded strange as though they did not belong to her voice, 'Only a pensy blossom, only a faded flower . . .'

We moved away to other ant heaps where we sat to watch the sunset and Mittee stopped singing while she counted the colours in the brilliant sky. Afterwards she danced a mazurka in the veld, her lips sweetly smiling. 'I am dancing with the Governor,' she said. She tripped over a tuft of grass as she spoke and let herself go, abandoning herself to the earth as though she had meant to fall, childish enough still to be afraid of my laughter.

Her sunbonnet was askew and she undid the strings for the first time that day. Mittee took great care of her fair complexion, so that the skin on her face was almost as white as that of her body, the thick whiteness of velvet. Each night she rubbed her face with mutton-fat and camphor and to lie next to her made me feel sick; yet I dared not leave her and lie under the waggon for fear that a puff-adder might coil up on me for warmth or, worse still, Jansie come near enough to touch me.

'This time tomorrow, Paul and I will be talking,' said Mittee, panting as she whirled. 'I suppose he is looking south even now, thinking to himself, She is coming nearer to me every minute.'

'How vain you are. We'd better go back, it's getting dark. Look out you don't tramp on a snake.'

The smell of grilling meat was on the air and the taint of mealie-meal porridge that had burned the bottom of the pots. We hurried from the silence that crouched on the darkening veld towards the upleaping fires where the people talked and laughed and screamed, blending their voices to the lowing of the kraaled oxen.

Mrs Coester, comfortable now, sat on a kaross, with her sons and daughters grouped about her. She had Mittee's plate of mealie-meal and meat ready for her but I could see that Mittee would not enjoy it for Jacob sat down beside her and, to show his fondness for her, nudged her or put grass down her neck, which was enough to make Mittee choke with fury.

I made off for the Kaffirs' fires to get my share of food, but before I reached them Jansie sprang before me. He caught the flesh over my stomach between his fingers and rolled it as though I had no feeling. 'Loose me,' I hissed, pulling away from him. The stuff of my dress ripped and he laughed with a voice pitched like a mare's whinny. I went close to the fire and stayed there until it was time to go to bed, afraid of him even when there were people nearby.

We saw Plessisburg the next afternoon as the sun turned, a collection of buildings that clung one to the other, on guard against the jealous veld. Such a day that was, a cool day, more silver than gold. There was silver in the clouded sky and I thought, Our Father is far away from us today, He sits up there tender and sad, unwilling to punish us with terrible happenings for our sins.

'Hi, Mittee,' shouted Coester. 'Here comes Du Plessis riding out of Plessisburg to meet you.'

Mittee sat up straight and folded her hands in her lap; but her mouth crept to one side and she sat there not knowing that a deep dimple detracted from her dignity.

'Lean out a bit, Selina, so that he can see where I am,' she said.

I poked my head out. Paul Du Plessis rode a bay gelding, a big horse, and he looked a fine sight as he came through the veld on the side of the road, raising his whip in greeting to the burghers. Each time he raised the whip the horse rose, eyes showing white in panic. Then Paul would master him with a cruel, sure hand, always smiling as though the battle brought him enjoyment.

'Where is he? Is he talking to somebody else?' Mittee asked, peevishly.

'No, he is fighting his horse, it seems a nervous animal.'

'Well, lean further out, I'm sure he can't see you. What's he doing now?'

I did not answer because I was watching Paul as he rode towards us. He was a tall man, over six feet, deep-chested but still delicately built then for he was only twenty-two, slender in hips and wrists. He was dark-haired and his eyes were dark but not with the soft darkness that you see in the eyes of the coloured people; rather it seemed that a lamp had been lit behind them so that they gave fiery warning of his passionate soul. My heart throbbed with the hoof-beats of the horse as he came alongside the waggon.

'Mittee.'

She leaned out and gave her hand to him. 'I'm so glad to see you, Paul.'

Mrs Coester giggled, crawling forward so that she could peer out at Paul.

'What's the matter with you, Paul Du Plessis? Why don't you get off that horse and climb into the waggon and give her a kiss? Heaven, when Coester was courting me . . . Give the girl a kiss, it's what you're wanting to do, isn't it?'

'Oh, Auntie Marta.' Mittee's fist clenched and for an awful moment I thought she was going to hit Mrs Coester.

'Well, now, what about it, Mittee?' Paul cried.

'Ag, don't talk nonsense. This old one here sometimes makes me very tired.'

Mrs Coester protested. 'Mittee, don't talk of your elders in that fashion. After all, it was only said in a joke and what, if I might ask, could be more natural than for a boy to kiss his promised wife? Coester, when a young man . . .'

We then heard a story about the Coesters' courtship to which everybody listened with a respect that restored Mrs Coester to a good humour. When she had finished, Mittee began to talk quickly to Paul, for Mrs Coester, once started, could go on for hours about the events of her placid life.

'What have you been doing while I've been away, Paul?'

'Now, you'd never guess. I went down to Durban. Truly,' as Mittee's eyes widened, 'and there was a boat in from China. I got a piece of silk for a dress for you from the captain . . .'

'Is it yellow?'

'Yes, bright yellow.'

She laughed with pleasure and he bent low to take a kiss from her. It was an awkward kiss but Mrs Coester, at least, was happy.

'Well, that was what should have happened in the first place. It's young people's ways when all is said and done.'

Paul had fast hold of Mittee's hand, jerking her dangerously between the rhythm of his horse and the oxen.

'Mittee, climb up in front of me and I'll gallop you into Plessisburg in style.'

'People would think she was mad,' said Mrs Coester, briskly.

Mittee laughed. 'What would your father say, and the minister?'

They bantered with each other, more at ease after the months of separation, so much in keeping with Mrs Coester's idea of lovers that she settled back in contented silence. Once Paul glanced at me.

'Her skin is a lot darker. She used to be quite fair. Funny how they get darker as they grow up.'

Seeing that I hung my head, Mittee touched me kindly on my knee. 'Selina is nice-looking now, not quite so thin. My grandfather always used to say she was a disgrace to the household, it looked as if we starved her. People do change when they grow up.'

'I suppose we have to call you grown-up now you're nineteen, hey, Mittee?' His eyes were on her lips, on her dainty breasts, on the curve of her thigh.

I looked down at my hands. The tops of my hands were shiny, like silk. I turned them over. The wrists were not brown but yellowish, threaded with violet veins. I was browner than I had been. When we were children, Paul and Mittee and I, we had played together without thinking that their brown skins were sunburned, while the darkness of my skin came from within. We soon learned of the difference. Even in those days I slept on a mat at Mittee's bedside for she was a lonely little girl and fonder of me than of anyone. Grandma Van Brandenberg had been good to me because it was my mother who had saved Mittee when the Kaffirs killed her parents on the Wolkbergen. She hid behind a waterfall with Mittee and me and so we escaped. We both swore that we could remember hiding there but Grandma Van Brandenberg always said, 'Pure nonsense, how could such small children remember anything?' I was three and Mittee not two years old when the burghers brought us sorrowfully to Plessisburg where we had been born.

Looking at my brown hands, I thought of my mother. She was half Shangaan, a woman almost black but in the remote corners of my memory she lived in beauty, mysterious as God. I was seven when she died and Grandma Van Brandenberg slapped me because I screamed; and then gave me some sugared fruit to eat. Mittee took me to the orchard and made me laugh by trying to stand on her head. Grandma Van Brandenberg. Virtue and experience had hewn at her face until it was as forbidding as the stony crags of the Wolkbergen. With the Bible in one hand and a strap in the other, she had guided Mittee and me through our terrified childhood.

We had entered Plessisburg. The people came running to meet their relations and friends as the waggons swung into the square; loud-voiced in their greetings and laughter. My head became dazed with all this excitement after the quiet Wolkbergen and Mittee's face flushed, though she pretended to be calm as if arriving in Plessisburg for Christmas were an everyday occurrence.

The magistrate came forward to greet her. He held out his arms and lifted her from the waggon.

'And how goes it with my little daughter?'

'But well, thank you, Uncle Siegfried. I've had a happy time and I've brought back another load of ivory and skins.'

'How proud it is,' the magistrate laughed.

He was a widower of sixty years, handsomer than Paul, strong as a mountain; with the undimmed, ardent eyes of a boy.

We had still a few miles to travel to the farm but first Mrs Coester must be got out of the waggon. Mittee stood beside the magistrate and it fell to Paul to pull Mrs Coester from the waggon while I pushed her. The important moment was when she sprang to the ground for then her helpers might fly in all directions; but this time we got her upright without any trouble.

Mittee climbed back to her seat. She let her hand fall on Paul's shoulder.

'When are you going to give me the new silk?' she asked.

'I thought you would want to know when we are going to put up the banns.'

Mittee's nose lifted in the air. Paul had spoken without laughing, his unpredictable temper putting a sharp edge to his voice.

CHAPTER II

When Mittee wore the yellow silk dress, she put on such airs that she would not speak to me except to give me orders. As soon as Paul gave the material to her, she cut it out and we sewed on it in a fever until our eyes were red and had to be bathed with cold black tea. There were fifteen frills on the skirt alone and all run by hand. Plessisburg had never seen such a dress but still Mittee was not happy.

I remember her sitting on the edge of the bed one night, carefully folding the new dress. In her calico nightdress and with her hair hanging in plaits on her shoulders, she looked such a wistful child that I said, 'Nonnie, is there anything the matter?'

All she answered was, 'Hurry up and blow out the candle. It's easy enough to waste other people's stuff.'

I unrolled my bedding and undressed in the dark to show her that I had her interests at heart. She lay quiet and I wondered if she thought of ghosts as I did. We were not afraid of Kaffirs for Gouws had his house only a few hundred yards away, and a call would have brought him and his eight sons on the run. But ghosts were another matter, even Gouws would run away from them.

Mittee's voice came low through the darkness, 'Selina, if I tell you something, promise you will never say a word.'

'I promise, Mittee.'

'You'll be struck dead if you do. Selina, Paul had been drinking peach brandy when he came to sit up with me tonight.'

'There's nothing in that, Mittee. All the young men drink a little peach brandy at Christmas time.'

'But if his father knew. That's not all. He put his hand down my dress . . .'

'Hi, Mittee.'

'I kicked him on his ankle and he said he was sorry and I mustn't tell his father.'

'His father would sjambok him.'

She sat up and I looked into the white blur of her face. 'Selina, I don't want to marry Paul. And the banns will go up in the New Year and I've taken that dress from him. I wish I could go somewhere else.'

'Mittee, is there anybody else you fancy?'

'No. But I don't want to get married. I'm afraid.'

'All girls feel like that, Mittee.' Her hand fell over the edge of the bed into mine. The fingers were strong though they were so soft. 'It's Christmas that makes you feel like this, Mittee, and coming back and the new silk dress, it's made you too excited.'

'It isn't that. When he touched my breast tonight, I felt that I hated him and it should have made me want him. It made my flesh creep, probably because of the drink.'

I thought of Jansie. 'I know what you mean. It shouldn't be like that.'

I crept close to her and leaned my head against her hand until she fell asleep.

The next morning she nagged me and cuffed me and made me call her Nonnie Mittee every time I opened my mouth because she had talked about Paul. He was late coming to sit up with her that night. She had put on the silk dress and she sat in the front room waiting for him. When Paul brought a candle to the house, Mrs Gouws was Mittee's chaperone. She was not the sort to chip in on the lovemaking for she was always so worn-out with cooking for her nine menfolk and her useless daughter Aletta that she fell asleep even before Paul came to the house; and slept right through his visit, sometimes long after the candle had gone out.

Mittee came into the kitchen, where I stood grinding coffee beans. 'Selina,' she hissed, 'go to the gate and see if he is coming.'

'But, nonnie, I don't like to go out in the dark.'

'You do what I tell you and stop your insolence. See if he is coming down the road.'

'Ag, nonnie, he'll come just now.'

'Do as I say. Instantly.'

'I thought you said last night you didn't want him.'

She forgot that she was in the yellow silk dress, she forgot the fine airs that went with it. Her hands tore at my hair.

'Wretch. Black devil.' I opened my mouth and let out howl after howl. 'Hold your tongue.' She pulled the harder at my hair.

Mrs Gouws ran in, still tottering with sleep. 'Almighty, what are you doing to the poor creature now? First you pet her, then you torment her. Fatherland, I have never seen anything like it in my life, no never.'

Mittee took me by the shoulders and ran me out of the kitchen. 'Go and sleep outside. Don't you dare come near me again. Ever.' She flung the last word after me like a stone.

'Poor Selina,' said Mrs Gouws. 'She's a good girl. You shouldn't use her so, Mittee.'

Mittee stamped her foot. 'I'm going to bed.'

I walked down to the spring. With my hand I scooped up cool, sweet water and drank my fill. Then I lay down on my back and let my mind wander into those untravelled spaces that lie between the treetops and the stars.

Mrs Gouws called me. 'Selina. My God, now I have to spend the night calling the girl in. Selina.'

'I'm coming, missis.'

Mrs Gouws sighed as I ran into the kitchen. 'Come when you're called, girl. Nonnie Mittee wants you in her room. Now I'm going to my own bed because there will be no sitting up tonight. The dear Heaven knows I'll be glad when there is a wedding in this house.'

Mittee was in bed, sitting up straight and crocheting ferociously. 'I want you to wait on the stoep, Selina, and if Baas Paul should come, tell him that I said he can go to hell.'

'Yes, nonnie.'

She folded up her crochet work, jabbing the needle through the ball of cotton. 'He can go to hell.' On the word Hell, she flung her work across the room and then fell back on her pillows.

'Selina, I'm sorry I pulled your hair, bring your poor Mittee a few drops of Essence of Life in a little water. I feel faint.'

I ran to the medicine chest in the corner of the room and then into the kitchen to fetch the water, all without saying a word. She drank the mixture, swallowing with down-turned lips as the bitterness touched her tongue. Then she patted my hand.

'Pick up my silk dress from the floor, like a good girl, and fold it. And pass me my crochet, I can't sit here doing nothing and I won't sleep. And then go and wait on the stoep and tell him what I told you.'

'Yes, nonnie.'

The silk whispered as I smoothed the dress and folded it. Suddenly I hated it, the bright yellow silk that Paul had brought all the way from Durban for her.

'I stamped on it,' said Mittee, crocheting now without venom. 'I don't think I like yellow as much as I thought I did. On second thoughts, Selina, don't use the word Hell. Tell him instead that Nonnie Mittee is very angry and never wants to see him again.'

'Yes, nonnie.'

I waited a long time on the stoep, counting all the sounds that went to make up the night song of the veld so that I need not think of ghosts. There were crickets singing, frogs at the spring, a night bird that flew over with a heart-broken cry, Lah-di-dah, Lad-di-dah, Lah-di-dah; the whirr of insects to which I could give no name; and far away on a rand behind the house the laugh of a hyena. Then to these sounds was added the hoofbeats of a horse. Paul, I thought, and ran inside to tell Mittee that he was coming.

She had fallen asleep with her hands beneath her cheek, as Grandma Van Brandenberg had taught us to sleep so that our hands should not get into mischief during the night. Her crochet work lay on the blanket but the ball of cotton had rolled across the floor. I rolled it up and folded the work. Then I blew out the candle and went again to the stoep. Paul was at the gate, dismounting. I walked half-way down the path to meet him.

'My nonnie went to bed, she got tired of waiting for you, basie.'

'Got tired of waiting for me, did she?' He stood in silence, close to me. From his body came the heavy smell of peach brandy, released in sweat. He whispered, 'Walk with me as far as my horse, Selina.'

I went with him willingly, though I knew even then what he wanted with me. When we had passed through the gate, he took my hand and pulled me into the grass beside him. I remember him always as he looked that night to me, the harsh outlines of his face softened by starshine. In remembering him so, I remember myself, the gentlehearted virgin.

'Basie, I must go,' I said, but my words were like the rustling of the wind through grass. I knew pain and a bitter, useless regret. Then I forgot that I was Selina.

Afterwards, he stirred me with his foot and said, 'You mustn't tell anybody about this, Selina.'

'No, Paul.'

'You must call me Baas Paul,' he said uneasily.

'Baas Paul.'

'I'll give you a little present.'

He went to his horse with lethargic steps and I heard the creak of leather as he mounted; his soft curses at the horse; hoofbeats on the road, growing fainter. I stayed there on the veld, remembering his touch upon my enchanted flesh.

A shadow slunk along the road. It was Jansie, returning from Plessisburg. He whistled as he passed the gate, probably for me. So still did I lie that it seemed an outrage that my heart should beat, that the grass should move in the wind. I did not look again towards him but stared at the sky until the stars spun and reeled above me. He whistled again and moved away slowly.

I lay there until the dew began to fall. Now I became cold and went inside to light up the stove, for dawn was breaking. As the wood caught, my clothes steamed in the heat and a smell rose up to me of my body and of the earth upon which I had lain. I began to sing, 'Jan Pierewit Jan Pierewit', a tune that set my feet jigging as I prepared a cup of coffee for Mittee.

She was sitting on the edge of the bed when I went into her

room, her plaits clenched in her hands, a sure sign that she was thinking hard. A stiff breeze blew through the open window, whipping the hem of her nightdress, but she did not seem to notice it. I closed the window quietly.

'Thank you, Selina.' She drank the coffee with a greedy sound. 'You didn't sleep here last night. I would have been frightened if I had woken up in the dark but it was morning before I opened my eyes.'

I knew that we were to be friends that day. 'I didn't want to come in and wake you up, Mittee.'

'Did he come, after all?'

'Yes, but it was late and you had fallen asleep.'

'Selina, after breakfast, put on the iron and you can do my silk dress. I'm going to the dance tonight but I won't dance with him. I'll show him. I bet the Coetzees were dancing last night and that's where he was. Tonight I'll make up to Dietloff Eberhardt.'

'Mittee, Mittee.'

She pulled off her nightdress with one gesture and stood naked, gleaming white. I turned my eyes away.

'Find my dress, Selina, my blue print dress. And bring me a dish of cold water. I'll wash myself all over.'

'You want to be careful, washing yourself all over and standing about naked. You'll catch a chill and die.'

'It's healthy. When I wear that silk dress to the dance tonight the other girls will faint with envy. Hurry, hurry now. Later on, we'll go for a walk to the river.'

I felt no weariness after the sleepless night, only an exhilaration that sent me flying about my tasks. First the breakfast must be prepared; mealie-meal and thick venison cutlets, for Mittee was a hearty eater. While I was making the gravy, Jansie brought the milk to the kitchen door. It was frothy, yellow milk because the grass was good that year. I dipped out some to drink there and then.

'That's right,' he said, looking me over with lewd eyes, 'fatten yourself up a bit or I won't be hanging round you. There are girls as round as peaches in Plessisburg and any one of them would have Jansie if he only winked at them.' He slapped my thigh. 'But tonight I'll show them that I belong to you. I'll dance only with you. I'll thrash anyone who so much as looks at you.'

I went to the stove and stirred the gravy with all my might, to keep out of his reach. 'You'll finish up in tronk behind bars if you go on like that. Where are the people dancing?'

'On the other side of the square. Fanie got an accordion, a present. There'll be fine music.'

'And I won't be dancing all the time with you.'

He swore at me and went away. Sis, I thought, let him put his yellow hands on me and I'll kick and bite him. That morning I felt as brave as a drunk person.

When breakfast was over, I tidied Mittee's room for this was always my work. She would never let the Kaffir girl into her room. Only I must clean it and put in fresh flowers each day, cabbage roses and daisies. During this time, she played the piano. The music that she played was pretty, gay and lighthearted as though laughter were in her fingertips and she would never know what it was to cry.

While I was ironing the silk dress, I heard the commotion of somebody arriving. The fowls flew about the yard with distracted squawks, the dog barked, the Kaffirs screamed, Ahe! Aletta Gouws flashed her face at the window for a few seconds.

'Herry's here.'

The iron went faster over the dress though I did not dare scamp the frills, for Mittee had a sharp eye. Herry's here! How often we shouted that out when we were children. Herry's here! It meant excitement and stories of adventure, too stirring to be true; trinkets, sometimes a piece of silk; or sweets.

I carried the silk dress to Mittee's bed and then ran outside to join the women standing around Herry. He was telling a wonderful story, his eyes darting from face to face. There was not one that he left out so that each person had the feeling that the story was meant for her alone. If he read disbelief in any face, he stared unwinkingly until its owner gave up the ghost of doubt and let her mouth sag open and her eyes pop wide in appreciation.

'. . . Yes, there I was, too tired to go on in that heat, so I sat down on a log and fell asleep. I woke up when it was dark and to my surprise I found that I was travelling along at a great rate, though I was still sitting on the log. The log, people, was a boa constrictor so huge that I had not seen either its head or its tail. You can imagine with what horror I jumped down from it and ran in the opposite direction.'

'Hi', and 'My God', were all that his listeners could say when he had finished. They began to paw over the articles on the tray he had slung about his neck, everybody wanting to buy at once.

He found time to say to me, 'How goes it, Selina? You've grown up all of a sudden.'

'Not all of a sudden, it's a year since I saw you.'

I always felt awkward when I talked to Herry in front of people because he would not let me call him Baas and if I called him Herry, Mittee or Mrs Gouws turned on me for being insolent; so I spoke to him jerkily and not with the friendliness that I felt. I was the last one to get to the tray. I stood fingering the laces and ribbons while the others went off with the oddments they had bought, cackling like geese as they compared prices. If one of them discovered that she had been cheated Herry would catch it, and knowing this he hastened to load up the little donkey that went with him from one end of the Transvaal to the other. He thrust a bundle of lace into my hand and a screw of paper, in which lay two small gold earrings.

'Hi, Herry, a present?'

'Of course. I haven't ever taken money from you, have I? Is the nonnie still good to you?'

'Yes. Just like my sister sometimes.'

'Well then, give her this book. But tell her to hide it. It's a love story and it would frighten the minister and the ladies of Plessisburg out of their wits.' He smiled. 'And you mustn't believe that story about the boa constrictor: it wasn't true.'

'I knew, Herry.'

'But the others believed it. They bought well after that. It makes them interested, you see. When I start telling the story, I always wink my eye and then God knows that I'm not telling lies but only getting the people interested.'

Thereupon Herry winked but I did not dare laugh for I knew that he was in earnest and he had indeed made this private contract with God. Mittee was calling me but I stood at the gate watching him as he made his way with the little donkey to the riverbank, where he would camp. He was a small man, with a wrinkled red face, from which stared his sun-faded eyes, haunted to their depths. Auntie Lena had whispered to me once that he was my father, but often as I searched for a likeness in him to myself I could find none except our smallness. I believe he was my father because ever since I can remember he brought me a present when he was passing through Plessisburg, and there was a present for Mittee too, but only after I had told him that she was good to me. He was an Englishman by birth but he spoke the Language so well and had roved the country so long that he was not regarded as an Outlander, though every Christmas Day he finished up in the tronk. He would drink brandy and then dress himself up as a minister of religion to preach in the square of the doom that was coming to Plessisburg, all in English, which luckily for him nobody followed well. It was his shouting that made the policeman arrest him for everyone knows that Christmas Day is not a time for shouting. It was his duty to preach, he told me, for he had been a minister once and this I think was true because I never knew him lie to me.

Mittee was working herself into a temper because I did not come immediately she called, but when she saw the English book she was all smiles. She even allowed me to preen myself before her mirror when I had clipped the gold earrings through my ears.

She was friendly as we walked to the river and when we lay beneath the willows she read aloud from the book, haltingly, explaining the scandalous meaning. It was called *Under Two Flags* and it was the sort of book that holy Grandma Van Brandenberg would have burnt.

Mittee could not struggle long with the English. She put the book aside and lay with arms outflung. Above us the swallows wheeled and darted, so black against the sky that it seemed they were shapes cut out to let through the darkness of space. From where we lay we could see the waggon that had carried Grandpa Van Brandenberg to the graveyard. The wheels had sunk into the mossy earth and the sighing willows dipped down to touch the rotting framework. You could lie there for a day without seeing anybody pass for the bank climbed steeply in steps to the roadway, shutting it from sight; and nobody came down there because the place was haunted. On Dingaan's Night, it was said, the ghost of Grandpa Van Brandenberg sat upon the waggon and sought to waylay passers-by, so that he might tell over again the story of Blood River.

I turned my eyes from the waggon and looked into the sky. There I saw the face of God. I put my hands over my eyes, whimpering, for it was a face of thunderous vengeance, searching out my sin.

'What's the matter?' Mittee asked. 'Did something sting you?'

'No. I saw the face of God in the sky.'

This silenced Mittee for a few minutes. Then she said respectfully, 'Selina, that's a wonderful thing. You must tell Dominie Brandt.'

'It's not a thing to speak of, Mittee, even to the minister. God is on my track, hunting me down. His eyes pierced to the very marrow of my soul. There was no loving-kindness in His face but only vengeance.'

'Then it was not God you saw or He would have looked at you with pity,' declared Mittee, but she kicked the English book under a tuft of grass. 'Most probably the ghost of my grandmother. She always said she would look down from Heaven and try and guide us from evil. It's getting near Dingaan's Day and I suppose she will walk with my grandfather, it's only natural . . .'

'You're a wicked girl, Mittee, you're joking. You'll be punished.'

'It's you who will be punished for mistaking Grandma for God. Selina, do you suppose Grandpa really sits on that waggon and waits to tell the story of Blood River? I can imagine him there, with his long white beard and his muzzle-loader beside him, sitting up as straight as a young man.' She changed her voice and her very expression, achieving a frightening likeness to her grandfather. 'Children, come close, and hear the story of what took place at Blood River on the sixteenth of December, 1838. There was a commando of five hundred of us under Andries Pretorius, mark his name well for he led us to victory that day. Five hundred of us in laager with our backs to the river and every man with his thoughts on God and his hand on his gun, as the Zulus came over in their thousands just as the dawn was breaking. The river ran red that day and the dead warriors lay as thick as pumpkins about us, for we were avenging the murder of Retief and his men and the massacre at Weenen, where they had stamped on the faces of the dying women and children. You see this old muzzle-loader? So often did I load and reload that the rag burst from its mouth in flames and my hands were blistered from the heat of the barrel . . .' Her voice trailed into tenderness and for a moment we were caught up by the memory of the tough old man, sitting on the front stoep with his muzzle-loader in his hands as though Dingaan's impis would come rushing over the hill. Mittee sighed, 'I am suddenly sad. Sing a little song, Selina, so that we can be happy again.'

'I don't feel like singing.'

She whispered, 'I know what we'll do. Let's see if the skull is still there, Selina.'

'No, no, Mittee.'

This skull had haunted us since childhood. When she was only five, Mittee had unearthed it by chance and putting it on her head, had danced with it. In my terror I ran to Grandma Van Brandenberg where she sat crocheting, her back against a willow tree, and pointed to Mittee dancing with the skull. 'My God,' said Grandma, but not in a pious voice. She threw her apron over the thing and carried it down to the river, meaning to cast it upon the water. But she paused, thinking of her duty now that the first flurry of fear had left her. 'Father, this was once a creature of Yours,' she said to the sky and placed the skull upon the ground while she thought out the best plan. Horrifyingly it rolled away and disappeared behind some rushes. Grandma went forward timidly, step by step, with Mittee and me following behind her, snivelling but curious. The skull had rolled into a hole in a mound on the bank as though it had deliberately retreated from us. She left it there and went to the minister to beg him to bury it in a Christian way but the minister would not. He said that you could not bury a skull or even a whole skeleton unless you knew whom it was part of, for how were you to know whether the bones belonged to a murderer or a suicide or perhaps even to an ape? So Grandma left the skull where it was and year after year it remained in its hiding place. It was the hope of my life that the river would wash it away or somebody else find it and with decency bury it; but whenever the mood took Mittee to look at it, there it was, laughing at its own joke. When the nightmare rode her, she vowed that never again would she look at the skull but on the next sunny day she was by the river, she peeped in at it and made up some new fantastic story about it.

'Mittee, I'll report you. It's a scandal.'

'Come with me and have a look at it and I'll call you Sister.'

I went sulkily with her to where the thing lay hidden. There it was, sure enough, frightful in its changelessness. One of the front teeth was missing and because of this you had the illusion that its expression changed, for if you looked at it from one side you were inclined to laugh but from the other side it was evil. I threw my apron over my head and scrambled up the bank as fast as my legs would take me. Mittee came after me, faithfully reciting, 'Selina is my sister, Selina is my sister.'

The words had lost their magic, even the terrifying outlines of the skull were less sharp. I thought, I have left childish things behind at last.

Mittee began a story. 'The skull belonged to a Kaffir who was setting out to kill a devout Boer when a crocodile seized him by the leg . . .' I slept and awakened to the spitefulness of a smart slap on the buttocks. 'Come home if you want to go to Plessisburg with me tonight. We'll have to be getting ready.'

I was savage for sleep and I could have torn her face because she had woken me up. I dragged myself homewards, lagging far behind her, and when I reached the farm I took no notice of her calling but hid myself in the grass near the spring. There I slept like the dead, caring nothing for her or for Jansie, who had thought he was going to dance with me that night.

On Dingaan's Day, the road through Plessisburg was lively with people making their way to the sports ground; in waggons, carts, traps and on foot. The sun had shot into a splendid sky, blazing within an hour of its rising. Those who had set out early in the hope of reaching the field in the cool of the morning were disappointed for it was hot by seven o'clock and tempers began to fray early. Mothers, marshalling their children in tens and eights and sixes, took their temper out on the distracted nursemaids. One little girl, I remember, in a dress of blue German print, covered by a frilled pinafore and with frills to her snowy drawers, must needs make straight for the water furrow and fall into the mud. Such a screaming went up from the mother that several people rushed forward, thinking the child drowned. The mother shook the little girl and then stood looking with fury at her mud-spattered clothes; but she was not allowed to stand there long for the cheeryhearted crowd jostled her onwards, making light of her misfortune.

This was not a day for best dresses because the dust would become thick later on; but the print dresses were new, their colours bright after the first wash, frills standing out stiff with starch, sun-bonnets sparkling from bleaching and blue.

I walked on the edge of the water furrow, carrying Mittee's blanket and her bottle of eau de cologne and a great supply of fresh handkerchiefs. That happy day. My apron was so white that it hurt the eyes to look at it and I wore a pair of Mittee's old shoes with cracks across the soles but smart on top and glittering with polish.

Coester's voorloper had got himself into trouble by blocking the road with his oxen. Dazed by the crowd, his mind was not strong enough to make the decision necessary to pull the oxen round and he stood with mouth hanging open in a grin while half the population of Plessisburg roared advice at him. At last a youth sprang forward and himself turned the oxen. Still the waggon did not move for now Coester was down from the driver's seat, threatening the frightened boy with his whip. Mrs Coester, who always raised her voice for the weak, screamed at her husband and, heaving herself unaided from the waggon, began to wrestle with him for possession of the whip. The little boy ducked into the furrow out of harm's way and the crowd gathered round the Coesters, exhorting them until the road rocked with laughter. 'The best wrestling match of the day,' they shouted. 'Enter Mrs Coester for the event at the sports and she'll put the Wolkbergen on to victory.' Coester gave in good-humouredly and, to the cheering of the crowd, the waggon moved on again.

I found myself next to Aletta Gouws. She was a big girl, mad for men since she was twelve years old, and more than her mother or eight brothers could manage. She had hold of Jacob Coester and she was pressing herself so hard against him that I thought to myself, If you don't get spoken to for wanton behaviour today, my name's not Selina.

I teased her, shaking my head at her inflamed face. 'It's no good, Aletta, he's sweet on Mittee.'

'Mittee's backside.'

She flaunted off without giving me a chance to answer her. I marched along furiously, thinking of all the things I could have said to her. Then I forgot all about her. A voice, sweet and thick as a comb of honey, spoke my name.

'And where is your nonnie?'

'She went to the service and she is driving to the ground in the magistrate's waggonette.'

I was glad to be walking beside Fanie. He was a beautiful youth then, as bright as the day. Near him walked Frikkie Du Plessis, the only man whom Fanie ever called Baas. Frikkie did not look happy although he had on his arm golden-haired Letty Van Aswegan, to whom he was betrothed. He was one of the magistrate's sons, a year or two older than Paul, and it was said that his father had forced him to propose because he loved Fanie too well.

'You see, Mittee rides in the waggonette,' said Letty at the top of her voice, 'but I must go on foot amongst the Coloureds.'

Fanie, proud from years of easy companionship with Frikkie, drew further away from them.

'You'll have me in the furrow if you come any closer,' I said, and nudged him with my elbow.

He strode along in silence, taking such long steps that we soon left Frikkie and Letty behind. The crowd was dispersing over the strip of veld that lay between the sports ground and the road, releasing the children who frisked like calves as they let loose their pent-up excitement. Fanie leaned against an outcrop of rocks from where he could see the target range.

'Either one of the Du Plessises will win the shooting,' he said with the positiveness of a man who talks of sport to a woman.

'Paul will.'

'More likely Frikkie.'

We laughed and Letty, passing by with Frikkie, stopped to glare at us. 'Those creatures are laughing at me.'

It was lucky for her that she had stopped. Fanie and I both saw the stirring of the dust at her feet as a sluggish puff-adder moved. Fanie leapt as he saw it, his body bounding into the air with the power and grace of a springbok's, and as he landed beside the snake he bent in the same movement to pick it up by the tail. He flicked the snake once through the air before he dashed its head against a stone. Then he returned to the rocks and stood with arms folded, the pace of his breath scarcely altered.

Letty had stepped back and now she stood with a look of affront on her face as though Fanie had meant some insolence to her in his method of killing the puff-adder. Frikkie must have felt this too for I saw his shoulders shake with secret laughter as he gingerly put a stick under the snake's belly and carried it to a flat stone. People on their way to the sports ground stopped to look with gloating triumph at their crushed enemy.

Aletta Gouws sagged against Jacob, whimpering as though she had never in her life seen a snake.

'It moves, it's alive.'

'Don't worry, little heart,' Jacob soothed her. 'It will wriggle until sunset but, really, it is dead.'

Aletta looked with big eyes at this embodiment of wisdom. It was all I could do to keep my face straight for I had seen her do battle with a ringhals and, except for a little sweat, show no sign of distress. In fact, she went in immediately afterwards and ate a bigger meal than most men could put away. But Jacob was intoxicated by this helplessness. He did not go back to the Wolkbergen with his people after Christmas but stayed on with the Gouwses so that poor old Gouws found himself with another hulking son on his hands.

A young mother, carrying her first baby in her arms, pushed her way through the group of people to see what it was that had attracted them. As her gaze fell upon the snake, she instinctively clapped her hand over the baby's eyes, guarding them from the stain of ugliness. Fanie noticed the exquisite gesture, I know, because he threw a large stone over the snake to hide it from view.

Mittee was beckoning me and I hurried away to the sports grounds. 'Where have you been?' she grumbled. 'The jukskei has started already. I'm going to sit in the cool under that tree and watch. Spread the blanket out for me. Look, there's Eberhardt throwing now. Bravo,' she called as he scored a lie.

He took this for an invitation to stand by her until his next turn. Mittee liked this small, purring man but as for me I always felt that he made himself a master of women by his very likeness to them. The strictest mothers in Plessisburg trusted him, misled by the passionless smoothness that hid his aggression. Mittee imagined that he pined from his hopeless love for her because he had once proposed to her but it was not Mittee he wanted so much as her farm which, though small, was level and rich-soiled and adjoined his own sprawling tract of land.

The heat grew powerful, shimmering over the cracking earth so that it was painful to walk across the field to watch the events. Everywhere babies screamed at the top of their voices while their nurses or mothers searched frantically through the clothing for pins, exhorted by officious grandmas. Here and there you saw an old woman, suffocated in her black dress, lying fast asleep in the shade of a tree; or one eating snacks from the basket and so aggravating the heat that she was likely to fall in a faint. The sports had become confused and there were two or three events going on at one and the same time. You saw girls running from one group to another as their loyalties were torn between relative and lover.

The target-shooting had begun but over in the corner of the field the Plessisburg wrestlers were meeting the Wolkbergen champions.

I wanted to stay and watch the target-shooting but Mittee decided she must watch the Coester boys.

'If only out of respect for their mother and father,' she said, opening up her sunshade. 'And bring the eau de cologne and some handkerchiefs, the dust will be thick over there when they get going.'

I limped after her, my feet throbbing against the vicious pinch of my shoes. You should have seen Aletta. Her face had gone beyond redness into purple, streaked with sweat and dust. She strained with Jacob Coester as he fell into his opponent's hold and clicked her fingers, shouting with joy as he broke away. The strange thing was that nobody took any notice of her antics beyond a smile except her mother who brought her to her senses now and again with a smart slap between the shoulder blades. Even pallid Jessie Tyson, the most down-trodden girl in Plessisburg, was watching with eyes that glistened, a different Jessie from the girl who recited cool poetry at her mother's musical evenings. It shows you what bulging muscles and hairy chests will do to the most carefully guarded girl. I glanced at Mittee to see how she was taking it. The single cloud that floated over the Wolkbergen was not more aloof than she. With dainty fingers she dabbed a scented handkerchief on her temples.

'You've got vinegar in your veins, not blood,' I said in her ear.

She was too much astonished to be angry. 'Vinegar?'

At that moment a hoera went up near the shooting range and her mind was distracted from my remark. 'We'd better go over and see what is happening. It must be at the interesting part now or they wouldn't be cheering.'

There were only two competitors left in the contest, Paul and Eberhardt: and their scores stood equal. I shifted from one aching foot to the other but in a few seconds I had forgotten everything in the world except the bright desire for Paul to win. Mittee, with her arm through the magistrate's, jumped with excitement and suddenly called out, 'Shoot like the devil, Paul.' Two old women standing near me said discontentedly, 'A schoolmistress, too,' but even Dominie Brandt paid no attention, though he looked with disapproval as Aletta burst through the crowd, dragging Jacob behind her. Quite beside herself, she yelled, 'Hotnot' and then, 'My Christ' as her mother clipped her.

Now they raised their rifles to shoot the last round. The whole scene became clear to me, as though I were apart from it; the sky, blue-white with heat, the gay dress of the women interspersed by the sombre clothes of the old or those in mourning. There was Paul's finger on the trigger. I could not watch. I closed my eyes and prayed, Let him win, let him win. Behind my eyelids were the colours of the rainbow and the outline of Paul's head, drawn with a pencil of gold. One after the other the bullets whined to their mark, while the crowd chanted the score in loud, wild voices like Kaffirs gone mad at a beer-drink. I did not open my eyes until they shouted, 'Hoera for Plessis'.

Mittee was dignified again. Tenderhearted, she offered her hand first to the defeated Eberhardt before she turned to Paul. He swung her from her feet and those standing nearby were scandalized by the sight of her legs kicking up to reveal openwork silk stockings.

I nudged Paul's arm. 'Almighty, Baas Paulie, behave yourself, first she swears and now legs showing to the whole of Plessisburg.'

'Voetsak, you bastard.'

The sound of my voice had quenched his triumph. He spoke in a slow, savage voice, deliberately choosing the words that would hurt me most.

Mittee cried out angrily, 'Don't speak to her like that,' but I threw my apron over my head and ran from the sports ground. Fanie had gone from the rocks and I was glad of that for I would not have liked him to see me with tear-drenched face and crippled feet after I had set out so bravely to enjoy Dingaan's Day.

I would go back to the farm, though it would be lonely there because everybody took a holiday on Dingaan's Day. As long as Jansie is not there, I thought, as I unbuttoned the hated shoes and made my way to the solitary road. The coloured people were congregated in the market square, where they were supposed to be overseeing the preparation of the great fires where the meat would be cooked that night; but from what I could hear there was very little work being done. I hesitated, thinking I might join in the fun but a feeling of not belonging to my own race was strong upon me; and the certainty that Jansie would be there, boisterous from merrymaking.

Herry was in Mittee's yard, dressed in his minister's clothes. He was rehearsing his sermon for Christmas Day but he had not yet reached the full flood of his denunciation of Plessisburg and its people. For audience he had Klaas, who was half Hottentot and as ugly as sin itself; sitting there with a bottle of peach brandy that Herry had given to him and not understanding a word of what was said. You could see that he enjoyed the shattering heat of brandy and sun. Herry traced a cross in the air when he saw me but further than that took no notice of me.

I sat in the cool of the back stoep with tears of bitterness in my eyes because I had to spend the best part of Dingaan's Day watching these two make fools of themselves. Herry took a delicate sip from his bottle from time to time, sneezed and then tossed a lurid phrase to Klaas. When Klaas drank, he poured the brandy down his throat as though it were water, licked his lips and held the bottle up to see where the brandy stood. Suddenly he launched his body into the air to a height of about five feet, bringing his heels together in mid-air and shouting 'Christmas!' As he landed on the ground again, he shouted even louder, 'New Year!' And so he went on for about half an hour, his leaps growing shorter and shorter until he fell in the dust, flat on his back. Herry said a prayer over him and went away.

Now indeed the place was dreary, quiet but for the clucking of the hens and the call of the guinea fowl. Klaas was asleep, his senseless face an offering to the sun and it seemed to me that his skin was frying in its own sweat. I became afraid for him so I dragged him by the feet, inch by inch, into the shade of a fig tree. The bottle rolled over and over, the brandy spilling out to intoxicate the earth. So must the breath of the devil smell. I picked up the bottle. I had never tasted brandy, not even buchu brandy, for Grandma Van Brandenberg, and Mittee after her, had believed in Essence of Life. I put my head back and drank what remained in the bottle.

Father of Pity. I had burnt my mouth to ashes and the inside of my nose was stinging with pain. I prayed, choking, as I ran to the tap for water. The brandy was slowly burning a path of fire into my stomach and arms and legs. I tried to do the same as Klaas but after shouting 'Christmas!' and 'New Year!' once I got tired of that.

I knew it was Dingaan's Day but I did not remember why I was alone on the farm. Selina should be with the folk in the square, dancing in the light of the purple-winged sun; not alone in this place where there was none to hear her laugh or to see how gaily she polka'd.

I ran nearly all the way to Plessisburg so that by the time I reached the square, the flames of the brandy had burnt down to the steady, heart-warming glow of embers. Some of the young people were already dancing though it was not yet dark and on the other side of the square the fires blazed, licking at yards of sausage and steak. Mittee was amongst the dancers, more brilliant than any girl there for she had changed into her yellow dress. The hem was already stained by the earthen floor from which the dust was beginning to rise although it was only a shadow swirling about the ankles of the dancers, only a tickle in the throats of the old people who sat on benches round the dancing space. I watched until the dust became a cloud, tearing at the lungs. Wimpie Maritz put aside his violin and called for water and salt to lay the dust because you could scarcely hear the music for the coughing that was going on. There was one old woman there who coughed so violently that I was frightened she would spit her heart out.

Paul drew Mittee into the darkness, disregarding the derisive calls from the young men who were sprinkling the floor from big buckets of water. He walked hand-in-hand with her across the square and I followed them. I was so jealous of her that I meant to tell her that Paul belonged to me; for so it seemed to me as I wafted along on the fumes of the brandy. I was saved from such foolishness by the magistrate.

He called out. 'Where are you, Paul?'

Paul did not answer but Mittee said, breathlessly, 'We were just going for a little walk in the cool while they sprinkled the floor, Uncle Siegfried.'

The magistrate sought them out in the darkness. 'Ah, here you are. Paul, you must look after the little daughter better than this. I had to stand by while the poisonous tongues got to work.'

'Ag, Father takes it too seriously,' said Paul sourly. 'They were only joking, after all.'

'Silence!' said the magistrate as though he were speaking from the Bench. 'Are you trying to argue with your own father?'

Mittee contritely took the magistrate's arm and went back to the dancing space with him but Paul stamped off by himself. The music had started again, Wimpie Maritz on his violin and Frikkie on his accordion. It sounded beautiful out there in the darkness.

I caught up with Paul on the road. 'Paulie, where are you going?'

'Go away, Selina.' For answer I danced a polka in front of him. 'I'll kick you, so true, Selina. Get away from me.'

'Ag no, my basie, don't you talk to Selina like that.' I put my breast and thigh against him, undulating slowly like a sun-drugged snake. Where I learned such behaviour I don't know but that brandy certainly made of life a simple affair. He put out his hands to ward me off but I slipped beneath them and wound my arms about him.

'You smell of brandy, you little devil,' he whispered.

Suddenly he began to laugh. We danced down the road, beyond the strains of the music, to the patch of veld that bordered the river.

There was somebody coming towards us. Paul pressed my body into the grass and lay flat beside me. The brandy and the passion had cleared from my brain so that I could see clearly and with piercing shame the ruin that would come to all his hopes if he were found there with me. A light shone straight on to us and we looked into Herry's face.

'Fornicators!'

He said this word in the Language but the rest of his speech was in English, delivered in stern tones. Then his voice changed, he spoke rapidly as though he were saying something off by heart.

'He's marrying us to each other,' I exclaimed, picking out an English word here and there. In spite of myself I laughed.

Paul saw nothing funny in it. He sprang at the old man, shouting, 'Thunder and lightning,' and would have taken him by the throat if I had not clung to his arm. Herry ducked away amongst the trees but we could still hear his voice chanting through the wedding service.

Paul said roughly, 'You'd better get back to Plessisburg. I'll follow on later.'

'Not by myself, basie. It must be past midnight and they say the ghost of Grandpa Van Brandenberg walks tonight.'

'I'll walk with you until we see the lights in the square and then you go on by yourself. And keep your mouth shut, Selina, I've trusted you.' He said not another word except, 'We'll have to think of some way to keep Herry from shouting it all over Plessisburg on Christmas Day.'

'I'll speak to him, basie, he has always been very kind to me.'

He left me to go on alone to the square. I found the folk gathered about Fanie, who was recounting a joke that made them stamp their feet with merriment. Nobody noticed me steal into the circle of light thrown by the fires.

Jansie caught sight of me first. He said angrily, 'Where have you been all day and all night? I've been looking for you.'

'I went to the farm because my nonnie was nasty to me.'

'I never thought of going there. I looked in every backyard in Plessisburg for you.'

'I'm as tired as a dog and hungry. Is there any sausage left?'

'Here you are, Selina,' Auntie Lena called. 'Here's a nice piece I saved for you. Where have you been? We missed you during the dancing. Did you have fever? You want to hear what Fanie and his baas are up to. I call it flying in the face of things you don't understand.'

I snuggled up to Auntie Lena. Though she was small and frail, with a face as wrinkled as an ape's, there was in her the warmth of motherliness. Not even a dog would walk by her without receiving a caress. She had reared fifteen children of her own, besides Fanie who was the child of her imbecile sister; and she claimed that she could number two hundred living descendants and that she was related to half the families in Plessisburg both white and coloured. She was related to me in an obscure way on my mother's side and she certainly bore a resemblance to the Van Brandenberg family. She was born a slave but she served Grandma Van Brandenberg forty years after she was freed and she was the only one from whom the old woman ever took advice.

'What is this joke that they are talking about?' I asked.

'Come here and I'll explain the whole thing to you,' said Fanie proudly.

Frikkie and he were well known for their practical jokes but this, Fanie told me, was to be the biggest joke ever played in Plessisburg. It seemed that Eberhardt had been boasting of the number of ghosts that he had laid and now there was a bet on that he would not lay the ghost of Grandpa Van Brandenberg. Eberhardt was to go down to the haunted waggon and sit there at midnight for half an hour. Good enough, but the cream of it was that Fanie would cover himself with a sheet and rise up behind Eberhardt in the moonlight. Then we would see how brave Eberhardt really was when it came to ghosts.

'What if the real ghost appears, Fanie?' I asked.

He held up a bottle of peach brandy. 'Frikkie has given me a bottle of brandy to keep up my courage but there will be nothing left by the time I start out because everybody has had a sip.'

'Give me a sip, too.'

'No. To me you are like a beautiful flower, Selina, that no wickedness must touch.'

When he said that, a feeling of sadness came over me and I turned away from him. He started up a tune on his accordion and before I could escape, Jansie was upon me. He seized my hands and swung me round in a breathless tickeydraai. His face streamed with sweat, his mouth hung wide open in laughter. You couldn't help liking him a little bit when he was so happy. Poor Jansie. He picked me up and set me on his shoulder. From there I could look down on the whole scene and yet remain a part of it because I shared the rhythm of his gyrating body.

The moon came up, shapeless in drifting clouds, its pale radiance touching the folk so gently that each one became beautiful; even imbecile Rebecca, Fanie's mother, who tottered amongst the dancers as though seeking something. The music grew slow and sad until everybody stood still, listening wistfully.

Fanie put his accordion into its box, handing it over for safe-keeping to Auntie Lena. Frikkie was on the edge of the crowd cautiously beckoning him.

'You're a fool to go, Fanie,' said Auntie Lena, as she put the box under her skirts where nobody would touch it. 'It's wickedness born out of brandy, that's all.'

Fanie laughed at her. 'Watch Rebecca or she'll go wandering off and getting lost while I'm away.'

'A will like a stone,' grumbled Auntie Lena. 'He was like that as a little boy.'

Fearfully we watched Fanie and Frikkie steal across the square to the road. The thought of ghosts had dampened our merriment. We sat waiting for Fanie's return and not even Jansie tried a hand at lovemaking. We huddled close together, whispering of shrieks heard through lonely houses, of ghastly sights seen on the veld in moonlight. There was nobody there who had not seen a ghost or whose auntie or grannie had not seen one. Old Auntie Lena told of a Thing that floated over her house on the same day each year; Jansie of a man with an assegai in his back who appeared to his uncle on the Wolkbergen. I remembered Grandma Van Brandenberg's vision of a Kaffir whom she had seen on two occasions drive a white cow through the backyard. When she dropped down dead one evening, everybody said she must have seen the vision again and the shock had killed her.

The moon wrenched free from the clouds. Now the light was so clear that I could see the wrinkles on Auntie Lena's face as it twisted with fright.

We heard wild cries. There in the moonlight we saw Eberhardt running towards the market place as though the devil himself were giving chase with a pitchfork; behind him, a sheeted form. Though we knew this must be Fanie, many people sprang up and ran in different directions, but nobody alone.

'Baas, baas,' Fanie was shouting, 'wait for me, the right one is coming after me.'

There was a ghost, a real ghost, behind Fanie. Then indeed you saw fright. Auntie Lena fainted straight out and nobody went to help her. Jansie fell on his knees beside me, he who scoffed at prayers. People were running everywhere to escape the doom of looking upon Grandpa Van Brandenberg.

It was Frikkie. I heard him laugh. He had a laugh like a horse neighing, you couldn't mistake it. I stopped my anxious prayers.

'That's Frikkie Du Plessis, not a ghost,' I said to Jansie, but he kept his head covered with his hands. 'Baas Frikkie, take that sheet off. You've frightened all the people, basie. Look, Auntie Lena has fallen in a faint.'

'Give her a drop of this,' Frikkie laughed, taking the sheet from his head. 'It's some brandy left in the bottle Fanie dropped when he ran. Mind you, I got a fright myself, but just for a minute. My brother Paul was hiding in the bushes near me and I thought it was old Grandpa Van Brandenberg himself. So Paul has the last laugh, after all.'

We did not dance again that night but by the next morning we could laugh at the story. At daybreak I went down to the riverbank to speak to Herry but he was not there. I searched for him all over Plessisburg but nobody had seen him. There was only a week to go before Christmas Day and I looked for him each morning, sure that he would come, for as long as I could remember he had preached on Christmas Day.

He did not preach in the square again. He was dead but I thought then that Paul had frightened him away from Plessisburg; though I should have known. A donkey hung about the riverbank for weeks afterwards until it was taken to the pound but one donkey looks much like another and I did not guess it was Herry's.

CHAPTER III

Mittee and I were going to Pretoria. The arrangements for the adventure began after the town had emptied and everyday life had taken the place of festivities. We began to prepare quietly enough but as the day of departure rushed upon us, our excitement became so great that we had Essence of Life three times a day.

I had four new doeks and two new aprons, as well as a petticoat that had belonged to Mittee and was frayed at the hem. Three days before we left I tied up my bundle but it had to be undone again because I had left something out. It seemed those last three days would never pass, that something must happen to prevent our leaving. I thought of floods; of Mittee changing her mind about taking me; of either of us falling sick. I could not eat. The dancing over Christmas and New Year had made me thin enough but now you could have put a needle through me.

Then suddenly it was time to go to the coach. Nothing was ready. My bundle was not tied up, after all. I had forgotten to iron my best doek. Mittee's carpetbag would not close. And there was Paul at the door, with his father.

Mittee screamed, 'Gouws, where are you? Come and help me close the damned bag.'

'Mittee, don't swear like that. Your voice carries so, the magistrate will hear you.'

She made a terrible face at me. 'Hold your mouth and get one of the Gouwses to help close up this thing.'

She kicked the bag and I rushed out of the room, fearful that I would be the next to catch it. Gouws was found, the bag was closed and away we went. I sat in the back of the spider, while Mittee sat between Paul and the magistrate.

Most of the women in Plessisburg had come to see Mittee off and there were three or four coloured people to wave to me. Those who had travelled shouted advice as I climbed up beside the driver. Auntie Lena came running up at the last moment with a bottle of red lavender and a basket full of peaches and biltong. Jansie was too shy to come right up to the coach. He had a paper parcel under his arm and by his grinning and pointing I knew it contained a present for me. Just as the coach was about to move off, he plucked up enough courage to shout huskily, 'Hi, Selina, catch,' and threw the parcel up to me. It was a roasted guinea fowl, still warm from the pot. The paper flew off but the guinea fowl landed right in my lap.

A yell of delight went up from the white people as well as from the Coloureds and the last I saw of Plessisburg as the coach moved off was poor Jansie chasing the coach with the paper.

'Fatherland, you've got enough food there to take you to Capetown and back,' said the driver, a coloured man.

I clung tightly to the side of the seat for being so high up gave me a feeling of unsteadiness but I tried to enjoy it and I kept saying to myself, Here you are, Selina, riding in one of Zeederberg's coaches, you'll always be able to talk about it.

The horses had no sooner got going than the driver slid his hand along the shiny seat, pressed his fingers under my bottom and pinched me.

'Ag Christ, man, stop your nonsense,' I screamed.

Mittee put her head out of the coach window, 'What's happening?'

'He pinched me, nonnie.'

'Stop it this minute, filth, or I'll report you,' Mittee threatened.

The driver shook with silent laughter. He made the journey a misery. When I moved out of his reach so that he could not pinch me, he jabbed me amorously with the whip. Only when the road became tricky did he leave me alone and then I enjoyed myself. When you got used to it, it was grand to be sitting up so high behind six fresh horses, with the wind slapping at your face. Your whole life was left behind you and you dashed with the flying hoofs to the horizon. Beyond the horizon was another horizon and beyond that yet another.

Pretoria. Wherever you looked there were big buildings, sharp against the sky; and on the pavements people wearing their best clothes. The street was never empty, you could always be sure to see at least five or six vehicles following one after the other.

'Busy, isn't it?' said Mittee, coolly.

I shook my head to show my wonderment. Mittee allowed me to stare for a little longer before we hurried off to the station. We were to catch a train to Welgedacht, a few miles out of Pretoria, where her aunt lived. The vibration of the train went through my tensed body like a file jarring against steel. I was alone in the carriage and I was so frightened that I admonished myself aloud, Selina, God will look after you. All the same I was glad when the train stopped. I leaned out to see where we were, thankful that the trees and fencing posts were still again. We had stopped in the veld, where there was nothing to see but thick green grass and an iron shed.

Then I thought, My God, there has been an accident; for Mittee was running alongside the train, waving and shouting.

'Get out, get out, Selina, you'll be taken on to Johannesburg.'

I rushed to the door but I could not open it. The engine whistled like a mad thing. Mittee, mad too, jumped up and down as she shrieked, 'Turn the handle the other way.' I tried that and the door opened suddenly. Out flew the basket and the guinea fowl rolled despairingly under the train. There were peaches everywhere. I grabbed my bundle, leaping to the ground as the train gave a lurch. Mittee steadied me with her arm as I landed. 'Pick up the food,' she said and I began dazedly to gather up a few of the peaches but Jansie's guinea fowl I left lying on the railway track for it reminded me of the time he killed his dog.

'Mittee, I want to piss.'

She said between her teeth, 'Shut up, screaming a thing like that out. You're not on the farm now. You'll have to wait.'

'God, no. I'm wetting my drawers.'

'It's the excitement,' she said resignedly. 'Well, go behind that shed. It serves me right for bringing such a pumpkin with me.'

There was nobody at the siding to meet us and we had to wait for some time in the burning sun. Mittee, frantic about her complexion, had just said that we would go back to Pretoria and stay at the hotel when we saw a trap flying down the road, with red dust scurrying after it. Mittee's aunt, Mrs Van Brandenberg, jumped down before anybody could give her a hand, tripped but recovered herself again before anybody could even think of helping her, and showered absent-minded kisses on Mittee's face. She was a sharp woman, I knew, but her mind at that moment was on her daughter Andrina, who was descending from the trap, assisted by a young man. They were all stylishly dressed but he had on holiday clothes; black broadcloth and a wonderfully embroidered waistcoat. This was Leon Dressel, cousin to Andrina. He greeted Mittee but he did not take his passionate eyes from Andrina, and I could see why Mrs Van Brandenberg was so worried unless she could see exactly what was going on.

Though I was put with the luggage on the floor of the four-wheeler I enjoyed the drive to Welgedacht more than the coach ride. The horses were trotters, groomed to the sheen of silk and with ribbons plaited into their manes as a welcome to Mittee. She was appeased by this attention and made no more mention of the hotel.

Welgedacht lay well back from the railway line. We drove in through the lower gates along a broad road that wound through gardens so luxuriant that the veld beyond the fences seemed a desert. But you should have seen the house. It was a tall white house with gables and the rooms were so big that you were afraid to speak above a whisper. And furniture. Man, it just stood everywhere.

I was taken to the kitchen and put into the care of Andrina's girl, Polly. She was a handsome girl and good-natured. She served me delicately with coffee and rusks. To show her that I, too, was used to a decent house, I crooked my little finger when I lifted the cup and said, 'Do you mind if I dip?' before I soaked a rusk.

'Pretoria is a quiet place,' she told me. 'Now, Johannesburg – I tell you, there are some wild goings-on there, man. It's a scandal. I worked in a house there. They had never heard of church, I don't think, and the men were terrible like mad things. Outlanders, of course. The missis was kind, I was as fat as butter but I couldn't stand the wildness. It is because there are not enough women to go round and then the gold drives men mad, I think. My mother would have turned in her grave to see her daughter amongst such sin so I gave notice. I don't mind a little drop of wine, that can't do you any harm but further than that, no. It's always the men. Black, white or coloured, they can't behave themselves.'

'I know.'

'They're strange creatures,' said Polly. 'They like to see you dressed up in a nice dress but, truly, all the time they're thinking of taking the dress off. Now, where is the sense of that. That dress looks nice on you, they say, and the next thing they're trying to take it off.' Polly sighed. 'It doesn't pay for a coloured girl to have good looks, especially a good figure. The way they look at you, with their eyes half closed and their teeth clenched. It's a disgrace.'

I drank more coffee. Polly, who seemed to have an easy job, showed me some new patterns in crochet while she told me her life story. Then I told her mine though I did not mention Paul. From decency we pretended to each other that we were virgins and the talk flowed smoothly, untroubled by the sarcastic remarks of the house girls and the cook. They were jealous of us sitting there with nothing to do except talk while they had to work hard and when Polly and I offered to do the peas for them, they answered with a string of filthy words as though we had insulted them.

The next day, Mittee went to the shops. She came back with a beautiful silk dress and a bonnet, the two worth sixty guineas; and beaded shoes that I knew she would not dare to wear in front of Mrs Brandt, the minister's wife. For me she had bought a bright blue silk piece.

'It's for you to wear on my wedding day, Selina. You can make it up with a flounce in the front and with your gold earrings, you'll look grand. And look at this, Selina. Pink powder. You put it on your cheeks and it looks like a healthy colour. See?'

She rubbed the powder on to her cheeks with wadding. It made her face glow but she did not look like Mittee.

'Hi, Mittee, it makes you rosy. You're quite different.'

'It's not as loud as cochineal. I'm always going to put it on. People will think the change of air has done me good.'

'Let me try a bit, Mittee.' I dabbed my cheeks.

'My God, take it off,' Mittee cried. 'It's turned you mauve. That's funny. Are you sure it's pink on me?'

'Yes, it's pink on you all right,' I said discontentedly.

'Wipe it off with a damp lappie.' Mittee tried on the beaded shoes. 'See, a butterfly worked out. Do you know that Andrina is in love with her own cousin?'

'Anybody can see that.'

'Her mother will never allow them to marry. She told me of a case where cousins married and had a two-headed baby.' She shuddered. 'You'd think it would put Andrina off but she just laughed. I'm going with them to see the lantern slides this evening. I'll tell you all about it tomorrow morning.'

'You'll be frightened to sleep in this strange room by yourself,' I said, spitefully.

'No, I won't. I don't believe in ghosts any more. Besides, I can always light a candle, everything is plentiful in the house; and I brought my Bible with me.'

'Somebody might have died in this room. I remember Eberhardt telling you a story about a man who slept in a strange bed and he was cold all night though it was summer. The next morning he found out that a man had died in the very bed.'

'That was in an hotel. My aunt wouldn't do a thing like that to me, she's a Christian. And don't try and frighten me, you cat. You can't sleep in the room with me, my aunt would faint with shock. So hold your mouth about ghosts.'

When she told me about the lantern slides the next morning, I cried. 'The hell, Selina, what are you crying for?' she asked impatiently.

'I want to see the lantern slides.'

'You can't, they wouldn't let a coloured girl in.'

I cried the harder at that. 'I want to see the lantern slides.'

'Father of Pity,' said Mittee to the ceiling, 'she wants to see the lantern slides,' but her heart melted at the sight of my tears and she took my hand in hers, telling me a story about a coloured girl who dressed herself up as a white person and went to see the lantern slides.

'What was the coloured girl like?' I asked with unwilling interest.

'Very pretty, really. She was small and fine-waisted, and her nose looked as if someone had put their thumb on it and pressed it up . . .'

'You've got the same nose yourself,' I said hotly.

'Mine turns up very slightly.' She caressed the tip of her nose, making the skin shine. 'But your nose is a different matter, you'd drown in the rain. To get on with the story. She had beautifully wavy hair that fell into loose curls over her shoulders, and red cheeks that looked quite nice with her brown skin.'

'You're only jealous because you are so pale yourself.'

'Do you want to hear the rest of the story?'

'No, your stories are always silly,' I said.

'This one could be true. Now look.' She sprang out of bed, pulling my hair back as far as it would go. 'How pretty you would have been if you were white.' She sprinkled bath powder over my face, smoothing it into my cheeks. 'My God, you're a sort of grey. I know what I'll do. The camphor fat.'

'I hate the smell,' I cried but she flipped her finger into the jar of camphor fat.

'Now, the powder over that. You look quite white. Honestly, at night nobody would guess. Look in the glass.'

'Hi, I look like a corpse.'

'Don't wipe it off. I'll put this straw bonnet on and a veil. Let me look in your hair first, Selina, you never know what you can pick up.' Her hands went through my hair quickly. 'You're clean. Put on the bonnet. Now you wouldn't know you were a Coloured.'

Andrina threw the door open without knocking. She sat on the bed, kicking her legs so that the calves showed. She pointed resentfully at me as though I stood between her and happiness.

'Why is the creature done up like that?'

Mittee explained, a little ashamed at being caught by her cousin at such foolishness, whereupon a scheming look came into Andrina's eyes.

'You know, she does look white. Let's take her to the show, just for a joke.'

'Take off my things.' Mittee pouted at me. 'It was only a game, Andrina.'

'But think of the fun. We'll ask mother if we can do it and then for once she may let us go into Pretoria alone for she would never dream of letting Karel come with us if we have Selina.'

She was thinking of seeing Leon. There was a silence in the room as Mittee and I stood by looking with helpless guilt upon Andrina. She leaned against the pillow on the bed, her body moving slightly with the rhythm of desire, her eyelids dropping and her lips opened as though for kisses.

'Take off my things,' said Mittee loudly.

Andrina sprang up suddenly and seizing my hand dragged me from the room. 'Ma, ma,' she shouted, 'did you ever see a thing like this?'

She pushed me into Mrs Van Brandenberg's room and stood laughing beside me. 'Mittee has dressed her up to take her to the lantern slides. You would never know she wasn't white. May we take her tonight? Say yes, say yes. It will be such fun.'

'It's a long time since you thought of fun,' said Mrs Van Brandenberg, finding her words slowly. Warmth came into her face and now I felt sorry for her. She must grow weary of the fight against her daughter. 'But it would be silly, Andrina . . .'

The girl flung her arms about her mother's neck, crooning in her ear like a child begging for sweets, 'Say yes, ma, say yes.'

A flush rose into Mrs Van Brandenberg's neck and spread over her florid face until it looked almost purple. It struck me then that this was the first time I had seen Andrina willingly address her mother; or had seen her anything but sulky when Leon was not by her side. Mrs Van Brandenberg softened a little but as she pushed Andrina from her, her eyes were as clear as ever, her smile as masterful.

'Of course, it is impossible.' She turned the smile to her son Karel as he came awkwardly into the room. 'Good morning, old son.'

'Good morning, ma.'

You would never have thought that he was Andrina's brother. He was a year younger than she was and it seemed that Nature in the fashioning of the girl had used up all that was fine and passionate, leaving clay for the boy. You could not say he was half-witted for he knew how to do the ordinary things of life; how to be polite and jump up to take cups round at coffee time or open doors for the women; how to eat with refinement; how to dress well. But the mild brown eyes, set in a ruddy face as yet hairless, had no more spark of life in them than a pool of mud. Polly said of him that you could dance naked in front of him and he would continue to stare at you as though you were fully clothed, carrying a tray of dishes.

Andrina could twist him round her little finger. I saw her eyes on him when her mother refused her permission to go to Pretoria. She nagged at him during the day until he went to Mrs Van Brandenberg and told her that he had invited Leon to spend the evening at Welgedacht. Mrs Van Brandenberg became agitated for she was visiting in Pretoria that evening and where she had refused to listen to Andrina, she now began to encourage her.

So, with all this scheming, I got a chance to see the lantern slides; disguised in Mittee's bonnet and the veil and smelling to the high heaven of camphor. Mrs Van Brandenberg drove with us as far as the hall and waited until she saw Andrina safely into the hall, thinking Leon was at Welgedacht with Karel.

We had scarcely seated ourselves when Andrina mumbled that she was going to post a letter and before Mittee could answer, she had hurried down the aisle and was out of the door. Mittee got up to follow her but I pulled at her arm.

'She's going to meet Leon, Mittee, how simple you are not to see it. The girl only used this as an excuse to get away from her mother.'

'Hi, what deep ground there is in her,' breathed Mittee almost in admiration.

There was time for no more conversation for a man had come on to the stage and as easily as though he had known us all his life began to tell us about the pictures we were to see. From the first picture the show was spoiled by a man in the seat behind me. The polished Outlander on the stage was explaining a picture of the Holy Land when this man leaned forward, tapping me on the shoulder.

'Would you mind removing your bonnet, madam, I can't see a thing past that brim.'

Mittee spoke to him over her shoulder. 'It is impossible.'

'Why, pray?'

'She's bald.'

'Bald?'

'As an egg.'

'Well, that's a terrible affliction for a woman.' He let us watch the pictures for a few minutes before he said, 'Well, she's got a wig on, hasn't she?'

Mittee did not answer. The Outlander was saying, 'We continue our journey to Jerusalem . . .'

'How did such a thing happen?'

'Sickness,' said Mittee.

Then he wanted to know what sort of sickness and when it had taken place. Mittee nudged me and I laughed out loud, causing the people round us to hiss and use such ugly words as Mad and No Upbringing. My interest in the pictures could not keep pace with my laughter. I laughed into my handkerchief, I strangled myself with my own hand; but it was no use. Mittee had to lead me out while Bethlehem was being shown. Then we had to stand for an hour, Mittee cursing me all the time, while we waited for that wicked Andrina. I liked it there for the streets were marvellously lit up with electric light, something to tell them about in Plessisburg.

At last we saw the lovers coming towards us, Andrina and Leon.

They were beautiful. With arms linked, stride matching stride, they looked more like brother and sister than cousins. She was fairer than he and an inch shorter but their slender bodies had been cast from the same mould, his skin was as pale as hers.

'Hi, how wonderful,' said Mittee, speaking out my thought. 'Look, Selina, they are like one person . . .'

That outing gave Polly an idea for a wonderful game which passed happy hours for us when the house was empty. We would dress up in our nonnies' clothes and pretend we were white girls. They would have been mad with rage to see us. Down the stairs we would float, taking care to show the slenderness of ankles in open-work silk stockings, as they did and then getting into a fluster because some man might have noticed. For the sake of a tickey, the Kaffir girl would serve us with tea in Andrina's sitting room down-stairs. I laugh even now to think of Polly and me in that room, to which Andrina invited only those she wished to honour. It was a room as pretty as the lid of a chocolate box, all satin and ribbons and net. In our borrowed clothes we looked quite at home there.

We were playing this game one afternoon when a cab drew up in front of the house and from it descended three gentlemen so well dressed that I scarcely recognized them for a few seconds.

'Rich people,' said Polly, peeping through the curtains. 'Only rich people could afford to hire a cab to drive them all the way out here.'

'The richest in Plessisburg,' I said proudly, for there was no mistaking the Du Plessises as they advanced on the house, chests bursting with the glory of marvellous waistcoats and heads crowned with beaver hats. The cabby came behind them with a large parcel. 'It's the magistrate and his two sons, Frikkie and Paul.' I said his name last, softly, but Polly did not seem to notice the tenderness in my voice.

'I wonder what is in the parcel,' she whispered.

There was time to say no more for when the Kaffir girl had explained that the people were out, the Du Plessises sauntered back and forth along the stoep. Polly, with a quick gesture to me, slid out of the room, leaving the door open so that I could follow her; but I stayed for a while to listen to Paul's voice, growing louder as he passed the sitting room and then softer as he turned the corner of the stoep. My hands were clasped beneath my chin and suddenly there were tears splashing on my fingers. Did he ever think of Selina when she was not by?

I heard the magistrate say, 'Let's take a stroll through the grounds, they are beautiful at this time of the year.'

'I will wait here for Mittee,' said Paul. 'She will not be long, the girl said.'

The tears dried on my hand. There was no sound on the stoep and I peeped out to see Paul sitting on a chair facing the door of Andrina's sitting room.

'Paul.' I was shy of him and yet eager for his admiration. I swished the skirt of Mittee's blue silk dress and ran my hand over the feather of her hat. He put out his hand to me but I stayed in the doorway. 'In these clothes I look like a white girl, don't I?'

His hand dropped and bitter pride twisted his mouth. 'No. You could never look like a white girl.'

I began in a shrill voice, 'I will tell Mittee, I will tell everybody . . .' but the look on his face stopped me. 'Hi, basie, don't look at me like that, you know that Selina would never do anything to hurt you.' My body drooped in the fine clothes and I could not see him for tears.

'You mustn't cry about it. But leave me alone, Selina. I'm finished with you.' I ground the knuckles of my forefingers into my eyes to stop myself from crying but the tears only came the faster. Paul crossed the stoep and took my hands in his. 'You are just like a little child. Now don't cry, I'm not angry any more.'

'You said you were finished with me.'

'I've come to fix the date for my wedding.'

'You will never be finished with me, basie.'

I pulled my hands away from him and ran through Andrina's sitting room. I wanted to take off Mittee's clothes now, to get rid of the smell of them from my body; for I knew that he had recognized the dress and the hat and the scent of lavender.

'Where have you been? Man, I was getting quite worried,' said Polly, meeting me at the head of the stairs.

'Ag, it was nothing.'

She watched me sourly as I put on my own print dress and white apron. 'You've been up to something. Listen, there's the waggonette now, you'd better hurry.'

We walked to the window on the landing, from where we could see the magistrate and Frikkie coming towards the waggonette as it drew to a standstill. Mrs Van Brandenberg was the first to come out, tripping over her own feet in her haste.

'Siegfried,' she cried. 'And which of your boys is this?'

'Frikkie, greet Mrs Van Brandenberg. And this, Margarita, is Paul.'

Paul shook hands but Frikkie was not in the mood for careful manners. He kissed Mrs Van Brandenberg and then shouted, 'Hotnot, Mittee, we've brought the silk for your wedding dress.'

He made a rush for Mittee as she got out of the waggonette but Paul was there first. He swung Mittee from her feet.

'Nice men, hey?' said Polly. 'Man, how I love jolly people. We'll go downstairs and get into the kitchen so that we can wait on table. I want to get a good look at them.'

We pushed the Kaffir girl out of the way and began to prepare the coffee ourselves. Mrs Van Brandenberg bustled into the kitchen.

'The best cups,' she breathed, 'and whole preserved oranges, pressed figs . . .' She was busy with her keys as she spoke, unlocking cupboard doors behind which the treasures of the pantry were kept safe from the servants. Polly and I had a try at everything before we carried the trays into the dining room.

We had to remove the silk from the table before we spread the cloth. 'Feel it, Selina, if your hands are spotless,' said Mittee, with glowing face. 'What beautiful quality. And twenty-five yards.'

I felt the silk. The touch of it melted into my fingers and I longed to wrap it round my naked body. Beneath it, a woman would be a desirable, boneless creature. . .

'Help Polly with the cups,' said Mrs Van Brandenberg, sharply.

'Well, Selina, and how do you like Pretoria?' asked the magistrate, as indulgent as though I were still a child. I remember that he used the same tone to me when I was small. He would pull my plaits and say, Neat, neat, what a neat little coloured child.

'I'd rather be in Plessisburg, baas,' I answered.

'That's right.' The magistrate arranged his beard carefully so that his coffee would not soil it. 'I'm glad you like the silk, Mittee. Paul chose it but all of us went into the shop, Chudleigh's it was, and it was I who spoke to the shopman. Show us the best silk in the shop, I said, rich silk for a wedding gown. This way, sir, says the Outlander, and he walks in front of us as if he is made of jelly. Two years in the saddle on commando would make something of you, my little old one, I thought. And suddenly there is no time to think. Bale after bale of silk is brought down, Paul shakes his head and grows angry. Nothing is good enough. At last they bring out the right stuff.'

'I tell you, that whole shop knew Paul Du Plessis was there buying a wedding dress for his girl,' said Frikkie sarcastically.

Paul retorted, 'We thought you might be tempted to buy a dress for Letty.'

'If there is one way to hurry the wedding on, it's to buy the girl her dress and perhaps I will when I've been waiting three years,' said Frikkie.

There was a silence as we went back to the kitchen and when we heard the magistrate speak again, the holiday boom had gone from his voice and I knew that Frikkie was catching it.

'Beautiful silk,' said Polly, as she halved a preserved orange with me. 'Are they really a rich family?'

I described to her a chest of drawers that Paul had shown to Mittee and me when we were children. It had been left open by mistake and in it were hundreds of golden sovereigns, piled one upon the other and wrapped in red silk handkerchiefs. 'You can ride from sunrise to sunset and you are still on their land,' I boasted.

'The Van Brandenbergs are better off,' said Polly, loyally. She rubbed her chest for the preserved orange had been too much for her. 'Why, they've got four houses in Pretoria alone and I don't know how many in Capetown and he has made money out of the gold. One of Andrina's dresses is worth more than two of Mittee's.'

We were close to quarrelling but I silenced Polly. 'My nonnie has the stuff for her wedding dress but yours is playing around and not even betrothed.'

Mittee did not have the wedding dress made up because she was having such a fine time going about with the Du Plessises. Man, how I envied her, although I knew that she was not happy.

I went into her room one morning to see why she was late for breakfast. She had been sitting so long in her corsets and frilled drawers that her arms were covered with goose pimples. One stocking was on but the other she had over her hand, the mesh pulled tight. She looked into it as though she saw some message written there.

'They are waiting breakfast for you, Mittee.'

'I don't want to eat.'

'If you're going to Johannesburg today, you'd better have something to eat.'

'I am not going to Johannesburg.'

I said bitterly, 'I know what is the matter with you. You were sitting there thinking that you will soon have to be married now that you have got the silk for your wedding dress.'

'Hold your mouth, insolence.' She picked up the comb from the dressing table, throwing it at me as though she was glad of the excuse to hurt me.

'You are a devil,' I cried, running out of the room before she could do anything else to me.

I was in Andrina's sitting room when she came downstairs for I had taken over the arrangement of the flowers from Polly. I peeped through the doorway and made a face at Mittee but she turned round and caught me.

She said calmly, 'I knew you were there, Selina, and get out of my sight. I'm in no mood for nonsensical girls.'

I went into the room again and after I had set the flowers out, I began to polish the beautiful ornaments that graced the room. Presently I heard the magistrate talking to Mittee. I stole to the door to listen, for his voice was quiet and serious. He sat on the bench beside her, leaning towards her so that I was taken by the illusion that he loved her.

'What is the matter, little daughter? Why did you not come to breakfast?'

'I didn't want breakfast.'

'Why are you so downcast? All the brightness is gone.'

'Uncle Siegfried, I am often afraid when I think of getting married. If only I could wait a little while longer.'

'The time for waiting is past, Mittee. I had been married for a year when I was your age. My dear child, when you have once taken the step and your life is busy with a big household and children, you will wonder why you were afraid.'

'Is there nothing else to expect from marriage but the care of a house and children?' asked Mittee, speaking with difficulty because she was shy at giving utterance to the longing that lay deep within her.

The magistrate answered her softly, 'We all hope there is, Mit, and we all search for it, even I who have been married three times and am old now. Some I have loved and not been loved in return, others have loved me but I could not love them; and so I think it is with everybody. Paul loves you, let that be sufficient. The other is only a dream.'

'Have you seen Andrina and Leon together?'

'It will pass away.' He took her hands in his. 'I should not persuade you but of all my children I love Paul the best. I know he is reckless and arrogant but you will put a curb on him.'

'Uncle, you are a good advocate.'

He was still serious although she was smiling. 'I want you to remember this, Mittee, and I will tell him the same thing. If he makes you unhappy, you must come to me, just as you would to your father. I promise you that I will look after you like my own daughter.'

Mittee's white hands still lay within his and I saw that his fingers were gnarled and old, marked by the years that he had lived, while the remainder of his body was vigorous and straight. Mittee sat quiet, drawing strength from those old hands, as she was to do many times when real sorrow came to her.

Andrina came on to the stoep, dressed for the outing. 'Aren't you ready, Mittee?' She smiled, with that spice of malice that reminded you of her mother. 'Anyone would think that you and Uncle Siegfried were courting.'

Hastily, the magistrate withdrew his hands. I was astonished to notice that he was embarrassed by Andrina, who seemed to know that she had power over him for she continued to smile at him while he looked steadfastly at her shoes.

Mrs Van Brandenberg allowed Polly and me to ride on the floor of the waggonette because we were to go with her to her eldest daughter's house and help with the spring cleaning. So it was that we were able to see the holiday party off on the train. My eye was taken by Frikkie who looked longingly at the beard of an Arab standing with folded arms near him. He was a dignified man and the beard was glossy and thick, oiled so that it sparkled. As the train moved out, Frikkie leaned from the window and put a lighted match to that glory. A cloud of sweet-scented smoke went up from the Arab's face and he cursed Frikkie with terrible words as he clutched at his beard. Mrs Van Brandenberg, thinking it her duty because she knew Frikkie, went up to him and offered him a tickey whereupon he turned his curses on her. Then she took it out on me because I laughed. The last we saw of the Du Plessises was the magistrate cuffing Frikkie as though he were a mischievous boy.

They went back to Plessisburg the next day, which was just as well, for Frikkie had bought himself a bicycle and a pair of knickerbockers made of check material. He was a sensation in Pretoria and I could imagine what Plessisburg would think of him when he took to the road. Aunt Lena told me that the Water Fiscal ran for the minister, thinking the devil was coming towards him when he saw Frikkie on the bicycle, with Fanie whooping beside him to clear the way.

Mittee, who always loved Paul better when he was absent, wrote long letters to him and put on airs with Andrina because she was engaged. She basked in Mrs Van Brandenberg's approval of the match.

'He's the sort of husband I would like for you, Andrina,' said Mrs Van Brandenberg, enviously. 'Not an easy man, I can see that, but a man who will make his mark wherever he goes. I can't stand a softie and that's just what my nephew is and I wouldn't like him for you even if you weren't related. Give me a son-in-law like Paul Du Plessis and I'll be happy.'

Andrina smiled and looked at no other man but Leon.

Mrs Van Brandenberg reminded me of the coach driver sitting up on his box, master of the horses. She managed her family with a harsh tactlessness that made the men fear her; her husband, a man meek at home but shrewd at business, and her son Karel, that huge and docile fellow. Andrina, of them all, called for strategy and she would answer her mother back, word for blistering word, taking no heed of the commandment that was quoted to her twenty times a day. She was a tall, proud girl, whom Mittee envied for her casualness about the clothes bought in Europe the year before.

Polly was feathering her nest for Mrs Van Brandenberg paid her sixpence a week to spy on Andrina. From Andrina she received a shilling a week so that she would say nothing of what she saw. Mrs Van Brandenberg did not trust Polly and soon after we arrived she came to me, looking about her to see that she was not observed. She was fashionably dressed but the grandeur of the plum-coloured silk and the flower-heavy hat could not hide her countrified look that persisted although she had lived in towns for years and even travelled across the sea. She had been a Plessisburg girl and one imagined her more at home in a print, with a sunbonnet shading her strong, homely face. I do believe she was jealous of Andrina's fine limbs and careless grace.

She pressed a tickey into my hand. 'Selina, I know you are a good little daughter. Like your mother. I remember her well, a faithful creature.' I looked down gratefully and Mrs Van Brandenberg, impressed by this sign of humility, squeezed my hand over the tickey. 'Now, don't get too friendly with that Polly. My daughter has spoilt her and she is not to be trusted. I trust you. And this is what you must do for me. Today your nonnie and I are going to see the President. I can't put it off but Nonnie Andrina is sick, at least she says she is sick and she has locked herself in her room and won't come out. I want you to stay by her all the time, understand. And if you do it properly, I'll give you another tickey perhaps. What I want to know is, if there are any visitors. Understand? Basie Karel will be here but in a thing like this, it's no use relying on the men, she leads them by the nose. You understand what you must do?'

'Yes, missis.'

'All right. Now hurry upstairs because your nonnie wants you to hook her up. Say nothing about what I've asked you to do.'

I was only too glad to get away from her whispering. As I went upstairs, I tied the tickey into a corner of my apron. I would share it with Polly or give her the whole amount, for truly, taking silver for such a purpose made me feel like Judas Iscariot, though of course Andrina could in no way be compared with the Christ; and if I did spy on her it would be for her own good. After all, who does not know the value of a neighbour's turkey cock straying into the yard? In the end, I bought Auntie Lena a present with the tickey, a little packet of sweets.

Mittee was wearing her new dress. No need for the pink powder today. Excitement had put colour into her face, brilliant on the cheeks and fading to palest pink over her nose and chin. I liked her better when she was pale but I had not the heart to say so for this coffee-drinking at the President's house was important to her. When she stood ready, she looked more beautiful than any girl I had seen, in spite of her rosy face. It was because she was not thinking of her looks for once but of coming face to face with the President.

The waggonette had scarcely turned through the gates when I heard Andrina moving about her room. I sat down near the window, sewing a button to a glove. I made a long job of it for the room was cool and I could look across the rich lawns and bright flower beds. Presently through the garden came Andrina. Her dress was white, a dazzling muslin: her hat was garlanded with poppies and cornflowers and tied with a black velvet ribbon. She was uncorseted and beneath her finery her eager hips rolled like any crude Kaffir girl's.

I bent over the glove. It was a small glove, marked by the impress of Mittee's fingers. Poor little Mittee. She came of stock as lusty as Andrina's, yet she was half dead, thinking of love like a gift of scent wrapped in pretty paper. I put the silly little glove in the box with its fellow and went after Andrina. I did not tell Mrs Van Brandenberg what I saw; a long, slender leg, bent in ecstasy, pressing through the screen of bushes. Then I heard her laugh, low and sweet. So had I laughed with Paul.

I ran across the empty lawns, in a sweat of shame at the thought that Andrina would come out of her hiding place and find that I had spied on her. Only when I reached the kitchen did I feel safe. I fell into a chair, and wiped the sweat from my face while I tried to recover my breath.

Polly, who was ironing, looked at me in surprise. 'Heaven, your face is blotched with red. Was a man after you?'

'No. The old one gave me a tickey to keep my eye on Andrina but I got frightened. I've seen that girl in a rage and she is like a lioness. I caught her there in the bushes.'

Polly tried the iron with the tip of her forefinger, producing the little sound of singing that is pleasant to hear when you are ironing a difficult dress. She bent with satisfaction over a frill, as though what I had told her was nothing.

'You're not the one to be frightened. She will give you ten shillings for keeping your mouth shut. She'll do anything to keep it away from her mother because if that old one knew she would never let her see Leon again. She has only to wait another year or so and she'll be twenty-one and then she can marry him. But a year would be a long time for her to stay away from Leon, I think she would die. She has been carrying on with him since she was sixteen, every chance she gets. She's got fire in her veins, that Andrina. Ask her for ten shillings and she'll give it to you like a lamb.'

'Hi, Polly, I couldn't.'

'I'll ask if you like,' said Polly, looking at me slyly.

'No. She would chase you out of the house.'

Polly laughed. 'She'll give me the ten shillings, especially when I tell her that it was you who saw her.'

'My God, don't do it, Polly, she'll hit me.'

Polly pointed and I looked through the open door to see Andrina returning. She had picked some flowers and she carried them carelessly so that one or two fell behind her. She twitched at her skirt and sang as she went round the corner of the house.

'I've got it,' said Polly the next day, holding up a bright half sovereign. 'I'll tell you what, we'll go to the circus this afternoon.'

'The circus. Oh, Polly.'

'Well, why not? They're all going, so it's good enough for us. This is a grand circus with music and real tigers doing tricks. I heard about it from a boy who does the sweeping.'

Andrina and Mittee went off with Mrs Van Brandenberg, all dressed smartly as though they were going to church. Polly and I were not far behind them, though we had to hurry on foot behind the waggonette, not even stopping for the stitches in our sides. We had to go in secret because Andrina had refused Polly the afternoon off, none too pleased at having to part with ten shillings.

We reached the circus just before it started. Polly and I were given seats on the top tier, the last two left there, and we were crammed against people so that our sweat mingled with theirs in happy brotherliness. It was not long before somebody passed a handful of monkey-nuts over, a man with his eye on Polly. What happiness to sit up there looking round the tent as we broke the monkey-nuts open. I chewed mine well so that the afternoon would not be spoiled by indigestion. They were lovely monkey-nuts, I remember, roasted just right and some slightly burned. These I kept to the last for if there is anything I like it's a browned monkey-nut.

We had not much time to look about but we picked out Andrina and Mittee. They had their parasols with them and leaned on the rail elegantly. They were on the ground and I did not think that their seats were as good as ours but Polly said they were sitting amongst the important people. While we watched, the man behind Andrina touched her on the shoulder. A look came on her face as though somebody had put bad meat under her nose.

'I know what he's doing,' I said joyfully to Polly. 'He's asking her to take her hat off.'

'She isn't going to do it, I know her.'

Polly flipped a shell at the man who had given the monkey-nuts. Flattered, he handed her some more.

'You're right, she won't even look round. Just watch the old one, she's telling him off for daring to speak to her daughter. If he only knew. He's embarrassed by what she has said, he's moving his seat away.'

The circus began. You could have marched a hundred miles to the glorious music, you could have fallen off the seat at the antics of the clown whose boots were yards long. Then up went a big cage and an Outlander, all shiny and with a buttonhole in his lapel, began to put the tigers through their tricks. The music stopped and there was not a sound to be heard from the crowd as they watched this wonderful thing. The tigers growled and showed their teeth but the brave man in their midst treated them like tame cats.

That was all Andrina and Mittee saw of the circus. A big tiger lifted its tail and sprayed through the bars on the two proud girls. Of all the people in the circus it had to be those two, so eaten up with vanity, and all over their parasols. It caught each one equally. At first I thought they would faint but no, they were both healthy girls. All they did was scream and spring up from their seats but, of course, it was too late. Everybody was laughing at them. They swept out of the tent, holding their parasols away from their dresses with the tips of three fingers as though the handles were hot. Mrs Van Brandenberg, with an anguished look at the entrancing tigers, followed the other two slowly.

'I suppose we should go home, too,' said Polly. 'Andrina will be in a terrible temper about the tiger and having to pay the ten shillings.'

'If I'm killed I'll stay to the end,' I said, for I could not have left that dazzling place.

So we stayed to the end and it was dark when we reached home. Auntie Lena believed everything I told her about the circus, except that one of the elephants played a game with a ball and bat. But it is true. You never saw anything so old-fashioned.

When I walked into Mittee's room, I expected her to fly at me for taking the afternoon off without permission but she said absently, 'Oh, there you are, Selina.' She was sitting at her table with a letter between her fingers. 'I've fixed my wedding for Nagmaal.'

I could hear Polly catching it from Andrina but I felt no pleasure in my escape from Mittee's tongue. 'Is that the letter, nonnie?'

'Yes. And I'm glad it is settled at last. I think I had really made up my mind after the magistrate spoke to me. No use telling you what he said because I know you listened to every word. There's not a man in Pretoria to touch Paul, I'm very lucky, even my aunt admits it.'

I thrust my face close to hers. 'I'm glad the tiger pissed you wet, Nonnie Maria.'

She went paler at that. Then words burst in a storm from her. 'I'll give you your wages. You can leave immediately. Immediately, spying on your betters.'

All I could think of to say was, 'Maria, Maria,' until she lost her temper completely and pulled my hair and shook me. Not a sound did I make and at last she fell back on the bed, laughing breathlessly.

'Why are you calling me Maria?'

'Because it is your proper name,' I said sulkily.

'Well, stop it. That tiger, Selina, I was never so ashamed in my life.'

'Polly and I nearly died of laughter.'

'It's not the sort of story I would like to hear going round Plessisburg.'

'How they would laugh,' I said with spite.

CHAPTER IV

I walked alone on the hill behind Welgedacht. When I looked back I could see Pretoria, snugly encircled by hills. Before me was the flat veld but my eyes could not travel unimpeded to the horizon as they did in Plessisburg for they were arrested by the green of the trees surrounding Welgedacht, by the farmhouses, by the grazing cattle and by the road that led to Johannesburg, a red road running like a mouth across the face of the veld. The sun blazed from a dead sky but I would not seek the relief of shade though my face was moist with sweat and tears.

Mittee had left the silk for her wedding dress lying in its wrappings on the foot of her bed. Twenty-five yards of silk for one dress, did you ever hear of such vanity? I burnt as though I was already in the fires of hell. It was only because of her vanity that she wanted to get married. How could he love the vain and empty thing, when all she wanted to do was prink in front of the glass? Everybody must come into her room to see the stuff; Leon must cast his opinion on its quality, even Karel's thick fingers must pronounce on its excellence and Polly had to see it a dozen times to exclaim in admiration. I grew sick with rage and hatred whenever I looked at it.

I had torn the silk to pieces that morning when I was tidying up her room after she had gone out. It was strong and I had to use my teeth on the weft to start the silk ripping. When it was in shreds, I turned my feet on it as though I were crushing a caterpillar.

As I walked on the hill, I knew with bitterness that I was as brutish as Jansie, finding relief in destruction. Had he suffered like this after he killed his dog? When Mittee ran into the house that afternoon, she would call out as she always did, 'Selina, get the parcels from the waggonette, I've brought a little surprise for you.' She always bought something for me when she was shopping even if it was only a screw of sweets or a necklace of cheap beads.

I threw myself on the ground in agony because I had no hatred left for her, only love. The hours dropped upon me one by one but still I lay there in the dry grass, careless of the blistering heat and of the ants that crawled over my still body.

There was somebody watching me. I sat up, smoothing the damp hair from my forehead. A man was sitting amongst the rocks, leaning his head well back to catch the shade from an overhanging ledge.

He was so fair that his hair at the roots was white, shading at the ends to the colour of ripened grass. In the sunlight he looked as though gold dust had been sprinkled over him for even the smallest hairs on his arms were bright. No beard hid the skin soft as a girl's and by this I knew him to be an Outlander who had not been long in the Transvaal.

He has gone from the Transvaal for ever, back to that land of cloud and mist where the winds come shouting over a cold sea; yet surely he speaks sometimes of that hill behind Pretoria where he found a poor coloured girl crying in the sun and spoke for the first time the name of Mittee.

'Come and cry in the shade,' he said with friendly mockery. 'Why do you choose such a very hot place to be miserable in?'

'Because I'm not a pink and white wax doll,' I spat.

He laughed and I could not help smiling just a little. So many Outlanders have corpse-like faces and if they do laugh, it is with a short bark as though they must get the joke over and hurry on to the serious business. This man was lazy in his fun and the laughter lodged itself in the wrinkles round his eyes.

All the same, when I sat down near him I kept a rock under my fingers, to be ready for him if he should spring at me and try to rape me. You never can tell with men and I have always heard that a blue-eyed man is not to be trusted.

He asked me my name. He was not afraid of speaking the Language, though he was not good at it, mixing it up with a bit of English, High Dutch, Kaffir and, I think, some words that he had made up for himself; but he understood what I said to him.

'You're English. We've got an Englishman trading in our town. His name is Tyson. Do you know him, baas?'

'No. And try and call me Doctor Castledene, that's my name, not Baas.'

'I can't say it.'

'Call me Doctor Basil then, that's my Christian name.'

'Besil. That's easy.'

'Why were you crying, Selina? Tell me and I'll help you if I can.'

He turned his face to me, the laughter gone from it. My fingers left the stone for I saw that this stranger was a good man. The baby skin and gentle eyes belied the noble strength of arched nose and fine mouth. Here was no weakling as I had at first supposed but a man whose power was tempered by kindliness and pity.

'Nobody can help me. I've done a terrible thing. I've torn up the silk that my nonnie was given for her wedding dress. When she sees what I have done, she'll be very angry. But it's not only that. She trusts me like her own sister and when we are alone I call her Mittee.'

'Mittee, that's a funny little name.'

'She chose it for herself. Her real name is Maria but she says it is ugly. She used to make me call her Mittee when we were children. Never in front of Grandma Van Brandenberg, of course. She would have thrashed us for such vanity. And as soon as the old lady died, she made everybody call her Mittee.'

He was smiling again. 'What does she look like?'

'She's got big eyes, as big as that.' I made a circle of my finger and thumb. 'And black hair, straight and shiny like a crow's wing; a pale, beautiful skin. She's very vain of her appearance. The minister has lectured her in public about it twice. She will be daughter-in-law to the magistrate of Plessisburg and she will have a waggonette to ride in, very important. She has spent all her money on eight silk dresses, the vain thing, I never heard of anybody having eight silk dresses. It's all she cares about, fine clothes and fine furniture.'

'Well then, perhaps it will do her good to lose the silk you have torn. In fact, she sounds so vain and empty that nothing could really hurt her much.'

I began to cry again. 'Oh, you don't understand. She bought me blue silk to wear on her wedding day. And beads and sweets. She took me to see the lantern slides and lent me her clothes. Sometimes she forgets I am a coloured girl and calls me Sister. I love her and I hate her, you could never understand.'

'Then she is lucky that your violence fell on that piece of silk. Why don't you get work somewhere else?'

'I knew you would not understand. I have been with her all my life and my mother was with the family before I was born. I couldn't leave her, not unless she forced me to go and Mittee would never do that.'

'If you are to stay with her, you must purge yourself of envy.'

'You speak like a minister,' I said bitterly. 'Who are you to set yourself up so?'

'A missionary, a doctor really. More of a doctor than a missionary as yet, I'm afraid.'

'Where is your church?'

'I haven't got a church yet. I have only just arrived in the country. Next month I go to my station, a hundred miles to the north of this town Plessisburg about which you speak. But now I'm picking up the languages and learning a little bit about the people.'

'There are few white people north of Plessisburg. You will be lonely and probably drink or take a Kaffir wife.' The clear eyes looked through me, not with arrogance but with a deep inward conviction of strength. It was the same look that Mittee had in her eyes sometimes and it always made me angry for it seemed to put her beyond the reach of temptation. 'Oh little doctor,' I said, leaning forward and laughing through clenched teeth, 'I daresay you won't drink or take a Kaffir wife. You are like Mittee, your blood is like vinegar . . .'

'Perhaps you will like me better if I promise to marry one of my pupils and drink myself to death,' said the missionary.

I was shocked. The man was joking. 'Hi, fancy a missionary saying a thing like that,' I said. 'You're like her, I tell you, you're like Mittee.'

'You won't tear up my best silk shirt, will you?' he mocked.

I sprang to my feet. 'And I won't sit here talking to you any more. It will be a surprise to me if you ever convert any heathen.'

'At least I have stopped you from crying. Here, take my handkerchief and wipe your face, it is streaked with dust and tears.'

'I'll use a corner of my apron, thank you.'

He stood beside me, holding out his hand to stop me from going. The laughter was dying out of his face and I was comforted by the sincerity in his eyes. 'Confess to Mittee what you have done and perhaps she will forgive you.'

'Yes. I will have to. She will hit me, perhaps she might even tell me to go.'

'If she turns you out, if she beats you badly, come to me and I will help you. I will find you work at the Mission Station until you get into a house. I will wait for you on the hill here. Promise me that you will let me help you.'

'Thank you, Doctor Besil.'

As I walked back to Welgedacht, I did not feel forsaken by God any more, for surely it was He who had sent the young missionary to help me in my need. I would drink my draught of bitter aloes and perhaps I would be forgiven.

I waited for her in her room, with the silk in an untidy heap at my feet. The words that I would say to her chased themselves round and round my brain but when she flung the door open at last and ran into the room, I could not utter a sound.

She closed the door behind her and put her handbag on the bed. 'Who has done that?' she whispered, pointing to the silk.

I could not speak. I sank to my knees, reaching up my clasped hands to her in the agony of my silence.

'You. You bastard.'

She pulled me to my feet by my hair and slapped my face until I was almost fainting. It was Mrs Van Brandenberg who pulled her from me.

'Shame on you, Mittee, to hit the creature like that.'

'Look what she has done, torn my silk to pieces.' Who would have thought that Mittee's voice could be so shrill?

'Hi. My time, what on earth made you do a thing like that, Selina?'

Andrina looked in through the doorway. 'She needs a good sjambokking.'

Their voices flicked at me until I quivered with hatred. I thought, If I ever get the chance, I'll poison Mittee and gloat over her as she dies.

Mittee said, 'Go out of the room, everybody, and I'll find out why she did it. She won't say a word while you're here.'

'All right, but I warn you, Mittee, not to lay a finger on her.' Mrs Van Brandenberg stooped over me. 'Her whole face is swollen up. You want to look out, she'll turn on you. It would be better to send her away.'

The door closed on them. I crept past Mittee, expecting her to spring at me again but she sat as still as a stone.

'Bastard, why did you do it?'

I went into the passage without answering. She flew after me but Mrs Van Brandenberg was lying in wait and caught her arm.

'Let her go now, Mittee, she'll be stabbing you if you keep on at her.'

Late that night, Mittee came to the little room where I slept. I knew she was there by the smell of camphor but I thought I must be dreaming until she spoke.

'Selina, I've brought ointment for your face. Oh, to think I hit you like that, all for a piece of silk. I'll light the candle so I can see to rub the stuff on your face.' With hands as delicate as fluttering moths, she smoothed the ointment into my cheeks.

'You should not do this for me, nonnie. I deserved it. I was jealous and I have no right to be jealous of you.'

'Jealous? But I bought you the blue silk . . .'

She could not understand. Almost I cried out, I love Paul, I have lain with him. It was pity for him rather than for her that kept me silent.

So it was that I did not take my bundle with me when I went to meet the missionary. I think he fell in love with Mittee, though he had never seen her, when I described her remorse and tenderness.

A parcel of silk came for her from Chudleigh's and as soon as she showed it to me, I knew who had sent it.

'Where did you get the money to replace the silk?' she asked sternly but her eyes were softer than her voice.

I laid my hand on my heart. 'It did not come from me, nonnie. I will swear it on the Bible.'

'Then where from? It is the same silk and the same amount as Paul gave me.'

I shook my head and she went to her aunt, but Mrs Van Brandenberg was as much mystified as she was. They questioned Andrina in vain. It was late afternoon but their curiosity was so great that Mrs Van Brandenberg told the boy to inspan at once. They were dressed anyhow as they dashed into Pretoria to find out at the shop who had sent the silk.

Leon Dressel got the credit for it. A fair man, clean-shaven, said the assistant, who was in a hurry to get home. Leon had side levers and a wisp of beard but he was the only fair man they knew of who could have bought the silk. Though Leon denied it, Mittee kept a soft place in her heart for him and always took his part against Mrs Van Brandenberg after that.

Many years later, in that dreadful cave in the Wolkbergen, Doctor Besil told Mittee that he had bought the silk for her wedding dress and that his pockets were empty when he had paid for it. Sometimes I dream that I said to Mittee, an English missionary bought the silk for you; and that she went with me to the hill behind Welgedacht and spoke to him. Would she have loved him then?

Let me remember him. He was tall and strongly built but there was an easiness about him that added grace to his movements. He walked quickly always, each step distinct from the other and while he spoke he kept his hands still, never gesticulating as we do. I remember his hands more clearly than his face. They were beautiful hands, with long up-curling fingers that healed whatever they touched. Once I saw him cut open a female monkey that could not give birth to her baby. Fanie found her dying on the veld and we took her to Doctor Besil. The sight of blood and wounds makes me sick but I watched him work over her, his hands so deft, his face so tranquil. He delivered the baby monkey and then sewed up the poor little mother; and he came often to visit her while we nursed her, pleased and proud to find her still alive.

He came to know the bitter mixing of evil and good, yet while I knew him he did not lose that air of youthfulness that would make the most cantankerous old woman smile at him. This youthfulness lay not altogether in his fairness for he retained it after the sun perished his colour; nor in his lack of sin for it was still there after he had broken the commandment; nor was it in his gentleness. He became a soldier. Perhaps it lay in his fearlessness.

He used to say that we who are born on the veld are afraid and face each day with anxious prayer. That was why he preached to us from the Books of hope and scarcely ever frightened us with the Old Testament. I thought his sermons were too weak for the Kaffirs in the valley and that was why he did not gain many converts, though they trusted him as I have never seen a white man trusted by Kaffirs.

I saw him again the day before we left Pretoria and said goodbye to him, never thinking that our lives were linked. But I fell asleep that night with the wish that I could have loved such a man.

Polly woke me up. She had not gone to bed early because she was courting with the Malay gardener and as she was sneaking up the driveway, she heard a terrible row going on in Andrina's sitting room.

'Come and watch the fun,' she said. 'The old one has caught Andrina with Leon at last.'

We stood on a bench in the shadow of a tree from where we were able to look across the stoep directly into Andrina's sitting room. Leon was held prisoner by Van Brandenberg and Karel. He must have put up a good fight before he was taken for chairs were overturned and the net round the couch was torn from the silk, giving the room the look of a lady roughly handled. Mrs Van Brandenburg had Andrina in a wrestler's grip. The girl had been caught naked for wrapped around her was the brocaded tablecloth, difficult to handle because of its stiffness. It slipped down constantly to reveal the flash of her breast or thigh.

'You will be excommunicated,' shrieked Mrs Van Brandenberg, her voice spiralling thinly through the open window.

'Street woman,' yelled Van Brandenberg and I think he surprised even himself by the thunder that came from his scraggy throat.

Leon bravely took the sting from their words. 'Stop up your ears, my love, don't listen to the old things.'

This sent Van Brandenberg almost mad. 'Hit him, Karel,' he cried. 'Kill him.'

Karel balled his fist, regarding it with a mild eye. He swung the fist to and fro as though it had no part with him but its momentum slackened and his fingers straightened. He looked at his father with the eyes of a dying ox.

'I can't do it, pa, not to Leon.'

Van Brandenberg himself took a swing at Leon but it was so ineffectual that Mrs Van Brandenberg said impatiently, 'Take him away. His father will thrash him.'

As they began to move towards the door, Polly and I scrambled down from the bench and ran with breathless laughter to my room. We could not sleep for laughing over Andrina's downfall.

The household was astir early the next morning and I found Mittee hollow-eyed from lack of sleep. 'Auntie has been at Andrina all night, you never heard such lamentations. They are coming to Plessisburg with us.'

Andrina refused to pack or even to dress herself. The place was in turmoil. Polly and I ran backwards and forwards with dresses to be sponged and ironed, while the kitchen girls jeered to see us so busy. Andrina sat sulkily in her bed, reading the newspaper. Her mother had to dress her and it took Karel and her father to drag her down to the waggonette. There was another scene at the coach but when she saw a crowd beginning to collect, her pride saved the situation and she got into the coach of her own free will.

Even Polly talked of finding another job, for a person had to walk as softly as a cat amongst those snappish women. Mittee was an angel in comparison with them. There was Andrina, tight-lipped over her separation from Leon. She could not even get a letter to him because his father opened all his letters and sent Andrina's back to Mrs Van Brandenberg. She had made Polly pay her back the ten shillings out of her wages and every time she passed me, she gave me a push; for she thought that one of us had given her away.

There was Mrs Van Brandenberg, smarting over her daughter's immorality but cruelly triumphant over her unhappiness. She quarrelled often with Andrina, sometimes at the top of her voice and sometimes in penetrating, vicious whispers that made the house unbearable.

There was Letty Van Aswegan who had come to stay while she sewed Mittee's wedding dress. She was a good needlewoman but a terrible companion for she dropped acid into everything she said so that Mittee was afraid every time she opened her mouth. She had always been jealous of Mittee but now that Mittee was to be married before her, she was venomous. Her spitefulness never ceased to come as a shock for she was a pretty girl with blue eyes of a wonderful softness and fine golden hair so that you expected sweetness from her. The only time we got a smile out of her was when Frikkie came to sit up with her. She came from a poor family so the match was a good one for her, but to offset her poverty she was known as the most virtuous girl in Plessisburg. Other girls might flirt at Nagmaal or Christmas time but not Letty and perhaps that is why Frikkie suited her, for a more luke-warm lover you never saw.

One afternoon, as Letty was putting the finishing touches to the dress, we heard Mrs Van Brandenberg's voice rise up in a cry of anguish.

'Andrina has struck her,' said Letty, almost swallowing a pin in her satisfaction.

'Surely not.'

Mittee tiptoed to the bedroom door but as she tapped on it there was the sound of the key turning in the lock. 'Auntie. Is Auntie all right?'

Mrs Van Brandenberg's voice came like a ghost's. 'Go away, why must you pry into everything?'

'There is something up,' said Letty joyfully. Her little pointed teeth glittered as she bit off a piece of cotton.

I caught Polly's eye and followed her to the backyard. We sat down with our backs against the wall of the orchard, stretching our legs to the consoling touch of the sun. Polly leaned towards me, whispering with pitying malice.

'Andrina has got herself into trouble.'

'Hi. How do you know?'

'Am I a fool? I look after every single thing of hers, don't I? I could have told the old woman this two months ago.'

'That's why the old thing screamed out like that. Now she will have to give way and let her marry the cousin.'

'Not if I know her. That stone would sooner give way. I shouldn't be surprised if she doesn't try to palm Andrina on to some other man.'

'Now, who?'

It was pleasant to sit there discussing the misfortunes of the rich and powerful. 'Thank God I'm a pure girl,' said Polly, but I knew this to be a sinful lie. She looked at me from the corners of her eyes. 'Now if I didn't know you were a good girl, Selina, I'd say you were pregnant too. You've got that drawn look about your face but, of course, I know I'm mistaken.'

'You hell,' I said and went away from her. I never felt the same towards Polly after that piece of spitefulness, although she was right.

By morning Mrs Van Brandenberg had got over the shock and she met Letty's bright, questioning eyes with a flat stare. 'When is this one going home, Mittee?'

Mittee blushed crimson for Letty's sake. 'Why, Auntie . . .'

Letty had meant to go home the next day for the dress was finished but now she said, 'If Mittee doesn't mind, I think I will stay until after the wedding, there is a lot I can do for her.'

There were still three weeks to go to Nagmaal but poor Mittee tried to smile. 'You are very welcome, Letty.'

Mrs Van Brandenberg made a noise like an angry rhinoceros and went out of the room. As far as I know, she never addressed another word to Letty. It did not seem that we prepared for a wedding for we thought all the time of the door that shut Andrina from us. There was something terrifying about that blank door behind which the haughty girl lay in silence. You did not hear her voice, only Mrs Van Brandenberg's. She would sit in the room with her daughter; talking, talking until your ears were revolted by the soft, insistent sound and you had either to shut it out with your fingers or go out of the house.

Because of this, we spent hours by the river, taking our handwork with us so that the time should not be wasted altogether. It was pleasant enough there although we had to put up with Letty. Her chief delight was to send me back to the house for something she had forgotten and always just as we had seated ourselves with our work ready to be started.

One afternoon she sent me back for a reel of crochet cotton. I was still grumbling as I came up the pathway at the side of the house but I forgot about Letty and her nonsense when I saw Andrina sitting on the stoep. She was pale, it is true, but her pride was as fierce as ever when she faced her mother.

'I will marry Leon if I have to go to the President himself for permission.'

'Never.' Her mother's voice cracked out like a whip. 'You will never marry him.'

The florid face was close to Andrina and she moved back distastefully. 'You are jealous. I know. You hate my father, and you are jealous because I love Leon.'

'I have known love. Oh yes, I have known love . . .' I could not catch what it was that she said to Andrina but it must have been something terrible for Andrina fell back, whimpering, 'No, no.'

Her voice died away and I saw that she had fainted. I ran forward but Mrs Van Brandenberg stood where she was, as savage as a lion about to maul its kill. Letty did not get her crochet cotton that afternoon because I sat by Andrina, fanning her and giving her water until Polly came home. She would not let her mother near her all that night but in the morning Mrs Van Brandenberg took charge again.

We did not see Andrina for a few days after that. When her mother was not in the room with her, the door remained locked. Once or twice Mrs Gouws went in there and then we would hear Andrina sobbing.

'I'm going to put a stop to this,' said Mittee one evening when Mrs Gouws was in the room.

Letty was out on the front stoep, watching the road for Frikkie's coming, and she missed the scandal that she had been waiting for for two weeks. I smiled when I saw her stroll to the gate just as Mittee went into Andrina's room.

I crept into the passage to listen. There was Mittee's voice, brave and clear.

'Andrina, can I help you? Are you ill? What is the matter?'

Then Mrs Van Brandenberg's voice, smug with power, 'Is this

how you treat your own family, bursting into the room and looking at me like that?'

Andrina spoke, each word as bitter as aloes. 'What they have done to me, Mit. They talk to me of excommunication. Ask her and her what they have done to me.'

'What is she talking about, Auntie Gouws?' Mittee asked, and you would have sworn it was Grandma Van Brandenberg speaking.

Mrs Gouws snivelled, 'Don't blame me. Hi, Mittee, don't blame me. It was your aunt who tempted me. Five pounds she gave me to do it and you know how poor we are.'

'It had to be done, Mittee,' said Andrina harshly. 'She is Leon's mother. Leon is my half-brother, Mittee.' Not a sound came from any of them for a few moments and then Andrina's voice went on. 'Get that girl Letty out of the house for my sake, Mittee. If she finds out anything about this, even the smallest thing, there will be a terrible scandal and even you will suffer.'

Letty was coming up the pathway with Frikkie and I called out to Mittee. She came out of the room, leaning on me as she walked. I took her to her bedroom and flew for smelling salts.

'Did you hear, Selina?'

'Yes, and if I were you I would get rid of Letty at once. Tell her to go tonight because already she guesses something is wrong.'

'Poor Andrina. Oh, poor Andrina. I used to see that damned old Auntie Gouws go in there but I never dreamed of anything like this. Hi, her own half-brother, Selina.'

'That's what the old one must have told her the day she fainted. To think she's allowed in the church.'

'I never dreamed there was anything the matter with poor Andrina except temper.'

'You call me a simpleton, nonnie. Why do you think Letty stayed on? Nobody could be as virtuous as she is and not have a suspicious mind.'

'She will have to go.' Mittee stood up and pulled her dress resolutely over her hips. Her steps, usually so light, struck the floor with sharp little taps as though to give rhythm to her voice.

'Good evening, little one,' said Frikkie, who was sitting on the stoep with Letty.

'Frikkie, you will have to take Letty home tonight.'

Frikkie burst out laughing. 'I thought it wouldn't be long before the womenfolk fell out. How many are there in the house?'

He held up his hand and flipped the names off on his fingers, making a face as he came to Mrs Van Brandenberg's. Nobody laughed at him but I could not help smiling as I peeped through the curtain. 'And that's not counting Polly and Selina.'

Letty turned on him before she attacked Mittee. 'Don't class me with the Coloureds, everybody knows they are your friends. And as for you, Mittee Van Brandenberg, I won't be at your wedding to see the dress I made for you, though I worked my fingers to the bone over it. I know what I know. It's a case for the minister.'

'You get out of this house tonight, Letty Van Aswegan,' retorted Mittee.

Frikkie's body straightened and his merry eyes grew cold. Now you could see the likeness to his family in the arrogant gesture he made towards Letty. 'Go and pack your things. Have you no pride, that you stand there arguing after you have been told to go?'

He halted Letty's tongue long enough for her to go into her room to pack but before she was half-way through she was spitting out insults like an infuriated cat though there was nobody in the room with her. Frikkie went outside and waited beside his horse. The trap came round to the door and Mittee, timid now, went to Frikkie to apologize softly for her treatment of his betrothed. His hand fell upon her shining head with all his old affection.

'It is nothing, Mittee, I know that little one and in a way I don't blame you. Though I wish you had been kind to her.'

'Hi, Frikkie, it is not my fault. It is my aunt, they don't speak a word to each other. I am worn out with it.'

'Letty has a good heart,' said Frikkie helplessly. 'It's only her tongue, it's forked, I think.'

Letty heard Mittee's laugh as she came out of the house and then you should have heard her. Mittee stood by and let her say what she liked for she knew herself to be in the wrong; but that night she made a bitter enemy.

Certainly the house was more peaceful with Letty out of it. Even Mrs Van Brandenberg remarked now and again on Mittee's trousseau but from Andrina we still heard nothing. Her mother got her out of bed on the day of Mittee's wedding. She was pale and so thin that her dress hung on her like a sack. You could not help feeling sorry for her in spite of her pride, as hard as marble.

You could not help feeling sorry for Andrina. There was nobody to feel sorry for Selina as she waited outside the court-house while the magistrate married Mittee to Paul; nobody to feel sorry for her as she followed the bridal procession to the church to see the knot doubly tied.

Still I smiled and thought myself more fortunate than Andrina for nobody would take from me the child that I was carrying, and I would see Paul every day for Mittee had laughed at him when he suggested that I should remain with Mrs Gouws after she married.

CHAPTER V

The swallows were gone and the veld had turned brown. I lay in the cold grass beside the spring though the air grew sharp, as the silken winter sky was shot through by the sunset. Mittee called and called me again, her voice pitched on a note of anger. Ag what, let her call until she is black in the face, I thought, I won't wait on their table tonight. The way she carried on now that she was married, with Paul hanging after her as though she were gold. I pulled a handful of grass out by the roots. As easily as that I could destroy him. I could go to Mittee and say, I am carrying Paul's child. Then she would pack her things and leave his house that very night.

I could not stay here. I thought with longing and pity of the child I must bear. Was there any place beyond Plessisburg for a coloured girl and her baby? I could not stay to face Paul's hatred and the speculation of the townspeople. Soon I must go away because already the little heart beat with mine and the limbs fluttered. I was never lonely now and I was unafraid, like a person who has the assurance of love.

Mittee was coming down the path with the short, hurrying steps of temper. Although she had been married for little more than a month, her face wore that look of pious knowingness that had marked Grandma Van Brandenberg's.

'You sit there. The baas will be in from the kraal in half an hour's time and not a fork laid on the table.' I stood up slowly, stiff from lying so long in the damp grass. The wind tugged at my dress with spiteful fingers. Mittee stared at me, her eyes bright. 'Selina. It can't be. Perhaps it is only this light. Come here.' Her hands went over me deftly. 'You are. You're going to have a baby.'

'I know that.'

'Still waters, deep ground, underneath the devil's turning round.'

'Hold your mouth.'

She cuffed me. 'Don't you dare to talk to me like that. Come up at once and set the table. We'll go into this later when the baas comes in.'

'The baas' backside.'

She passed beyond words. She did not even hit me; but she slammed the door in my face when I tried to follow her into the house. The Kaffir girl waited on the table that night while I sat with Jansie, eating roasted mealies as though I had not a care in the world. When he tried to touch me, I seared his hand with a mealie from the fire.

He laughed, rubbing his hand against his thigh. 'One day I'll get you, Selina.'

The back door opened. Mittee and Paul walked slowly down the yard towards Jansie's fire. They stopped and we heard them arguing in low voices. Paul was urging her back to the house but it was not because of what he said that she turned back. She looked at Jansie and me, sitting in the fire-light with mealies in our hands; then hurried to the house, closing the door with a bang that was like a slap in the face. Bastard, she had called me when I tore her silk, but I still remained Selina to her, a person who could move her to anger or love. Seeing me beside Jansie, she cast me from her, distastefully. Wait a bit, Mittee, you're not finished with me yet, I thought.

Paul stood awkwardly on the other side of the fire, his hands deep in his pockets. Jansie got to his feet with a submissive 'Baas' rattling in his throat. His face was as bland as a baby's for he was trying hard to work himself into the job of Paul's right-hand man. I remained seated, smiling as I picked the mealie-pips one by one from the cob.

'Jansie, there is a good place for a hard-working married couple on some land I've bought about a hundred miles north,' said Paul, throwing aside his awkwardness. He spoke in the clipped, assured voice of a righteous man but still his eyes looked into the fire and not at us. 'The nonna and I both think it best that you and Selina should get married. There is already a shack on the land and you could have a few morgen to work for yourselves.'

Jansie, overcome by such generosity, let loose a tremendous laugh. 'Ever since I saw Selina, my baas, I've been telling her that she must marry me.'

'Well, the sooner the better.' Paul's sombre voice staunched Jansie's exuberance. 'You can take some time off tomorrow to make arrangements for the wedding and I'll give a sheep towards the feast.'

Jansie grinned again, but dubiously, for Paul's manner was harsh though his words betokened a kindliness that bewildered Jansie. 'Tomorrow I'll go up to the Mission, my baas, and arrange the whole thing.'

I had said not a word but Paul walked away quickly as if the affair was settled. I noticed that he did not go into the house. Oh, he knew that I was carrying his child and he would fight his bitter pride there in the darkness. My anger at his happiness in possessing Mittee melted to tenderness because he was afraid of me. I longed to go after him to tell him that Selina would never hurt him, that he need not come with bribes to a coloured servant in order to make himself safe from her. Sweetness would chant through my blood if I could put my hands upon him again and whisper, Lamb of my heart, my love. But he would push me away, perhaps call me bastard. Tears went softly down my cheeks. If there had been no Mittee, would he have loved me then? It was a joke in Plessisburg that Paul Du Plessis was so proud that he would have been a bachelor if he could not have the most beautiful girl in the town. Would he have loved me if there had been no Mittee? There was a story that one of the President's generals had turned his back on Pretoria and married a Kaffir girl because he loved her. If there had been no Mittee, would Paul have taken Selina, who was more beautiful than any white girl? But he was giving me to Jansie, who was cruel and ugly.

'I've got three pounds saved up,' said Jansie, plans bubbling from him now that he had got over his astonishment. 'We'll buy a cow with that. I'll smear out the floors for you. We'll go to my mother at Christmas time. She's got a sewing machine that she's keeping for my wife, and some petticoats. Always she says, Jansie, it's time you brought a grandson to comfort my old age. She's old, my mother, with hair as white as a cloud. In all the world there is only Jansie for her. My treasure, she says to me, bring home a good wife to this little house and we'll have Christmas even if it's in the middle of the year. She's bought her own small holding and ducks and geese and fowls. All these will be Jansie's when she dies.' All the while he was speaking, he pawed at me but I kept my knees drawn up to my chin and my arms folded with the elbows sticking out like a chicken's wings. At last he said anxiously, 'Selina, why do you sit there like a piece of stone? You're coming to live with me, I'll buy you print for the curtains, I'll do all the hard work . . .'

I screeched at him. 'Loose me. I'm going to my room. I've got fever or something, my head is aching.'

As I stumbled away from him, he clutched at me. 'Don't get sick, Selina. I'll ask the missionary to put up the banns and you must come with me tomorrow. All Plessisburg must know that Selina has said Yes to Jansie at last.'

I shut him out of my room, leaning against the door until I heard him go away. It was a big room where a bywoner had once lived and there was a window opposite the bed. Good enough for a white person, said Mittee, when she showed it to me. You're lucky to have such a good nonnie, Selina. She had put in some old linoleum and curtains; a chest of drawers and a bed. Selina was a lucky girl.

I opened the door timidly and making sure that Jansie was

nowhere about, I crouched on the threshold in the darkness until I heard Paul's footsteps.

I called out softly, 'Basie.'

'You. What do you want, Selina?'

I came close to him. 'I will not go with Jansie.'

'Say one word about me and I'll take you before my father and you'll be put in prison. Nobody will believe you.'

'Except Herry,' I whispered.

'Herry will not pass through Plessisburg again.' Each word was torn painfully from him. 'It's no use, Selina. What's done is done and I've paid for it with bitter remorse, tonight and many times before. Do you think I will let a little madness at Christmas time spoil my life?'

'I will not marry Jansie.'

'But you must have a husband and someone to look after . . .' He could not bring himself to speak of his child.

'I'll go away, basie, tomorrow as soon as it is light. There is nothing but bitterness for me here, seeing you with Mittee.'

'You dare to speak of her.' He stood uneasily for a moment, fumbling in his pockets. 'Here it is, a sovereign. I thought I had one on me. Go tomorrow, Selina, and if anybody finds this out, I warn you . . . I trusted you too much. You've put a curse on me.'

I pressed the sovereign into my palm so hard that it was a disc of pain in my flesh. 'You blame me. I should have told Mittee, I should tell her now so that she could know you for what you are. I would have loved you, basie. She doesn't love you, she's only proud of being married . . .'

He choked me into silence. He might have killed me if Jansie had not whistled. Jansie was carrying a candle covered by brown paper and by its light he saw us together. He watched, surprised into silence, as Paul pushed me aside and strode away.

'What were you doing with him?'

Something in his voice brought that dog Wagter clearly to my mind. I answered nervously, 'He gave me a wedding present, Jansie. Look, a sovereign.' The gleam of the coin pacified Jansie for the moment. He took it from me and ran his thumbnail round the ridges.

'A sovereign. Fatherland, I never knew Du Plessis so generous, or any white man. I'll look after it.'

'No, let me have it. I need it to buy some things. Give it to me, my dear Jansie.'

'She calls me Dear. No, I'll look after it. I thought we could sit in your room and court a bit, that's why I brought the candle, just like a white man.'

I did not give him a chance to argue with me. I ran into the room and banged the door.

'Go away, Jansie. If you come inside I'll scream the place down. You'll get a hiding.' He was pushing against the door. Terrified, I forced honey into my voice. 'When we are married. Soon, dear, dear Jansie.'

He grumbled but he went away. I put the chair under the door-knob and closed the window but for a long time I could not sleep. Mittee was still mean with the candles and I had only a short end but I lit it. By its light I packed my bundle so that I could leave the farm with the first show of the morning. I got into bed fully dressed to lie counting the hours while the candle burnt down to a charred wick sputtering in the melted wax. I might have dozed for I don't remember the first lurch of fright as the chair rattled beneath the doorknob. Panic was on me as the door opened a crack, straining against the chair. I thought, It's Paul standing beyond there in the darkness, come to kill me; or it's a ghost, hunting me down for my sins; or Jansie, after me like a dog.

It was Jansie. He took the paper bag from his candle, which he set upon the warm wax, slowly pressing it down until it was firmly fixed.

'Scream, Selina,' he said, baring his teeth.

I shook my head. He pulled me up by the shoulders and brought his face close to mine. I could see the pores in his nose, coarse as the skin of an orange; the pitted cheeks; and an obscene mole from which hairs sprouted as stiff as wire.

'I have been looking at the sovereign and thinking, Selina. Why does a white baas give us money to get married, a sheep, a piece of land and a shack to live in? Why, Selina?'

'Because I was so long with the nonnie,' I whispered.

'I thought of that. But why is it the baas that makes the presents and stands so close when he speaks to you?'

'The nonnie was a bit cross with me tonight because I was cheeky,' I said a little more boldly as I realized how difficult it was for him to reason. 'Did you put the money in a safe place?'

'Yes. It is in the tin with my other money, buried in a secret place.'

Through the open door I could see a curve of sky, beautiful with the savage blaze of the stars. I longed to be out there beneath it, lying on the bitter, clean veld. Following the direction of my gaze, he went to the door and shut out the sight of freedom.

I closed my eyes. There was no sound but the hissing of his feet as they slid over the linoleum. He bent over me again.

'You would never have Jansie. Was it because you wanted the white man?'

'No, no, Jansie,' I panted.

With one frightful gesture he ripped the dress from my body. I brought my feet up and kicked him in the chest, crooking my fingers to tear at his lust-crazed eyes when he came at me again. Above my screams, he yelled in jubilation. I will always remember those few seconds, I will always remember that hateful body from which the hot sweat trickled.

He threw me to the floor and sprang high, coming down upon me even as I turned to protect my baby. Pain beat at me, there was blood and vomit in my mouth, muffling my screams. He sprang again and again. Lightning behind my eyes swirled me to the very brink of nothingness but always I came back to the staggering pain; and the pain was turned into sound as I screamed to God for mercy.

I did not hear the sounds that meant deliverance but Jansie did. I saw him run for the window, crouched like an animal. He went through the glass head first as the door flew open. Paul stood there, his mouth wide open in a battle cry to the few Kaffirs who had braved the darkness with him. He sent a shot after Jansie and then ran for him. But Jansie got away. I heard him howl and curse as somebody laid hold of him and then a yell from Paul as he broke free. Again there was the shattering report of the rifle.

Paul came into the room and looked down at me with eyes as cold as a snake's. 'Fetch one of the women to see to her,' he called out to the Kaffirs.

My voice was like the croak of an old, old woman.

'He found out. It was that money . . .'

Then I heard Mittee, her voice as sharp and fresh as dew. 'Is it Selina? Oh my God, what has he done to her?'

'Kicked her almost to death,' said Paul, 'but there's no need for you to worry about her, my treasure, I've sent for one of the old women to look after her.'

She knelt beside my writhing body, sheltering me from Paul's stare. There was no resemblance to Grandma Van Brandenberg now for God had set upon her face a look of such compassion that it was like drinking sweet water to see her.

'Shame on you, Paul, to have all those men looking in on her. Send the rabble away, can't you see what is happening to the poor thing?'

Paul's bad-tempered yell sent the Kaffirs scattering to their rooms. 'You shouldn't come running out, little wife, you must leave these things to me. The girl will be all right, these old women know what to do.'

'I wouldn't let a Kaffir touch Selina. You must send a boy for Auntie Gouws at once. And get two of them to carry her up to the house on the mattress, we can look after her better there.'

'I will not,' Paul shouted. 'She is not coming into my house.'

Mittee stood up. 'It is not your house, it is also mine and it is for me to say who comes there. If you won't do as I ask you then I will do it myself.'

She picked up the lantern and she was calling out to the servants before he gave in. He spoke his orders in such angry tones that the Kaffirs hung their heads, afraid that he would knock them down if they said boo or baa.

Mittee had pulled a bed on to the back stoep and she was making it up herself when they carried me to the house. The sheets were cool on my aching body and as the Kaffirs put me down I said to Mittee in my broken voice, 'Thank you nonnie.'

'Nothing to say thanks for,' she said, smiling at me.

'Well now, come to bed and I will wait up for Auntie Gouws, wife,' said Paul, and he took her arm to enforce his authority.

'Loose me,' said Mittee coldly. 'Why should you want to stop me from doing my duty?'

'Is it your duty to obey me or to look after every coloured thing that gets into trouble?'

His voice was so rough that she drew away from him and sat down on the chair at my bedside. He stamped away but she sat by me through that long and desolate night even after Mrs Gouws came. Sometimes it seemed that I slept; but the dusk that blanketed the pain was made horrible by a vision of Jansie. I forced myself to waken, willing rather to face the edged agony that awaited me.

Mittee had sent a boy in the trap for Mrs Gouws and at last she came. She was breezy in the face of calamity, as befitted one who had laid out a hundred corpses.

'Hi, Selina, what have you been up to, dragging me out of my bed at this hour?' she shouted, as loudly as though she were calling Gouws and the boys to their evening meal. 'We'll see what can be done to make you more comfortable.'

There was nothing much that she could do for me. The terrible hour was upon me. I had but to reach out my hand to touch the blackness of death. Mrs Gouws' voice seemed to grow fainter.

'My God, the poor thing is going to die. We'll give her brandy.'

'Drink the brandy,' said Mittee, holding up my head. 'Stop being such a fool, Selina. Drink it.'

Then everything was clear; Mittee's face, sharp-pointed in the candlelight; the beads of sweat sparkling on Mrs Gouws' upper lip. She pushed Mittee into the kitchen.

'Out,' she panted. 'A bride . . .' Then she said, 'It's all over now, Selina. I'll blow the candle out and we can go to sleep. Let this teach you a lesson.'

I could see the dawn in the sky, rolling in on the backs of smooth clouds. I closed my eyes against it and there was Jansie standing over me. No need to be afraid of him now. Paul was already in the saddle. He would hunt Jansie down; flog him and have him put in prison. Jansie would not be strong and cruel when Paul had done with him.

God was hidden from me, except in Mittee's charity. Could that radiance come from foolish little Mittee; the child who had stamped her feet when Grandma Van Brandenberg sewed the sunbonnet on her hair; who had giggled in church; pinched me during prayers; sworn, fibbed, peeped in at the forbidden skull? Upon her brow God had set the crown of His favour and upon me the yoke of wrongdoing and suffering, upon me who had sought Him in tree and cloud and star.

Paul returned from the chase in the afternoon. The day had become misty, made bitterly cold by the wind that blew from the Wolkbergen. Paul went into the kitchen and stood before the fire, with a cup of coffee between his hands, inhaling the steam as though he would wring the last ounce of warmth from the coffee. He spoke to Mittee and Mrs Gouws but he looked directly through the open door at me.

'I'll have to go to my father first to make a report, and then to the Mission. They'll have to bury him.' He laughed, bringing a shocked exclamation from Mrs Gouws. 'I don't mind shooting a creature down but I've always hated to see or touch a dead body.'

'Now to me, it's a pleasure to lay a person out properly,' said Mrs Gouws reprovingly, 'for if there is anything that offends the dear God, it must surely be a dead man's eyes staring straight up to the heaven and his arms and legs laying in all sorts of unseemly positions. It's an art to lay them out so that the bereaved can look at them in the coffin without dreaming about it for weeks afterwards.' Her voice was so cheerful that death might have been part of the fun of a holiday; though Paul shuddered and put aside his coffee without drinking it.

Mittee, who always wanted to laugh at solemn things, laughed out loud and then tried to pretend she was coughing. Mrs Gouws snapped, 'Hysterics,' and a moodiness fell on them all.

Paul took Mrs Gouws back to Mittee's farm soon afterwards and then rode to Plessisburg to see his father. Mittee went to bed though it was not yet dark. I could not sleep. I sucked the bitter fruit of loneliness as I lay watching the sky. Night came on and the sky darkened to unfathomable blackness, merging with the earth in a fine, sighing rain. If I had screamed and run away when Jansie first came to my room, perhaps he would not have killed my baby. I cradled the pillow in my arms, whispering, my baby, my baby. And thinking of the ugly thing Mrs Gouws had whisked away, I howled like a dog.

Mittee came to me. She was in her nightgown, her hair in ruffled plaits.

'Almighty, Selina, shut up. You nearly frightened me out of my wits. Oh hell, I thought, it's Jansie's ghost come to haunt us. Have you got a pain? I think I'll give you some Essence of Life. Auntie Gouws doesn't believe in it, but I always take it every month and who could be healthier than I am?'

'No, thank you, nonnie.'

She put the candle on the chair beside the bed and sat at my feet. The brightness of the candle was reflected in her skin, that shone with camphor fat. Nauseous as the smell of the camphor was, its familiarity brought back those happy years when we had travelled on the Wolkbergen.

'I was thinking of my baby, nonnie. If only I had that to look forward to. Now there is nothing.'

'There will be other babies, Selina. Next time you must pick out a good man, though Jansie seemed gentle enough.'

'He was very cruel. He killed his dog the same way on the Wolkbergen.'

'Then you should have had nothing to do with him. And perhaps you were a little to blame, Selina. The way you spoke to me last night, you were in an insolent mood. I said to the baas, The sooner Selina is married the better and we'll go and speak to her about it, but he wouldn't let me come at first. And then I didn't want to. When I thought of you and Jansie, somehow it seemed wrong that you, so beautiful and delicate, should have given yourself to him without even being married . . .'

Her voice went on and on, swinging me into a deep and healing sleep from which I awoke the next morning only when the girl came to light the fire.

She woke me up deliberately, the black thing, and when Mittee told her to bring me coffee, she gave it to me with a laugh of contempt.

'Oh, what trouble you got yourself into, oh, what trouble,' she sang in Shangaan so that the white people would not know that she was tormenting me.

I swore at her in her own language but Mittee understood the swearwords. 'Why swear at the girl? Truly, Selina, you are changed.'

She was dressed for going out and because of the sleepless night, she had put pink powder on her cheeks. She was going to visit

Andrina for Mrs Gouws had told her that the girl had taken to her bed and would not speak to anybody.

'Look after Selina well,' she admonished Anna before she left.

As soon as she was out of the house, Anna lifted a shoulder at me to show her withering scorn and then made off to the yard. I heard Paul coming soft-footed towards me. I was not afraid of him then. He stood in the doorway, looking at me with brooding eyes.

'There's going to be trouble about Jansie. My father has ordered an enquiry. You will be called as a witness.'

'Yes, basie.'

'What will you say, Selina, when they ask you why Jansie kicked you?'

'I will tell the truth, basie.'

'About me?'

'No. I will say he was jealous but I will not say of whom.'

'They will trick it out of you.'

'I can only try my best. It's too late for me to run away now, they would go after me.'

He put his cold hands on mine. 'Stand by me, Selina.'

'Basie, I could have spoken a long time ago. I could have told Mittee and she would never have married you. You must not be afraid of Selina.'

Now his face was so close that I could feel his beard on my cheeks. 'Afraid. Yes, I am afraid. Sometimes I have looked at you and thought, In all the world she is the only one who knows anything against me. I asked Mittee not to bring you with her but she laughed. Selina, she said, why she is like my own family.'

'I meant to go away. Every day I said to myself, Take your bundle and go to Auntie Lena's. But it was hard for me to leave my nonnie after all these years. And you. Oh, I should have gone and then I would have had my baby.'

He said, 'It is not finished between us yet, Selina.' His hands, warming over mine, held a promise and his eyes were bright with this lying promise.

'Basie, I will be faithful to death,' I said.

'Lay your hand on your heart.'

He left me for we heard the girl singing in the yard. As I lay sleepless, I dreamed that I had another child by him, a daughter who would be light enough to marry a white man. He had said, It is not finished between us yet, Selina. I dreamed also that a man came to me with a parcel of silk for my wedding dress. I was a white girl and my name was Mittee.

CHAPTER VI

The walls of the courtroom were white, the tables and chairs varnished black. I saw these as its symbols, the white for truth, the black for falsehood. I had lied and I had not been struck down, though I expected it at any minute. The magistrate was suspicious of me for he kept asking me the same questions over and over again.

I licked my seared lips as he leaned forward, watching me shrewdly. 'Why did the deceased assault you in the way you describe?'

I thought, He means why did Jansie jump on me but I'll pretend I don't understand. 'Baas?'

Then Verster started on me again. He was the Public Prosecutor and a great one for having things right. He had already told me a dozen times, in a voice of thunder, to call the magistrate Your Honour, though the magistrate waved his hand to show that it signified nothing what I called him so long as the matter was straightened out. From his calm face you would not have known that he was angry with Paul for having taken the law into his own hands but all Plessisburg knew that he would be more severe with his own son than with a stranger.

He came to the point, using clear language. 'Why did the boy kick you?'

'I told you. He was jealous. He was always jealous though we were going to be married.'

'Of whom was he jealous?'

'There was nobody, baas,' I answered shrilly. 'He was jealous of everything I touched, baas, even the dog I was telling you about, my oubaas, Your Honour.'

Verster threw up his hands hopelessly but the magistrate leaned back as though he were satisfied. He had sifted and resifted everything I said, like a person passing boermeal through silk to get the finest white flour. Now he will send me to prison, I thought, as I looked into his face. The glowing eyes were hooded and you could read no emotion in them.

He said nothing about prison then and I was allowed to go back to the waiting room. This was a small room, whitewashed and bare except for the benches round the walls. The courtroom had been cold but here the sun came through the window, warming the benches through so that it was pleasant to sit down. I began to sweat gently.

The orderly moved away from the door. 'The magistrate is giving his verdict,' he said. 'You can go in and listen if you like.'

I wiped the moisture from my face with the corner of my apron. Nothing would make me go into that courtroom of my own free will so I went outside and waited by the trap for Mittee and Paul.

Soon afterwards, a few people came out of the courthouse, amongst them Mrs Gouws and Eberhardt. I went forward to listen to what they said.

'For his own father to have to do it,' wailed the tender-hearted Mrs Gouws.

Eberhardt said with satisfaction, 'They'll send him to Pretoria for trial.'

'What a blow for the good old magistrate. Such a thing has never happened in all the world. It makes you afraid of what might be in store for us all.'

'Don't cry, treasure,' said Gouws tenderly. 'He will get off. It is only a formality.'

Eberhardt was a subtle as a cat. 'What a good thing it was that everybody seemed to forget what a magnificent shot Paul is or they might have thought he deliberately aimed for the boy's heart.'

He stopped guiltily as Frikkie ran down the steps, guiding Mittee. 'Go carefully over the stones, Eberhardt,' he called, shaking his fist.

'There's going to be a fight outside the courthouse,' cried Mrs Gouws, her voice rollicking up and down the street.

Eberhardt moved away from her to join the gossiping crowd for he had no use for this forthright way of settling things. Frikkie looked after him with longing but for once he controlled the first wild impulse that leapt to his mind and hurried Mittee to the waiting trap.

Mittee climbed on to the front seat and sat up straight so that nobody should mark her agitation. 'Hi, I didn't think your father would give such a verdict against his own son,' she declared.

'The law isn't a family affair,' said Frikkie. 'It serves Paul right, he shouldn't have gone after the boy alone. At least he could have sent somebody to report it but he must always do everything his own way.'

'Don't turn against him, Frikkie. It's been a terrible shock to him. He went as white as paper. To be out on bail for manslaughter, when you think how proud he is. After all, he only did his duty.'

'You mean he did the policeman's duty.'

'If you had seen what the boy did to Selina, you would have saddled up and shot him down yourself. He was like a mad dog, this Jansie.'

Frikkie's voice was serious. 'Paul will have to have reliable witnesses. It's a grave charge, even if it concerns a Coloured. He's in there, talking it over now with the notary. You'll be one of the witnesses again, Selina.' He turned to me so suddenly that I jumped. 'And see that you call the magistrate in Pretoria Your Honour.'

Mittee laughed at that and the gossipers looked across at her in an aggrieved fashion as though she had been caught laughing at a funeral. Their own faces were dark, as though Paul had been sentenced to hanging. Plessisburg always made the most of a tragedy.

Paul came home that night in time for the evening meal. When he would not eat, Mittee poured out a teaspoonful of Essence of Life for him but he pushed it aside. He sat until late with the brandy bottle, raving against his father. I was on the back stoep, huddled into a blanket, for Mittee had told me to sleep in my own room; but I knew that I would never sleep there in peace again for Jansie haunted me.

I could hear Paul's voice through my fitful sleep and I pitied Mittee, having left her looking confusedly at the scorned Essence of Life. It was her first lesson in bowing her head before Paul for he was in no mood to truckle to anybody. Now and again, she dared to lift her voice in defence of the magistrate but Paul shouted her down.

In the morning, the magistrate drove out to see him. Paul calmed down after he had spoken to his father about the case but he was never as free with his affection after that. He began to prepare his defence, gathering all sorts of evidence against Jansie, some of which came as a surprise to me.

By the time we went to Pretoria for the trial, my body was healed. The bruises turned from red to black and then became a saffron stain upon my skin, painless. Only the milk in my breasts and the slackening of my muscles, secret and shameful, reminded me of the suffering through which I had passed.

In Pretoria Mittee, too, gave evidence and Coester came forward with a story about Jansie's viciousness to a young Kaffir girl many years before. As always, the luck was with Paul. Jansie had been imprisoned once for striking a white man and that was the reason why he had left his home in Pretoria to work on the Wolkbergen. It was from his poor old mother that they dragged this evidence; a woman as thin as a secretary bird and in a passion of grief that was mistaken for violence. Paul was let go with a reprimand.

As we came out of the courthouse, the old woman cursed us from the gutter. I thought of the sewing machine that she had saved for her daughter-in-law and briefly shared in the emptiness that was her portion now that her only child was dead.

Jansie's voice said through her curses, '. . . In all the world there is only Jansie for her. My treasure, she says to me, bring home a good wife to this little house and we'll have Christmas even if it's in the middle of the year . . .'

We took the road to Plessisburg; and Paul and Frikkie, who had drunk brandy, sang all the way. But I whispered to Mittee, 'He was the old woman's only child, nonnie, no wonder she cursed us,' and she was quiet, her face shadowed so that you could see what she would look like when she herself was an old woman.

Christmas in the middle of the year. It was like that on Paul's farm when the springbok came over. They came from the uninhabited north, perhaps driven south by drought, thousands of them dancing and leaping across the veld, their tails like white handkerchiefs thrown over their rumps. To save the winter grazing, Paul rallied every man in the district to cut down the pests and for days they rode out until the herds turned north again, leaving the ruined pastures to mark their path.

Mittee had her hands full, for many of the farmers' wives, too timid to stay alone, had followed their husbands to Paul's farm. There were enormous meals to be cooked, a dozen babies to be bathed in the morning, napkins to be washed. Polly threatened to give Andrina notice for she was pressed into every kind of task. No sooner did she loll in the sun than some woman came out of the house and spying her there with nothing to do, gave her a bundle of washing or set her to iron; or watching the baby. She would slink behind my room with her comb and mirror so that she could do her hair but even then she would be found out and berated for a lazy, good-for-nothing creature.

Polly took great pride in her hair. It was so thick and frizzy that she had to part it into separate sections before she could get the comb through it. One day I caught Fanie doing her hair for her, kneeling in the dirt beside her. His mouth hung open and a thin trickle of spit fell on to his chin as he concentrated on getting the comb through the frizz. Polly squealed at the tugs but more from pleasure than from pain for she had been making up to Fanie ever since she first saw him. I had never seen Fanie take notice of any girl but me and though I did not love him, I could have kicked Polly.

'Give me the comb, you're making her hair go into knots.'

I seized the comb from him and ran it down her scalp and then briskly combed out a tuft of hair. She screamed as I went round her head for the teeth of the comb left little red ridges on her scalp as I made the partings. She would not let me finish but snatched the comb from my hand and flounced off, murmuring ugly words. I went to my room for my comb and made Fanie do my hair for me.

That evening there was dancing but I was too tired to join in. Frikkie was playing his accordion in the dining room and I stood in the shadows watching the white people through the open window. Mittee had lit four candles to impress the company but I could see that she was anxious about them. The wind blowing through the open window set their flames dancing, melting the wax so that it spewed wastefully down their sides. She came to the window to pull it down but Paul was behind her, pressing his body on her as he leaned over to pull the sash down. Then he ran his hands from her breast to her thigh and I saw that look on his face that I had thought belonged to me alone.

There was a shout from Frikkie. 'Blow out the candle, wife,' that brought a howl of laughter from the young people but a throwing up of hands from the older women. Mittee was confused but Paul took her in his arms and waltzed with her round and round the table. The faces of the women, young and old, softened as they watched them. Frikkie muted his accordion to a heart-breaking pitch, half in fun and half in earnest. From where comes that feeling that you are linked to Eternity? Sometimes it springs at you from the lonely, starlit veld, sometimes it is in the melancholy chanting of the Kaffirs. It was there that night as Paul and Mittee danced, with their shadows flying along the wall beside them.

They stopped as Mittee caught her hip on the end of the table. Paul stroked the spot, looking over her head and daring Frikkie with a look to say anything. Andrina got up suddenly and went from the room.

I went away, too, down to the spring to lie in the cold grass, sad because I was Selina. It was late when I heard them talking near me; his voice and hers, separating and then blending. They were beautiful words that he said to her, 'Look, little heart, if I hold up your hand to the sky so, it is filled with stars . . .'

I must not stir my aching limbs or call out to them that I was there. I must wait until they were gone and then I must pack my bundle, I must go away.

'But little wife . . .'

Her edged voice stabbed the air. 'No, not here. If a Kaffir should see . . .'

Those were her feet swishing through the grass as she ran away from him. I thought he would follow her but he did not move away from the spring.

I said softly, 'Paul.'

Each Tuesday Mittee drove out to her farm to see how the Gouwses were getting on and to visit Andrina and Mrs Van Brandenberg who were still living in her house. There they would stay until either Leon or Andrina married somebody else, or so Mrs Van Brandenberg had decided.

Usually Mittee took me with her but on the Tuesday after the hunt she went alone. 'You must rest, you're like a starved dog. A disgrace to the farm.' She caught my thin face between her hands. 'Sit by the spring in the fresh air and do some doilies and the darning. Your bones are almost cutting through your skin.'

'Mittee, it is that room. I have nailed a board over the window where Jansie broke it and I put the chest of drawers in front of the door every night, but still Jansie and his mother float hand-in-hand from nowhere and stand at the end of my bed, looking at me so mournfully. Their faces are green . . .'

'How can Jansie's mother haunt you when she is alive?' Mittee asked disbelievingly. 'You imagine it, Selina. Keep the Bible under your hand and say your prayers, then nothing can harm you.'

'Let me have another room, nonnie.'

'There is only the room that Jansie used to have; nobody will go in there because Anna says she saw him in the doorway. Now I must hurry. If I see Auntie Lena I'll ask her to send one of her grandchildren to sleep with you until you are over it.'

I sat by the spring when she had gone, concentrating on my crochet work. I saw only the beads and heard no sound except the rhythm of my own heart. Surely God looked down on me now. I had paid back what I owed. If I had been wicked, I could have broken Mittee's heart and sent Paul to prison. But I was not wicked.

In all the world there was only one Selina, of all the millions who had lived before and the millions who came after her, there would never be another being exactly like she who sat crocheting beside the spring. Her breasts were like golden satin, the nipples like the heart of a dark rose; her waist so small that a man could span it with his hands, her limbs delicate and glossy-skinned. Her soul was a star, brilliant in her eyes. This was Selina, rich and unassailable.

'Selina.'

His voice fell across my dream like the lash of a sjambok. I bent my head over my work but the pattern of the beads blurred and wavered.

'Yes, basie.'

'Put aside what you are doing and go and get your bundle. I'm sending you to the Wolkbergen. There's a transport rider passing here with his waggons in half an hour's time.'

'Basie, why must I go? Did I say anything in the court against you? Have I said one word to anybody?'

'I can't have you here.'

'You are afraid of me,' I sneered.

'It is you who should be afraid of me, Selina.'

'Why? Will you shoot me down the same as you did Jansie?'

He pulled me to my feet, scattering my work in the grass. I cried out and twisted away from him to pick up the beads that were precious because of their rare colour. When I looked up, he was smiling and I felt the blood leap thunderously through my body. My hands became clumsy in picking up the beads. He bent down to help me and before I knew what I was doing, my starved hands were upon him.

'We will be found out,' he groaned, sweating. 'You devil, you leave this farm today or I'll choke you and throw you into the river.'

'I will go, Paul, if you stay here for a little while with me.'

They put me in the last waggon in the line. I sat with my elbows on my knees, my bundle by my side, looking to the east long after Plessisburg had dropped behind us. I watched for the land-marks for I meant to leave the waggons at the first outspan and return to Mittee.

The rhythm of the oxen was pleasing. I gave myself to it and sang softly under my breath. The veld, unbroken by kopjes, spun to the horizon. It was as empty as the sky and I wished that I could trek on and on in solitude until I reached the soul's resting place.

The scene changed as we turned west to the mountains. We were moving into thornveld and our small company became livelier, for the scattered trees and kopjes broke the spell that the wide sweep of flat veld had put on us. The driver of our waggon sent us a song flying from lip to lip. A Kaffir girl, her head tied in a snow-white doek, jumped from the waggon and danced in the road, pushing out her buttocks, stamping her feet. We laughed and the driver, looking back, sent his whip hissing into the dust at her feet. She sprang aside nimbly but he caught her on the toe and she hopped after the waggon, holding her foot while she laughed to hide her discomfiture. There was one who did not laugh, I noticed. This was the owner of the waggons and he spurred his pony to the side of the driver, speaking to him earnestly, but all he got from the boy was a sneer.

It was early outspan. The owner was devout and made long prayers. I was happy standing there in the afterglow, singing my heart out in praise, kneeling down to pray again and again.

I lay that night beside the Kaffir girl but even if I had wanted to, I could not have slept for my nostrils are ever keen to pick up a scent. She smelt strongly, like a koedoe, enough to make you sick.

I had begged Paul to allow me to remain on his farm but as soon as he heard the transport waggons turning down the road, he hustled me to the yard and sent the hated Anna to tie up my bundle while he bargained with the owner for a seat for me.

'I will come back, basie.'

'Let it be at Christmas time for we are going to the Cape then,' he laughed.

The youth who had driven our waggon was on watch. He looked vacuously into the fire and from time to time played with himself but he did not fall asleep once. Later, when the moon had risen, the owner took over the watch. I have forgotten his name but his face I always remember. It was as noble as Doctor Besil's, with eyes as sweet as a child's. This was a man who saw God and I longed to creep to his feet to ask him the way.

I kept my eyes on him for there is always a time after midnight when a man on watch falls asleep, if it is only for a few minutes. At last the moment came. His head fell forward, he jerked awake and sat with eyes distended, then fell asleep again. I picked up my bundle.

Dawn was far off but the moonlight was strong. The grass was thick with dew, drenching my dress, chilling my toes as I cut across country. While the campfire was still in sight I pressed bravely on, anxious to get away, but once I was over the rand into the open veld I became afraid and I was tempted to turn back. A sound in the grass behind me made me jump and then I almost fainted for I looked back to see a slinking shadow on the veld.

'My God, a lion,' I said aloud.

As I spoke the creature fawned up to me. It was the transport rider's dog, a large brindled animal with one ear floppy and the other sticking up straight. I told him to voetsak but he would not go, so I threw a clod of earth at him. He lay down, putting his head on his paws. As soon as I began to walk again, he followed me. In the end, I ceased trying to make him go back and was even glad of his company for I thought he would warn me if a snake should lie on our path. I placed my feet tenderly on the veld, obsessed by this fear of snakes; of the swiftness of the mamba, of the slowness of the puff-adder. Then as I went on, there was added to this the fear that I would come upon lions, though we had heard no roars at sunset and the district was thought to be cleaned out.

The moon set. Now the veld grew so dark that I could not go on but must sit down in a horror of cold and blackness, my arms about the dog's neck. Perverse creature, he pulled himself away from me and ran back to the camp, though I called to him desperately.

Up from the quiet veld sprang Jansie, as real as the thorn tree against which I leaned. I closed my eyes but I could still see him plainly. I prayed but my prayers were of no use for he had the terrible power of the dead and the wronged.

He had lit a fire when Paul found him and he was crouching over the flames to warm himself before going on. How frightened he must have been when he looked up to see that horseman riding down upon him, how frightened he must have been from the time that he crashed head first through the window until the bullet found his heart. No wonder he haunted me whom he had loved.

I sank into a shivering sleep where he walked with me through vast and lonely places. I awoke sobbing to the reality of the darkness and the stillness that lies over the veld before the dawn. I watched and watched for the light as though it would burst on me in broad beams that would release me from my fears but it came grudgingly, in tones of black and grey that gave to the trees and bushes the shapes of waiting beasts.

Dawn came in on a chill wind that set me running to make myself warm. At the foot of an incline, I steadied my pace for my breath was tearing at my lungs. I passed the remains of a fire, made by some passing Kaffirs I thought, and was clutched by another fear; rape, perhaps a bloody death. Oh, the endlessness of that bare veld, so solitary but from which danger might spring at any moment.

I topped the rise and there I saw the grave. I knew that it was Jansie's for the golden stones were not weathered and the cross was bright with whitewash, placed there by the hands of the coloured Mission folk, more loving-kind than I to their brother. I walked round and round the grave, thinking sorrowfully of Jansie lying beneath the stones, his violent, lustful body seething with worms, his untamed spirit howling in the outer wastes.

I knelt down. 'Oh God, have mercy on him and on me, Thy sinful daughter. Oh Father of Pity, help us.'

As I prayed I saw a puff-adder move amongst the stones, its back marked with a pattern of awful beauty. The forked tongue shot out in mockery at my prayers.

'Paradise, it's the devil himself. Oh dear God, oh little Jesus, watch out for me now.'

I shrieked and ran from the place.

It was two o'clock in the afternoon when I came into Mittee's kitchen and I had not stopped walking since I left Jansie's grave. Mittee and the girl were round the stove looking after the jam that they were making.

'Now look, it's Selina,' Mittee cried.

Anna laughed. 'We had a dog like that once, he came home even after we thought we had drowned him. He used to eat eggs. We had to get the baas to shoot him in the finish.'

'Essence of Life,' said Mittee, catching me under the arms.

She put me on a chair and I sat back with my arms dangling, my mouth hanging open. 'Mittee, give me some food,' I whispered.

'There is no mealie-meal cooked. I'll fry some meat on top of the stove, it won't take long.'

The smell of the beefsteak that she set on the hot stove made my stomach crawl with hunger. I began to cry, harsh gulps and hiccups wracking me.

'Hi, Mittee, I'm hungry. I can't wait.'

'Run outside and get her a mealie from the Kaffirs' tin, they're cooking down there,' Mittee told Anna. 'She can eat that while the meat cooks.'

Anna, laughing at the top of her voice, came back with a steaming mealie held in the corner of her apron. 'Here, eat that.'

I ate backwards and forwards on the cob, scarcely chewing the juicy yellow pips. When the last of them was gone, I sucked the water from the cob. Almost instantly gas came from my stomach with a belch that shook my body, while pain gripped my chest.

'The mealie pips have formed into a solid ball. Now I'm going to die, nonnie, I can't live.'

'It's wind. I'll get some peppermint drops. Watch the meat, Anna, that it doesn't burn. And the jam.'

The drops of peppermint, sprinkled on sugar, spread their warmth through me and the pain went away. I could not eat the meat nor could I speak any more.

Mittee said, 'I'll stir the jam, Anna, you take her down to her room.'

Anna jerked me to my feet and shoved me in front of her down the path. This seemed to be her idea of helping me. She kicked the door of my room open but I would not go in there, for nothing would have taken me into that room since I had seen Jansie's grave. She shrugged her shoulders, murmuring, 'Mad,' and left me to find my own way to the Kaffirs' room. The place was dirty and airless but I fell into a beautiful sleep, more strengthening than food.

Mittee woke me up, stepping fastidiously over the bundles of rags that the Kaffirs used for beds. 'You'll have to go, Selina. He's like a madman. A Du Plessis if I ever saw one. Come along, your bundle is already on the trap. I'll take you to Auntie Gouws.'

'Ag, Mittee, surely you can persuade him.'

'Persuade. He's like a stone. He never wanted you here in the first place, he says you're a troublemaker. Come on. He's put a sjambok on the kitchen table and he says he will use it on you if you're not off this farm in ten minutes.'

Paul was on the back stoep and as I staggered out of the room, he roared at me in such fury that I began to run, thinking of the sjambok. I cowered on the floor of the trap, while Mittee climbed up and took the reins. Paul ran down the steps, pushing her roughly from the driver's seat.

'I'll take her, you go inside, I'm taking charge of this.'

Mittee turned a bewildered face to him, shocked to find that she was afraid of him. 'I am going with you.'

His violence subsided a little when he saw that he had frightened her, but he took it out on the horse, thrashing it to a gallop that sent chickens squawking across the yard. Mittee gained more confidence for he put his arm about her, trying already to get back into her favour now that he was sure that he was to have his own way about me.

To Mrs Gouws they explained that I could not be happy away from the old farm but whether she believed them is another matter. You don't catch an old bird with chaff. She looked me over sarcastically, remarking that a rat would have more strength and what did they expect she could set me to do.

'She's the best ironer in the district,' said Mittee. 'And some day she's coming back to her old nonnie to iron, hey, Selina?'

'Pity you have to part with her at all for I'm sure it doesn't matter how my plain dresses are ironed.' Mrs Gouws giggled but she looked from Mittee to Paul in an inquisitive manner.

'Come on, we've got to get back,' said Paul, with temper in his voice.

I stood with Mrs Gouws, watching the trap as it raced down the road. 'I never thought to see the day you would leave your nonnie,' said Mrs Gouws, hopefully trying to draw some information from me.

My flat voice quenched that hope. 'The day has come and I have left her.'

Snorting, she went indoors and I walked into the veld to sit alone under a thorn tree for I was sorrowful. The veld had come to life. Here and there black showed where the grass had been burnt at the end of July but there were tufts of dazzling green. A korhaan, with feathers as brown as droughted veld, ran zigzagging on one side of me and partridges flew up suddenly as though flung into the air. Guinea fowl were calling from across the road and I caught sight of them sitting up in a wild fig tree. The speckles on their feathers made me think of the spotted silk dress that Grandma Van Brandenberg had worn to church, year in and year out, a dress that she had brought with her on the Great Trek, made of a silk that was indestructible. Mittee gave the dress to Mrs Gouws when Grandma died but she grew too fat for it and cut it up for cushions. The cushions shone through the twilight of Mrs Gouws' front room, to quench the glory of such frivolous things as the artificial flowers and the gold-and-pink china mugs. Still I felt that this was not the place for that silk, for there was always something sacrilegious to me about people sitting on that worthy and terrifying old woman's Sunday dress.

Under her rule Sundays on the farm were days of hushed voices and anguished searching through the Bible. Even the dog respected the brittle quietness, not daring to bark except with a hoarseness that testified to his efforts to vanquish his brutishness. The only creatures that made a noise on the yard were a godless baboon and a flock of geese. The geese Grandma could forgive but when the baboon profaned the holiness with monkey swearwords she would stand before him and promise him the thrashing of his life on Monday morning, to which he responded by rubbing himself lewdly against her for he had a strange passion for her; and she so virtuous.

Grandma prayed so long on Sunday mornings that the fire went out in the stove and a thick scum formed over the porridge as the steam went from it; but nobody complained at her table when they ate the cold porridge nor did you hear the vigorous clatter of plates that marked mealtimes on other days. If you did hear a spoon touch the bottom of a plate, it had a stealthy sound that would not offend God's ear. Once, I remember, a Kaffir girl dropped the cups she was carrying. She ran away before the crash had died on the fainting air, never to be seen on the farm again.

When church was over, Grandma would sit on the front stoep, still wearing the spotted silk dress, and with Grandpa's spectacles on her nose would read to her family from the Bible. This was a book so big that Grandpa had to carry it from the front room for her, a splendid book with pictures so bright that they made you wink your eyes.

There was a Sunday when the baboon got loose. Mittee and I said nothing as he sidled on to the stoep and sat down next to Grandma, leaning against her leg. Abstractedly, she put her hand on his head and went on to the end of the chapter. Then she looked down into the baboon's face. Such was her control that she did not scream out but sat staring at the baboon. 'Paradise,' she whispered, 'I thought it was you there beside me, Maria.' Because Mittee and I laughed, she thrashed us, as well as the baboon, on Monday morning.

Perhaps if Grandma had lived, I would not have sinned with Paul and Mittee and I would not be parted. Ah, Mittee, I said aloud, I'll miss you, little nonnie. How I wept that afternoon for the loves that I had lost.

That was an early summer. Heavy rains had fallen and the earth, exulting, threw up huge mushrooms and many wild flowers between the grass tufts. The Kaffirs shone with good living and the cattle were fatter than I had ever seen them. Wherever you looked there were young things; Aletta, married now to Jacob Coester, had borne twin sons; each day saw more calves in the kraals; there were puppies in the yard and every egg that was set hatched into a chicken. The moist, birth-giving season filled me with sorrow as I sat beneath the tree, remembering, for the ghost of my baby lay on the hazy air, far from my hungry arms. This was the month that it should have been born.

'Come on, Selina,' yelled Mrs Gouws, 'there's plenty of work to be done.'

I jumped up and ran to the house, for I knew that she had no time to be patient with servants.

CHAPTER VII

I was in Mrs Gouws' good graces because I had finished my work early. Three months under her had taught me to get through quickly, never stopping to stare or gossip.

'Take these fat cookies and sit out on the threshold and eat them,' she said kindly to me.

Gouws had left only five and I ate them slowly for they were good. He sat at the kitchen table, rubbing his chest every now and then because fat cookies disagreed with him.

'Heaven, Cobie,' he said to his wife, 'it's as if my mouth was filled with vinegar.'

'That's pure poison from your stomach.'

'Then I'm going to lie down until it passes over.'

'But here comes Frikkie Du Plessis riding down the road. He's come to see you about that heifer at last.'

'Well, send him into the bedroom, I can't sit up a minute longer,' said Gouws heavily.

The walls of the rooms were made of hessian so that you heard every sound that was made. I heard Gouws sigh himself into the bedroom, the creaking of the bed as he descended upon it and the explosion as he relieved himself of the wind that was troubling him. He said, 'Excuse,' in a shamed voice, though there was nobody with him. Mrs Gouws began to giggle in a high, childish voice and it was all I could do to keep my face straight.

Frikkie rode into the yard. He threw the reins to Fanie who came behind mounted on a donkey.

'Day, Selina,' Frikkie said and winked as he passed me. He was free and easy with all, not like the magistrate's other sons who were so full of pride that they even set themselves above some of the white people.

'It's you, Frikkie,' roared Mrs Gouws. 'Well, here's a cup of coffee. You can take it with you to the bedroom. Gouws is there, he's feeling pretty bad.'

'Thanks, Auntie.'

Frikkie passed through the house, calling out cheerfully, 'May I come in, Uncle? I've brought Fanie with me to drive the heifer to my farm.'

'Well, it's a difficult matter,' said Gouws, groaning. 'She's no longer a heifer. She has calved since you bought her. Now how do we stand?'

'We can make a deal surely, Uncle.'

'Not today,' Gouws moaned. 'I'm in the most terrible pain. It's like flames running up and down my chest.'

I knew that Frikkie had sat down on the end of the bed by the scream of the springs. 'I'm sorry that Uncle is not well but let us talk the matter out now. I've ridden a long way.'

Mrs Gouws yelled out, 'Make him an offer, Frikkie.'

'Thirty shillings.'

'That's robbery. Nothing less than two pounds. After all, the calf is a heifer and the cow is in milk: make it two pounds ten,' said Gouws in a stronger voice.

'It's a hard struggle,' shouted Mrs Gouws. 'Mittee was never one to give much away and she makes us give a good account even if she is rich today.'

'Health is more than riches,' consoled Frikkie.

'Gouws has neither and you have both.'

Frikkie could think of nothing to say to that except to make a feeble reference to his poverty. 'Will Uncle take thirty-five shillings,' he said, trying to ignore the voice on the other side of the hessian that sounded out the words 'Two pounds ten' as soon as he mentioned a sum of money.

Frikkie's nerves were not strong enough and he gave in at two pounds three shillings. He said generously, 'I hope that Uncle will be in better shape for my wedding at Nagmaal.'

'The dear God knows I wish I was.'

'I'll tell you what I'll do. I have some good pills and I'll send them over in the morning. Take them every day and you'll be able to eat with the best of them at the wedding.'

'If you could cure me of these pains I'd give you that heifer.'

'You put your trust in the Lord and eat less,' boomed Mrs Gouws. 'And don't go throwing your money away on pills you know nothing about.'

I had saved half a fat cookie for Fanie and now I ran into the yard to greet him. He ate the fat cookie, nibble by nibble, rolling up his eyes to show how good it was. Then he put his hands behind his back.

'Guess which hand.'

'What have you got?'

'Sweets.'

I pointed to his left hand. 'That one.' He thrust something soft and squashy into my palm. 'Christ, a caterpillar,' I screamed.

Fanie laughed until he rolled on the ground. He was clever with animals but in other ways he was simple and he had learned these tricks from his baas, so you could not be angry with him when he teased you. He recovered and put a heart-shaped sweet into my hand. On it was written in High Dutch, 'I Love You'.

'What an expensive sweet, Fanie; where did you get it from?'

'Frikkie buys them for when he is sitting up with his girl. It's like a game. They sort out the sweets and they can have quite a loving conversation without the mother hearing a word.'

'It's a very pretty sweet, too pretty to eat.'

'Keep it then and think of me. Frikkie has to use them because there is only one room in his girl's house, they're so poor. He had to sleep there one night because the drift was in flood. He had a terrible time. They put him in the same room as the girl but on a new sheepskin and every time he moved the sheepskin crackled and then the old man would cough. Frikkie says that afterwards he didn't even think of the girl but he didn't sleep a wink all night because when he tried to turn round the damned sheepskin crackled. He was glad when daylight came, I tell you.'

Polly had been watching us through the kitchen window and seeing us laugh she could not resist joining us, though she always said the Plessisburg boys were too silly even to flirt. Fanie played the caterpillar trick on her but he did not give her a sweet so I shared mine with her after I had licked off I Love You for she was always generous with the chocolates that Eberhardt brought Andrina every Monday evening when he came to sit up with her. He did not regret Mittee now for she was a poor prize in comparison with Andrina. Polly often let me into Andrina's bedroom, from where you could hear all that went on in the front room, but the courting was dull and precise as Eberhardt himself; and the best thing about it was the abundance of chocolates to which Polly could help herself without Andrina noticing the difference.

The next morning Fanie brought the pills, which Gouws was to swallow after every meal. They were large and difficult to swallow but they did him good and he decided to take a bath on the day before Frikkie's wedding, when the sun was at its hottest.

When he said, 'Today I'll bath,' Mrs Gouws' face grew serious. Neither she nor Gouws took the bath as lightly as Mittee. He had danced unbathed at Mittee's wedding because a cold snap set in just before.

Mrs Gouws sent me into the front bedroom to prepare the place for her husband. The windows had to be closed and the crack in the wall stuffed with rag for if a draught should fall upon Gouws' body, it might mean pneumonia. Then I carried the tin bath in; and one of the yard boys followed with a tin full of warm water. Mrs Gouws came next, to test the water, making sure that it was not too hot or too cold; and to examine the room for any leakage of air.

Gouws went in and she closed the door on him. Nothing further was heard for some time but a mighty splashing. Then came the call, 'Cobie, my clothes.' Mrs Gouws snatched up the clothes that she had placed in the oven to warm, hurrying to the bedroom with them, for there must be no danger of anything cold striking his body.

He ventured out of the room, clearing his throat to see if he had caught cold. Mrs Gouws scolded him.

'Fancy letting your beard get wet. You should have kept it clear of the water. That's the way to get the toothache.'

'My beard itched. I washed it,' said Gouws, seating himself near the fire.

'Washed it. All the world, do you want to die of pain, man? Here, let me part it and comb it for you.' She must have dug the comb into the flesh for Gouws bellowed in agony. He was not a man who could stand much pain. Contrite, she rubbed the tangled beard.

'I don't know how we're going to do it without hurting you.' She considered the beard, head first to this side and then to the other. 'It's gone into knots. I'll try combing it lightly.'

Gouws shrank from her. 'You're not going to touch it. The pain is terrible.'

'My treasure, what shall we do?'

'Perhaps a little oil,' suggested Gouws.

'There's not a drop in the house, I gave the last to Aletta for the babies. I'll have to send Selina into Plessisburg.'

I pulled my dress straight and stood ready, hoping that she would not change her mind. A trip into Plessisburg was a rare thing when you worked for Mrs Gouws. She hastened to her bedroom and brought out two tickeys from the secret place where she kept her money.

'Here's the money, Selina; wait while I write a note for sixpence worth of oil. But you must hurry and no dawdling or gossip on the way.'

I put the tickeys into my pocket with the note and set off at a run, which I kept up while in sight of the house. It was always a good plan to run while she could still see you, then she would send you on the next errand. I watched my shadow slide away from me, faster and faster. I ran with laughter in my throat for I was going to catch that shadow. It spun away from me and I had to stop to get my breath. I stood in the middle of the road, shaking my head from side to side to get the comical effect that the two points of my doek made where it was tied in front of my head, like two horns. The sun was hot and I sat under a thorn tree to eat a chocolate that Polly had slipped into my pocket. It had begun to melt and I was glad I had stopped to eat it before it was spoilt. I ate slowly, grudging each swallow that carried away the smooth sweetness.

The turning sun warned me that I had stayed there too long. I would have to hurry the rest of the way for Mrs Gouws had an arm on her like a leg of mutton and when she boxed your ears your head sang for an hour afterwards.

As I sped along the road, the tickeys chattered merrily in my pocket and I thought, They have come loose from the paper, I should stop and make them secure. But I did not stop, for the thought of Gouws waiting to have his tangled beard combed out made me feel anxious. One of the tickeys flew out of my pocket into the veld. 'Little Christ, where has it gone?' I bent down to search in the grass but I could not see it. I went through that grass like a person looking for nits. The tickey was gone. I spent as long as I dared, but I had to go without it for the afternoon was growing shadows. I would have to buy only a tickey's worth of the oil and hope for the best. Fearful that something might happen to the remaining tickey, I put it into my mouth for safety. I had just made up my mind that I would tie it in my doek, and I had the tickey lying firm and cool on my tongue one minute and it was sliding down my throat the next. I tried to make myself sick with my fingers but though I retched a little there was no sign of the tickey. What to do now? Thinking of Mrs Gouws, who counted her wealth in tickeys, there was nothing for it but to sit down and cry.

A trap was scampering down the road from Plessisburg. Even at that distance I could recognize Mittee coming towards me like an angel. She stopped the trap beside me and leaned out.

'Almighty, Selina, why are you crying?'

'I've lost the money. Mrs Gouws will thunder me up when I get back. It was for oil for the old baas' beard, it's in a terrible tangle. I will get such a hiding.'

'Well, it serves you right. Where did you lose the money? Perhaps I can get down and help you find it.'

I pointed to my stomach. 'One tickey is in here and the other was spirited away in the veld some way back.'

'There's a curse on you, Selina. Never mind, jump up beside me and I'll drive back to Plessisburg with you and buy the oil. You can pay the sixpence out of your wages one day.'

The whole world was different now. There was I, who had been so hopeless, sitting up beside Mittee, without a care except to wonder whether we would get to Plessisburg before the shop shut. There was no need to worry about that when Mittee was driving. The horse always knew who was behind him when she was driving for she was not one to be content with a steady jogging along. The gossips of Plessisburg, when they got tired of talking about her vanity, discussed the speed of her driving as though there were something faintly scandalous about it. And well they might. You had to hold on to the seat when Mittee was in a hurry.

Within a few minutes, I was breathlessly asking Mrs Tyson for a sixpence worth of oil for the oubaas' beard, explaining to her what had happened while she dourly read through Mrs Gouws' note, not a word of which did she understand because it was written in High Dutch.

As we got down from the trap, we saw Gouws with a sawn-off shotgun in his hand. I fell to my knees, sheltering behind Mittee's skirts for protection.

'Don't shoot, baas, I will explain . . .'

He blundered past us as though he neither saw nor heard us and I got up, relieved that it was not me he was after. I had never seen the man in such a rage, it was enough to make you tremble although it was not directed at you.

Mrs Gouws was in the kitchen, praying as she cooked the evening meal. 'Here is the oil, missis,' I said timidly.

'Do not let him commit murder, oh Father,' she exhorted. 'You're back? Put the bottle down where it won't be broken. Father, help me in my misery.'

'What shall I do now, missis?' I spoke more loudly, rejoicing that I was getting off without even a scolding.

'Watch this pot while I go and reason with the baas. Was that Nonnie Mittee who walked past? A terrible thing has happened, Selina. The pills that Baas Frikkie gave him turned out to be lizards' eggs and he's going for Frikkie with a sawn-off shotgun. And on the eve of the wedding. Only God can stop murder. He was feeling in his waistcoat pocket for a pill and as he took it out, it broke and there was the baby lizard. He has swallowed four and what is happening inside his stomach I cannot think.'

'What's the matter?' asked Mittee, peeping in at the door. 'I can't get a chance to talk to anybody, not even Andrina. She's down by the river talking to Eberhardt.'

'Just now, Mittee,' shouted Mrs Gouws, charging through the door, 'I've got to talk Gouws out of this madness.'

'It's a terrible mix-up, Mittee,' I said. 'Gouws' beard is in a tangle and he's been taking lizards' eggs instead of pills. He's going to Plessisburg to shoot Frikkie.'

Mrs Gouws hurried again into the kitchen. 'Leave the food, Selina, and come and help me into my corsets. I'll have to dress before he inspans. He's determined. I'll have to get the minister on to him.'

'There are a lot of things I want to talk to Uncle about this afternoon,' said Mittee peevishly. 'He must stay while I'm here.'

'Get him to stay if you can and I'll be glad. But he's like a mad thing and who wouldn't be, I ask you, with lizards' eggs hatching inside?'

So Gouws drove off with his wife and I walked with Mittee on the riverbank. We were not alone for Eberhardt sat with Andrina under the willows, pursuing his decorous courtship under the eye of Mrs Van Brandenberg.

He was telling a ghost story, pleasant to hear in the bright sunshine. Mittee and I sat down to listen, though Mrs Van Brandenberg shook her head as though we were spoiling lovers' talk. This was when Eberhardt was at his best, for he was a good storyteller. His narrow, parsimonious features became lively and he used his voice like an instrument, now soft, now loud.

'I am riding through the veld in Natal,' said Eberhardt and his hand went delicately over Andrina's fingers. She snatched her hand away, rubbing it against her skirt as though a worm had crawled over it. 'I am riding through the veld in Natal,' he repeated, careless of the rebuff, 'and all of a sudden I hear a baby crying. I look about but I can see no baby. And I ride on. The baby begins to cry again and this time I get off my horse to see where it is. There, lying abandoned on the veld, is a little Kaffir baby. I bend over it to pick it up for even if it is black it is, after all, human . . .'

'A kind heart,' said Mrs Van Brandenberg for Andrina's benefit.

'But as I bent over the thing,' Eberhardt's voice was like a flute now, 'it turns into a little monster. My God, it is Tigoloshi, whom the Zulus dread.' Here came a pause while we shivered in spite of the afternoon sunshine. 'Fortunately, I had the sense to carry my Bible on me and I throw the Bible at the unholy thing, whereupon it vanishes. I run to my horse and putting spurs to it, it's gallop, gallop all the way to the nearest farmhouse twenty miles away. The horse dropped dead in the yard but everybody said it was a wonder that I escaped with my life.'

Paul had turned his horse into the grass while Eberhardt was telling the story. Now, sitting close to Mittee, he laughed.

'It's a useful thing to carry the Bible on the veld, Dietloff, I must remember that; I usually take my rifle.'

Andrina joined her laugh to Paul's, a sound like splintering glass. She began to flirt with Paul so cunningly that Mittee did not notice, though her mother fidgeted. Eberhardt, to draw her attention back to him, put his hand into the small of her back. In an instant the peace was shattered. Andrina buried her fingers in his beard, tugging until he yelled. It would not have been so bad if Paul had not laughed again, throwing his derision like salt into Eberhardt's wounded pride. Andrina was well pleased, not so much because she had hurt Eberhardt, I fancy, but because she saw her mother grow purple with anger.

'Apologize at once,' said Mrs Van Brandenberg in a thick voice.

Andrina leaned back, clasping her knees. For the first time since she had parted with Leon, I saw a look of pleasure on her face. I turned my eyes away, sick with pity for her as I glimpsed the emptiness of her life. She might never know love again or any emotion but this hatred for her mother.

Mittee hissed at Paul, 'You should be ashamed, laughing like that. Come away from them and perhaps she will apologize.'

Paul walked with her a little way down the riverbank, though he was still laughing. Mrs Van Brandenberg said over and over again, 'Apologize at once,' commands to which Andrina paid no attention as she looked serenely upon the rage that twisted Eberhardt's features. Mittee beckoned me to follow her.

'It's a disgrace to laugh like that in the man's face,' she admonished Paul.

He became sulky. 'The way you lecture, you often remind me of your grandma.' I smiled for he had given words to my very thoughts. She took his hand and they walked on without me. Leaning against the trunk of a willow tree, I watched them, bitterness welling up in me, for they passed over the very spot where Herry had found Paul and me on Dingaan's Night. The frill of Mittee's muslin dress brushed over the grass innocently and carelessly.

He remembered, for he tried to turn Mittee back. She danced away from him, holding her skirts out as she had done when she was a girl, but he seemed to take no pleasure in her grace.

'Come back now,' he said harshly. 'My father is expecting us to the evening meal.'

Andrina, seeing Mittee dance, ran away from her mother's nagging voice and joined in, while I clapped and sang, 'Music so false, they were dancing a waltz . . .'

Paul walked moodily to his horse and mounted. He called out again to Mittee and then rode slowly away.

'Yes, it's time to go,' snapped Mrs Van Brandenberg, but Mittee shook her head.

'There's plenty of time yet. I'm going to walk a little way along the bank.'

Andrina's gaiety had faded and she sat down alone, while Mittee and I walked on. Mittee was silent until we reached the haunted waggon. She picked out the place where we always used to sit.

She sat down on the grass and spread her skirt round her carefully. 'Sometimes I wish that I was not Mittee.'

'Would you rather be Selina, who has no home and no people?' I asked bitterly.

'Paul is like Grandma. You are never free from him. I have to do only what he tells me, I'm like a monkey on a chain.'

'I thought he was very kind to you, Mittee.'

'Only when everything is going his way. I'll never forgive him for making you go, Selina. I miss you. I'm so used to having you with me. Sometimes I call out, "Selina," before I realize that you are not there.'

'I miss you, too, my nonnie.' She looked so downcast that I said, 'Shall I look in the hole and see if the skull is still there?' not because I wanted to look at the grisly thing but because I thought it might make her smile.

'Yes do, Selina,' she said listlessly. 'And then I must hurry back because I've got to be at this big family meal that the magistrate is giving for Frikkie. There will be ninety-seven of the Du Plessis relatives there. Fancy, I am related to all those people now.'

I clambered down the bank and peeped into the cavity. At first I saw only a white blur but as my eyes focused the blur took on the shape of a complete human skeleton.

For a moment I hung over the edge of the bank, filling my eyes with that dreadful arrangement of bones, then I ran to Mittee and clutched at her while I jumped up and down in time to my screams, like a person who has been scalded.

She pushed me aside and went to look for herself what was in the riverbank to frighten me so much. When she saw it, she took to her heels, caring nothing of what became of me; we ran desperately as though the skeleton would come out of its hiding place to chase us.

Gouws was back from his journey of vengeance. He had been soothed by Frikkie's explanation that the whole thing was a mistake; and by the gift of a sucking pig and a box of genuine pills. He cracked each pill open while his wife was oiling his beard and then had to throw them all away for the taste was too vile.

His adventures were as nothing beside the finding of the skeleton. I was the most important person in the house that evening, once Mittee was gone. I was made to tell the story over and over again, long after everybody's bedtime. Mrs Gouws, when she had finished combing the beard, sat listening in a charmed silence and never once fell asleep although she had had a hard day. Even the kitchen girl, who scorned me for my mixed blood, looked at me with respect so that when I got over my fright I enjoyed myself, though it was not to be for long.

It was when I was in bed that I realized as clearly as though somebody had told me that the skeleton was Herry's. I remembered Paul's face when Mittee and I came running up from the riverbank. Then I was glad that I shared the room with the kitchen girl. I hated her as much as she hated me but that night I listened to her night sounds with a sense of comfort; her tortured breathing, the grinding of her teeth, the sudden mumble of Shangaan words.

There was a hole in the tin roof through which I could see a patch of sky; but that night I did not see the stars, only Herry's gentle little face. Had he cried out when those strong hands battered at his old body? I could not pray for I thought God must be far from us indeed not to have stretched out His hand that night to save the weak and innocent.

He had killed Herry and Jansie. Would he come that night to destroy me, whose word would put him on the gallows? When the dogs barked, I shivered, thinking, He will come like Jansie did. At times it seemed that he was already in the room with me and I shrieked to the Kaffir girl, to be answered and soothed by her swearing.

At dawn I took my bundle and set off for Auntie Lena's house so that he would not know where to find me. I was glad Frikkie was to be married that day because that meant Paul would be at the wedding until late at night and he would not have time to come looking for me. My way lay over a narrow pathway that the feet of Auntie Lena's many relations had beaten during their passing across the veld to and from Plessisburg. Her house stood on a hill. It was made of clay and poles, with no windows so that the rooms were dark and hot all the time; but I would be safe there for she had her sons and daughters-in-law always with her and you could never be alone in Auntie Lena's house.

She was sweeping the threshold when I came to the gate. She swept with furious strokes, taunting the dust that was her bane.

'That will be the last of you, lying thick as soon as I turn my back. All the world, Selina, what are you doing here carrying your bundle?'

'I've finished with them, Auntie. I didn't even wait for the money she owes me.'

'Almighty, surely that couldn't happen. Why, you were born on the farm.' She put the broom aside. 'Come inside and you can tell me everything.'

She moved quietly for her grandchild was asleep on the kitchen floor. It must have been smeared out the day before because the smell of dung and ox blood was still so sharp that it burnt your nostrils. One of her relations had probably stolen the blood from the beast that Frikkie had killed for his wedding feast. Still, the place was inviting for Auntie Lena had so few possessions that each one was precious to her and kept spotless.

She made coffee and in that close little room, the smell of it was so strong that you were satisfied before you drank it. Auntie Lena did not talk about my affairs but about her relations. She had not yet heard about the finding of the skeleton and for that I was glad. The heat pressed me into drowsiness but I did not get a chance to sleep because soon the house became noisy with awakening children. Little boys rushed into the kitchen, whistling like colts. Auntie Lena spoke to them absent-mindedly, 'Silence, you'll wake your mother,' although their mother stood in the doorway. Her mind was not on them or on me but on some far-off incident that had happened to her youngest son when he was a child.

There were peach trees growing behind the house. I slept there for a few hours until Auntie Lena brought one of her great-grand-children for me to watch because its mother was off to Frikkie's wedding. She was a sickly child and nervous from too much nursing. She began to cry as soon as Auntie Lena left her, struggling in my arms. To pacify her I showed her a beetle rolling a ball of cowdung a hundred times bigger than himself and she watched as he climbed over and over the ball to give it momentum, until she could resist him no longer. Greedily, her hand closed over the ball and shining beetle. The dung had grown hard with rolling but she pressed it until it shattered. She screamed shrilly as I plucked the beetle from her hand and threw him high into the air. I imprisoned her in my arms, chanting, 'Doedoe baba, doedoe baba,' holding her so tightly that she could not fight against the rhythm of my voice and rocking body. Her eyelids fluttered and then opened wide. I rocked more violently, convinced that she would never go to sleep but she gave in suddenly with a long sigh, snuggling into me.

So still was the place now that it seemed as though God held a finger up, calling for quietness. I was glad of the warmth of the child against my body for suddenly I was afraid again. Would Paul be dancing at his brother's wedding? Would he be standing apart like a man awaiting some disaster or would he be watching amongst the coloured people for me? I was safe now, surely, for he would not seek me out in broad daylight. Then I saw him.

A twig crackled beneath his foot as he left a sheltering tree. Gone was his pride. The flame in his eyes had died to a smouldering watch-fulness.

'I had to talk to you, Selina.'

'You want to kill me like you killed the others, Herry and Jansie.'

'I could not help it. I went back to the river that night when I left you and I tried to force him to leave Plessisburg. I tied the pack to the donkey and drove it along with him down the road but he fought with me. I did not know that he was so frail. I did not mean to kill him, he was dead before I knew what I had done. Oh Christ, I'll always remember the feel of that dead body when I carried it from the road. I was going to throw it into the river but I thought, It will be washed up. Then I remembered that hole in the bank. It could have stayed there for years, nobody ever goes to that part of the river. I had to bend down and push his body into the hole . . .' He was speaking eagerly, like a man who speaks of his love, with gusts of breath that shook the words from him.

I held the sleeping child against my body like a shield. 'They say that Herry was my father. While we both live, there will always be this thing between us and one day you will kill me.'

'Never. Little heart, have you forgotten? I avenged our child. If it had lived, I would not have seen it in want. If the world were different, I would have loved you.'

I shook my head at his lies. 'No, Paul, there is only one in all the world whom you love and it was because of her that you killed Herry and Jansie, too. It is not for your sake that I will keep silent, but for hers. I will never speak of that night to anybody, I will be as faithful as I was when they asked questions about Jansie.'

'Nobody will guess it is Herry, for I took his clothes off and burnt everything from his pack. I drove his donkey away but that came back to the river.' His voice was eager again as though he found relief in talking.

'Now I will go away from Plessisburg as you wanted me to. There is nothing for me here but bitterness.'

He leaned over the sleeping baby and kissed my lips. It was the first kiss that he had ever given me.

'Hi, Selina, you must not hate me. Think of me sometimes when the moonlight lies on the river for I think of you then. And I will always remember how you danced down the road in front of me.'

'I will think of Herry.'

He stood up, still uncertain of me. 'The next moonlight night I will wait for you, Selina, over there on the veld by that big wild fig tree.'

'And they will find Selina dead and nobody will know why Selina was there.'

'I will wait there for you, Selina.'

His quick eyes had seen the flutter of a skirt in the doorway of the house. He was under cover in the trees as Auntie Lena came on to the yard but she had caught a glimpse of him, though her old eyes had not recognized him. She sat down beside me.

'Who was that with you?'

'It was Fanie.'

'No. I could see that he was wearing an embroidered waistcoat and good clothes. He was a white man, Selina, and he must have come from the wedding. Why should a white man leave the wedding to come and see you? What are you up to now, Selina, haven't you had enough trouble?'

I knew a way to stop her from asking questions. 'You know, Auntie, yesterday Mittee and I were walking by the river and we found a human skeleton in a hole in the bank.'

'God, no.' The old thing looked at me with the big eyes of an owl, all thought of anything else wiped from her mind. 'Whose, Selina?'

'Now, that's a thing they don't know yet, Auntie. Perhaps some Kaffir who was drowned and washed in there by the river.'

'Perhaps somebody who was dragged there by a crocodile years ago,' she said, a little disappointed.

'Well no, it can't be that. There are no crocodiles in the river now and Mittee and I looked in that selfsame place just before Christmas and there was no skeleton there then.'

'It must be somebody we know.' She rubbed her dry hands together until they crackled. It was well known that if you wanted to cheer Auntie Lena up, you must tell her of a calamity that had befallen one of her friends.

I did not listen to her wild conjectures. Sunset had fallen on the Wolkbergen. I turned my face to the bright mountains, wistfully, like the Coesters' chained monkey did when he stared towards the krantzes where his tribe lived its thrilling life. I was too young then to know how swift is our passing, how old are our griefs.

Polly told me the next day that Letty had been angry even on her wedding day, for the guests had no heart for the dancing but gathered in groups to speak about the skeleton.

'It serves her right,' said Polly as we walked together to Plessisburg. 'The vinegary thing deserved to have a skeleton at her wedding.'

'If you would only speak of something else,' I grumbled.

'What else is there to speak of in this place but skeletons?' she said contemptuously. 'The men here are all half dead or married so fast they don't even give you a look.'

She had her pay tied up in a corner of her apron and she was off to Tyson's shop to spend it. Tyson, smug because it was the end of the month, greeted her civilly.

'Will you bring out the ribbons?' she said, sweetening her voice and arching her brows.

It was wasted on Tyson who was interested in Polly only because she was a good spender. He brought out a tray of ribbons and left her to examine them while he hurried to the other end of the shop to attend to Eberhardt who had come in with Meyer the Water Fiscal.

'Tobacco,' said Eberhardt in English, and then without lowering his voice but speaking in the Language to the Water Fiscal, 'I tell you, man, I had to drag the thing out alone because Du Plessis, and you know his arrogance, stood by as squeamish as a woman. He had something to do with it, you mark what I say. Wasn't he down at the river on Dingaan's Night and Herry was camped there that night? I had it from the policeman that it is Herry's skeleton and nobody else's.' He took his change from Tyson and stuffed the tobacco into his pocket.

'Why should Du Plessis want to do anything to Herry?' asked the Water Fiscal.

'Now that is for the magistrate to find out,' said Eberhardt triumphantly. 'We can only tell what we know.'

The Water Fiscal's face was alight with wonder and excitement as though he had picked up a bag of gold. 'What a terrible thing it would be for the Du Plessis family if it were true. There was that coloured boy that he killed . . .'

'Well, there he was down by the riverbank, I tell you.'

They went out of the shop and I followed them to the door, leaving Polly to murmur over the quality of the ribbon by herself. The minister passed them and the Water Fiscal, to show he was minding his own business, officiously removed a stone from the side of the furrow. Then I saw them turn in at the policeman's house. By the time I got home, even Auntie Lena was saying that Paul Du Plessis was to be hanged.

All the coloured people had congregated at Auntie Lena's house to talk the matter over. They sat over fires grilling meat they had saved from Frikkie's wedding feast, happy in the knowledge that they would not be missed for the white people were holding a service in the church. There were many strange faces there because it was Nagmaal but one face seemed to spring out from all the others at me; and I remembered the last time I had seen Herry. Did Klaas remember?

Fanie, who had been before the magistrate for questioning that afternoon, was the centre of attraction. 'They are looking for somebody who saw Herry on Dingaan's Day,' he told us. 'He was seen in the morning but never again and you know he never missed preaching on Christmas Day. When the magistrate asked me, I began to shiver and shake though I had not seen him for a year, and I was kept back after the others for more questions. I was glad when they let me go, I can tell you. Now, if they can find somebody who saw him and spoke to him . . .'

I felt sorry for Klaas as I watched him. He was remembering that Herry gave him a bottle of peach brandy on Dingaan's Day. Probably that was all he could remember, he had been so drunk. Presently I saw him get up and edge away into the darkness.

'When they hang people, they sometimes bungle it,' said Auntie Lena. 'It was like that at Slachter's Nek. Hanging's a terrible death if they bungle it. They bungled it at Slachter's Nek, that's why we trekked away from the Cape.'

'The magistrate will see to it that his son is properly hanged,' said Polly.

So the talk went on until the last sausage was eaten and people slept as they sat. It was late before the last of them had left.

There was a moon that night, shivering behind clouds, and by its treacherous light I made my way to the wild fig tree. I went in fear, not of ghosts, but of Paul. Twice I turned back for I thought, When he has me at his mercy, he will kill me to make himself safe for only I can give evidence against him.

He was waiting for me, standing still beside his horse. I went close to him.

'I came because I heard from Fanie that you had been before your father. I will say nothing. I came to tell you that. Now kill me if you want to for I might as well be dead. I am afraid of you, all the time, awake and asleep.'

His voice was stronger than mine. 'If you had not come I might have killed you, Selina.'

A fit of shivering passed over me and I hugged my body close to stop it.

He said, 'I had to face my father again like a criminal and I thought to myself, Selina is the only one who can give me away. But I never thought of killing you, Selina. He had the four of us in, Eberhardt, Frikkie, Fanie and me. He questioned us for two hours but I think he is satisfied, and it won't go to court. There is nobody who knows why Herry died, nobody except you and me, Selina.'

He put out his hands to me but I backed away. 'No, basie, never again, never.'

I walked away from him quickly. My back crawled but I did not look round until I came to the door of Auntie Lena's house and then I could no longer see him, only the veld, shadowed by the clouded moon, secret and dangerous.

Auntie Lena was awake. She beckoned me to her quietly for the house was full to bursting with sleeping people.

'Where have you been? Have you got stomach trouble?'

'Yes.'

'Green peaches. I've seen children die in screaming fits and convulsions from green peaches but they will eat them and I can remember as though it was yesterday the taste of a green peach and the bitterness when you came close to the pip.'

I sat down on the threshold beside her, grateful that I did not have to go into the stifling little house. I tried to listen to what the old woman was saying for now that my fear of him had left me, I felt creeping over me again tenderness and longing for him. It was evil for me to love him and a deep, inward melancholy came upon me that night, never to leave me.

'Babies, babies, babies,' said Auntie Lena. 'I bore fifteen children and nursed them and none of them died. And I saw them all grow up and marry and then there were more babies and now it isn't wonderful any more though I remember the first time I saw a baby born and afterwards I went outside and prayed and prayed because I thought it was so wonderful. I remember that first baby. Henry Dressel. And I brought his son into the world. Leon Dressel.'

'Leon Dressel, Auntie?'

'Yes, I brought Leon Dressel into the world. This was how it happened. The Van Brandenbergs went to Durban for a holiday and while they were away Henry Dressel and his wife and sister Margarita stayed in the house. The sister married one of the Van Brandenberg boys and what a hard woman she is. She's living on the farm now with her daughter. Only the other day, as I was making my poor old way to Plessisburg to buy a few skeins of cotton, I saw her on the stoep. Do you remember me, nonna? I said. No, she shouted, How would I remember every old coloured thing that stops to talk to me? Then I sat down. You should remember me, I said, because I brought your nephew into the world, your own brother's child, don't you remember? And you ran round crying and fainting because the woman hadn't come and when she did come, I had the baby bathed and ready to put into its mother's arms. They called him Leon after your own father. There's not much old Auntie Lena forgets, I said. Then she took me by the scruff of the neck and pushed me out of the place. She forgot how frightened she was that night and how she said to me, Lena, I will never forget what a good girl you have been. And now she says, You're talking nonsense, they should put you in a place for mad people.'

'Leon Dressel.'

'That was the name,' said Auntie Lena, taking a pinch of snuff. 'Leon, after the old father.'

'And she had no children before she was married?'

'No. I saw her married from the Van Brandenbergs' house. He was a runt and she married him for his money, it was said, he was good at trading, I remember. Though she used to be in love with the magistrate . . .'

'Poor Andrina,' I said, suddenly sleepy.

When Klaas had been missing for a week, a warrant was made out for his arrest and though he was never caught and tried, the policeman told everybody in Plessisburg that the case was solved. There was a witness. A little Kaffir, who had been looking for his mother's strayed goats, had seen Herry give Klaas a bottle of peach brandy.

This threw cold water on the gossip that had been raging in the town. It had been said openly in the shop that the magistrate had cut both Paul and Frikkie out of his will because they had killed Herry in horseplay; that it was the coloured boy who had done it, for the bale of silks he carried. Young Plessis was the most likely one, though, after all, did he not shoot a boy and get taken to court while his wife laughed about it? The minister preached a thunderous sermon against gossip during which the whole congregation looked guilty, so Mittee told me.

I met her on the road while I was shopping for Auntie Lena. She had a parcel of print that she had just bought from Tyson and she tore a corner in the paper to show me the pattern.

'You never think of anything else but clothes,' I said. 'It's time you gave your mind to serious things, nonnie. I want to tell you something.'

'Well come into the shade, because I'm burning black here.'

While we walked beneath the poplar trees that bordered the road, I told her how Auntie Lena had brought Leon Dressel into the world. 'So you see your aunt is a liar, Mittee, and there was no need for Mrs Gouws to work that wickedness.'

'Hi, I can't believe it. Wait until I tell Andrina this.'

'The best thing would be to make sure it is true first, because Auntie Lena's memory gets muddled.'

'We can look up the records,' said Mittee. 'I'll go straight away and ask the magistrate.' She thrust her parcel into my arms. 'You hold this and I'll go in now.'

She came out of the courthouse with her face flushed. 'It's true, Selina, why didn't we think of it before. Why didn't Andrina think of it?'

'Who would think a mother would tell such lies?'

'Now I must make a plan. To tell you the truth I'll be glad to see Andrina settled because she has been flirting with Paul and making more scandal, all to spite her mother. The quickest thing would be for me to go to Pretoria and see Leon's father and tell him the whole story and also to tell my uncle. I am sure that not even he will stand by Aunt Margarita when he hears what she has done.'

Mittee went to Pretoria soon afterwards and then all Plessisburg was scandalized to see Paul ride down the road towards Mittee's farm. It was thought he went to see Andrina and not even Auntie Lena knew that he rode past the house, far into the veld.

Would I live again those nights of terror and passion? Each time I said to him, I will never come here again. But when the moon was high and nothing stirred on the veld but the night wind, I would leave my mat in Auntie Lena's house and run down the path; across the road to the great wild fig tree. There I waited, fearful of every sound, fearful of the ghosts of those dead ones; fearful that one night he would kill me in his bitter self-abasement. Sometimes he did not come and I would creep home, hoping that this was the end of it.

He could not keep away. I think it was because I knew all the evil in him. But I was as lonely as a ghost, even when I lay beside him, listening to the slowing down of his breath.

I was glad when he said to me, 'This is the last time, Selina. Mittee comes home tomorrow. And then I am trekking away from Plessisburg and you must forget all this.'

'Oh Paul, I hope you find a happy life,' I said.

Paul trekked north. He took with him his bywoners and other poor families, to be spread over the fertile valleys of the Wolkbergen. More followed him, lured by the promise of fat pastures that never knew drought or rinderpest, until the movement became known jokingly in Plessisburg as the Little Trek.

The waggons left Plessisburg on a day of sunshine and rain, more silver than gold. Still you could not say, The rain is silver and the sun is gold for as you said it, the rain turned golden, yet in another moment the sky and grass, the very air you breathed, was silver. 'A monkey's wedding,' cried the children, clapping their hands in delight at this magical blending of sun and rain.

The people assembled in the square before leaving and even Auntie Lena forced her old legs to take her to Plessisburg though she was bad with rheumatism. I joined in the hymns but there was no passion of faith to send my voice soaring above the others. I kept well back amongst the coloured people, afraid to face him when Mittee was by. He looked strong now as he stood with his arm through hers, this man who had grovelled on the veld, seeking ease of body and soul from me. There was nothing by which I could remember him when he was gone, not so much as a trinket or a handkerchief, and perhaps I might forget the touch of his hands and the sound of his voice. I wished then that I was already like Auntie Lena, mumbling ceaselessly over trifles.

The prayers were over and from the passers-by came snatches of talk that were flung into the air, isolated by a penetrating spite from the jumble of words. '. . . They say he is after gold, he has struck a reef . . .' '. . . The only answer for Plessis is to trek on . . .' '. . . game by the million and fertile, he wants everything . . .'

There was Letty passing with Frikkie, her mouth already showing the acidity of a woman married but unloved; and Mrs Van Brandenberg, dressed up in Pretoria style, but with a face as sour as vinegar; behind her, Andrina. This was a different Andrina. She walked with Leon. Eberhardt, obviously still hopeful, purred after them, his scheming eyes blinking against the light like a cat's.

I drifted with the crowd to watch the departure of the waggons. Aletta and her husband were going with Paul and she was already in their waggon, suckling one of her babies, though he should have been weaned long since. The other screamed and kicked in the arms of his nurse.

'Until I see you, Nonnie Aletta,' I said.

She did not raise her eyes from her breast. I could see that she found a sensuous delight in feeding the child and that the screaming of the other was but a promise of further joy.

'You should be coming with us.' She did not care if she never saw me again; or her mother and father or the road through Plessisburg. Her whole world was bounded by the babies and Jacob and herself. 'My babies are fat. Now poor Drina Coetzel didn't have a drop and she had to bring her baby up on donkey's milk. I could have fed another two. Drina's child is thin but she can't see that. She thinks it looks very healthy but if it were my child I would be frantic with worry . . .'

I walked away from her. Some of the women had begun to weep at parting with their relatives but as the men swung into their saddles, they set up a lively tune. Auntie Lena blubbered beside me, clutching at the broken threads of memory that drew her back to a morning more than fifty years before when she had set out on the Trek in the Van Brandenbergs' waggons. I called out shrilly to Mittee as their waggon moved to the centre of the road but she did not hear me and she passed out of Plessisburg without a word of farewell from me.

One by one the waggons took their places in the line. The song gave way to a hymn and I sang now, so clear and true that Auntie

Lena said, nudging me, 'You should go to the choir practice at the Mission and you could sing in the square on Christmas Eve.'

The misting rain fell like a knife behind the last waggon.

I did not go home with Auntie Lena. I walked across the veld, on and on, until my legs ached. I thought, I will walk until I die. I went towards the Wolkbergen but sunset was in the sky and still the mountains seemed no nearer than when I had set out. The rain had stopped. Brilliant clouds tumbled one against the other in the west but the eastern horizon was serene and presently I saw a figure emerge from its clear gold.

It was Fanie, coming towards me with the tireless stride of an animal. His eyes picked me out when he was mile away and he broke into a run.

'You little vagabond,' he said, dropping to the grass beside me, 'why have you run away again? Auntie Lena sent me after you and it's lucky for you I'm good at picking up a spoor.'

'I walked here to die, Fanie.'

'Why should a flower want to die?'

Never had I heard words spoken so gently. A great stillness enfolded me.

'Selina, why should you want to die?'

'In all the world there is nothing for me. I loved Mittee and she is gone from me for ever. I can have no children after what Jansie did to me. No husband, because I am bewitched.'

'Who is it that you have loved, little heart?' he asked mournfully. I shivered and with quiet hands he put his coat about my shoulders. 'Oh, love me, Selina.'

I sank against the earth forlornly and held out my arms to him. When I am as old as Auntie Lena I will remember the beauty of his face as his moment came upon him.

'Hi, Fanie, where did you learn such gentleness and grace?'

He sat up, a little apart from me. 'There are some people who say that Fanie is as soft as a woman. That is why they spoke against Frikkie and me. If I am gentle, Selina, it is because I pity women. I first learned that pity for them when I was a little boy. I was in the house with Auntie Lena when her last child was born. I learned that night that love for a woman means blood and pain and sweat. I was ashamed of being a man, when I grew older and understood. I am ashamed of the man that fathered me. I have seen how women smile and look proud when you praise their babies.'

'But all these things are natural.'

'Yes. But thinking about it has kept me away from girls and people talk about me. You are the only one and it's no good because you don't love me.'

'Let us go back, Fanie.'

I was not afraid of the darkness when I was with him. I was not afraid of anything when I was with him. I wanted to say, You've set me apart from the brute beasts of the field, Fanie; but I was tired of words and we walked in silence until we saw the light Auntie Lena had set in the peach tree to guide us.

CHAPTER VIII

Time dries tears and vanquishes dreams. I cannot say for certain when I ceased to grieve but I remember that one afternoon I ran singing over a hundred little paths to the rondavel where Fanie lived with his mother. I had filled my apron with yellow peaches, the first to ripen, and as I ran I thought with wonder, I have forgotten Paul and Herry and Jansie, I have forgotten even my baby.

Mittee. I could think of her without jealousy at last, remembering only the beautiful smile and the touch of rich-skinned hands when I lay sick after Jansie kicked me. How did she fare, poor little Mittee who walked blindfold along the precipice of Paul's love? They had come to Plessisburg at Christmas time and at Nagmaal but Auntie Lena was sick and I stayed with her when the others went to the town to pray or to dance. Only once while he was in Plessisburg I ran into the veld and waited for him beneath the wild fig tree but he did not come to me.

We ate the peaches and then Fanie played the accordion but his heart was not in the music. After the first piece, he threw aside the accordion with a jangle of notes and told me that the minister was threatening to have his mother taken from him. It was all Letty's fault. She reported him when she found him in bed with his mother.

'It was only to keep her safe and warm but that cat wouldn't believe it,' said Fanie with tears in his eyes. 'You ask Auntie Lena. My mother wanders away during the night if I don't watch her and sometimes I'm too tired to keep running after her. The catch on the door was broken and the night before last she was restless, so I lay on the rushes beside her after I had brought her in from the veld four times. That Letty thing hates me and she walked all the way here to shout at me for being late for the milking though it's none of her business. That's how she came to find me in bed with my mother and you should have heard her. The minister says he will shut her up away from me.'

'Have you spoken to Frikkie?'

'All he says is that I had better take a wife the same as he did. He says he married Letty to shut people's mouths but there is nothing he can do to shut hers.'

I laughed. 'Why don't you take a wife, Fanie?'

'Would you take me and my mother, too?'

I thought he was joking but he called to sit up with me that night; in his best clothes, with Rebecca hanging on his arm. I took him in spite of Rebecca, remembering the tenderness of his love. He was as sleek as a well-fed buck then and as strong, a man you could feel proud to call your husband.

We were married in the Mission Church three weeks later and I wore the blue silk that I had had for Mittee's wedding, with the gold earrings that Herry had given to me. Frikkie gave us a sheep and Polly begged a jar of wine from Andrina for the feast at Auntie Lena's house.

My God, that Polly got drunk. She turned the wedding into a wild affair for she stamped as she danced, infusing a mad rhythm into everybody's feet. Even Auntie Lena tried to dance and had to be carried to her bed with a sore back. I lay on the bed beside her, for it was past midnight and Fanie showed no signs of wanting to leave. The wine had made me drowsy and yet I felt merry because of the music, but the best I could do was to sing under my breath, 'And I hold my body like a pheasant-bird and I make up to the girl with the red sash . . .' The children screamed as they ran amongst the dancers, pursued by their mothers who were afraid that they would be trampled. Somebody was yelling, 'Bread and meat, people, why don't you eat something?'

'And I hold my body like a pheasant-bird . . .' I forgot that it was my wedding night and fell fast asleep.

The next thing I knew it was daylight. There was a noise of snoring and as I went into the eating room I had to pick my way through about twenty people who lay asleep on the floor, some in disgraceful attitudes. In the centre of the room I came upon Polly, tightly locked in the arms of Fanie. At his back was Rebecca, struggling in her sleep as though the nightmare rode her.

I crept from the room. The morning air, fragrant from the kopjes, was as cool as heaven. I spat into the dust to get the taste of wine from my mouth.

The knife with which Fanie had skinned the sheep was lying on a bench by the front door. Auntie Lena had cleaned it in the sand to a wickedly gleaming silver. I picked it up and waited for Polly to come out of the house. She was the first to stagger out, rubbing her eyes and smiling as though she was the bride.

'I'm going to cut your throat like a sheep's,' I said, holding up the knife so that the sun would show off its polished edge.

She put her hand over her throat and her mouth fell open and you could see the inside, smooth as pink satin. She gave a primitive cry of fear as I advanced upon her step by step, jerking my neck with a menacing movement. 'Run,' said Fanie, coming to the door, and then to me in a voice of silk, 'my little night-ape, why are you so angry? My little flower, give Fanie the knife.'

'You hell,' I answered through straight lips but I did not take my glassy eyes from Polly.

She screamed and fled down the path, with me after her. I did not mean to stab her, only to give her the fright of her life, and I think Fanie knew this for he made only a half-hearted attempt to take the knife from me. Then he leaned dispiritedly against the side of the house.

I chased Polly to the road, laughing like a devil when I saw her skirts fly up to show the silk openwork stockings she had stolen from Andrina. Her ankles were as thin as sticks and I taunted her with this when she drew away beyond my reach. I stood on an ant heap, waving the knife when I yelled, and she did not slacken her speed while she was in my sight.

When I returned, Fanie said with an air of anxious authority, 'Get your bundle and we'll go home.'

'Home,' I sneered, flinging the knife on to the bench. 'Ag sis, you don't think I would go anywhere with you. Get somebody else to chaperone your mother.'

'You are so pretty in your blue dress, Selina, that it seems a shame you pull your face so,' he said, smooth as the notary. 'Now smile and come home with me.'

'Such godlessness,' said Auntie Lena, sitting on the knife handle so that I should not take it up again. 'I saw it happen once before in the Cape when I was a girl. It was at my half-sister's wedding but there the bridegroom was found in the veld a week after the wedding, with his throat cut from here to here.' She raised a quivering finger and carefully drew the shape of a horseshoe on her neck.

'Dear time,' said the wedding guests, looking at Fanie with bright eyes.

They sat down in the sun, waiting to see what would be the outcome of the situation. Some were patient enough to wait in satirical silence but others must give advice to both Fanie and me. Fanie answered them but I said never a word.

At midday, he went home glumly with Rebecca, and the crowd, disappointed, went back to work and to the thrashings that awaited them for being late. To punish Fanie, I did not follow until the next morning. As I walked along the paths, carrying my bundle, I was discouraged at this bad start, thinking that I had been mistaken in him. I little knew that I was leaving behind me fear and loneliness and walking towards years of peace and fatness.

Purposely, I passed the spot where I used to meet Paul. A pool of rainwater had been caught in a big hole between the wild fig tree and a camel thorn. As I approached, the sun, firing the muddy pool, made of it from end to end a sheet of bronze, not altogether brilliant but darkened at the edges by purple shadow. I leaned over and looking into the pool, saw every leaf of the great fig tree; and the clouds and the sky. There, reflected in the pool, I saw the magnificence of space more clearly than in the wider sweep of the sky. When I drank, the water tasted of the dawn wind, chilling my fingers and lips.

I laughed aloud as I came into the rondavel, in derision at Fanie's eager face. 'You who talked so of love, to lie with Polly who goes with any man . . .'

'It was nothing, I swear it. I was so drunk that I thought she was Rebecca. So true, Selina.'

'I wish she could hear that,' I said discontentedly, sitting down on my bundle.

'I'll tell her,' he promised. 'I'll say, You must excuse me, Polly, I thought you were my mother.'

I smiled unwillingly at that and he knelt beside me, whispering every word of endearment in the Language. Who could resist those gentle hands and that voice of honey? I had meant to be cold and proud with him but there I was, stroking his shoulder and calling him the lamb of my heart.

We slept on the rushes until the sun was high and it was Rebecca who awakened us. She stood in the doorway, jabbering. I was a little afraid of her then but soon I learned that her mind was so dimly lit that she was incapable of malice. She had been like that since birth, Auntie Lena told me, and nobody knows to this day who fathered Fanie. Somebody must have grabbed her while she wandered on the veld at night and it must have been a white man because Fanie is so light. Yet you could look the men of Plessisburg over a hundred times and not see one capable of such an act. Somebody drunk, Auntie Lena would say, shrugging her shoulders.

'She's hungry,' said Fanie.

He led her to the three-legged iron pot that stood near the door and squatted beside her, feeding her with cold mealie-meal. She ate with difficulty so that he was forced to catch her lolling head and hold it while he edged the spoon into her mouth.

His love for his mother is something to remember always. From it he received no gain for she did not know him and fed as willingly from me or anybody else; yet he would have died for her though she hardly knew the difference between life and death. His love for her went so deeply into the heart of pity that though I often grew angry with him about it, I would not have had him otherwise.

The rondavel was poor and not even clean. All Fanie possessed, besides his accordion, were a few blankets, a spoon, a cup, a bucket and the iron pot. The floor was of earth, filthy with the peel of peaches.

I went outside and pulled down the branches from a thorn tree to fashion a broom. With this I swept the floor but still the odour of blue mould embraced the stagnant air of the windowless room. I took off the old woman's clothes and washed her body for I could not bear her near me as she was. She was small and so light that I could move her about easily, though I hated touching that ugly body from which the dark-brown skin hung in folds, a covering that seemed intended for a bigger-boned woman. I looked at her in wonderment, overpowered by the mystery of her being. She was Auntie Lena's sister, she was Fanie's mother, one of the accepted sights of Plessisburg, yet she was farther removed from us than a dog. It was terrifying to think that her body had known the impact of passion, that those breasts, shrivelled as droughted mealies, had nourished Fanie.

'Don't stare at her like that,' he said sharply.

'Ag, I'm only trying to help her.'

I pushed her away from me and while she lay naked in the sun I rinsed out her clothes. She rolled her eyes up so that only the whites showed and for a terrifying moment I thought Gouws was right when he said that a bath could kill you.

'Is she all right?' I asked.

'Yes. She will squeak, like this, if she is hurt. But cover her up. Somebody might pass this way and see her.'

I felt like saying, There is nothing about the dried-up old imbecile to make anybody look except in astonishment, but I held my mouth about that.

'I'm going to wash her hair,' I said and plunged her head into the bucket, scratching the dirt loose from her scalp. She squeaked so loudly that Fanie tore her loose from my grip.

'Devil, you're hurting her. Put something over her, it's not right to have my mother naked out in the open like this.'

I rolled her in a blanket but still he was not satisfied. 'Why a blanket? Look, she is beginning to tear at herself with the itch. Take the blanket off her.'

He pulled off his shirt and gave it to me to put on her. It was his best shirt, one that Frikkie had given to him for the wedding. The front was frilled and except for a small rent at the back it was like new. I thought it was a pity to let Rebecca wear such a good thing but I dressed her in it to please Fanie and then sat beside her, keeping the flies from her face with the branch of a tree.

Fanie was happy to see me so kind to her and when she had fallen asleep he took me to see his pets. There were a hedgehog and a springbok that he had found crippled after the drive in the winter; a secretary bird that would eat from your hand; and a guinea fowl with chicks. I held one of the chicks against my face, a downy little thing that seemed to be no relation to its speckled mother. It was the colour of a biscuit, striped with brown. They were all shy of me. The hedgehog rolled himself into an obstinate ball, the guinea fowl set up an alarm, the buck hid himself behind a bush. We sat still in the grass until they were soothed again but only the springbok came up to me, and then with a beating heart, ready to spring away if I moved a hand.

Fanie had been given the day off, so we went to lie in the shade of the thorn trees. It was late when we remembered his mother. The poor thing had crawled under a thorn bush and her body was scratched as though she had been cut with a knife.

'Your good shirt is ruined, what waste,' I said and he looked at me angrily as he took her in his arms, rocking her like a baby.

I lay on my stomach in the shade, as though I were interested in the ants that hurried by on their important business. She was less than they. Surely, buried deep, she must have a soul for which God could probe. He would take her to Himself one day, for that soul knew no evil.

'What can it know of good, then?' I said aloud.

'What are you talking about?' asked Fanie.

'Only your mother's soul,' I answered, and his face darkened beneath my mockery.

Sleeping in the rondavel with Rebecca was like being with a pig for she snorted all night long. But I learned to be grateful for her noise because that meant at least that she was with us and that we did not need to go looking for her in the middle of the night. This was the only preference that she showed. She liked to find a place of her own to sleep. The old nuisance. I had to teach myself not to hate her for what was the use of hating a thing that had less feeling than a dog?

Fanie and I prospered. Our rondavel was clean, with a smeared floor and two beds; Rebecca sparkled. Frikkie sold us the strip of land upon which stood the rondavel and we paid him out of our wages. To help make more money, I went out to work nearly every day of the week. Strangely enough, my best job was with Andrina, whom Polly had deserted. That Polly. She caused a terrible scandal in Plessisburg by running away with an English trader from the Lowveld and that was the last we ever heard of her.

Andrina could not do enough for me now for Mittee had told

her the part I had played in her affairs, and there was a little present every time she paid me. She was to be married to Leon at Nagmaal and she was like a butterfly for happiness when she was away from her mother. She told me that she had taken a vow never to speak to her mother again and if I knew Andrina she kept that vow. It was wonderful how she did it but she certainly never spoke to her mother while I was there. 'She can come to my house, she can sit at my table, she can play with my children, but I'll never open my mouth to her again, Selina,' Andrina said. They were a hard lot, that family.

Nagmaal saw her wedding take place; and the christening of Frikkie's first-born, a son. Though we worked so hard, Fanie and I found time to be happy together. At Nagmaal he came with Rebecca and me to the Mission, all of us dressed like respectable people and at Christmas time we were the gayest at the dances. Then there were picnics by the river and the pets to play with in the evenings when everything was done.

It was marvellous how quickly one Nagmaal slipped into the other so that one had little time to ponder on the changes that were taking place in Plessisburg. You saw girls whom you thought of as children going for confirmation, or you heard of their banns being read.

I went down year after year to meet the waggons coming in from the north but neither Mittee nor Paul were on them.

When I asked Aletta why Mittee did not come to Plessisburg, she shrugged her shoulders. 'They have a son,' she said, 'a sickly child.' A shadow rippled across her face, disturbing her smugness, and she embraced the child nearest her as though warding off the evil eye. She had four children now and she was fatter than her mother, with huge breasts that gave her an air of importance.

I was aware of that shadow always as soon as Mittee's name was spoken. There is something terribly wrong, I thought; the child has turned out to be coloured or an idiot, but you would think they would at least bring it one Nagmaal for baptism.

It was Fanie of all people who gave me real news of her at last. 'I saw Nonnie Mittee talking to the magistrate,' he told me one day. 'They were taking the coach to Pretoria.'

'Was her husband with her?' I asked quickly.

'Oh yes. And they were in mourning, the deepest black, all three of them.'

'Ask Frikkie what has happened,' I implored him.

Frikkie told Fanie that the child was dead and that Paul was taking Mittee to Europe to get over her sorrow. I thought, At least one of her dreams has come true for she always wanted to travel across the sea. Then I thought no more of her for a long time and I missed her again on her return because she stayed only one night in Plessisburg before setting out for the valley.

Plessisburg was prosperous when the drought set in. The railway from Pretoria had reached us and there were two big shops in the town. It was a common sight to see bicycles on the road, sometimes you saw even a Kaffir riding an old one.

Fanie and I had four cows and I remember him saying, When a man owns cattle, he is like a tree with deep roots, for he must think of his cattle first before he makes a move. Fanie did not like the cattle because he is by instinct a roamer but I took great joy in them and in all our possessions.

Gouws was a fool in many ways but he was a good prophet when it came to crops and land. The seasons had been good for years but he threw it up in Plessisburg and followed Paul to the Wolkbergen the year before the drought. Through the magistrate, Mittee sold her farm to strangers and you could pass by there without the people calling your name, which was a strange feeling to me at first. Frikkie laughed at Gouws but even he grew serious when no rain had fallen by December. The minister was already holding services for rain but not a shower fell in answer to our prayers.

In the evening the clouds would come sullenly over the Wolkbergen, swamping every star in the sky. That was the time that every farmer, big or small, stood out in the open with face upturned, waiting for the deathly stillness to be broken by the chant of the rain. Perhaps there would be one or two crashes of thunder and the mountaintops would writhe beneath the lash of lightning for a few seconds; a few drops of rain might fall upon our supplicating palms. But within the hour, the sky would be bright again. We awakened each morning to the terrifying sun that burnt down the grass to the earth so that the cattle moved in clouds of dust in their search for food and water. Some men trekked south but Frikkie remained, putting off the evil day.

It was March before we moved on. Frikkie headed north for he had had a message by runner from Paul that there had been rain on his lands and though the grass was not plentiful, it would support what was left of Frikkie's herds. We travelled slowly because the cattle were weak; Frikkie and Letty and their two children in the first waggon, Fanie and Rebecca and I in the second. I did not want to go because all but one of our little herd was dead and this one I could manage to keep alive by hand-feeding her. I was sure she would die on the trek to the valley. I would have stayed on alone but I would have starved. Plessisburg had no work to offer, with hungry Kaffirs swarming there, offering their services in exchange for food.

We passed these starving Kaffirs for mile after mile along the road. Frikkie sat with his gun ready, night and day, forbidding us to give them food but I often threw the children a piece of bread or biltong from our scant stock; and I caught Letty at it, too. It hurt me then to see Rebecca fed, while the bleary-eyed children fought in the dust over a few mouthfuls of food.

The road ended after we had passed Eberhardt's farm. I had often travelled straight through the veld but never had I gone into anything like this. The earth had died. Nothing moved upon the plain but our waggons, dragged painfully by the heartbroken mules; and the remnants of Frikkie's herds creeping forward, a few bitter miles every day. Frikkie had thought we would be in the valley within eight days and that there would be some grass for the cattle along the Wolk River but when we reached the river on the tenth day, we found the bed dry except for a few muddy pools, and the grass shrivelled.

We were tense that night as we sat around the fires and the children, troubled by our silence, would not go to sleep. We were all thinking that between us and the valley lay miles of sun-whitened veld, deserted even by the game, a death trap for the cattle and perhaps for us.

You could not believe that ten days could change people so. When we set out, Letty had been a pretty woman but now her gold hair was darker and the creamy skin tracked over with lines. The two children, Pieter and Petronella, who had been bright-cheeked, had gone straw-coloured, that peculiar shade that comes over pallid skin enriched by sunburn. Little Petronella sat on her mother's lap but Pieter, true son of Frikkie, would leave her from time to time and seek mischief. It added to our trials that we had to listen to Letty nagging at him to come close to the fires.

'A lion will eat you, if you stray,' she said not once but fifty times.

Only Rebecca remained unchanged. The mules did not have a stronger constitution than she did. She was as well as though we were on a Sunday morning's ride to church, the senseless old creature; yet it was on her that Fanie lavished all his pity and for her that he saved something from his food.

You can never be angry with him for long. When he saw that Rebecca was safely asleep, lying in her blanket like a bundle of rags, he lay down by me with his head in my lap. Frikkie passed the accordion over to him.

'Give us a few tunes, it will cheer us up, old mate.' That could not pass Letty without an astringent remark. 'Old mate, to every last Coloured.'

Fanie pulled the accordion across his chest. The plaintive notes came as a relief in that immense stillness and I put my hand gratefully on Fanie's head. I thought, We carry our lives with us wherever we go. Fanie and I were at peace with each other but you could feel the restlessness that tortured Letty as she looked across the fire at Frikkie. I felt sorry for her for he should have been sitting beside her. They were not like married people. I tried to think of Frikkie married to a woman he loved but I had never seen the woman to match that good-natured carelessness. I could imagine Letty married to Eberhardt for they were alike in the same way that Andrina and Leon were alike. I remember that I had once seen her walking with Eberhardt and thought what a good pair they would make; but of course Eberhardt would never have taken her because she was poor. He was still looking for a rich wife.

Her voice pierced suddenly through the music. 'You have brought us into the wilderness to die.'

'Play "The Monkey's Wedding", Fanie,' said Frikkie as though she had not spoken.

Letty's fury was as unexpected as a storm in the mountains. It was terrible to listen to her for, truly, the woman had no decency. She screamed out the secrets of man and wife for all to hear, she screamed that it was Fanie he loved. When she said that, Fanie put aside his accordion and crouched down as though he was going to spring at her.

'Be still,' said Frikkie. He picked up his rifle and sent a shot over her head. 'Hold your mouth or I'll blow your brains out.' He had to shout now for the children were crying with terror.

We had peace from her tongue at last. That terrible journey did one thing for Frikkie, at least. It made him Letty's master and whenever her nagging grew too much for him, he would threaten her with violence, which would quieten her down for a time though she was never entirely cured. The habit was so strong on her and she was so righteous herself that she could not help nagging. But I was sorry for her that night as I lay beside Fanie.

We followed the course of the Wolk for several days, going more easily for the cattle seemed to chew some sustenance from the dry grass. Our cow was still alive though Fanie had to get her to her feet every morning and she grew weaker after we forded the river bed and began to climb the thornveld that sloped towards the mountains. We were looking eagerly for Paul now because Frikkie had sent a runner from Plessisburg to tell him of our coming but we saw no sign of life nor even of waggon tracks though the mountains seemed near. At outspan we would think that only another day's journey could lie ahead of us. At the next outspan it was the same, just another day and we would climb the ridge and look down into the valley.

Sixteen days after we left Plessisburg, Frikkie and Fanie dragged the mules to the top of the first ridge. Paul had told Frikkie of the wonderful natural entrance to the valley, an opening between the mountains so easy to pass through that you went straight from the plain into the valley without climbing; but there was no time to look for this easier way. I got down from the waggon and walked behind our cow because she was staggering. When she went to her knees, I doubled her tail over and bit it until she stood up again. I took no notice of my own bursting heart or the sweat that ran in streams down my face for I would rather have lain in the veld myself than leave her there for the vultures to pick, this last link with the days of our prosperity. Other cattle fell in that last push to the top of the ridge but our cow was still on her feet.

We stood amongst rocks but down the slope we could see rich grass, russet and green. Even the children were silent. There had never been such a moment in our lives as this, when we looked back over the desolation through which we had come and then forward into the valley, where we glimpsed the chimney of a house. It took us another day to traverse the ridges that separated us from the broad road cutting the valley bottom as far as the eyes could see.

The first person we saw was Doctor Besil, the missionary. He came running from his house to greet us. I knew him at once. The sun had faded the peachy boyishness from his cheeks but he had still that look of having been reared in a country of frost and mist. In his voice, too, was the ring of the frost, so that everything he said was sharp and clear.

'Du Plessis,' said Frikkie, extending his hand.

'Castledene,' said the doctor, heartily shaking hands. Frikkie was a little awkward with him because he distrusted all missionaries, even good ones. 'The whole valley is awaiting your arrival. Your brother is watching for your waggons at the pass. I shall send a runner to him at once. They would have gone out to meet you but your runner got in only yesterday evening. He was down with fever before he got half-way here. It's a wonder he got here at all.'

Letty said peevishly, 'Who's that? Where is Paul, you'd think he would have been here to greet us.'

She descended from the waggon and Frikkie reluctantly introduced her to the missionary. 'You must come to the Mission House, you and all your people,' he said. 'There's hot water on the stove and you can have a wash.' He grinned suddenly, looking at Pieter, and well he might for the naughty child had stripped off all his clothes the night before and covered himself with axle grease. There was no hot water for washing and his face and hands remained streaked with black and brown. 'You could come and be one of my pupils,' said the missionary, taking his hand.

Pieter liked him but Letty was affronted. 'No child of mine could look coloured, no matter how dirty he was. We've had no water to wash in for the last two days and before that it was nothing but muddy water.'

Frikkie soothed her. 'Think of it, Letty, hot water, probably rain water.'

'Oh yes, rain water,' said the missionary.

'Selina, come and help me with the children,' Letty called.

Doctor Besil did not remember me but he smiled at me as I passed him. It was not long before we had the children clean for the housegirl gave us a hand. Though she was lame, she was quick and intelligent and even Letty had no fault to find.

The missionary and Frikkie were talking together in a friendly way but Letty soon put a stop to that. She screeched first at Pieter and then at Petronella while everybody kept silence, overawed by that terrible tongue. Fortunately, the lame girl had made some tea and Letty had to stop talking long enough to drink hers.

It was an hour before Paul rode up to the gate. I was sitting in the waggon so that he did not see me then. He sprang from his horse and fell upon Frikkie, cuffing him and wrestling with him playfully. You could not help smiling at the meeting of the two brothers but I noticed that the missionary became aloof as soon as he saw Paul.

Paul. I loved him still. I tried hard to see him as he was, a man more repulsively wicked than Jansie but disguised by the refinement of his features. But you might as well have asked Fanie not to love Rebecca because she was a hideous old imbecile.

Frikkie went on with Paul to his farm but he left Fanie with those cattle that seemed too weak to continue. We camped that night behind big fires for game was plentiful in the valley. During the drought, Doctor Besil told us, they had come pouring in from the plain; herds of zebra and wildebeest, bringing after them lions and jackals and hyenas to pester the farmers. Doctor Besil came to speak to us and to drink coffee, as easily as though he were paying a call on a white family. I asked him if he remembered me.

'Selina. Selina. Of course.' He smiled. 'The girl who cried in the broiling sun. You used to work for Mrs Du Plessis, she talks of the way you can iron. None of the girls from the Mission can iron as well as you, she says.'

'You speak the Language well now.'

'The only time I hear English is when I read it aloud.'

We told him about our prosperity before the drought overtook us; and pointed out our cow to him, sorrowfully, for it did not seem possible that she would see the night through.

'Do you think she will live?' asked Fanie, who knew more about cattle than Doctor Besil did.

Doctor Besil was so used to comforting people that he assured us that the cow would bring us many calves but, of course, we must have faith in God, whereupon I prayed throughout the night. But Fanie said that the missionary knew the tricks of his trade for he could not be wrong either way and we would feel guilty if the creature died through our lack of faith.

The cow did not die. Fanie brought her calf to Doctor Besil a year later, in memory of that night.

Paul had built a gabled house, bigger than the magistrate's. At the front gates crouched two stone lions, quite at home except for the barbed wire fence running on each side of them. I knew at once that Mittee had caused them to be put there, for two such lions guarded Welgedacht. How Frikkie laughed at those lions, while Letty admired them and envied Mittee.

We reached the farm in the late afternoon after a slow trek with the grazing cattle. When Fanie turned the mules out, he went to sleep with Rebecca under the waggon but I sat on an ant heap near the fence. Smoke was curling up from the kitchen chimney. It stained the sky with bluish smudges and then vanished as though a hand had rubbed it away. That would be the girl beginning the evening meal, I thought. Now and again I heard her voice, high-pitched, when she came to the open door to throw something to the dog or to call for a bucket of fresh water. I knew that voice, it belonged to Anna who had been with Mittee since she was married. What would Mittee be eating for her evening meal? Ape, I chided myself, leave them alone, you have been happy away from the white people.

She walked out of the house, holding Petronella by the hand. Her dress was blue and she wore a white hat, plumed with blue ostrich feathers. It was the same old Mittee, vain as a peacock though she lived in the wilderness.

'Nonnie,' I called, running forward, 'I've come a long way to visit you.'

The dimples hollowed her cheeks but it was not the same smile that shone out at me. 'It's Selina. Yes it is Selina.'

We stared at each other in silence. She had not thickened. There was still about her something of the quick grace of wind in trees, of water sweeping over rocks.

She said, 'How you've changed. You're almost black. You should keep out of the sun like I do.'

'It's five years since I saw you, nonnie, and I've worked hard since then. Married, I suppose you heard.'

'Aletta told me. No family?' said Mittee, politely.

'None. And you, nonnie?'

'My son died.'

'It's a terrible thing to lose a child, nonnie. But you, at least, can look forward to other children.'

'No,' she said harshly. There was sadness and fear beneath the bland mask of her beauty and I wondered what she had suffered during the five years of our separation. She hurried on, 'This is a sweet child of Letty's. But the boy. My heaven, what a naughty child. They are both like the Du Plessises, big-boned and dark-skinned. See how the upper lip is long and curls at the corners. My son had the same mouth.'

'It runs in the family. I used to long to see your baby, nonnie, but every time I went to meet the waggons from the valley, you were not with them.'

'No. It was because of Siegfried. He was not strong.'

To push the ghost of the dead child from us, I said, 'Do you think the baas will let me stay with you now? I'm sick of working for that Letty.'

'I'll speak to him and tell him you are respectably married. He always used to say that you were the sort of girl who would cause trouble amongst the boys and I suppose he was right. How pretty you were, Selina, though I would never tell you then. All I can say is thank God you're here, you can iron my dress, it's very difficult and none of the others can do it properly.'

CHAPTER IX

I should have stayed in Plessisburg even though it meant starvation. There my life had been simple and the most I could feel was a longing to slap Rebecca or to shout at Letty to hold her mouth, if only out of pity for others. The richness of my life lay in keeping the rondavel spick and span, in building up the pennies to a pound, in darning and ironing and washing better than any coloured girl in the district; and there was richness, too, in Fanie's love.

Now I must suffer again the wild storms of the spirit that set me apart from everybody. Now I must feel that glow of love when Mittee put her hand on me carelessly or called me dear old Selina. The room I shared with Fanie and Rebecca became a shadowland. The change was slow, at first only a feeling of pleasure in being allowed to handle Mittee's fine clothes, in catching the scent of them from the steam beneath the hot iron; camphor and lavender. If she was not there when I carried the dresses to her room, I walked about noticing what was new or picking up some little box or trinket that she had kept by her since girlhood.

The longing for Paul crept upon me again and I threw myself into Fanie's cool arms night after night so that I should not seek him out. He had grown from a narrow stripling to a man of brazen strength with a formidable air of pride but still I saw the recklessness come into his eyes sometimes when he looked at me. I kept away from him.

He was angry with Frikkie for bringing us because we all offended him in some way. I brought back to him memories of a dangerous lust that had almost destroyed him; of an old man murdered and a terrified boy shot as he stood up to surrender. The proud set of Fanie's head he mistook for impudence. Rebecca was an eyesore and a nuisance about the place. Frikkie quarrelled with him before he allowed us to remain.

Frikkie had fallen in love with the valley. He wrote to his father, asking him to sell the farms round Plessisburg for here a man could grow rich easily, with fat land to be taken from the Kaffirs for a few shillings a morgen. Besides this, there were vast numbers of elephant in the forests beyond the mountains. Paul had made enough money from ivory to pay the cost of his house. Ivory had paid for the road and for the building of a dam big enough to irrigate the valley from end to end. Even that unlucky muddler, Gouws, was prosperous and independent for the first time in his life, through ivory.

When winter browned the veld, the men left their farms to go after elephant, returning for the ploughing in the early summer. Fanie went with them, and during the months that they were away Mittee drew me once more into the circle of her life. She was as lonely as she had been when she was a girl for vinegar was sweet compared with Letty. Letty now spoke of herself as the Bywoner and would suddenly clutch Pieter to her, mourning, No home, no place to lay your head on all this earth; she would finger the material of Mittee's dresses, her lips downturned as though Mittee's reasons for wearing silk were immoral. Mittee could not have conversation with her that did not finish in an argument and many a day she sent Letty off to visit Mrs Gouws or Aletta, but so artfully that you would not have guessed she was getting rid of her unwanted visitor. She would say, 'Oh, what a lovely day it is, I will drive out to see Mrs Gouws if you will stay and look after the house for me, Letty.'

'The Bywoner does as she is told.'

'Not Bywoner, Letty, you are my honoured guest. How selfish I am, it is you who should be riding about enjoying yourself and I who should sit at home. Now, I insist, you must not argue . . .'

When Letty had gone, we sat on the front stoep together, crocheting as of old, with Rebecca in the corner, imprisoned behind a barricade of chairs. It was comfortable there for that was a winter of freezing nights and sunny days and it was good to get yourself warmed through before the sun turned. The conversation always started with a piece of scandal about the absent Letty and Pieter, who got on Mittee's nerves. After that, Mittee would begin to tell me stories about what had happened to her since we parted. They were not silly stories like she used to tell and I could listen without falling asleep. As she talked I noticed for the first time the shadowed lines beneath her carefully tended skin.

She took me into the room where her baby had slept for the two short years of his life. The furniture had been changed but she showed me where the cot had stood and brought out some of the things she had kept for remembrance.

'Siegfried.' Mittee's voice stroked the word. 'Paul was on commando when he was born. He was born a month before his time. I remember lying there thinking what Paul would say when he came home to a son. Auntie Gouws had taken the baby out of the room and I was sick of lying there alone so I shouted to her to bring him to me so that I could hold him and as she came into the room I said, You'd better lace me up much tighter than this because I have no intention of spreading out like some people. I noticed that she was crying, and thinking her feelings had been hurt I said, a little impatiently I'm afraid, I didn't mean Auntie's figure.

'Without a word she handed the baby to me and something in her face made my fingers cold as I undid the wrappings. The poor little legs, oh the poor little legs. I didn't cry, Selina, but I'm still sad when I think of him. I never cried over him but I couldn't help being sad though I made up my mind as I looked at him that first time that I'd make the best of it. The body is not everything I said to Auntie Gouws, but nothing would stop her from crying.

'He was a week old when Paul came hurrying home to see him. He screamed like a woman, Selina, when he found out. Because Siegfried cried so much I moved into this room with him. Night after night I sat with him, so alone that the turn of a curtain in the wind seemed company and I came to know every sound on the veld.

'Paul was ashamed of him. That was the terrible part to bear. At first I had no thought of going to Plessisburg for Siegfried was too weak, but he grew stronger when he turned a year and I got ready to take him to be baptized at the next Nagmaal. We didn't go. Paul did not forbid it but he spoke for a week about nothing else except Frikkie's son and the Coesters' solid children. He said, I've suffered enough without taking that thing for everybody to stare at and laugh at. Afterwards, he went down on his knees and begged my forgiveness but, Selina, I have never forgiven him for saying that, though I have tried to.

'In his third winter, Siegfried got croup. That was a bitter winter with snow on the mountains and even Aletta's children, who never had a day's illness, had to be nursed through colds, so I did not worry much at first. In the daytime, he took his food and seemed as well as ever but the croup would strike him sharply at night and sometimes I thought he would choke to death. There wasn't always time to call Anna to help me and I would have to get Paul out of bed to keep the fire going while I ran from kitchen to bedroom with hot poultices. But I gave up doing that because he said it was Kaffir's work, so Anna slept on the kitchen floor to be ready at a moment's notice. Croup is a terrifying thing, Selina, but Auntie Gouws said most little boys get it and not to grow too frightened.

'I did grow frightened one night. It was the worst of the winter, with wind and rain. For hours I poulticed Siegfried and kept alight the steam kettle, so cold myself that I was glad of the hot poultices on my hands. His breath came out in a long, whistling sound and the ipecac seemed to make no difference. When the whistling died down at last I thought I had broken the phlegm but then I noticed that his breathing was very shallow. Anna came in and looked at him and she shrugged her shoulders as though everything was already finished.

'I went to Paul's room and told him to go for Auntie Gouws. Don't worry, Mittee, he said, cripples are strong. But he brought a brazier into the room before he left and put it near me to keep me warm while I waited.

'You know what old Auntie Gouws is. She looked at Siegfried and said, Pneumonia. I'll try my remedies but it's a case of folding your hands and waiting in prayer until the crisis is past, Mittee. After an hour she stopped praying and said, I'll tell you what, send for the English doctor, his medicines are quite good and he has often helped me with a difficult case.

'I had to quarrel with Paul before he would go to the Mission House for he and the missionary have clashed over the building of that dam. But in the end he rode for him.

'It was the first time I had seen Doctor Castledene face to face but I don't remember anything about him from that night except his hands. His hands are so strong and yet so delicate. It's strange, even now, I often dream about his hands.

'He put Auntie Gouws in her place straight away. She kept saying, Comfort the little mother, sometimes they get over it. He said, You have a very doleful voice, Mrs Gouws, the child has pleurisy not pneumonia. We'll see, my little doctor, said the old Auntie and he gave her one look. After that, she did everything he told her while he tapped the lung. It was wonderful to watch, though I was so anxious. I've never seen anything so skilful.

'He came often to see Siegfried. Is there anything more beautiful in the world, Selina, than to see gentleness in a man and yet know at the same time that he is strong? He stopped coming to the house before Siegfried was really well. I'll look in tomorrow, he said, but he did not come again until I sent a note asking him to baptize Siegfried. How angry Paul was with me and he stood like a black shadow in the room during the baptism. I have never had a chance to speak to Doctor Castledene again.

'The magistrate came in August on his annual visit. It was the happiest time since Siegfried was born. We would sit under the peach trees and he would put Siegfried on his knee and teach him little rhymes and let him play with his beard. My little namesake, he called him. Then one day he took my hands in his as he always does when I am in trouble. Things are not right here, he said, so we must make a plan. He had read of a surgeon in Germany who could perform miracles by an operation and why shouldn't I take Siegfried to Europe? I ran for Paul straightway and we began to talk about it, though Paul said very little that first time. A few days later, he told me that he had been to see Doctor Castledene and ask his opinion. It was a long time since I had put my arms round Paul's neck but I held him very close to me when he told me that. He said, But he doesn't hold out much hope, Mittee, he says it is possible that the child may walk but he will always be deformed.

'Anyway, we decided we would go to Germany. The last thing the magistrate said before he left was, Try and make Paul feel his responsibility more, Mittee, make him do little things for the boy. It was good advice, I knew, and without asking Paul I moved Siegfried's cot into his room. We passed a terrible night because Siegfried was made restless by the strange room and he cried all the time. I took him into bed with me but he was still wakeful and in the end I thought it would be best to put him back in his own room.

'Paul wheeled the cot without grumbling and I was about to carry Siegfried in here when I was struck by the thought that Paul had never held him. Surely if he held the poor little body in his arms, it would awaken his pity and love. So when he came back I said, Carry Siegfried in and tuck him up, beloved. Selina, minutes and minutes went by before he held out his arms for his son. Siegfried was crying and it was all I could do not to follow after them but I lay quiet. The crying stopped and I thought, He is sitting there until Siegfried falls asleep. I must have dozed off for a little while because I don't remember Paul coming back to our room. Let us go out of here, Selina.'

I followed her to the stoep. We took up our crochetwork again.

'Crochet is soothing,' said Mittee, going very fast. 'Oh, Selina, I wish I had not talked to you about Siegfried. I wish I could forget that night. I lit the candle when I woke up because I was suddenly worried about Siegfried. I had never slept away from him before. How still the house was. I knew that stillness from nights of watching, it meant that dawn was not far off. Paul lay with his back to me and I saw that he shuddered with cold in his sleep. I put an extra blanket over him before I went out of the room.

'Siegfried was dead. He had turned on his face during the night and the pillows had smothered him.'

'Hi, my nonnie.'

'It was my fault, I should never have left him alone. But I didn't know that the pleurisy had left him so weak, though he always found it difficult to turn over because of his legs. It was my fault but when I screamed for Paul, I blamed him for not waking me. I remembered every little thing he had said and we shouted over the dead little body like two mad things.

'I still grieve, Selina, and it has never been the same between Paul and me. Blood is thicker than water, Mittee, he said, and I wish that I was dead too. But he never thought that when Siegfried was alive. He said, We will have other sons of whom we can be proud . . .'

'Then you will be happy again, nonnie.'

'No, I will bear him no more children, because of Siegfried.'

CHAPTER X

The house was painted in the early summer when the men returned from hunting, for the President was to visit the new settlement. Paul had great hopes of this visit because he was planning a road from the valley to Plessisburg but he needed a grant of money to carry on the work.

We lived in turmoil until Mittee had got the house cleaned to her satisfaction. One would have thought that President Kruger was a man who would peer into corners and examine the rims of vases to see whether dust had lodged there; crawl under beds in spare bedrooms in search of fluff; look in the press for undarned linen; and number the cobwebs in the servants' rooms. Only Anna kept her presence of mind, for she was used to Mittee's ways and having little affection for her did not care whether Mittee scolded or praised.

On the morning of the President's arrival, the road was lined by the burghers and their families, for next to the completion of the dam, this was the most important event in the history of the valley. All the world, you never saw such a grand sight. There was a thundering of hoofs as the State Artillery swept down the road. The sun, that had been hidden by spiteful clouds, came out just as they flashed into sight, their helmets shining. They wheeled their prancing horses to surround the house. These were showy horsemen and to watch them was enough to take in for one day. As soon as they had taken up their positions, the horses, so full of fire a moment before, became as still as the scrag of the mountain.

Now the burghers rode up, perhaps four hundred of them, men with beards of such magnificence that I wondered if they had been chosen for that reason alone. They were more sedate in their handling of the horses, as befitted those upon whom depended the defence of the Republic; but superb horsemen, unconscious of their appearance.

They flanked the road on each side as the President's waggonette dashed into sight. It was drawn by six horses and escorted by the very pick of the State Artillery. With him was his Staff and the magistrate, all grave-faced men these, accustomed to weighty affairs.

Paul had come to the threshold of the house and stood bareheaded waiting to greet the President. I had meant to watch their meeting but my horrified gaze was drawn to Pieter, who ran suddenly from the garden towards the cordon of State Artillery. I thought, My God, Letty will be in mourning, for the mischievous child slapped one of the horses on the rump. I rushed forward to save him, certain that the horse would lash out at him. It did no such thing. Even when Pieter, seeing me after him, ran under its belly, the horse did not move an inch. I was in terror but Pieter, finding this a fascinating new pastime, ran first under this horse and then under that one, sometimes coming through the forelegs and sometimes through the hind legs. It was the most extraordinary thing so see them stand so still but Mittee told me afterwards that they were specially trained to stand like that for parades and State occasions.

I sat and watched him, assured that by some miracle he was safe; and thought happily of Mittee, for at that moment she was the most important woman in the Transvaal, with the President sheltering under her roof and her house surrounded by the State Artillery.

The midday meal was almost finished but Mittee's plate had not been touched. If she could have shouted at Pieter it would have been better for her but she had to keep her face in lines of graciousness, knowing that Letty might start a scene that would be heard in the dining room where the President was eating. By some misadventure, Pieter's chair had been placed behind Mittee and throughout the meal he infuriated her by putting the plate under her ear, yelling, 'Rice and gravy'. Mittee, falsely smiling, helped him to rice and gravy no less than six times, but whenever she went to pick up her knife and fork the plate whizzed past her ear. She told me to move Pieter to another place, whereupon he set up such a scream that Mittee gestured to me to leave him where he was. To show Letty what she thought of the child, she refused to touch her food but Letty did not seem to notice.

Mittee stalked from the table to the side stoep. As soon as I had cleared the table, I followed her and sat on the stoep, looking with interest at the burghers and the members of the State Artillery who sat about in the grass. They were subdued after the huge meal they had eaten and now they looked like ordinary men who had travelled a long way, showing signs of weariness and the stains of the road. I could pick this one out as being a good husband and that one as being a drunkard.

Peace had fallen on the household. A clatter of plates told of the girls washing and stacking, soothing to listen to when you're not doing it yourself.

'I'm going to my room to have a little nap,' said Mittee. 'Afterwards I must go and see that everything is ready for the banquet tonight. Heaven, what a feast. Twelve ducks, four turkeys, fifteen fowls, pigeon pies . . .'

Letty rushed on to the stoep. 'I cannot find him. Pieter. He's gone. I can't find my Pieter.'

'Be quiet, the President is conferring with my husband in the front room,' said Mittee grandly. 'Pieter can't be far. He didn't come out here.'

'I'm afraid he has fallen into the well or something like that,' said Letty, purposely working herself into hysterics.

The men on the lawn began to search for him in the grounds but I did not look there. I knew him well. Pieter must always be with his father, to share in the jokes. I stole on to the front stoep and peeped in at the window of the sitting room, to which the President had retired to talk over the affair of the road, we supposed. Sure enough, Pieter was there, sitting on a stool at his father's feet. The room was quiet. The magistrate slept, with a red silk handkerchief over his face; the President's head was sunk low. Even Pieter slept, while Paul and Frikkie waited drowsily for them to awaken and talk about the road.

'The whole lot are in there fast asleep,' I said to Letty.

She wiped her tears away. 'The little treasure-lamb. I'll tell the men they need not look for him. They were going to drag the well. But first let me see him there with my own eyes.'

'When nothing comes to something, then look out,' said Mittee, and I saw with astonishment that she was jealous of Letty's handsome little boy.

The devil must have laughed at those two women. Letty was speechless with envy when Mittee, shining like a young girl, was presented first to the President and his Staff that evening.

The President condemned Paul's dam. Though the other farmers in the valley had contributed towards its building, Paul always looked upon the dam as his own. Doctor Besil had opposed him bitterly because the Mission House and a Kaffir kraal lay half a mile from the dam, in direct line with the wall that was built across a narrow neck of land between the mountains and in time of flood would have been in danger from the waters. The President knew of Doctor Besil's letters of protest to the magistrate and as soon as he saw the dam, he berated Paul. Mittee accompanied the party and she described to me how the President, in top hat and broadcloth, hopped across the stones, waving his stick irascibly while he pointed out the danger.

It would do Paul good, she said, for since he came to the valley he had recognized only the slight authority shown by the magistrate on his flying annual visits. His face grew vicious with baulked pride though he had no cause to complain for the President promised to send engineers to advise him, as well as speaking favourably about the grant for the road.

Paul went with him to Pretoria to carry the matter through. He was away for three months and during that time, Mittee fell in love with Doctor Besil. I think she had been in love with him from the night he came into her baby's sickroom but she had pushed the temptation from her.

She ran a school for the children of the valley and when I saw her teaching in the classroom, it seemed to me that she would never lose the look of girlhood that is proud and yet frivolous for she had never been in love. Within a year that look was gone.

You never saw such weather. The nights were showery, softening the impact of the brilliant days. Frikkie grew lazy without Paul to spur him on and instead of overseeing the weeding of the mealies and the milking of the cows, he organized grand picnics and jukskei tournaments in which all the farmers took part, as though bewitched by the strange beauty of the season. Kaffirs loafed on the yard or went home to brew beer; their womenfolk on the lands stood idle, leaning on their hoes. If there had been a minister in the valley, he would have called the people to church service every day to remind them of their morals.

Mittee sent the children home early from school and then to ease her conscience, she would start some useless and complicated piece of embroidery, working like lightning as though everything depended on its being finished before the light faded. One afternoon, I remember, she set us all to scooping out pumpkins in which she intended to store peaches. I agreed with Letty when she said the idea was ridiculous but Mittee read out the instructions from a newspaper that the magistrate had brought with him and the solemn High Dutch was so convincing that we set to work; all except Anna who refused resolutely to be mixed up in such nonsense.

'We'll have fresh peaches when other people are opening their preserves,' Mittee promised. 'We'll take them to Plessisburg with us and astonish everybody.'

'I will be the most astonished if anything ever comes of it,' said Letty disagreeably.

We each knelt with a pumpkin in front of us, clawing the pulp out as though we were engaged on some important task. The pumpkins were filled with peaches and carefully sealed down, then put in the loft in the shed. A few weeks later Frikkie went up to see what was causing the smell. We heard a cry of fury. Instantly we knew that as he swung himself into the loft he pulled one of the pumpkins down. Those pumpkins were never properly cleaned out, as I told Mittee at the time.

'Heaven, those peaches,' cried Letty, running towards her husband.

She delicately removed a piece of rotting pulp and a stone from his cheek. Frikkie swept his beard with loathing.

'My beard is ruined. I will have to wash and comb it. Whoever is responsible for this . . .'

Though we laughed, we felt guilty at this waste of food and time, at this stealing of a holiday from the rigid calendar of the year. Frikkie, seeing the slothfulness on the yard, kicked the Kaffirs to work; Letty began grimly to sew on a pile of unfinished shirts; Mittee kept the school open all day; she set Anna and me to preserving fruit and making jam though the pantry shelves stood full. But it was done with ill-will, in conflict with the bright excitement of the weather.

Mittee needed a new housegirl. She had trained a raw girl who was quick and willing but who had such a sweet tooth that the sugar was not safe from her. It disappeared by the pound. Mittee could never catch her at it but every morning when the sugar was measured out for the day, the amount in the bin had dropped. The lock on the bin was broken and there was none other to be spared from anywhere, so she wrote her name on top of the sugar, thinking that this would stop the thief. The next morning the printed letters were still there but the sugar was less. It was a long time before Mittee discovered that the girl had mastered the six letters of her name. She caught her red-handed, flattening down the sugar and laboriously tracing MIT; but Mittee let her go no further. She chased her there and then, annoyed at this cleverness in one who a few months before had not known how to turn a doorknob and had fled screaming when the piano was played.

She sent Fanie with a note to the missionary, asking for a trained housegirl. 'But she must not eat sugar, not a grain,' she wrote, underlining each word. Doctor Besil sent back the lame girl with Fanie. When Mittee saw her, she hissed, 'The Englishman has gone mad,' and called for the Cape cart to be inspanned. She put the girl in the back and Petronella and me beside her. All the way there, she made up the speech that she would hurl at Doctor Besil's burning ears. She would confound him by saying in English, Doctor Castledene, you may not understand that I have a big house to keep clean, or Doctor Castledene, my time is valuable and you play jokes on me . . .

She said none of these things when she saw him. Perhaps she grew ashamed when she noticed how gently he took the cowering girl from the cart; or perhaps she was reminded of her own crippled son.

I know her voice was soft when she said, 'I need a strong girl, Doctor Castledene.'

'Your note said that it was important that the girl should know something of housework and yet not be fond of sugar. So I sent you the girl out of my own house, because I know she never touches sugar.' He clipped his words, like a shopman snipping ribbon.

'She is not strong enough,' repeated Mittee.

'You said nothing about strength, Mrs Du Plessis. It was the sugar you underlined. Look, I have your note here. And she must not eat sugar, not a grain.' He glared at Mittee but as she told the story about the thieving housegirl I saw laughter hovering in his face and Mittee, noticing it too, went red. 'I sent you that girl at a sacrifice, Mrs Du Plessis, and all you do is frighten her. She is defter than many girls. Come into my house and see how she keeps it.' When Mittee shook her head, he laughed outright at her and then spoke in English. 'You make me feel like an ogre.'

'An ogre, doctor?' said Mittee, flustered at having such a strange word to deal with.

'A giant, one who would gobble you up if he got the chance.'

Mittee snapped at him suddenly, 'Do you think I am a silly little farm girl, to believe you would eat me up? I have been to London and Paris and Berlin, you forget. You know very well that my husband is furious with you over the dam and he would not allow me to go into your house.'

Doctor Besil stood back from the cart. 'I apologize, Mrs Du Plessis.'

'But I would like to see your house.' In a flash she was down from the seat before he could help her.

Doctor Besil walked beside her and I followed with Petronella on my hip. I noticed how Mittee was walking as though the languorous summer air had quickened her senses and I grumbled under my breath.

First he showed her the garden. It was a passionate garden where wild and cultivated flowers bloomed in shouting colours. Red creepers foamed over the trees, the hedges were yellow with blossoms. As we went into the house I could not help thinking, because of that garden, You can never tell, perhaps he wants to get rid of the lame girl because he has been carrying on with her.

The house inside was stark. We saw stiffly starched curtains, deal chairs and tables scrubbed white, polished brown linoleum, gleaming like water. It was a house to frighten away all thoughts of lust. You could not have enjoyed even food in it. I was glad to get out of that house for it seemed to shut you off from Doctor Besil as though his kindness was a cloak to the crystal soul that demanded no comfort from love.

He asked the lame girl to bring tea, serving me with the same politeness as he showed Mittee; and if Mittee was surprised at seeing me in a chair beside her she gave no sign of it and sipped the tea as though she were accustomed to it.

'The tea is refreshing,' she said in her politest tones. 'With us it is always coffee, coffee.'

I could not help saying, 'I've often heard you say that you think tea is a ninny's drink.'

'Hold your mouth.' Mittee's politeness forsook her but she struggled to regain it as Doctor Besil, unperturbed, turned the conversation away from the delicate subject.

I am sad when I remember that afternoon. Beyond the garden the veld unfolded as smoothly as a kaross to the trees that staggered up the mountain slopes. We could see the big-horned native cattle grazing, herded by little Kaffir boys who were bright in Mission clothes. The stately Kaffir women passed to and from the waterhole, carrying tins and calabashes on their heads. There was nothing to keep Mittee there but she stayed until the shadows came from the mountain.

When she was leaving, she carefully took off her mitten and held out her hand to the missionary. 'I am sorry about the girl, Doctor Castledene, but we cannot have a lame creature in the house.'

'I thought you of all people would pity her for her lameness.'

She was still burning beneath the rebuke as we drove home. 'He was thinking of Siegfried when he said that. How heartless I must have sounded to him.'

'Ag, he's only a missionary, Mittee, why worry about it?'

'Always cheeky,' she said absently. 'What did we talk about, Selina? I know we talked of gardening.'

'And you boasted about your trip to Europe.'

'He told me how he taught the Kaffir children to read.'

'He said you shouldn't call them Kaffirs, that it meant they were heathens.'

'He asked me about my school and did you hear his voice when he spoke about Siegfried? Did you ever hear such gentleness? Selina, I don't think I'll ever forget this afternoon.'

'I often wonder about these missionaries, Mittee. That lame girl worships him. Do you think it possible for a man to live without a woman? I couldn't help wondering if he had a reason for getting rid of the lame girl.'

'I'll knock you off this cart, so true,' said Mittee. 'You watch your mouth, you thunder, you lightning, you halfcaste devil.'

'I wish the missionary could hear you now,' I said with satisfaction.

The next afternoon, Mittee said to me, 'I have told Letty that we are going to see Aletta Coester's new baby. But we shall call there on our way back. We will go to the Mission again to see Doctor Castledene about that girl.' I said nothing and she went on, her voice uncertain, 'I think I should explain to him why I can't have the girl, seeing that he was so kind to give her out of his own house. I would take her but can you imagine Paul's anger at having a lame girl in the house? You know how he hates anything that is marked, he said that if he had his way he would shoot Rebecca as you would a deformed beast. That's a real Kaffir idea, isn't it? He is angry enough with Doctor Castledene because of the dam and he would think it was a deliberate slight.'

'You need not explain to me,' I said, nudging her slyly.

'Ag, hold your mouth.' She gave the horse an unreasonable cut with the whip, sending him into a gallop that made the stolid Petronella shriek with excitement.

Doctor Besil was not at the Mission House. Only the lame girl was there and she shrugged her shoulders at Mittee's questions. The briskness had gone from Mittee's driving and she allowed the horse to settle down to a tepid walk as though she did not care if she never saw Aletta's new baby. We had gone about half a mile down the road when we saw coming towards us a little Kaffir boy leading a flock of turkeys. He wore a red shirt and a red cap as a guide to the turkeys and he walked with the jauntiness of one who knows he is more brightly coloured than any bird or beast on the veld.

'Where is the baas?' Mittee shouted.

'Nonnie?'

'Doctor Besil. Where is Doctor Besil?' I asked.

He smiled then and pointed to the mountain. 'He is up there.'

Mittee was disappointed. 'Will he be away for long?'

'Only for today, nonnie; he goes up there to read to himself in his own language. He told me.'

'Show me the place,' Mittee commanded.

When he shook his head, Mittee sprang down from the cart and grabbed him by the back of his neck. The turkeys scattered, gobbling with indignation, and Petronella was shaken out of her placidity for the second time that afternoon. She yelled when she saw her aunt's unusual behaviour, thinking something was amiss.

'You're making a fool of yourself, Mittee,' I shouted, patting the child to soothe her.

'The hell. I take no Kaffir's impudence,' she answered.

She bundled the poor little Kaffir into the back of the cart, holding on to his arm while she whipped up the horse. Away we went over the veld, bouncing over tufts of grass and missing ant heaps by inches. A herd of springbok stood in our path. We sent them flying, and caught only a glimpse of their white tails as we rushed on. Partridges flew up under the horse's feet, gorged vultures flapped helplessly from a carcass upon which they had been feeding, terrified by the wind of our passing.

I clutched at Petronella to save her from falling and tried to reason with Mittee at the same time. It seemed to me that the devil had pitchforked us into the past and that Mittee was driving like a fury into Plessisburg to be first at the shop when the new bales of materials came in. I had lost all memory of why we were galloping across the veld, and so had the little Kaffir in the back, I think, for he whimpered brokenly for his mother.

'Mittee Van Brandenberg, you'll have us all killed,' I gasped.

She found time to laugh. 'Mittee Van Brandenberg, indeed. I wish it was so. Don't worry, Selina, I know what I'm doing.'

She had to slow down because the ground was rising to meet the first low krantzes on the mountainside. I unloosed Petronella's arms from round my neck and tried to smooth my crumpled apron. Mittee turned to the Kaffir boy.

'Show me where the baas goes to read.'

By now he had a great respect for Mittee. 'I will take the nonnie to the very spot. And then she must let me go or the turkeys will all be dead.'

Stricken by his anxious little face, she brought out some of the homemade toffee that Letty had sent for Aletta to chew while she lay in bed; broke off a generous piece by smashing it against the side of the cart and watched his misery change to pure joy as she handed it to him. Petronella was appeased with a chunk, though I spoke sharply to Mittee for it was as bad as stealing. Her only answer was to give me a small piece as we set off after the Kaffir boy over a winding, stone-strewn path. I shrugged my shoulders when I thought of what Letty would have to say if she found out about this afternoon's doing.

Only the dear God knows what Doctor Besil thought when he looked up from the book the was reading to see four silent and breathless people scrambling over the stones to the ledge that was his sanctuary. He rose to his feet and his finger fell upon the hapless little turkey boy.

'Where are the turkeys?'

Tears sullied the toffee. 'Do not blame him, Doctor Besil, it's this one,' I burst out. 'She forced him to bring us here.' I gestured with my thumb towards Mittee, who had seated herself on a rock as decorously as though she were paying a call.

'Behave yourself, Selina,' she said, smiling at Doctor Besil.

It was the first time I had seen the enchanting smile since I came to the valley. It was the first time that Doctor Besil had ever seen her smile like that. Man, she was beautiful then.

She said, 'Go and look after your turkeys, creature.'

'It's a long distance for a child to walk, even when the legs are black,' said Doctor Besil tartly.

'He's got the toffee to suck.'

Doctor Besil shook his head. 'You're very heartless, like all your people, in your dealings with the natives.'

'Ag, they are used to walking. You're an Outlander, you don't understand them. Heartless? Why, that girl Anna who goes to your church has worked for me for years, ever since I was married. Would she stay if I were unkind to her? She has cattle of her own from the presents I have given her and she will be rich when she goes back to her own people one day. But I'll drive the boy back if you like. He can stay and play with Petronella while I talk to you.' She smiled again as she smashed more toffee against a stone and offered it round. I had not the heart to spoil her smile by telling Doctor Besil that it was not hers to give away.

'It's good toffee,' said Doctor Besil. 'Did you make it?'

'My sister-in-law made it.' This without a blush. 'But I must tell you why I came. I could not take that girl. You see, my husband would not put up with a lame girl in the house. It would fret him. He did not even like having my son in the house. You remember . . .'

Doctor Besil spoke in English. 'Of course. I should have thought of that. How clumsy of me. I remember him saying to me one day that all imperfect things should be destroyed. We argued about it.'

'I am not speaking against him but I don't want you to think I am heartless.'

Her humility touched him. 'Does it matter much what I think of you, Mrs Du Plessis? We meet so seldom.'

'Oh yes, it matters,' said Mittee, earnestly, 'because that's the most important thing about me. I have a great deal of pity for the sick and I nurse them, black or white, you ask Selina here.'

'I know. The natives speak well of you and they like your medicines much better than mine because they taste viler. You must give me some of your recipes.'

'You're laughing at me,' said Mittee, 'but I'll tell you a good purgative I made up. It has a terrible taste I know but even Mrs Gouws uses it . . .'

She stayed talking to him until the krantzes turned chilly and dark as the sun faded behind the mountains. Then we had to hurtle through the veld again, Doctor Besil in the back of the cart with the turkey-boy, waiting to drop off as soon as we came to the road. Petronella was overtired and hungry, crying in my arms all the way home.

We found Frikkie waiting on the front stoep, for the last light was gone as we jogged past the stone lions. Letty was at his elbow, asking why we were so late and how the baby looked and did Aletta enjoy the toffee. Mittee fibbed to her as easily as she had done to Grandma Van Brandenberg.

It made your heart ache to see them together. They made no plans for the future, dallying with their love as though they would not have to part soon. She did not see him alone and I thought she was mad to risk so much for the sake of seeing him and of hearing him speak. I scorned him for the restraint that kept him from even a handclasp at greeting. Theirs was the greater wisdom. Beautiful days dawn in soft shades and beautiful music with quiet chords. The pattern of their love was perfect but I did not understand that then, as I played string games with Petronella to keep her amused so that she should not bother them while they talked.

November came to an end in a burst of brazen sunshine and Mittee drove to the mountains for the last time. The waggons stood ready for the Christmas journey to Plessisburg where Paul awaited her. It was as well. Letty knew that Mittee lied to her about these frequent outings and she linked Mittee's name ominously with the missionary's because the child prattled of him. Fanie warned me that she was forever nagging at Frikkie to follow Mittee for his brother's sake but so far he had held out against her. Several times she had told Fanie to drive after Mittee but he put her off by telling her that the donkeys and horses were lost. Once she got as far as having two oxen yoked to the scotch-cart. They were young oxen and as skittish as girls at a dance. When a mamba passed between their legs as they went through the veld, they put their tails into the air and bolted.

Poor Letty. She had Pieter in the scotch-cart with her and she rolled him into the veld but she could not pluck up the courage to jump herself and sat with her legs dangling over the edge of the cart, screeching at Fanie that he was a bastard, a thunder and a lightning. The oxen were stopped at last by a big thorn tree and both Letty and Fanie were flung into a patch of devil-thorn. She did not follow Mittee again but she bided her time, strong in the knowledge of her own virtue.

Mittee knew that she was suspected but she did not seem to care. She stopped making excuses for her absence.

'I am doing no harm, Selina. Petronella and you are always there.'

'You have gone mad, Mittee. Your husband will see harm in it. He will sjambok you when he finds this out.'

Again that foolish cry, 'What harm am I doing?'

On that last afternoon, she seated herself as usual on the rock, while he sat in the grass, an unopened book beside him.

'I have learned to love this place, Basil. I will always remember it though I suppose this is the last time I will ever come here.'

'I always loved it. The veld is shut away from you here. There are times when I can't stand the sameness of the rolling grass. But when I come here alone, Mittee, there is always a ghost with me and I find myself talking to somebody who isn't there and who probably never thinks of me as she goes about her busy household.'

She smiled. 'I'll always think of you, I always do. But I will see you sometimes in the valley when we come back from Plessisburg.'

'As soon as the dam is demolished I am leaving the Mission. I have asked to be transferred to the Congo.'

'And I will never, never see you again.'

'Mittee.'

I said briskly, 'It's time to go home, nonnie, we're making an early start tomorrow and this child has to have rest.' I took Petronella's hand and walked down the pathway, looking back every now and then to see if they were following. I shouted once to her but she did not even turn her head. Ag well, I thought, let them have a few moments together, it will be the last time. The next day, God be thanked, we would be on our way to Plessisburg.

I waited by the cart, expecting her every moment. An hour passed and another. The child screamed with hunger but all I could find to pacify her was an orange. When she had eaten that, I rolled her in a crocheted rug and nursed her to sleep. I was frightened for in the far distance I heard the beat of lions' roaring and in the fading light the bushes seemed to be moving in on me. The horse was restless and I had to stand at his head, terrified that he might go off, leaving us stranded on the veld. I cursed Mittee for her foolishness. There would be no argument now when Letty babbled to Paul.

A shivering of prophecy passed through me. The future held violence and terror. I swore that when I reached Plessisburg I would stay there no matter what Fanie said and even if he reported me to the magistrate.

The stars were out when Mittee came down the path with Doctor Besil. The stars could have fallen out of the sky one by one for all she cared, the mad thing.

I said shrilly, 'Here I am holding this child and lions roaring. We'll all get fever from the night air.'

'Lions,' said Mittee, coming down to earth. 'They'll come after the horse. Oh my God, let's hurry.'

I was as sour as vinegar. 'You wait, you're going to get into trouble, Nonnie Mittee.'

We had to go slowly and carefully over the veld, leaving the horse to pick its own way but still we were jarred time and again when the wheels rolled over unseen stones and bushes. I crouched at the back of the cart with Petronella pressed close to me, while Mittee and Doctor Besil shared the driver's seat. It seemed that we would never reach the road but travel forever through the tense darkness, oppressed by the sound of wild life bounding through the grass at our approach.

I fell into an uneasy doze and when I awakened we were on the road. Mittee stopped the horse, urging Doctor Besil to leave us now, for through the stillness we could hear coming towards us the sound of a galloping horse. Their bodies blended sadly together and then he was gone, with Mittee's voice lingering on the air, 'Goodbye, Basil.'

Frikkie had come looking for her. He sprang to the road, all his good humour gone.

'Where have you been? Almighty, when your husband hears about this.'

'Don't shout, Frikkie,' she said, taking the liberty of a sister-in-law to stroke his beard. 'It wasn't my fault, the wheel came off the cart.'

'Lightning!' There was no sting in the swearword because of that gentle hand in his beard. 'You said you were going to visit the Gouwses and the Gouwses are even at this minute sitting with Letty in the dining room and they have been there since five o'clock. They're spending the night to be ready for an early start.'

'We found them away,' said Mittee glibly, 'so I drove towards the mountains and we had a picnic. That's how we came to lose the wheel.'

'And who put it back for you?'

'Selina and I did it ourselves, didn't we, Selina?'

When they were alone, Frikkie was open in his disbelief of her weak lies but when he walked behind her into the dining room he was her champion against Letty's spiteful questioning. Frikkie, that master of practical jokes, was a valuable person to have on your side; and though Letty sat with slanting mouth to show her contempt, the Gouwses were all over Mittee, blaming themselves for not being at home.

'Poor Mittee, you must have been frightened,' said Gouws, himself so simple and honest that he was more easily deceived than a child. 'If it hadn't been for my lumbago I would have ridden after you as soon as we got here.'

The old woman said nothing but Mittee did not have to fear that mild face. Even when she was a little girl, Mrs Gouws had covered up the childish sins that would have sent Grandma's strap hissing through the air.

She would have to watch out for Letty. 'I will try to keep the peace,' said Frikkie, following Mittee into the kitchen where I was preparing a meal, 'but Paul will hear about these comings and goings, this toffee that Aletta never received. It's that that annoys Letty more than anything.'

'Ag, it will all be forgotten tomorrow in the excitement of going to Plessisburg,' said Mittee, avoiding his bright, curious eyes.

'All the same, I'd like to know what you've been up to, you little vagabond.'

The waggons were on the move at daybreak. We saw the sky split above the far-off mountains to the east and colour come tumbling into the greyness. It made our progress glorious, as though God Himself marched with us, for Mittee had set the children to singing a psalm and their voices quivered in the air with sweet angel notes. '... He maketh me to lie down in green pastures: He leadeth me beside the still waters ...'

The sky turned blue before the psalm ended. Waggon after waggon joined us on the road, their drivers calling out in good fellowship. Horses pranced and bucked beneath their masters' playful teasing; mostly youngsters these, exuberant over the holiday. But everyone was jovial in some measure and even the old women, whose main concern was their comfort, roused themselves from the lethargy of age to cackle out a few jokes. The only ones untouched by the occasion were the babies who sucked their fingers or screamed from some uneasiness as though to be riding to Plessisburg was an everyday occurrence.

We passed the missionary's lonely house. He was in his garden and he took his hat off, waving to us as we passed. 'Until we see you,' the happy folk cried, 'have a merry Christmas, Doctor.'

'Why doesn't he come with us?' Fanie asked. He was already hungry with the travelling and split cold sweet potatoes to share with Rebecca and me. I did not answer for I was peering out of our waggon at Mittee making a fool of herself over the missionary. She waved long after everybody else had stopped and I thought, Well, let her, it's none of my business if Paul kills her.

The mountains run together, leaving a narrow opening through which a waggon can pass with only a few feet to spare on either side. The walls of this opening are steep and bare, so high that the sun is shut off and you enter into shadow on the most brilliant day. Once through there and you look over thornveld, stretching grey-green for mile upon mile. On this day, as we trekked into the suffocating heat of the plain, we saw no wild life except a scarred old elephant, grim and alone; plodding eastwards to some other stamping-ground. But there was plenty of game about if you looked for it, said Fanie, and he went off to beg Frikkie for the loan of his rifle. But Frikkie wanted to do the shooting himself, so Fanie spent the day dreaming about the rifle he would own some day.

It was a relief to outspan after that gruelling day but I took no pleasure in that halt for my holiday cheerfulness had been subsiding hour by hour as I remembered our trek across the plain during the drought. I think Letty remembered too, for I could not hear her voice raised in nagging and perhaps she thought of the time that Frikkie first defeated her.

Gouws called out suddenly, 'There's a runner coming towards us.'

A throb of excitement ran through the laager for what could he bring but a message of war or sudden death, when we would be so soon in Plessisburg? 'The President is dead,' said Mrs Gouws, that bird of ill-omen. This was accepted as a fact by the more simple-minded of the women and they began to pray with lamentations.

To cut short the waiting, Frikkie rode his horse bareback to meet the runner. We saw the boy flash forward in a proud burst of speed, holding high his spear and the cleft stick in which he carried a letter.

Every voice was raised as Frikkie rode back. 'Is it the President?' 'Are we at war with the English?' 'It's another raid on Johannesburg.' Frikkie sprang to the ground and held up his hand to quieten the clamour.

The letter was from Paul, with the envelope marked, Haste, haste! Speed, speed! to show its urgency. As Frikkie read it out, an awed silence fell upon us. There would be no festivities in Plessisburg that Christmas for smallpox had struck the town. Not a household remained untouched, the Kaffirs were dying like flies. The High Dutch gave to Frikkie's voice the solemnity of a rolling drum. 'Stand fast in the valley,' Paul wrote, 'and let your Christmas be one of prayer for the burghers of Plessisburg in their misery.'

There was a letter enclosed for Mittee and she told us that Paul would be leaving Plessisburg within the week. He gave a list of names, those who were already dead from the fever, but these she did not read out. She went to each person separately to tell them which of their relatives had been struck down. Oh, the misery. That was a night of prayer when we fell asleep to waken and pray again.

The next morning we returned to the valley, quietly as though the waggons carried the dead. All through that week we prayed and our throats were hoarse at the end of it. Men who had never before preached stood up before us during that week. The valley was a melancholy place for most of the farmers and their wives came from Plessisburg and many of them mourned already over the list of names that Paul had sent; while those whose families had not been mentioned waited anxiously for Paul's coming so that they might know how each one fared. We were afraid for ourselves, too, when Doctor Besil seized the runner as he came into the valley, to watch for the symptoms of smallpox.

In the second week, Frikkie and Fanie looked out for Paul from the top of the ridge day after day, but no waggon broke the monotony of the veld. The farmers began to talk of riding across the plain to meet him.

'He is dead, of course,' said Mrs Gouws, 'and probably all his Kaffirs too, torn to pieces by now by hyenas and vultures.'

It was Doctor Besil who sent us news at last. A Mission boy brought a letter to Mittee on Dingaan's Day. She took it from him at the back door and when she had read it, she sat for a long time at the kitchen table without speaking while she folded the paper into tiny squares. Letty stood by, nagging and impatient with suspicion.

'That letter is from Doctor Castledene . . . What is in the letter to strike you dumb, Mrs Du Plessis?' She put vicious emphasis into the names. No wonder Frikkie threatened to shoot her. 'A letter from the missionary . . . Besil, the innocent child calls him . . . How Paul hates missionaries . . . What is in the letter?'

Mittee spoke slowly. 'There is smallpox in the valley, Letty. Two Kaffirs came to the missionary's house last night, one so sick that he could hardly walk. He died this morning from smallpox. They had run away from Paul's waggons. He is lying on the veld, alone and sick. The missionary has ridden out to look after him. Now will you be still?'

Mittee was not devout. That is the only time I ever saw her pray from her heart, but it was not for Paul's life that she begged, I knew. Letty, her face blazing from shame, knelt beside Mittee in torment from the spite that was destroying her. I was harder than they. I looked down at their bowed heads and relived the calamities that had brought me dry-eyed to this moment.

CHAPTER XI

The smallpox passed lightly over the valley. You heard of a Kaffir dying here and there but none of the white people went down with it: though it was a long time before we could feel the fever on a sick person without that surge of panic.

Mittee and I often climbed to the top of the ridge and looked until our eyes ached for some sign from Doctor Besil and Paul. The veld had closed over them so completely that they might both have been dead. Frikkie had found them on the riverbank, where Doctor Besil had built a hut to shelter Paul, but he would not let Frikkie come near. He told us with an echo of laughter in his voice how the missionary had kept him off with Paul's rifle while he explained that he would carry the smallpox back to the valley. So every second day, Frikkie would ride within shouting distance of the camp. Doctor Besil, cupping his hands, would call out that Paul still lived and that he himself had not yet been sickened.

Then Frikkie developed a fever. Letty shut herself up with him and I whispered to Mittee that she seemed almost glad to martyr herself. We heard Frikkie yelling at her after the third day to open up the windows because he did not have smallpox, he had malaria. Whenever I brought a tray of food to the door, I could hear their voices. Letty's was gentle but persistent as though she would soothe Frikkie into an easy death. Frikkie's voice was weaker but it quivered with rage when he said the word Smallpox. The argument seemed never to end and as Frikkie grew stronger you could hear it all over the house.

At last Letty had to admit that he had malaria. She grudgingly opened the windows and the door and allowed the children to see their father. They screeched and ran away from him, for Letty had shaved his hair and beard, in readiness for the appearance of the pustules; and it was this that made Frikkie so bitter for he looked a sight, believe me.

Mittee and I took up our watch on the ridge again. We grew to hate the thornveld. 'It is like the sea,' Mittee said. 'It is vast and cruel like the sea.'

The picture of the sea was not clear to me; as wide as the plain below us but all water, no, I could not believe it. I remembered that Herry had once described the sea to me, and he had used the same words as Mittee. As endless as the veld, he had told me, but constantly changing in colour and form. Sometimes it was like a glass for smoothness and sometimes the water curled into waves as high as a mountain. When I was younger I had dreamed of seeing this wonderful thing, of putting my hands into it and tasting the salt in the water. Herry had promised that one day he would take me to Capetown.

It was a long time since I had thought of Herry but there was little else to do but think as we kept watch. Surely this was the hand of God avenging his death at last, punishing me by this waiting for my silence.

Mittee would sit for hours without changing her position, staring into the distance as unwaveringly as a baboon on guard; waiting, I knew, for the moment when she would see Doctor Besil come back alone across the plain.

'To wish for a person's death is as bad as murdering them,' I said one day, but she answered nothing.

Twelve times we walked to the top of the ridge. The whiteness of Mittee's skin was marred by a faint sheen of gold from the sun before we saw the waggon. At first it was only a stirring amongst the thorn trees, lost and found again with the rise and fall of the ground, then after an hour we saw the swinging oxen plainly and the figure of a man. The veld blurred and sharpened beneath the intensity of my stare and I could not make out who it was that God was sending back to the valley.

'Come, Selina, we will go to the pass and watch from there.'

I had to help her as we descended to the level place where we had left the cart, for she trembled with the violence of her excitement and fear. She gave the reins to me and I drove to the road, slowly because the veld was strewn with boulders and treacherous little stones.

On the road, the horse stretched out and soon we had passed between the gloomy rocks on to the plain. The waggon was approaching us and in the bright light we saw the shine of Doctor Besil's fairness.

'Oh Paradise, it is Paul who is dead,' I cried.

Mittee sprang from the slow-moving cart, running towards the waggon with the speed of a buck in flight. The wait-a-bit thorns clutched at her dress and petticoats but she tore herself loose, leaving behind her streamers of lace and bright print.

Doctor Besil was unmarked by the smallpox but the long vigil showed itself in his gaunt face by harsh lines newly drawn about his mouth. He halted Mittee, holding her at arm's length.

'Carefully over the stones. Your husband does not expect to see you yet and he is still weak and in agony over his disfigurement.'

I chanted, 'Rejoice in our Father,' but no word of praise came from Mittee's lips. She turned from Doctor Besil as though she was leaving him for ever, and walked with dragging feet to the waggon where Paul lay.

His lips were shrivelled by fever and his body wasted to a shell. In the ruin of his face, only his eyes remained unchanged.

'We thought you were dead, Paul.'

He pulled himself on to his elbow, searching that beloved face. 'You must find me hideous to look at.'

In an instant she was beside him, her fearless, compassionate hand on his cheek. I longed to cry out, She wished you dead while I prayed for you, hating her for the pity that comforted him. Doctor Besil drew me away from them.

'Always, always it is like this,' I whispered, 'God lays his hand on her and I am passed by. She knows his pride. One word, one look of horror and he would have let her go.'

'Hush. You must not hate her for that.'

'You saw how she ran to the waggon. She thought that you were alone . . .' He took my arm in a painful grip, dragging me to the cart, for my voice was growing louder. He put me up on the driver's seat, lifting me bodily, and then gave the reins into my unwilling hands, as he caught the horse a smart clip on the rump. The cart shot forward and I cursed him for a waxen-faced Outlander but he looked after me mildly. He understood me well. When I drew the horse into the stable, I felt nothing but sorrow for Mittee.

We grew used to the alteration in Paul's looks. Mittee was so gentle with him but so natural in her acceptance that even he became less sensitive. By the time that summer was over, his shoulders were straight and his body had filled out. He was afraid to face people but under Mittee's urging he called the farmers to a meeting, to tell them that work on the road could begin at once as the grant had been made. Slowly the glare of pride lit his face again.

Letty held her tongue until Paul was strong. Then one afternoon I heard her hissing like a spiteful goose while she gave Paul coffee on the front stoep.

'Mittee. Oh, the slyness. I'm going to visit Aletta Coester, she says, but Aletta never sees her. I made toffee for Aletta and she gives it to this Englishman, I tell you. Ask Frikkie, she came here at nine o'clock at night from the veld . . .'

Mittee had gone to visit Aletta that afternoon but I had to stay with Rebecca because Fanie was helping to build Frikkie's house. I saw Paul throw his cup of coffee over Letty. She stepped back from him in terror for he was calling her every name that the Bible has given to wicked women. She ran inside and locked the door on him, then feeling herself safe, screeched abuse through the keyhole.

'You call me a whore. The Father above knows my virtue. You go after her now and you will find her with the accursed Redneck.'

Paul kicked at the door until she fled to her bedroom, for the very walls seemed to shake with the magnificence of his wrath. He stood for a while, grinding the broken china beneath his heel, cursing Letty in the Language, in English and in Kaffir; but he called to the boy to saddle his horse and when he mounted he carried his rifle.

There was no time to worry about Rebecca. I left her wandering on the yard and ran across country to the mountains. Devil-thorns stung my feet and wait-a-bit branded my arms, the wind tore the doek from my head, three times I saw snakes glide from my path; but I stopped for nothing. He would go first to the Coesters' farm and then perhaps on to the Mission House. Fatherland, how I ran that day and all for nothing.

There was no cart on the veld and when I climbed breathlessly to the ledge, only Doctor Besil was there. I dropped into the grass beside him and stroked the trembling from my legs.

'I thought she had come here. Paul has gone looking for her with his rifle. God be thanked. He would have murdered her and you, too.'

'She does not come here any more.'

'It is better. She was so careless and her husband is a violent, dangerous man. Only I know what he is capable of, Doctor Besil.'

'There is nothing to be afraid of, because I am leaving the valley in a few months' time. I should have gone as soon as she came to live here but I thought our paths would not cross often. Du Plessis would have nothing to do with me from the start and so I saw her only once or twice as she drove by, until their child became sick. After that, I used to sit on my stoep and dream that she was not married . . . Come along, Selina, we must go down now, it's getting late.'

He walked with me as far as the road. All the way, he spoke of Mittee as a person speaks of water when he is thirsty.

'You will forget about her when you go from here, Doctor Besil. She will seem to you like a dream in a few months' time and you will be happy again. I know because the same thing happened to me. The only cure is marriage. You should be married for a missionary is no good without a wife.'

'I will give up my missionary work for a time,' he answered, 'perhaps even return to England. For now I am like you, Selina, I cannot say where right and wrong are divided.'

He began to talk about Mittee again and I was glad to get away from him, for she was haunting him as though she was already dead.

That night, Frikkie gave Letty a hiding. Fanie shook me until my head wobbled, for Rebecca was lost and we did not find her until the next morning. Only Mittee was in her husband's favour.

Paul invited Doctor Besil to Sunday dinner. He said it was to show his gratitude but really it was to punish Letty. Frikkie forced her to come to the table and though the turkey was cooked to a melting tenderness, she ate with long teeth and swallowed the milk tart as if it were bitter aloes.

It was an uncomfortable meal. Paul liked to pay attention to what he was eating but for the sake of politeness he would stop to address a remark in English to Doctor Besil, the phrases so thick with his accent that Doctor Besil was puzzled and answered him at random. When they had finished eating, such a terrible silence fell upon them all that even I, clearing away plates, felt myself grow prickly. Doctor Besil read the High Dutch on the label of the bottle of Essence, kept on the table since Paul's illness; Letty played with a fork as though she meant to throw it at somebody; Mittee busied herself unnecessarily with the cruet, while Paul leaned back in his chair, seeking some dazzling English phrase to entertain the guest. Only Frikkie was calm. His sardonic eye fell on one and all, as though this meal with a foreign missionary would make a good story to tell around a campfire.

Paul abandoned the ceiling and sought inspiration in Petronella. He put her on his knee and so set the unwieldly conversation under way. Silence would have been better.

She said, 'Besil' twice before he noticed it but Letty looked up triumphantly each time. Paul's glowing eyes fixed on Mittee.

'Besil? Where has she learnt to call Doctor Castledene Besil?'

'It's my fault, basie, I taught her.' My voice was shrill. 'I go to the Mission Church and everybody there calls him Besil.'

'Everybody?' Paul asked, ominously.

'But everybody, basie, to the last Kaffir.'

'It's my Christian name,' said Doctor Besil and his eyes twinkled as he studied the Essence of Life label.

That was the finish for Frikkie. Choking 'Excuse', through his laughter, he went from the room and left the others to a silence that fell like a blanket over their wits. He stood in the kitchen laughing silently while I packed the dishes on the table.

'For shame, basie, to laugh at a visitor at your brother's table.'

Frikkie defended himself. 'I was not laughing at the missionary. It was the thought of Paul sitting at the table with a man the Kaffirs call by his Christian name. Did you see his face?'

'You shouldn't laugh at anything on a Sunday. A fine example you are to your children and the servants.'

When the missionary had gone, everybody seemed to forget that it was Sunday and a family row started that could be heard at the end of the yard. Frikkie caught it from all sides, even from Mittee. I got a long lecture from Paul about my familiarity in calling a white man by his Christian name and though I bobbed up and down in all humility I could have laughed in the face of his hypocrisy.

He continued an uneasy friendship with Doctor Besil, sending him gifts of the first pickings from the lands and the orchards, beef or mutton when he killed and a sucking pig from the best sow. Still his debt remained unpaid for Doctor Besil fastidiously returned his favours with cut flowers from his garden, prime turkeys or if he had nothing else to give, a buck that the Kaffirs had snared.

CHAPTER XII

The dam was not yet demolished and work on the road only just begun when Eberhardt rode into the valley with the news that the Transvaal was at war. The despatches that he carried sent a ripple of unrest running from farmhouse to farmhouse. There had been talk of war in Plessisburg at Nagmaal but it seemed remote to me, in spite of Eberhardt's plumed hat and serious face.

Letty cared nothing about the dam or the road. She was thinking about her unfinished house and she went for Frikkie as though he had made a plot with the English to spite her. 'You can't go on commando until my house is finished,' she stormed.

'This is war, Letty. You don't realize. Every rifle is needed for the Transvaal,' said Eberhardt. You could hear his voice all over the house as his importance burst from him in wild stories of clashes with the English. Letty stopped talking about her house.

The next morning, Paul climbed to the loft and brought down Grandpa Van Brandenberg's muzzle-loader and powder horn. Then he and Frikkie talked for an hour, arguing and planning. At the end of it, Paul called Fanie to him. Leaning on the gun, he explained to Fanie that he would be left in charge of the Kaffirs on the farm for a while, as both he and Frikkie had been called up. To uphold authority, there was this muzzle-loader and a shotgun which would be kept in a corner of Mittee's bedroom to be handed to him only when a desperate situation arose. Fanie's eyes grew big when he took in the responsibility of his position but he was happy enough when Paul left him to clean the gun for there is nothing he loves more than to handle firearms. Fanie did not behave well. As soon as the men had gone, he begged Mittee to let him have the shotgun for target practice, but he used up every last cartridge, shooting game. She refused to allow him to touch the muzzle-loader as Frikkie had mixed only a small quantity of powder. When Paul came home, she said nothing about the empty shotgun for it would have meant trouble and Fanie had, after all, given her first pick of the game he shot.

When we watched the first column of men march out of the valley, we thought they were going for only a short time. They cantered down the road on their finest ponies, rifles at their knees and bandoliers at their waists, as easily as if they were going on a hunt or to oversee the road-building. We sent them off with psalms and then went about the everyday tasks, though with a feeling of uneasiness for many of the farms were now unprotected by menfolk. Letty made the house more miserable by keeping up the psalm-singing throughout the day, her voice dreary with the expectation of woe.

'You'd think not one of them was ever going to ride back again,' Mittee whispered to me, but that night she was glad enough of harmonium and hymn, realizing how much we leaned on the men for their protection.

The war came upon us slowly. At first there were men in the valley but after the first year even old Gouws, with all his aches and pains, was out on commando. We missed going to Plessisburg for Nagmaal and Christmas but we got used to that; then sugar disappeared from the table as transports grew rarer and a new dress became a thing to dream about. There were no wax candles to plague Mittee with their wastefulness and even tallow candles were so precious that we lit them only in time of sickness. The bearing of the most trusted servants grew easier. The changes were so gradual that you could not say, On such and such a day we became careful with the candles or, It was in such and such a month that a Kaffir first threw a stone at a passing cart. The white women learned to modulate their voices for when the first insolent answer came there would be no redress. Mrs Gouws was moved to speak darkly of the massacre at Weenen and after she had visited, mothers clutched their babies to them tightly for she dwelt on a description given by a cousin, who had been there. This unfortunate woman had seen her babies' brains dashed out against the waggon-wheel and she herself had eighty-six assegai wounds to show. We came to know that woman as though we ourselves had spoken to her.

When the men came back to the valley it was for fresh horses and biltong and the brief comfort of their beds. It was useless to tell them of that vague threat of insolence for it disappeared with their coming. They were cheerful companions after the long loneliness and they, too, seemed unchanged until one day you saw as though for the first time that the jokes they made had a wry twist to them and that they laughed too often. Their eyes had grown watchful. Sometimes they spoke of the War; of the stealthy rides across the veld, of the blowing up of trains, as exciting as a vicious practical joke; of terrible men in skirts who fell upon them with long knives; of their friends and relatives who were dead.

Soon they were off again, riding loosely and with their right hands resting from habit on their rifles. When they were gone, the tension crept upon us again and we spoke softly to any Kaffir who had been kicked or flogged.

We owed much of our safety to Doctor Besil. He was unarmed

and sometimes he was the only white man in the valley but for more than a year he kept the ferocity of the Kaffirs in check. He was on parole but in time the women forgot that he was an Outlander, for if a boy became obstinate or dangerously surly, they could send for Doctor Besil, who would remove him to his kraal, often before a harsh word had been spoken. His help in sickness had been sought long before the war but now he took the place of a minister as well, despite the look of everlasting boyishness that his fairness gave him.

His love for Mittee was overlaid by friendliness. During that time, as far as I know, they never saw each other alone and sometimes I thought that I had dreamed that they were in love; yet suddenly I would be made aware of the deep feeling that lay between them. Dangerously and unexpectedly a silence would fall on them and you had the illusion that they had moved closer though they stood unmoving. It happened, I remember, when we set the mother monkey and her baby free. Letty and the children were with us and they clapped their hands as the monkey, with her baby clinging to her, raced for the security of the mountains.

'It's the most wonderful thing I ever saw,' cried Mittee. I thought, They are like Andrina and Leon; as though they were related to each other. I spoke quickly to Letty and began a game with the children, distracting her envious, bitter eyes. Fanie noticed for he spoke about it to me that night.

I saw it happen again one afternoon when he was setting a Kaffir girl's broken leg. He said, 'You'd better give her a tot of brandy, this is going to hurt a bit.'

'I don't believe in brandy,' Mittee answered.

'Don't argue, get me the brandy, Mittee.' There was a snap in his voice but he had called her Mittee and not Mrs Du Plessis.

'I'll go for it,' I said, but I might as well not have spoken.

Such small things made up the cycle of our lives. The wheel tracks running from the valley to Plessisburg disappeared for no transports came through. We knew from the occasional riders who came in that the struggle was growing more bitter on the Highveld and that the English were in Pretoria; but it was unreal to us until Jacob Coester was killed and Frikkie taken prisoner, to be sent across the sea to Bermuda.

The swaggering Kaffirs knew long before we did of the disasters that were overtaking the Republic. Those who were faithful crept into the kitchens at night, terrified by the talk that went on round the fires when a pot of beer was brewed.

Then one morning I went into the yard to find the dog vomiting. I rushed into the house for Mittee.

'Come quickly, nonnie, the dog has been poisoned.'

'Mustard and milk,' said Mittee calmly. 'And stop screaming, Selina, that won't save the dog's life.'

Fanie pushed a way for her through the rabble of Kaffirs who had gathered around the dog. She took one look at the animal and then emptied the mustard mixture on the ground.

'Which one of you has done this?'

Her eyes searched each face, seeking the hidden enemy. Silence had fallen on them, a silence that spread outwards to us; and beyond us to the grass and the trees and the sky. There was not one face there that we did not know, not one that we trusted completely. It might be that boy whom Paul had thrashed when he was last home or it might be that girl, an impudent, sleek thing, with eyes for the white men. It might even be Anna, for who knew what went on behind that sullen black face.

'Come inside, nonnie,' said Fanie, oppressed by the silence.

Its menace seemed to follow us into the house and it was a relief to hear at last the high chanting of a woman's voice as she swept the yard. Fanie stayed by the house for a week, though there was ploughing to be done, and sometimes he paraded with the muzzle-loader to frighten anyone who might be plotting violence. Doctor Besil questioned each Kaffir separately but he did not find out who had poisoned the dog.

'You must be careful,' he said to Mittee and Letty. 'Don't go far from the house and try to keep together, as much as possible. When next the commando rides in, some of the older men will have to stay in the valley. The temper of the natives is changing every day and wherever I go I hear old wrongs discussed.'

The peaceful days that followed lulled our fears, though we still went two by two to the little house during the night; and Anna took to sleeping on the kitchen floor for she complained that the Kaffir boys plagued her night and day. A sudden shout or an aggressive laugh would set us thinking about the poisoned dog.

On that bright July day, Letty had gone to her room because she had a headache, leaving Anna under the peach trees with Pieter and Petronella. I had charge of Rebecca for Fanie had been on the lands since early morning looking after the ploughing. As usual I had barricaded Rebecca behind chairs while Mittee and I darned the precious house linen. It was such a quiet afternoon, I remember, not a sound to be heard from outside but the throbbing of the doves in the peach trees. The stillness seemed to have tamed even Mittee for when the machine stuck she did not swear but bent down quite good-temperedly to work the needle free from a bunch of cotton. For a few seconds there were just the two of us in the world, concentrating on getting the needle loose; and then the terror was upon us, terror that we had known must come ever since the men went away.

At the first scream, Mittee stood up slowly, brushing strands of cotton from her skirt. I remained kneeling beside the machine, my face upturned to her. All the air was filled with Anna's screams. Oh, Grandma Van Brandenberg was wrong, I did remember hiding behind the waterfall with my mother.

'Kaffirs,' whispered Mittee.

She picked up her skirts as she ran, pushing past Letty who came from her room with her hair flying. 'My children,' Letty wailed. 'Oh Paradise, my children.'

'Don't go out there,' Mittee called but it was useless. Letty slipped past my clutching hands, and as I followed her to the back door I saw the poor thing snatch up a hoe from the yard as she ran towards the orchard.

Mittee was already measuring powder into the old muzzle-loader. Sweat ran down her face but her hands were strong with desperation. 'Now the rag over the mouth and then the bullet,' she said with hissing breath. Together we rammed the bullet down the barrel.

We came to the trees as one boy rose from Anna. There was another, with his left hand wound in Letty's beautiful hair while he fought with his right to take the hoe from her. Near them Pieter lay unconscious, his face beaten to a pulp. I looked anxiously for little Petronella and I saw her creep from behind a tree like a timid little meercat. She was crying, I knew that by the shape of her mouth, but her thin voice was lost entirely in the raging sounds that came from Letty and the Kaffir. As Mittee raised the gun to her shoulder, the boy who had raped Anna bounded off amongst the trees but the flat-faced Shangaan who had hold of Letty did not let go of her. He shifted his hand from her hair to her throat and so stopped her screaming. He was from the Mission, not ill-natured usually, but a little muddled in the head and now so frightened that he was dangerous.

The aching moments were made suddenly sweet by the lowing of oxen and the call of the herd boys. 'Fanie,' I screamed. My voice let loose a hellish explosion from Mittee's wavering finger and she fell back from the kick of the gun as though she were dead, blood streaming from her nose. The Shangaan fled through the trees with a terrible cry though the bullet had gone far over his head. Letty ran to Pieter. There in the dust lay vain and foolish little Mittee with the smoking gun beside her. She said, 'Go and see to Pieter, it's only my nose that is bleeding. And there's poor Anna.'

Anna had turned her face to the earth. I said, 'Anna, sit up. It's no use lying there, what's done is done.' But the shamed head clung to the earth.

'Rebecca?' Fanie shouted as he ran on to the yard.

'Don't worry about that old fool now,' I screeched. 'She's safe behind some chairs. Carry Pieter up to the house.'

'And then run for Doctor Besil, we won't be safe while those two are loose,' said Mittee, hiccupping and sobbing as she staunched her nose.

Everybody went from the yard except a few of the women who walked around Anna like curious fowls inspecting something strange in their pen. From time to time I touched her shoulder but she lay like a dead thing and at last I went to Mittee who was sitting with Letty and Pieter. The little boy had revived and lay quiet but every time Letty looked at him, she moaned, 'He tried to hit them, he tried to hit them. He kept them from Petronella.'

'You should cry,' advised Mittee, 'I've cried and cried for an hour and it does you good.'

'You. Why couldn't it have been you who saw those things? My own child with that Shangaan pounding at his face, pounding at it with his fist, and that other one with Anna. Why should it have been me and not you who saw those things?'

'You hell, don't wish that on me,' said Mittee, losing all patience. I spoke quickly, hoping to avoid the quarrel that I could see coming. 'Nonnie, come and do something for Anna, she won't move or speak.'

Mittee jumped up. 'Of course. Sit here with Nonnie Letty while I go and help her, Selina.'

'So you'll leave me while you nurse the Kaffir girl,' said Letty sourly. 'Leave me almost dead with my sick child and put the Kaffir first.'

'Ag, hold your mouth,' snapped Mittee, 'I've got to go and do something for her in any case. There might be a baby and the hardest heart wouldn't expect her to have to go through that.'

'So old Auntie Gouws has taught you her tricks,' said Letty with such spite that Mittee looked back at her almost in fear.

It might have been Nagmaal. Waggons passed between the stone lions day after day, until every farmhouse but ours stood empty for Doctor Besil had advised the women to go into laager until their menfolk came back from the war. There would be terrible tales to tell them; a coloured girl chopped to pieces on the Vermeulens' farm, cattle hamstrung on the veld, a revolver stolen from Mrs Gouws.

The first to arrive were Mrs Gouws and Aletta Coester with her six children. The eight of them were in deepest mourning and even their Kaffir girl was in a dress of the strange rusty colour that comes from bad dyeing. Piled on their waggons was as much of their household goods as they could carry.

Aletta's children tumbled into the hallway and rushed out again, though their grandma exhorted them to remember that they were in mourning. Aletta brought in bundles of clothes and tins of food that had been thrown into the waggon in the haste of flight; the Kaffir girl directed the boy shrilly as he carried a tin trunk into the house. You never heard such a noise.

'The baboon is quite happy tied up under the tree,' she told her missis.

'You brought the baboon, too,' said Mittee and seated herself on the tin trunk beside Aletta as though there was not a chair in the house. She put her arm about Aletta. 'Now stop crying, there's nothing to cry about. Everything will come right.'

'If every man does his duty,' Mrs Gouws finished the quotation pessimistically. She picked up the flower-decked hat that Aletta had worn in Plessisburg the last Christmas we were there. 'Don't give in,' she said, fanning the pale, fat face. A rose, loosely stitched, flew off with a sad little plop! on to the floor. It added so much to the sorrowfulness of the scene as it lay there that I picked it up and tried to restore it to the garland. Mrs Gouws flapped the hat impatiently under my hands. 'Let alone, Selina. I think Aletta should have some brandy, Mittee, she's been very low since The News.' Then she saw Letty at the door. 'Hi, Letty. What can a person say? Such a terrible thing. You are lucky that Pieter wasn't killed.' Letty nodded and Mrs Gouws went on with great enjoyment, 'Mind you, I've been expecting it, I've been expecting it all along. It's a wonder we weren't all murdered or worse.'

'Nothing could be worse than being murdered,' said Mittee briskly. 'Come along, Auntie, the food must be ready by now.'

Mrs Gouws looked at Mittee with indignation but she went eagerly to the dining room for she was just at the age when food is the most important thing in life.

'It looks like a school,' said Mittee in a voice of forced cheerfulness that showed she did not mean to let her temper get the better of her, even though Pieter and Petronella were giggling in the way that children will as soon as their elders get into a flurry.

'The baboon is loose,' said Pieter into his bread-and-milk, and from the way Petronella laughed we knew that he had turned the thing loose.

'That's dangerous, nobody can handle him when he gets off his chain.' Mrs Gouws sighed but she took more meat and pap.

'Fanie will catch him when he comes up from the lands, he's good with animals,' I said.

'It would have been better if you had brought a dog, our dog was poisoned, I suppose you heard,' said Mittee.

'He doesn't get on with dogs . . .'

There was a great noise outside and when we looked through the window, we saw the baboon running this way and that as he cleared the yard of all living things but himself.

'Shut the window,' yelled Mrs Gouws. 'He'll be in here next, biting everything he sees.'

I felt my stomach crawl for with the windows closed, the smell of the fried meat mingled with the cloying smell of women's bodies. Through the window I could see the baboon sitting on the fence. He stared into the very heart of space as though he understood the full meaning of life. I thought that he would not notice if I pulled the window up to let in a little air while I cleared the table but no sooner had I moved the window up an inch than he sprang menacingly from the fence.

It was difficult to clear the table because I had to step lightly and move the dishes cautiously as Aletta had chosen this time to go to sleep, with her great arms spread across the table.

'Don't wake her, creature,' said Mrs Gouws. 'She has hardly slept since poor Coester was killed and I let her snatch a few minutes whenever the fit takes her.'

You wouldn't have thought it possible for anybody to sleep with the noise the eight children made as they played 'Here comes the waggon'. Pieter had moved the chairs so that they could form a circle. The child seemed to grow bolder since the Shangaan hit him, probably because his mother always referred to him as The Little Hero and did not check his boisterousness. Of course, Aletta had had two tots of brandy, that's why she could do it, I suppose.

In spite of all my care, Letty woke the sleeper by screaming, 'Look through the window. The Redneck has got the baboon.'

It was a heartening sight. Doctor Besil had the baboon by the end of his chain and was leading him along like a dog, talking to him and even patting him from time to time.

'Thanks, my Christ,' said Mrs Gouws, stroking Aletta's hair so that she should fall asleep again. 'Tell the creature who has got him to tie him under the tree, please, Letty.'

'The Redneck has got him,' Letty repeated.

'Who? Oh, Doctor Besil. From the way you spoke I expected to see Tommies at the very door.'

'Well, he is a Redneck,' said Letty.

The children caught the word from her and when Doctor Besil

came into the room, they joined hands round him singing Redneck, Redneck.

Mrs Gouws slapped her grandchildren but Pieter and Petronella ran to their mother as Mittee raised her hand to hit them. Letty held them to her closely while she looked at the missionary with burning eyes.

'Have they been caught yet?' she asked.

'The two who attacked here gave themselves up to me this morning. Their own people turned them out of the kraal. They are going to Plessisburg for trial.'

'Trial?' sneered Letty.

He saw that sneer reflected in every face in the room, even in Mittee's. He was no longer their friend but a hated missionary who put himself on the side of the Kaffirs.

'That was the condition I promised when they gave themselves up. I promised their chief that they would have a fair trial. And there is no need for alarm any more. Your men are not far off, their fires were seen this morning.'

'Outlander,' said Letty as though she spat.

A thousand men rode into the valley. As soon as they were sighted from the ridge, the women packed up their waggons, ready for the return to their homes. They had lived for months with the constant fear of the Kaffirs hanging over them but they prepared to go without elation for so many men coming to the valley must mean that defeat lay behind them.

The road was more closely thronged than the streets of Pretoria that morning as the horsemen rode up to the returning waggons. I stood at the fence, watching for Paul, and my nostrils expanded as I caught the smell of dust and leather, unwashed bodies and sweating horses. A woman cried out when she caught sight of the one form she was looking for in the crowd and she held her baby high, calling, 'There's pappie, throw him a kiss now.' The child was only two months old but it was expected to crow with delight when a rough, black-bearded face was thrust against it. Instead it howled in terror and the mother cried, anguished, 'Hi, he doesn't know you, the little angel doesn't know his own father.' An old mother held her son off at arm's length, shaking her head at the gauntness that showed beneath the ragged clothes. 'But so thin, my little son, you are so thin.' Tears squeezed from her eyes into the wrinkles on her cheeks. Her tall son, touched beyond endurance that she should worry so over him, bit his lip as though he were still the boy she pictured him. There were sweethearts embracing, unashamed by the chaffing of those who had time to watch, having no kin in the valley. 'Carefully over the stones there, Sarel . . .' 'Aits, don't forget to ask your mother . . .'

I saw Paul leap from his horse, running beside it as it cantered, in his eagerness to embrace Mittee. There was for him only the shadow of her smile, though she laid her head dutifully against his threadbare shirt while he kissed her hair and called her the lamb of his heart, his beloved. She stroked the untrimmed, ferocious beard and scarred cheeks but never once did she look into the savage eyes.

'Welcome home, General Du Plessis,' I screamed out so that he would notice me.

His eyes flickered towards me briefly and I knew that he did not even recognize me. He lifted Mittee to the level of his face by placing her on the back of one of the stone lions and laughed at her attempt to retain her dignity in such a position.

Did he ever know that he held no more than the shell of her body? Oh, the love I would have given him if he had taken me, a love as beautiful as Fanie's for Rebecca. When I washed his shirt the next day, I wept for the burning miles that had soaked it with sweat and for the winds that dried it on his body. But she wept because Doctor Besil had gone from the valley.

'Keep still until they have eaten,' Mittee admonished Letty. 'After all, they have ridden a long way and they will enjoy a meal at a table for once.'

I was pouring out the coffee when Letty came into the dining room. Paul, good-tempered after roasted fowl and new bread, rose to his feet and said kindly, 'I am sorry that you are not well, sister-in-law.'

She stood in the doorway, the candleshine in her hair, no longer pretty because of her lined face and writhing lips. Her voice was like a rotten limb cracking from a tree.

'Has she told you what the Kaffir did to Pieter? Has she told you that her lover is protecting him at the Mission House?'

Mittee put her hand on Paul's. 'Two Kaffirs attacked Anna one afternoon. One . . . one of them . . .'

'One of them raped Anna, the other was waiting and laughing while he hit Pieter's face. That is all,' said Letty. 'And the missionary stands there with his mouth full of teeth, a man would have hanged them. Mittee won't hear a word against him.'

'Silence. It has nothing to do with Mittee. I will see that justice is done.'

'Wait until your coffee cup is cold at least,' sneered Letty. 'They must have their meal in peace, Mittee said, because having no child of her own, she knows nothing of a mother's feeling.'

'She has gone mad with the shock,' said a man who did not know her.

'I will have proper respect while we go into the matter,' Paul shouted, quite at a loss to know how to deal with Letty's venomous tongue. 'Now tell me from the beginning what happened.'

He interrupted Letty's story with a loud hurrah when she told about Mittee and the muzzle-loader. All the men crowded round Mittee, yelling their admiration as they tried to shake her hand.

'But why the old muzzle-loader, why not the shotgun?' Paul asked when the clamour subsided.

Letty answered for her. 'I asked her that and it was because Fanie had stolen the cartridges for the shotgun.'

'Not stolen exactly, he gave us the pick of the game he shot,' said Mittee. 'He seemed to have no control over himself and shot off every last cartridge before he knew where he was.'

'We will first teach this coloured boy a thing or two,' said Paul and I thought that he was pleased to have something for which he could punish Fanie at last.

He went to the back door and shouted for Fanie, holding his rifle in his hands. 'I believe you like handling guns,' he said, and Fanie grinned, thinking Paul was about to lend him the gun to get a buck or two for the crowd of men on the farm. His hand went towards the gun eagerly. 'Oh God no, that's not what I mean,' said Paul, raising the rifle. He shot off a round of ammunition; into the dust, a fraction of an inch from Fanie's toes; up into the air, just grazing his hair; and on each side of him, so that Fanie did not know which direction the next bullet would take. At first he leaped and yelled as he tried to run away but when he realized why Paul was doing this, he stood still, with arms folded to show his pride. It was not Fanie whom the men cheered but Paul, for his exquisite marksmanship. That was the first time I had heard Letty laugh since the Kaffir attacked Pieter. When Paul's gun was empty, she clapped her hands, calling out, 'Fine shooting, brother-in-law.'

Paul was already on his way to the front stoep, shouting to the men who had bivouacked on the grass.

'Saddle up. There are two Kaffirs at the Mission waiting to go to Plessisburg for trial.' A yell went up for the English were already in Plessisburg. 'Who will come with me, brothers, to hold the trial tonight?'

We stood on the front stoep as they rode into the dusk, singing. Long after they had passed from sight, we heard the rhythm of their voices, 'Take your things and trek, Ferreira, take your things and trek . . .' When we saw the sky grow bright with flames, Letty raised her clasped hands in thanksgiving, as if the fire from the burning kraal could scorch away the memory of Pieter's suffering.

She went inside but I waited with Mittee on the stoep. She said over and over again, 'Will he remember that he owes Basil his life?' We grew old that night with waiting, but it is sweet for me to remember now how we stood with our arms about each other for comfort; like sisters.

In the starlight we saw a shadow pass between the stone lions. 'Fanie,' I whispered.

Mittee ran to him. 'What has happened to the missionary?'

'He would not give up the Kaffirs, nonnie,' Fanie answered, 'so they have burnt down the Mission House and they took him prisoner. Then they held a trial in the light of the flames. They have gelded and flogged the boys. Now they are burning the kraal and driving the Kaffirs away.' Fanie's voice was passionless but as I reached out my hand to him, I found that he was sweating.

'And Doctor Castledene? What have they done to Doctor Castledene?'

'I don't know,' said Fanie, sulkily.

I left Mittee on the stoep while I went with him to our room. 'What is it, Fanie?' I asked. He patted Rebecca to see that she was safe.

There was anger and pity in his voice. 'That lame girl. She fought them like a wildcat when they began to wreck the missionary's house. Du Plessis sjambokked her. It made me vomit to hear her scream and Gouws and one or two of the others put a stop to it. Doctor Besil had to watch it, though, and he was like a mad thing, with two men holding him. As soon as they let go of him, he went for Plessis. After that, they tied him up, and Plessis said, Now we're even, because I would have shot any other man who hit me, we're even at last, little doctor. You see, Selina, the Englishman hit him twice before he was grabbed again, you should see his eye, it's like this.' Fanie held his cupped hand over his right eye and laughed aloud. 'And then, Selina, I paid Du Plessis back for shooting at me this evening. I cut Doctor Besil loose. It was simple. I was standing in the dark near the horses and I led Du Plessis' horse away from the others. Gouws had been left on guard over the horses and the missionary; but you know what he is like, as soft as a mother with her baby. He said of his own free will, I'll get you some water, doctor, and with a drop of brandy, it will put new life into you. Then he stood talking for a while about the brandy he always kept with him so that he could keep up with the others on the march. It's a medicine, doctor, he was saying as he went off to the well to fill his tin mug. He wasn't out of sight before I had started to cut Doctor Besil loose. It wasn't three minutes before he was in Paul's saddle. He is on his way over the mountains to the English now, and Du Plessis will never know who did it.'

'He wins all the same, Fanie,' I said softly, 'for his dam is safe, after all, now that the Mission station is finished.'

'Yes. But there are only a few of us who were there who will ever look back on this night without shame.'

'Why did you not tell the nonnie that Doctor Besil is free? Let me go and tell her now.'

'She will know soon enough,' said Fanie. 'It's always best not to trust a white person too much, no matter who they are.'

CHAPTER XIII

Mittee was to have a new dress. Paul had brought for her a beautiful violet silk and while she sewed on it, Paul told Letty and her its story. When Plessisburg fell to the English he had halted his troop at Eberhardt's farm. That night, they attacked the town, taking the English by surprise. Paul had come upon a coloured boy making off with an armful of loot that he had taken during the heat of the fight. Paul kicked the boy off and on looking the stuff over, found two pieces of priceless silk. 'These, womenfolk, were sheets belonging to an English officer, some lily of the field,' he said. 'You wouldn't believe it but there are his initials and the hemstitching to prove it. I said to the boy, Where did you get these? And he said, My baas, from one of the beds. Then I shouted, Hurrah, a new dress for Mittee.' The English chased them out of the town the next day but he brought the sheets with him and though a person might call it stealing, what was a soldier doing with silk sheets when women had to wear calico?

Is it any wonder that Letty was half crazy with jealousy? There was vain Mittee with her husband beside her, sewing on violet silk while she sat unheeded except for a pitying glance when anybody thought of Frikkie in far Bermuda. I could see the spite working up in her when I brought in the coffee but Mittee hummed a little tune as she sent the shuttle flying.

They sat in the dining room, to catch the warmth of the afternoon sun for the August wind blew harsh and cold. Except for Letty's face, as sour as vinegar, the house seemed happy, brightened by the murmur of the children's voices as they played in the passage with knuckle bones which they pretended were teams of oxen.

'The children sound as peaceful as doves' cooing,' said Mittee, taking up her coffee cup as she leaned back from the machine.

'And not one of yours there in spite of being married ten years,' flashed Letty. 'Paul should be told how he is being fooled.'

She ran from the room but Mittee's hand began to tremble, rattling the cup in its saucer.

'What does she mean this time?' Paul asked with his eyes on those shaking hands.

Letty found a ready listener in Eberhardt, that man whom all women liked but none loved well enough to marry; who in spite of the years of rough living had still the tame, sleek look of a cat; whose tongue was spiced with witty scandal. He rode in with dispatches to Paul and stayed a few days at the farmhouse, basking in the comfort of meals served from a table, the gloss of white sheets and the light voices of the women. He had news of everybody, from Andrina and Leon who were flirting with the English on a Committee investigating the concentration camps; to poor old Auntie Lena who had waved the Flag in all the bravery of its four colours when the English paraded in Plessisburg Square. When she was marched before the English colonel, she sang the Anthem in such a shivering old voice that she was given hot soup and told to go home. He knew how Jacob Coester had died, with his chest shot away, poor boy, on the same day that Frikkie was taken prisoner. We thrilled to the story of Frikkie's capture for he was no hands-upper. When Eberhardt told the story, you could see old Frikkie there, still smiling though the cannons lay smashed to pieces and the English were rushing across the veld towards him. He had a blood-stained rag tied about his head to staunch a bullet graze and his face was blackened by smoke when he stood up with his arms hanging at his sides, too much of a Du Plessis to put up his hands, said Eberhardt with the shadow of a sneer.

Doctor Besil had joined the English in Plessisburg. He had reported the burning of the Mission House and kraal not only to the English colonel but to the magistrate and amongst Eberhardt's papers was a letter smuggled from the magistrate. Paul tore the letter to shreds.

'What does he know of war, sitting there in Plessisburg?' he shouted angrily. 'If that Englishman sets foot in this valley, I'll shoot him in cold blood.'

Mittee cried out before she could stop herself, 'Remember you owe him your life, Paul.'

'It's not the first time you've reminded me of it, wife, though I've paid that debt.'

'Mittee is right and apart from that, you have no right to shoot a prisoner no matter what he has done.' Eberhardt could always flick Paul's temper which was so close to the surface that a chance word could set it going. His horse was standing ready saddled, for he was riding with a message to Aletta from her mother but he lingered on the stoep talking, regardless of the poor thing's whinnies and stamping.

'You should be ashamed to stand up for the English missionary,' said Letty, turning her bitter face to him. 'Would the magistrate have written like that if it was Mittee's son who had been touched, if she had a son?' Paul put out a hand to stop her and then gestured furiously to me to get off the stoep for there was no stopping that voice.

I went into the passage, closing the door behind me, but I could still hear her. Now at last she spoke of that terrible afternoon, not dryly as she had spoken before, giving the facts in a few sentences; but in every intimate detail, even to the help that Mittee had given Anna.

'And now you know why your house is childless, Paul. She is full of evil knowledge.'

She began to cry and I heard Eberhardt soothing her with broken words. The door opened and Paul came into the passage, striding past me as though he did not care whether I listened at keyholes. So must his face have looked when he killed Herry and Jansie.

Mittee came after him, closing the door with a sharp click. Her face was white for she knew that lies would not help her now but she was as calm as on the day she went for the Kaffirs with the muzzle-loader.

The children were playing on the yard. I had asked them to watch Rebecca for me while I did my work and they had built a kraal of thorn bushes around her. The old thing was scratching herself to pieces on the thorns as she tried to push a way out but I left her, thinking the children would be better there than in the house. Surely he would not be angry with Mittee for long.

I heard him shouting at Eberhardt, 'Get along on your own business,' and then I saw Eberhardt ride unwillingly down the road, loath to miss the rest of the quarrel. I thought, I wouldn't be surprised if he is not after Aletta Coester now that she is a widow with a farm of her own.

The house was quiet and I went timidly to the dining-room door. Only Letty was there.

'He's going to thrash her with a sjambok,' she gloated, 'and it's no use trying to help, Selina, he has locked the door. There. Listen. He said, Where did you learn these tricks, wife? But she did not answer. I said, From Mrs Gouws, of course, and I told him about that girl Andrina. Then in that voice of honey she said, I will have no more children by you because of Siegfried. I laughed at that. Don't be taken in, I said, she tried her tricks with Siegfried and failed . . .'

I snatched the carving knife from the drawer and held the point of it to the hollow of her throat. The ecstasy died from her face. At the sound of every blow and scream I let her feel the threatening sharpness of the knife, until the sweat poured from her face and her eyes rolled up to show the whites.

It was over. When the door opened, I stepped over Letty's fainting body to face him. The knife fell from my hands and I shrank away from him for it was not into Paul's face that I was looking.

'Oh God, it's Jansie,' I screamed.

He saw neither Letty nor me as he walked heavily from the house, the sjambok still in his hand. I went to Mittee's room to help her through her agony and shame.

An English force was marching on the valley and Paul rode out with his men to cut them off. We were not afraid of the Kaffirs for they were submissive after the lesson they had been taught and, besides, a body of men had been left to guard the pass. Our household felt no relief at this lifting of the tension for Mittee would not come out of her room while Letty remained under the same roof.

'You must get out of the house,' I told Letty. 'My nonnie doesn't want you in her house.'

All she did was box my ears, so I made a plan to drive her out. I gave Fanie an empty preserving bottle and asked him to put a live puff-adder into it.

'You are clever at catching wild things,' I said, 'and don't forget to screw the lid down tight, because I don't want the thing jumping out at me.'

'What's it for?' he asked suspiciously.

'It's a joke I'm going to play on Letty. She deserves a fright after what she did to the little nonnie.'

Fanie could appreciate a practical joke but he looked at the bottle with big blue eyes. 'Why not give her lizards' eggs instead of pills? It made even Gouws wild enough to kill when Frikkie did that to him.'

'I want to frighten her.'

Letty took her evening meal alone as the children were early in bed and when she saw the bottle on the table, she stared unbelievingly into the snake's eyes. I knelt beside her and whispered, 'Shall I take the lid off, nonna?'

She ran from the table without a word and I knew that she was too sick to scream. I hid the bottle in the spare bedroom and when she came back to the dining room with the yard boy, I was standing at the table, polishing a fork. She ate nothing more that night and when she went to her bedroom she carried a little footstool with her, from which she could examine the floor before she stepped on it.

The next morning I put the bottle on the tray when I took the coffee to the bedrooms. I left it standing on the table beside the steaming cup and she awoke to look straight at it. She ran screaming to Mittee's door, beating on the wood with her fists. 'Come out, Mittee, this devil is chasing me with a puff-adder in a bottle.' There was no answer from Mittee.

She could never be certain when she would see it. I put it into the drawer where she kept her underclothes and watched through the window as she packed her clean things away. She knew what she was touching as soon as she put her hand on the smooth surface and I felt almost sorry for her standing there with her mouth open in soundless terror. By the time she had got the Kaffir girl to come and help her, I had already removed the bottle and she had no idea where I had put it.

As the days passed and still she did not go, Fanie suggested silly things like putting a porcupine in her bed or dressing up like ghosts but I kept at her with the snake and on the fifth day she packed up her things. She went to Mrs Gouws for refuge and as soon as she was out of the house, Mittee came out of her bedroom.

'I am going away, Selina.'

'Where will you go, little nonnie?'

'To Plessisburg. The magistrate will help me to get a separation from Paul. It is finished between us now.'

'Men often beat the women they love, nonnie. He was disappointed in you.'

'I am going to his father with the whole story. Fanie can take me over the mountains and I will be in Plessisburg before Paul knows I have left the valley.'

'Fanie would never risk it.'

'Selina.' She put her hand over mine. 'It is not only because he sjambokked me. He said, You bear me another deformed child and I'll smother it as I smothered that other one.'

'No, nonnie.'

She put her head into her arms. 'He said that. You see why I must go, Selina. If I stay here and live with him and have his children, then the Mittee who sits here today will be as dead as though he had murdered her.'

'Yes, you must go, my nonnie. But wait until you can go safely over the plain, the mountains are too dangerous. Doctor Besil got through but that is a strong man, travelling on horse-back. A waggon could never do it.'

'It has been done. If you can persuade Fanie to take me, I will be safer than here.'

When I spoke to Fanie, he laughed. 'The little nonnie must think I am tired of the life. If the mountains did not get us, there would be Plessis riding after us and with what must I shoot back at him, the old muzzle-loader? Tell her to put such a mad plan from her head.'

'I am so sorry for her, Fanie, and I would go with her for, truly, I have grown to hate this valley.'

'I will take you away, then, but only when we can travel in safety, my little wife.'

We spoke no more of going over the mountains until Doctor Besil came to the valley again.

It was three months since the men had ridden into the valley and I went to the top of the ridge to watch them for there had been talk that the English were encamped along the Wolk River. Mittee had sent me so that she could be warned of Paul's coming. I took Rebecca with me to tire her out because she was up to her tricks again, wandering away in the middle of the night when she was supposed to be sound asleep. It was a hot afternoon and I sat down to breathe myself under the shade of a thorn tree. Not so Rebecca. She must find a place of her own. She stumbled from bush to bush but none suited her. She chose at last to hide herself behind an outcrop of rocks. I moved to where I could watch her for there were a great number of snakes about that year and Heaven knows what Fanie would have done to me if I had let her get bitten. Thereupon she crawled to the other side of the rocks, out of my sight. Ag what, I thought, let the old thing go where she likes, I don't care.

I leaned against the trunk of the tree, listening to the beat, beat of the veld. The mealies had cobbed and the chickens had grown big; Fanie had planted again. A few riders came into the valley from time to time, men who were too sick to go on fighting. They told stories of the desolation round Plessisburg. Farmhouses had been burnt to the ground and hundreds of women and children were living in tents. Defeat was driving the burghers further and further north.

. . . Paul's tragic face rose before me. He had been back to the valley only once since he had thrashed Mittee. When she saw him turn in past the stone lions, she ran to her room and locked the door on him.

He knelt beside the door, entreating her. 'Little heart, speak to me. Hi, Mit, let me see your face. My heart is full . . .'

Her silence terrified him and he threw himself against the door until it creaked and shuddered. She spoke then.

'If you come in here, I will blow myself to pieces with this old gun. I have it ready here.'

He laughed but he stepped back into the passage. 'Put on your new silk dress and come and sit with me. I will court you over again, my love.'

'I have burnt the silk dress.'

That made him angry. 'I give you one hour to open the door and then I will break it down.'

He waited for her to answer but she did not speak again.

'Your food is ready, basie,' I whispered when he came into the dining room.

The room was darkening. Mittee had eaten her meal early so that the girl could wash up in the daylight but I had to light one of the precious candles now. He did not touch the food I put before him.

'Where is the brandy?'

I pointed to the sideboard cupboard. 'The nonnie has the key.'

He smashed the door in with the butt of his rifle. I was afraid when he began to drink the brandy for his face became brutally seamed. It was for my little nonnie's sake that I took off my clothes and danced before him. Then I knew what Anna had suffered . . .

The rhythm of the veld quickened. A horseman leaped against the skyline, followed by others. They were Boers, as stark in build as the bitter, wind-twisted thorns that clung to the slopes of the ridge. They rode towards me and then turned down, disappearing with the stealth of wild game. A second group of horsemen topped the rise a few minutes later. I sprang up, as tense as though I were young again, watching the sports on Dingaan's Day. These were English, this was the war.

Clearly a word of command came across the still air, an English word, clipped off at the end. 'Halt!' The men reined in, suspicious, but perfect targets for those who waited. Bullets spat out towards them. Suddenly the foremost twisted in his saddle. Then another man fell, dropping from his saddle slowly as though he was tired. The echoes smashed like breaking glass against the rocks as the hail of bullets grew stronger. The Boers rode out into full view now but the English dropped behind the ridge. I saw a young Boer lad roll down the slope but old Gouws fell behind the others and doubled him.

The ridge was bare now except for the riderless horses and the fallen men. One Englishman was not dead for presently I saw him raise himself and crawl across the veld towards his horse. So painful was his advance that I felt tears spring to my eyes. I would have gone to help him but I was afraid that soon the fighters would come tearing over the ridge. He reached the horse but he had to try twice before he got into the saddle. His hat fell from his head and in that instant I knew him. It was Doctor Besil. I called out to him but he rode away without looking back. Soon he, too, had disappeared from my sight.

It was nearly sunset then. Clouds were rolling in from the east, low and black, but the west was ablaze so that while the veld was in shadow, the mountains stood as bright as at noonday. I went round the rock to get Rebecca and go home.

The old devil was gone. I hunted behind rocks and bushes but she was nowhere to be found. Rain began to fall, a few great drops, shaken from the overheavy clouds. I hurried through the grass and over treacherous rocks, calling her name, uselessly, for I knew she could not answer me.

I passed the dead Englishman and paused to cover his face with his hat or his staring eyes would have haunted me to the grave. Doctor Besil's hat was lying on the grass nearby and I picked it up so that I could show Mittee what her English lover had come to, and perhaps she would be cured of him.

I walked on and at last I thought I saw Rebecca. I ran cursing to drag her home. It was not Rebecca. Doctor Besil lay there on his back in the blood-flecked grass. The last light from the kopjes touched the sun-burned face, showing each line that hours in the saddle had wrought on his delicate English skin, the dust that caked his bright hair and the blood that had dried with the sweat in a streak across his forehead. He must have dismounted so that he could staunch his wound for his saddle bag was open and half his things were lying on the veld. A pad was pressed into the wound on his shoulder from which the blood oozed sickeningly. He will die, I thought. I was frightened for it was growing dark and here was I alone on the veld, far from help.

Something horrible and black came out of the bushes near-by. I murmured, It's Satan come after me, and then I saw that it was Rebecca.

Fanie, mounted on a donkey, had come looking for us. I ran towards him, calling Doctor Besil's name.

'He is lying wounded on the ridge there.'

'Almighty, what will happen next? The world is going mad . . .'

'He is bleeding terribly, I think he will die, Fanie.'

Fanie sprang from the donkey, and setting Rebecca upon it, urged it up the side of the ridge. 'We had better take him to Mrs Gouws to nurse. He will be safer there than in the house with the nonnie; Paul is not to be trusted,' I gasped as I scrambled after him.

The rain had started in earnest before we reached Doctor Besil. In the half-light, Fanie bent over him, probing his wound.

'It is nothing, only a flesh wound,' said Fanie. 'He is weak from loss of blood, that is all.'

He loaded Doctor Besil on to one of the horses and we set off dispiritedly for the Gouws' farm. The rain seemed to shrink Rebecca as though she was made of wool and she sank lower and lower on the donkey's back until she was only a blob in the gathering darkness. We crossed the road but that was as far as we could go through the blinding rain. Fanie halted at the shack where the coloured girl had been murdered by the Kaffirs.

'We'll have to take shelter here,' he shouted.

'Never, Almighty, never.'

'It's the only thing.'

He was as uneasy as I was but there was no hope of crossing the veld now. He left me to bring Rebecca in while he dragged Doctor Besil to shelter. I entered into a desperate struggle with Rebecca for she would not let go of the donkey's mane. The donkey turned round and round as I tried to free her hands. I would get one loose undoing the fingers separately, only to find the other wound into the mane.

'Let go, you stupid old thing,' I hissed with the rain. 'You lightning, thunder . . .'

I gave her a sudden push and she squeaked as she fell to the ground. The donkey threw up his heels and sprinted into the darkness.

Fanie had started a little fire from an old box and he added to it with pieces of wet wood that smoked rather than burnt so that the tears streamed from our eyes. We took off Doctor Besil's coat and tied up his wound roughly with a piece of his shirt. While we were doing this, he opened his eyes.

In spite of his bewilderment and pain, he made one of his gentle, quaint jokes. 'Is Rebecca safe under our eyes?'

Fanie laughed, delighted at this mark of remembrance. 'She's there in the corner but for how long nobody can say.'

'You should be ashamed of yourself coming to our valley in that uniform,' I said sharply.

He answered me with sadness. 'Perhaps in a way I am, Selina. A long time ago I spoke to you of good and evil, on a hill outside Pretoria. Do you remember?'

'I have never forgotten it.'

'Well, you were right, though I was so sure then. They are shadows, good and evil . . .'

He seemed to sleep. Fanie fell asleep, too tired to worry about the ghost of the murdered girl, but she joggled at my elbow all night and peeped at me from the shrouded corners. My life passed before me over and over again, as though I were about to die. Now Mittee and I were children, running to the forbidden river, now we were young girls, trying hard with the crochet work. There the two young women stood, with the silver light of childhood still shining on them as they turned their faces to the terrible years.

I pressed my hands against my breasts, my throat, my thighs. It was the body of a stranger that I touched. Surely Selina had died and this husk that cowered here was her ghost. The awesomeness of this thought made me wake Fanie so that I could draw some comfort from his beautiful, familiar face. But that was strange, too, a part of the world of ghosts to which I belonged. I covered my head with my damp apron so that I might not look upon the forbidden faces of the dead that walk.

'Go to sleep, little night-ape,' said Fanie indulgently. He himself was asleep as he turned round.

'Why are you crying?' Doctor Besil's voice was tender. 'You are a sad little thing, Selina. I used to notice those sad eyes in church. The other coloured people are happy, like Fanie here, but not you.'

I crept closer to him. 'You wonder why Selina is sad. When I was young I used to laugh so loudly that Mittee would shake me to quieten me down; I would stand on a kopje and reach my hands to the sky or lay my heart against the veld for I saw God in all the world about me.

'But now I am afraid of the ghosts. There are Herry and Jansie and the little child Siegfried. He murdered them all. Paul murdered them all. I lied for him in court because I loved him. God has taken vengeance on me and he is like Jansie now, as ugly and as brutal.'

'You are saying terrible things, Selina.'

'They are true. Mittee would not let him near her and I gave myself to him but it was as if Jansie had hold of me. It is not only the pockmarks and the sunburn, there is the same expression, ever since he sjambokked Mittee.'

'Mittee!' Strength surged into him and he raised himself on his elbow.

'She knows only half his wickedness,' I said bitterly, 'and you must not tell her that I have loved him because she trusts me like her own sister.'

'Why hasn't she left him?'

'How? She speaks of going over the mountains to the magistrate in Plessisburg but that is impossible. She is as delicate as a china doll . . .'

'We must find a way of getting her out of the valley.' He lay back again, waxen-faced after the effort of sitting up. 'I know the way over the mountains.'

'That is impossible. And it is impossible for her to go through the pass, there are men guarding it day and night.'

'I know. I led the company over the ridge but they spotted us. It may be months before we take the valley and yet it may be only a matter of days.'

'I am very frightened when he is home, Doctor Besil. I think he goes mad when he can't get his own way.'

'We must make a plan, as you people say.'

'How can we make a plan?' I said, but I was comforted and fell asleep at last.

In the half-light of the dawn, I stood outside the shack, uneasily looking down at that proud house in the valley. Should I go to Mittee and whisper, Doctor Besil is in the shack on the ridge? Surely it would be better for her and for all of us if we took him straight to Mrs Gouws.

Fanie came up behind me so quietly that I jumped. He had Doctor Besil's rifle and he ran his hand down the barrel and over the stock as though he was caressing a woman's body.

'I am strong as Plessis now, with this in my hands,' he said, dropping on one knee as he took aim.

'Hi, put the thing down, it's not a toy. Time you took the missionary to the old lady for nursing. His wound will get stiff.'

'That won't do.' He played longingly with the rifle. 'The quickest is to run across to our farm and tell the nonna. I've been thinking about it. She can bring the cart up here whereas the Gouwses only have waggons and the oxen would have to be rounded up. You run to the farm and I'll stand on guard with this fancy English rifle.'

'Perhaps you would like to go over the mountains to Plessisburg with it.'

'What nonsense are you talking now? Off you go to the farm and bring us back some breakfast.'

'We're not on a holiday,' I grumbled, but it was useless arguing with him because he was like a child with the rifle in his hands.

'Do as I tell you, Selina, I'm the baas when I hold this thing up so.' He pointed the rifle at me, squinting down the sights.

'Ag, you're as mad as your mother.'

There was nobody but me astir on the veld. The sun was not out yet and the grass hung heavily with the rain, touching my skirt with a cold kiss as I made my way uncertainly to the road. When I looked back I could see my path cut cleanly down the side of the ridge where I had brushed the water from the grass. The shack was hidden by trees but I could see Fanie, still posturing with the rifle; and Rebecca, who shambled about near him. I saw him put down the rifle suddenly and snatch something from her hands, just as an anxious mother snatches a pebble from her toddler. Well I knew Rebecca. She was as likely to put a piece of cowdung or a stone into her mouth as a piece of bread, yet Fanie always gave her the choicest of the food. No use telling him it was wasted.

I walked slowly along the road for I still had not made up my mind about what was the best thing to do; yet in my heart I knew

Mittee would never forgive me if I did not give her the chance of an hour alone with him. When it was too late to turn back, I began to run and soon I saw the stone lions glistening in their wet coats.

Anna was lighting the fire and she looked from the grate with sleep-sodden eyes.

'You'll get it. Staying out all night.'

'Hold your mouth.'

The night had imprisoned a musty smell in the house but in Mittee's room the curtains swept out grandly in the clean wind that blew through the open window. She lay curled under the blankets, her hands still lax with sleep.

I bent over her. 'Nonnie, there is something I have to tell you.'

She was not in a good humour at being so suddenly awakened. 'What the hell are you doing here, Selina? It's almost night still.'

'Doctor Besil is in the haunted shack. He was wounded yesterday; I saw the whole thing. And Paul is nearby, he will be here soon.'

'Basil.' She sprang out of bed as though I had put a pin into her. 'Almighty, I might have known you would have something terrible to say. And you say Paul is close; oh, the misery. Is he badly hurt, Selina?'

'Fanie says no. But he's feverish and tired. The bullet seems just to have grazed his shoulder and he lost a lot of blood. I think it is best to take him to Mrs Gouws.'

'Yes. He must not come here. Paul will not remember how he nursed him alone on the veld and stood by us when there were no men in the valley.'

'He is a khaki now, Mittee.'

'I don't care. To me he is still Basil. I will go and see him now before you take him on to Mrs Gouws.'

She had begun to dress and now she turned her back to me so that I could hook her up. She did not even glance in the mirror, winding her plaits carelessly round her head. They were ruffled with sleep and her face was so pallid that she looked ill.

I felt a sudden pity not only for her but for Doctor Besil. 'Don't let him see you looking like that, Mittee. Let me brush your hair for you and then put on some of the pink powder. The sickest man likes to see a pretty face and you look like a ghost. Hi, to think the day has come when I encourage you to vanity.'

'There is no time for vanity now,' she said, but she let me take the pins from her hair and brush it. I did it lovingly, feeling its voluptuous softness without envy. I coiled the hair low on her neck as though she was going to a ball, while she dabbed the powder on her cheeks.

Anna watched us with inquisitive eyes as we packed food into a basket. 'A picnic in the rain and so early in the morning. I've never heard of such a thing, nonnie.'

Mittee snapped at her, 'Don't interfere with me, creature.'

'Doesn't the nonnie want a cup of coffee?' she asked with sly humility.

'God, I'll have a cup,' I said. 'I'm dead for want of something to eat and drink.'

'The stomach is not so important, after all,' Mittee chided.

She hurried away while I was snatching a few mouthfuls of scalding coffee. 'What's the matter?' Anna asked. 'I've worked for her for years but I've never known her go off like this without a bite . . .'

I put down the coffee and ran after Mittee, to save myself from answering. Mittee was waiting for me at the fence and when she saw Anna's curious eyes fixed on us, she shook her fist, whereupon the Kaffir girl scuttled inside like a cat running from water. We had hidden bandages and medicines from her underneath our petticoats and we put them into the basket. Mittee bent down to pass through the fence while I held up the top strand of wire. Her skirt got caught on a barb and she swore as we worked it loose.

'How does he look, Selina?' she asked as she held up the wire for me.

'The same, only his face is burned.' Now I was caught on the wire. Mittee swore again. 'Stop it, nonnie. Now I'm loose. The skin is coming off his face in layers. He is a Redneck if I ever saw one.'

'A person can't help their skin. The dear God, is this shack much further, I can't walk like you, I never could. I'm getting a blister on my heel. And feel that sun. It's burning through the clouds. What a fool I was not to wear my bonnet and mittens.'

I could not help being spiteful about her treasured complexion. 'It will burn you all right. You'll finish up as black as me. Now this is where we cross the road.'

'My God, look at that,' Mittee exclaimed.

Fanie was riding down the road on his donkey, trailing behind him a dead python. He had shot the snake through the head and he had tied plaited grass to the tail so that he could drag it. He got down from the donkey and looked guiltily from the snake to Mittee.

'What have you been doing, Fanie?'

'I was trying out the rifle, nonnie. And I saw this going after that old dog of the Vermeulens'. I had to save the dog, they think a lot of it.' He waggled the snake in the dust.

'Ag, keep away with that gruesome thing.'

Fanie was proud of the python. 'Hi, nonnie, I'll make you a pretty belt out of this if you give me a clasp for it.'

I tried to kick him but he got out of my way without any effort. 'Put that gun away, you'll get us all into trouble, see if you don't. What if somebody had come along the road and seen you?'

'Come along, come along, I'm being burnt to a cinder,' said Mittee.

Fanie hung the python over a tree and followed us to the shack. Mittee was limping now but she hurried to the doorway and stood there without speaking as she sought out Doctor Besil's shining hair through the dimness of the shadowy little room.

He said in English, 'You shouldn't have come here, Mittee.'

'I could not stay away. We are going to have you moved to the Gouws' farm. She will look after you well. I would take you into my house but there is my husband to think of.'

She had not gone into the shack and thinking she was squeamish I pushed past her with the basket.

'Go outside for a few minutes, Selina,' she said and came slowly into the room. I saw her stretch out her hands to him and heard the throb in her voice when she spoke. 'Oh, have they hurt you, Basil?'

I thought with bitterness, If she had loved Paul like this, how different our lives would have been, we would not then be standing by this desolate shack, hiding an accursed khaki. She whispered to him while she dressed his wound and gave him food and coffee, never thinking of the others who had spent the night there with him.

Rebecca lay in the wet grass, her body writhing as though she sought relief from the darkness that swamped her mind, but no glimmering of consciousness made her writhe, I knew. She was hungry. I looked about for Fanie and saw that he had returned to his damned python which he was skinning gleefully. Perversely, I was angry with him because he was taking no notice of his mother.

The sun was fighting with the clouds in a sultry battle that brought the sweat from my pores. In all the world there was nobody who thought of Selina, shrivelled with heat and aching with hunger.

I went into the shack. Mittee did not stir from Doctor Besil's side. Mittee, who changed her dress if the slightest smear stained it, was half lying on the dirt floor, with her face against Doctor Besil's and her hands holding him close to her.

'I want some food. And the old one is dead with hunger.'

'Take a little from the basket. You can eat your fill at home,' said Mittee. 'And call Fanie. We must make a plan. Say absolutely nothing until we have made up our minds what we are going to do.'

*

Gouws had come back with a small party to bury the dead and to bring the wounded lad to his wife for nursing, while the main body of burghers went in pursuit of the English. He was still scratching his head over Doctor Besil's disappearance when he came to see Mittee that afternoon.

'It was Castledene who got away,' he told Mittee. 'And if I have to search every hut in this valley I will find him. The funny thing is, my wife said to me, Go and have a talk with Mittee about it.'

The room was so still that the brushing of leaves against a window-pane could be heard separately from the clock.

'How do you know it was Castledene, Uncle?'

'I was right on top of him when he fell, I couldn't mistake him. I thought he was killed but when I come up with the Kaffirs to dig the graves, there is only one Englishman there, with his face covered by his hat. The other one is gone, horse, rifle, everything. Paul will be furious when he knows who it is that got away.'

'He was our friend,' said Mittee softly.

'Mittee, we trusted him here but he has betrayed us. Letty said straight out that you would shield him. Ag, my little daughter, there are no two ways in war, you must hate the very name of your enemy.'

'Yes, Uncle.'

'I knew you would see it like that. You don't know where he is, do you?'

'No, Uncle.'

'Remember, he is your enemy.'

Gouws' eyes kindled but you could not imagine any Englishman flinching before that good old face. I thought of the time he had set out to shoot Frikkie with a sawn-off shotgun and had come home with a sucking pig; gratefully, for under him there would be no burning of kraals and if Doctor Besil fell into his hands, he might meet with a few surly looks but he would have the best of food and nursing in the Gouws' home. I said as much to Mittee when he was gone, perhaps a little distrustful of her but unwilling to show it.

'And when Paul comes home?' she answered. 'The English are closer than we think and one man killed in the battle for the valley will make little difference. Basil is willing to guide us across the mountains so that I should not have to face Paul again. But we will need Fanie to handle the waggon. Tell him to come here, Selina, we must go at once, before Paul comes back.'

Fanie was frightened when she told him that he must pick out the strongest oxen to take her to Plessisburg by way of the mountains. 'I would rather go over the plain and face the soldiers, nonnie,' he said. 'You would never get a waggon over those mountains.'

'It has been done. The Vermeulens came that way during the drought and hardly lost a beast.'

'If Baas Plessis catches us, he will kill us all.'

'He will be in the valley very soon, Fanie. We must go tonight or not at all. The General will have no time to go after us with the English so close.'

I said sourly, 'Besides, Fanie, there is the rifle and a gun makes one man as good as the other.'

Fanie's eyes grew bright and as though he had spoken aloud I knew that he pictured himself firing off a few shots at game now and then, rather than shooting it out with Paul.

Still he shook his head. 'No, nonnie, I will not do it.'

'There is this,' said Mittee. She pulled the dress from her shoulder and her face flushed brilliantly as Fanie looked at the mark of the sjambok on her white skin.

'Hi, nonnie.' His eyes filled with tears and he looked down at his clasped hands to hide such weakness. 'Nonnie, before we decide, I must speak to Doctor Besil. Two heads are better than one, even if they are sheep's heads. It will be safe to go to the shack as soon as it is dark for the old baas with the Bible in his hand wouldn't go there at night.'

'You can speak to him but you will find that he agrees. I showed him that mark and it was he who suggested my going at once. Get the oxen together first. We will start at ten o'clock tonight and be in the mountains before morning, with God's help.'

I raised my voice to a bargaining tone. 'There are our cattle, nonnie, two cows and three heifers . . .'

'I will give you a price for them,' said Mittee, impatiently.

'Thirty-five pounds,' I said boldly.

I nearly fainted with surprise when she paid without an argument for I was all ready for one. I sewed the money in a pocket in my drawers without letting Fanie see it for he is a spendthrift.

CHAPTER XIV

We travelled all night beneath crackling stars, glad to be on the move again after the tense secrecy of our preparations, for we could not load the waggon until the last Kaffir was asleep. We took only mealie-meal and biltong and coffee and sugar with us. Mittee, who had been so vain, packed three print dresses though she spared a sigh over the wardrobe where the silks hung. Everything was in the waggon when we heard the dainty tread of the unshod donkey carrying Doctor Besil, who sat awkwardly because of his long legs. Fanie ran beside him, with the rifle in the crook of his arm.

They came up to us like shadows. 'We've turned the horse loose and buried the saddle,' said Fanie.

He took playful aim at one of the stone lions and I said angrily, 'Stop playing the fool and get the oxen inspanned.'

I had not let go of Rebecca's arm all evening and I was glad enough to push her into the waggon beside Doctor Besil, while Fanie went for the oxen. While we waited I noticed by the light of the lantern that the rings were missing from Mittee's finger. With pity and remorse I thought of Paul when he tore the envelope open and found them with her letter. Fanie was chuckling while I helped him to inspan. It seemed that Anna had come to the doorway of her room as Fanie passed and not recognizing him in the darkness, had whimpered, 'The dead are walking tonight' and then locked her door.

We were over the first ridge with the fragile dawn behind us. Only Fanie had spoken during the night, hissing the oxen's names as he walked beside them, but the rest of us were silent to make our passing more secret. I did not sleep in spite of the soothing roll of the waggon for I felt that disaster was close to us. Paul might even now be riding into the valley, we might go only a few more miles and then his voice would spring through the darkness at us to halt our flight. In my fevered mind he grew to the stature of a mountain, invincible as God.

The first halt beyond the ridge found me shaking and speechless, far from the world of reality. Mittee brought out the bottle of Essence of Life and the very sight of this old stand-by was like a caress to my aching nerves. When the fire was lit and the oxen grazed peacefully along the grassy slopes, the strain went from my muscles and I sniffed the cooking mealie-meal hungrily.

'Wonderful stuff that Essence of Life. See what it has done for Selina already,' she said.

Doctor Besil smiled. 'You are a better doctor than I am, Mittee.'

They spoke with an everyday cheerfulness as though we had not to traverse those formidable crags whose shadow fell upon us while we ate our food.

Fanie rested the oxen for little more than an hour before we went on again. The going was fairly easy and the weather was cool so that the oxen, fresh from pasture, made good speed. That afternoon, before we camped, Fanie swept his hand to the north to show us the dim line of the great forests where the farmers went to hunt elephant.

They are separated from the mountains by a wide basin of dense thorn, where trees lock their branches with each other to make a barrier to the hunting grounds. Fanie had been with Frikkie far beyond the range of mountains that shaded the horizon, to a broad lake, fringed by marshes. Here the flamingos come, as bright as the sunset; the wild duck in their thousands and the wild geese. Man, he said, how wonderful it would be to live there and hunt with a rifle and call no man Baas.

Before that year was out, he had his wish. He joined up with some Kaffir hunters and went to the lake while I lived with the women in their kraal on top of the mountain. He was gone for many months and often I thought sadly, He has forgotten Selina, he will go further north with his rifle, never to return and I will always be alone. But when the women went to meet the returning men, Fanie was there with a pile of skins which he made into a fine kaross for me.

But the day I first looked towards the elephant country, I said snappishly, 'Wish that we were all safe in Plessisburg if you must wish for anything.'

We travelled comfortably for two days. Sometimes we glimpsed herds of galloping zebra and wildebeest as they broke through on to the open ground at the foot of the mountains, figures as tiny as toys pulled by strings; and each evening we drew closer to the roaring of the lions that had their lying places amongst the rocks below us. Though they remained far from us, confusion would come upon the oxen when they roared at sunset and none of us felt safe until the fires were lit and the oxen kraaled.

We were quiet that second night while we waited for the porridge to cook. The thickening dusk had brought a deep silence to the mountain, broken only by the everlasting song of the insects. The stillness lasted while the light held and we were at peace. I took no thought of yesterday nor of tomorrow, except that now and then there floated from memory the vision of the stinkwood table in the dining room, rich in the candlelight, with a smooth, thick damask cloth waiting to be spread over it for the evening meal.

As the darkness grew deeper, the mountain vibrated to the sounds of unseen animals. Night-apes screamed, there was a shower of stones from the krantz above. Something blundered through the bushes beyond our enclosure, causing us to move closer to the fire.

'What is it?' Mittee whispered.

'Ag, it might not even be a wild thing, nonnie,' said Fanie. 'Perhaps only some goats that have wandered away from a kraal.'

To allay our unease, Doctor Besil said, 'Bring out your accordion, Fanie, it's almost as good a medicine as the Essence of Life.'

We sang to the familiar tones, throwing our voices in a challenge to the throbbing night. Rebecca, as though the music had been a signal, moved sideways to the rough fence, fossicking for an opening through which she might get out to find a place of her own to sleep. I sprang up and danced about her, edging her towards the fire as I clapped my hands in time to the music. Fanie changed the rhythm. Now I swayed my body from side to side, moving my feet only an inch at a time. 'Aits, you people. Hotnot!' shouted Fanie and sent his accordion plunging into wilder notes. I pushed Rebecca down beside him and went to stir the mealie-meal.

'Is it ready yet?' Mittee asked. 'I could eat the whole potful myself.'

Her face was bright from the fresh air. She had washed it that morning in a mountain stream that had left its sparkle on her skin. Doctor Besil's wound was healing and he could move easily now, so that one could have imagined that we were on a prolonged picnic.

The mealie-meal had simmered to a delicious moist thickness without a trace of burning. 'Plates please, it's ready,' I cried. Even Doctor Besil, who ate our porridge with long teeth, asked for more that night, while Mittee cleaned her plate twice and would have had a third helping if there had been any left.

I said tartly, 'It's only mealie-meal, nonnie, not the rich food you always used to say you would eat when you grew up. And it's from an old tin plate, not fine china. All she would ever talk about was how grand she would be one day,' I said to Doctor Besil, 'and now, so true, she is happier than I have ever seen her, out here in the wilderness.'

Mittee laughed. 'I got it all from English novels, Basil. A funny little pedlar used to give them to me. He was murdered and Selina and I found his skeleton.' She went on, not noticing the silence, 'Oh, I was vain, so vain that the minister delivered two sermons against vanity for my benefit. All the girls went home from church and snipped off flowers from their hats.'

'Did you?' asked Doctor Besil.

'Not Mittee,' I answered.

Then Doctor Besil began to talk about his boyhood. He drew a map on the ground to show us where he was born. We all said the name after him; Yorkshire. He told us of a little town hundreds of years old, where a man took up the pattern that his father had woven and repeated it in his own life, where he could say, My great-grandfather was born in this house and my children will be born here. He told us of misty skies and grass as short and thick as a carpet, sweeping over low hills to the sea; a place like Eden where a man could set his foot without fear. He told us of a boyhood passed within sound of church bells; of white men who worked like Kaffirs and of cities so great that Pretoria would be swallowed up inside them.

'My God, it frightens you when you think how different the English are,' said Fanie, drawing his blanket about him.

Fanie rested the oxen for a few days for a terrible climb lay ahead of them, and some of them already had tender feet. Though we were uneasy at the delay, it was a welcome respite for Doctor Besil and before we went on, he was able to throw away his bandages. We set off again under dull skies and as we penetrated deeper into the mountains, we lost sight of the thornveld and the forests. Fanie followed the course of a dry mountain river cut between forbidding krantzes where troops of baboons hid themselves as their sentries gave warning of our approach. We would hear the scattered sounds of their flight and then until we reached the next bend in the river bed we would be conscious of their watching eyes. Now and then a shower of stones rolled down from the krantzes as a warning to us. Fanie told a story to wring the heart, all about a mother baboon whose baby was taken from her by a hunter. She fell on her knees and raised her hands, begging for her baby. The hunter was so much overcome that he returned the baby to her.

'Christ, Fanie, you've almost made me cry,' I said, and Doctor Besil asked gently, 'Where did the baboon learn such tricks, Fanie?'

'Instinct,' said Fanie, 'but keep your hand on the rifle for where there are baboons you will find leopards and they will make a spring at you even in the daytime if you disturb them.'

I walked well away from the trees after that for I have seen a sheep that was mauled by a leopard. We had got out of the waggon because the boulders rolled beneath the wheels and you were thrown about until you were black and blue. This was when Mittee encountered the first real hardship for her feet were soon blistered from the rough walking. She climbed back into the waggon where she was bounced about until her body ached.

A few showers of rain had fallen and at the beginning of the day I enjoyed the walking, but as the clouds cleared the sun beat down ferociously, making each step painful. The sudden heat had made the oxen uneasy and their restlessness passed to Fanie. He stopped once or twice, looking back as though he were expecting some danger. Then he urged the oxen on faster, cracking his whip over the two back animals so that their powerful struggles sent the others trotting, with the waggon pitching violently from side to side. Disaster was coming upon us.

A wheel slid between two big boulders and before Fanie could halt the oxen to free it, it was wrenched off. He cursed and came round to look at the damage while Doctor Besil pulled Mittee from under the bag of mealie-meal and put her on a rock to see if she had broken any bones. She looked as if she liked standing up there while he was touching her.

He smiled at her. 'Nothing wrong that a little iodine won't set right.'

Mittee started swearing in three languages as her legs began to smart where the iron pot had rolled on her. At first she would not walk but I grabbed her arm and pulled her along as though she were Rebecca.

'See, there's nothing wrong with you, nonnie. Come and sit on the bank while they mend the wheel.'

Doctor Besil gave me his bottle of iodine for her legs and when I dabbed the stuff on, the swearing broke out again. 'God, nonnie, behave yourself. The missionary is a refined man. What he must think of you.'

We looked about well before we sat down; up in the trees for leopards and in the grass for snakes but the place seemed harmless enough. I put Rebecca between us and we drank a little cold coffee to pass the time. Down in the river bed, Fanie and Doctor Besil were sweating as they pushed a log under the waggon to raise it.

'Your Englishman looks handsome now with the axle grease and sweat on his face,' I laughed.

'You're getting vinegary, Selina. Guard against it. Go down and get me some biltong from the waggon. I'm famished.'

'Hi, nonnie, I'd be ashamed to go scratching for biltong while they are working so hard.'

We were arguing about the biltong when the storm came upon us. It seemed to come out of a clear sky but I remember now that a breeze stirred the air, striking cold on our heated bodies. Then we heard an explosion like thousands of guns going off at once. Forked lightning ran across the blackening sky and in the same instant hail shattered on the rocks. Mittee and I, with Rebecca's frail body between us, clung to each other, shielding our faces from the hailstones.

The rain that followed was so awesome that I shouted in Mittee's ear, 'It's a judgment, the end of the world has come.' We tried to crawl to shelter but we could see only a few inches in front of us and we crouched down again with bowed heads. The roar of the rain deepened.

'The river,' I screamed, thinking of Fanie and Doctor Besil beside the waggon, but my voice was like the bleat of a sheep against the roaring of lions.

The first shock of the rain passed but through the grey mist we saw the river boiling just below us and not a sign of the waggon in the yellow, frothy waters.

'They're both drowned,' I cried hopelessly to Mittee.

'No, there they are,' she cried, pointing to the two dark shapes that wavered through the rain towards us.

In our thankfulness at finding them alive, we did not realize how close to death we all stood. The river had swept away our waggon and all our supplies. Fanie blamed himself as we sat shivering beneath the trees.

'I knew this morning when the oxen became restless. I kept saying to myself, Fanie, outspan. But no, I thought, that devil of a Plessis might be behind us and I held on. Now it's all gone, oxen, mealie-meal, even the rifle.'

'We should be down on our bended knees thanking God for our deliverance, instead of harping on what you should have done,' I snapped at him, for never in my life have I been so uncomfortable, drenched with water until it seeped into my very marrow and hungry, knowing there was nothing to eat. Rebecca made everything worse by rubbing up against me like a dog trying to get itself dry.

Reminded of the strength of my prayers for the cow on the night we reached the valley, I fell on my knees and they all followed me, with heads bowed beneath the unappeased skies.

Doctor Besil found a small cave, a hole in the face of the mountain, where we could spend the night. We clambered down to it in the late afternoon, grateful that the rain had stopped and that a stiff wind was blowing some of the water from our sodden clothes. There was no hope of making a fire for though Fanie and Doctor Besil both carried matches, these were soaked. That night I envied Rebecca for she slept more soundly than she would have done in her own bed at home, while we lay sleepless side by side, each drawing a little comfort from the other as we shivered in our damp clothes.

'Fanie blames himself,' said Mittee to Doctor Besil when she thought that we were asleep. 'I am the one to blame. It's not you I feel so badly for because you were in real danger from Paul, just as I was. But these two. When you think how all their lives they have been poor and now they must suffer this.' He did not answer, and she said, 'Does your shoulder ache, Basil? Do you wish you had never known me?'

'I would rather be here than anywhere else in the world, Mittee. Long before I had seen you, I used to think of a girl called Mittee, beautiful and wayward and kind. I took every penny I had and bought you twenty-five yards of silk for your wedding dress after Selina had told me about you.'

'Selina?'

'Did you call me, nonnie?' I said spitefully. The cave was quiet after that.

As soon as daybreak smudged the darkness, Fanie went outside. He came back with three dassies that he had snared and while he skinned them, Doctor Besil struggled with a fire, growing bad-tempered with the damp matches and wet wood. The sight of the flames curling through the smoking wood and the smell of the grilling meat were more satisfying than eating the skinny dassies; but the very act of eating breakfast put some heart into us and we made a plan.

Doctor Besil knew of this kraal where we live now; right at the top of the mountain. The Kaffirs were his friends and would give us help but it would be a difficult climb. Less dangerous, he decided, than trying to get back to the valley without transport and arms, for with luck we would reach the kraal the next day.

We set off as soon as we had eaten, along the river course in search of wreckage from the waggon. The vultures were our guide and many miles further on we came upon a shattered wheel lying against a rock and near it, cast upon a high, flat rock, lay my Bible, already drying in the sun. We took this as an omen and looked eagerly for other articles but there was nothing else to be seen.

Only one ox had been thrown on to the bank, the others had been swept over a krantz, down which the river plunges into a narrow, terrifying gorge. Fanie drove the vultures from the ox and with his treasured knife cut steaks from the ruined meat.

It was Mittee who found the axe. She had taken off her shoes and stockings so that she could bathe her blistered feet in the river for she was in pain. She bent down suddenly and picked the axe from the mud with both hands. Such a yell of delight went up from the men that the vultures that had settled in the trees nearby flapped off in terror.

We cooked the meat there and then, eating some of it before we started our climb over the inhospitable rocks. It was Mittee who suffered most. She paid the price that day for her vanity in shunning the veld, for with every step that she took, she drew in her breath with the burning of the blisters against her shoes. We went more and more slowly so that she could keep up with us but we had to stop for her while the sun was still high for she could last out no longer but sat rocking herself with agony.

I eased her shoes from her feet. Fanie turned his face away. The stockings were stuck to the broken skin with dried blood and she yelled like a child when I tried to take them off. 'Wait a moment,' said Doctor Besil. He went back to a pool that we had passed and brought water in his hat to sprinkle on her feet so that the stockings would come away easily.

We sheltered that night in another cave and though we had a fire we were as low in spirits as we had been the night before for we knew that Mittee would not be able to go on.

'I will be all right in the morning,' she promised, but when morning came, the blisters had turned into sores and there were frightening red streaks running from her swollen ankles.

Doctor Besil gave us each a small piece of trek ox and as we chewed it, we talked over a plan. He would go on alone to the kraal and beg donkeys and mealie-meal from the Kaffirs while we waited for him at the cave. This was our only chance now and as I watched him climbing steadily I sent a loud chant of prayer after him. He heard me for he turned and saluted me.

It was a day of hope. Never had I seen a sky so tender, beautiful as the robes of the angels, never had I felt sun so sweet upon my face. The call of the partridges was on the air, drowned when the raucous-voiced hornbills swept past in swarms. From the rocks across the chasm on the side of the cave came the tiny sounds of dassies playing in their hundreds in the sun but when I crept along to look at them, the rocks were bare in a few seconds as they tumbled into crevices and holes.

Fanie was angry with me for frightening them. He had tried that morning to trap a klipspringer but it was an unlikely chance, he said, and we would have to rely on the dassies for food until Doctor Besil came back. He had found the old dassies lazy and easy to snare if he came on them by stealth.

All the day he spent storing the cave with firewood and the next day he trapped dassies, cooking their flesh so that they would keep, for he was uneasy, prophesying more rain. It was as well he did these things for on the third day after Doctor Besil had left us, the rain started again.

That dreadful cave. Its floor was of black, pitted rock that bit into the flesh through the grass and leaves we had put down for beds. Its jagged roof scraped your head when you stood up straight. Even the firelight could not penetrate its shadows and when the rain started it was as black during the daytime as at night.

We tried singing psalms but the beat of the rain made our voices melancholy. Mittee tried telling us stories about her trip to Europe but the gift had left her and she would stop in the middle of a sentence, listening. Then Fanie would go to the opening of the cave and watch for Doctor Besil but without much hope.

'This rain might hold him up for days,' he said. 'There's a curse on us, so true.'

CHAPTER XV

A merry little fire jeered at our long faces as we chewed at the obstinate, dried flesh that was our evening meal. Every second mouthful that I chewed I forced between Rebecca's teeth for she would not take a whole piece in her mouth. She interrupted me constantly by moving with great cunning to the entrance of the cave. You could not imagine that any creature would be so foolish as to want to go into that rain, but there it was, you had to watch her all the time. In the end, I grew so angry with her that I pinched her. She gave me away to Fanie by squeaking.

'What did you do to her?' he cried.

'She must have scraped herself on the wall or perhaps I pushed her a bit, Fanie. I can't understand her, she wants to go out in the rain, I'm only trying to help her.'

'You pinched her,' said Mittee, as she wrung the last drop of nourishment from a little bone.

'She doesn't understand anything. You know that and yet you hurt her.' Fanie shook me as he spoke.

Mittee threw the bone into the fire, wiping her hands fastidiously on the hem of her dirty dress. 'Fatherland, how filthy I feel. As soon as the rain stops, we'll rinse out our dresses, Selina.' Her feet had healed but she still limped slightly as she crossed the cave. She pushed Rebecca on to her bed and patted her to sleep with a firm kindness that not even the old nuisance could withstand.

Fanie slept against the wall, with Rebecca next to him, while Mittee and I took the first watch. We spoke in whispers of the past and the future but neither had reality, for we were trapped by the walls of the cave and by the driving rain.

I dozed off, to waken with Mittee's hand on my shoulder. 'Listen, Selina.'

There it was, a sound that brought Fanie to the fire with an armful of wood; the roaring of a lion on the mountainside. It was the first we had heard since we left the thornveld behind us.

'There is only one. Don't be afraid, he will not come near the fire,' Fanie consoled us, but he built another fire, closer to the entrance of the cave.

We watched all night until the twilight of dawn came upon us in soft shades of grey. Then we saw the lion slink past through the bushes, his body crouched as though he was stalking.

Had I ever been afraid of shadows on the veld, of ghosts? Had harsh words and boxed ear ever made me cry? Had thirst and desolation seemed suffering? They were as nothing. The cave, the fire, Rebecca, Fanie, Mittee; they fell from my sight and I was alone, separated from all things by terror.

Close by, the lion roared and the walls of the cave threw back the echoes to us tauntingly. My heart, that had seemed to stop beating, now sent the blood shouting through my body and I was isolated no longer. The fire was burning strongly, throwing its light on to Mittee's sweating face. Fanie held the axe in his right hand while with his left he threw more wood on the fire. Pity for him burnt away my own fright for I could see that he was terrified but that he must pretend to be fearless for our sakes.

Mittee whispered, 'Oh, Fanie, he's after us.'

'I will look after you, nonnie. But we must keep on guard for this is an old lion and lame in one foot. He is hungry to come so close.'

If we spoke that day at all, it was about the lion. And where we had watched for Doctor Besil only now and then, we prayed for his coming with such intensity that we looked every hour, sure that God must send him that day with weapons and transport. But the long twilight of the day ended and still Doctor Besil did not come.

I kept Rebecca awake all day so that she would sleep without worrying us when it grew dark. The only way to keep her awake for long was to pour water over her face, and I dipped my hand into the calabash whenever Fanie's back was turned or when he fell into a doze. The rain came down harder and harder. Fanie said we might as well give up hope of seeing Doctor Besil until it eased.

We did not see the lion though we watched all night for him, nor did we see him the next night, but we could hear him roaring on the mountain. We were afraid to go out of the cave even during the daytime but Fanie made us walk on the rocks, so that we should not foul the cave. Rebecca would not sit down for a minute though we waited half an hour for her. We were getting drenched but she made off at once for a large rock beside the narrow chasm near the cave. It must have been this rock that she had set her heart on from the start for she patted the coarse ferns that grew about it and prepared to lie down there.

My temper rose when I saw how far Fanie let the old mad thing stray from the cave. If that fearsome dun-coloured shape would spring through the mist, what then? I shouted this at him but he said that the lion would not come out of its lair in the daytime.

'I've heard of it,' I shouted.

'Ag, the things you've heard.'

I was so angry when he brought her in at last that I leaned over and under his very eyes caught a good hold of her buttock, beneath her skirt, twisting and pinching the flesh until she squeaked and squeaked again. Fanie threatened me with the axe but I went on pinching her without saying a word. He tore her away from me and then in a fury to equal mine, shook me until every bone in my body rattled.

'Why do you hurt her? You wicked, pinching cat.'

I screamed at him, 'Why do you let her go out there where the lion can get her and you, too?'

'Hi, stop fighting,' said Mittee. 'Isn't it bad enough without all this screaming? Make up with Fanie and keep your mind on God, Selina. Pinching the defenceless old thing.' She rubbed the spot where I had twisted Rebecca's skin.

This soothed Rebecca so much that she fell asleep at once. I hissed at Mittee, 'The thing to do is to keep her awake in the daytime, then she's not a plague at night.' As Fanie was busy splitting wood for the fire, I sprinkled water over her face, whereupon she awoke and began to shuffle towards the entrance of the cave. Fanie forced her to sit beside him.

When he noticed the water on her face, he said discontentedly, 'She's been crying, you must have hurt her when you pinched her . . .'

'Ag, voetsak! You know she hasn't got enough sense to cry.' I turned my back on the lot of them and went to sleep.

We did not hear the lion though we sat far into the night, nursing the fire. Fanie put Rebecca to bed at the back of the cave and then made me sit next to him, curling his fingers into mine. We smiled at each other again. That night his beauty caught at my heart and I thought sorrowfully that never could I bear a child to him. It seems strange that that hideous little Rebecca should have given birth to such beauty. His skin is dark gold, his beard and hair rich to the touch; his fingers are long, with rosy nails like a white man's; his eyes large and soft as a buck's. How sad that such beauty must wither with no seed to replace it, but when I say that to him, he tells me not to mourn for he might have transmitted Rebecca's imbecility to his children.

I fell asleep, sitting up. When I awoke I watched the fire with contentment for it was still bright. Then I smiled to see Fanie and Mittee had both fallen into a sound sleep, worn out by the watching. Fatherland, if that lion should roar now they would jump out of their skins, I thought.

The rain had stopped and a savage wind was blowing. It swooped past the cave entrance with whistles and shrieks as though it carried a ghost on its back. From the mountain slopes came the sound of water hurrying in a thousand rivulets through the crevices in the rocks. The wind had torn aside the great cloud banks to show the moon, a guilty face peering into our cave.

I missed Rebecca's snorts and grunts and looked round at her bed. She was not there. I felt my way to the back of the cave, searching the rough floor on my hands and knees. Piece by piece I pulled the wood away and then I knew she was not in the cave with us. Like a mist an evil thought floated through my mind. Let her go, Selina, and she will not worry you any more. I gave it no time to take shape.

I went to Fanie's side and took him by the shoulder. 'Fanie,' I whispered, 'Rebecca is not here, Fanie.'

He sprang from sleep like an animal. He was at the back of the cave before I could put out my hand to stop him.

'It is no use looking. She is gone, she is outside. She crept away when we were all asleep.'

His eyes flashed in the firelight, hard as diamonds now, and the great vein in his neck swelled up as he mastered his fear. He picked up the axe, and with the smoothness of a night creature hunting, went out of the cave.

Mittee awoke suddenly as though somebody had shaken her. Her eyes were still dark with sleep as she looked up at me. 'What has happened? Where is Fanie, Selina?'

'Rebecca,' I whispered.

The firelight meant safety but I could not sit there while Fanie was outside. I crept to the opening of the cave but I could see nothing of him or Rebecca. Like a blessing, Mittee's soft hand stole into mine. Her body, warm from sleep, comforted my shuddering muscles.

Something stirred in the bushes by the chasm and then Rebecca squeaked. Something was hurting Rebecca and we heard its growling. The lion was growling as a dog does when he gnaws a bone, a sound so horrible that I vomited without warning.

Fanie brought Rebecca back. His step was light for she had no weight, she was like a doll, an ugly doll that had been torn to pieces. She was still alive though blood pumped like a fountain from her side and from her right arm. He stood by the fire, holding her in his arms and behind him I could see the moist, red imprint of his foot on the rock.

I was useless. I crawled away from them but Mittee was already tearing the skirt of her dress. When I looked again she had tied strips of the print above and below Rebecca's elbow and she was trying to staunch the blood with cobwebs pulled from the sides of the cave. There was blood on her now and sweat running from her temples in two little rivers. Fanie stood beside her, his face so blank that I was afraid that he had gone mad. I staggered over to him and caught his stained hands in mine.

'Fanie, how did you get her back?'

'That's right,' said Mittee in a faraway voice. 'Make him talk about it, Selina. You remember, Anna wouldn't talk about the Kaffir. This is the same sort of thing.' Her voice ran away from her suddenly. 'If Basil was here he would know what to do. If she would stop bleeding . . .'

I made Fanie sit by the fire and I tried to get him to tell us what had happened out there on the rocks. 'Tell us, Fanie, oh say something, we're afraid.'

The dazed look went from his face after a while but he would not tell us what had happened nor has he ever spoken to me of that night.

When the day had grown bright I went outside on to the rocks. The air struck crisply sweet into my nostrils after the smell of blood and woodsmoke in the cave.

I saw the body of the lion on the rocks across the chasm, half concealed by the bush behind which he had taken Rebecca. I walked timidly to the edge of the chasm. His head had been cleft with one stroke of the axe and he had fallen sideways though his hind legs were still drawn up and his tail outstretched in an attitude of feasting. The singing flies now took their turn at him. They flew in sickening masses from his mouth as I approached but some clustered round his eyes as if they had been glued. Their time was short for already the vultures were in the sky.

I pulled out the axe that lay buried in a mass of brain and blood to the haft for I did not want poor Fanie to have to clean it when we needed it. Then I washed it in a pool near the cave, scrubbing at it with a handful of fern until it sparkled. All the time, I fought against the sickness that the smell of the lion had brought on me. From nowhere a picture came to my mind of myself standing at a kitchen table, grinding coffee beans. Man, how I hungered for coffee. Even its sensuous smell would have been enough for me.

The axe was clean. I turned to go into the cave because the rain had started again, not steadily, but in edged, wind-driven gusts that made me shiver.

There, coming through the rain towards me, was Doctor Besil. He carried two assegais and he was driving before him two little donkeys, loaded with meat, and a huge calabash from which kaffir corn spilled with the movement of the donkey. Mittee had been watching for him and she ran into the rain with her arms flung wide in a tragic gesture. Was that Mittee, in the tattered, bloodstained dress? I was as vacant as Rebecca as I stood beside the donkeys while she hurried him into the cave, her voice labouring with her breath as she told him what had happened. There was a three-legged iron pot tied to one of the donkeys and I stroked its roundness with a feeling of pleasure for it brought back the memory of comfort, of kitchens with shining stoves.

'Bring in the pot,' Fanie shouted, 'we want hot water,' but before I could move he was untying it from the donkey's back.

I followed him into the cave. Doctor Besil knelt beside Rebecca, his hands as quick as a flame as he worked over her. He cut away the tattered flesh from Rebecca's arm and drew the deep incisions together with strands from Mittee's hair. It was an hour before he stood up and put his hand on Fanie's shoulder.

'I don't think that she will die of the wounds if we can get her back to the valley, Fanie.'

A faint smile came to Fanie's lips. The little cave was not so horrible, after all. Water spat and bubbled in the pot, the fire sang. Fanie went outside to offload the donkeys while I crouched down beside Rebecca. It was the first time I had been close to her since she was mauled and I tried to look at her without getting sick. Her wounds seemed clean but she lay in an unconsciousness so deep that her breath did not stir on my hand when I put it to her open lips.

I cooked some of the kaffir corn, careful of the grains as if they were gold. It was sweet on the tongue after the dassie flesh and we ate slowly, trying to bring some cheerfulness to each other with exclamations of delight. Doctor Besil, lowering his voice as though we were deaf, paid Mittee a compliment not on her efficiency in looking after Rebecca, but on her looks. For a learned man he sometimes showed a surprising amount of sense. The compliment did her as much good as the sudden appearance of a clean dress would have done. But our cheerfulness was forced and we did not speak loudly, afraid of our voices against the silence that shut us off from Rebecca.

When Fanie had washed out the pot and the fire was stacked high, Doctor Besil put his hand over Mittee's and turned his serious face to us. 'We will have to return to the valley, for Rebecca's sake.'

'There is no going back for you or Mittee,' I said, looking deep into his eyes. 'Even to wait here is dangerous. When he finds that Mittee is gone, I tell you, he will come after her even if the English are storming the pass. It would be better if we separate and you go on to Plessisburg while Fanie and I take Rebecca to the kraal on the top of the mountain.'

'We will have to build a sled to carry her,' said Fanie, 'and we would never get a sled up those mountains. We must go back to the valley, Selina, we could be there within six days.'

We talked about it this way and that but it was the only thing we could do. When the sled was built, Doctor Besil shared everything equally, even the money that he had in his pocket. For the first time in his life Fanie had ten golden sovereigns on his palm but I forced him to give them back and let him see the money that I had got for the cattle, though it seemed worthless to us then. They took the iron pot for they would be longer on the way, while we cooked our grain and stored it in a calabash.

On a clear, bright day we parted.

'You will be far from me but always close to my heart,' said Mittee.

'Nonnie, my nonnie, my Mittee.'

'Let us see you smile,' said Doctor Besil, patting my head.

He shook hands with Fanie and then set Mittee upon the little donkey, with her back against the iron pot, and they went their way. Fanie grasped our donkey stoutly by its rough bridle but I stood looking after Mittee. She turned again and again to wave before the rocks hid her from my sight.

I followed Fanie but I turned back for as I looked up at the cave, I saw the lion's skeleton showing vividly through the green grass where Doctor Besil had thrown it. I scrambled up to it and kicked it. The bones, still strong, scarcely moved. Overcome by hatred for the thing, I sprang upon its backbone. For a few seconds it supported my weight and then it crashed inwards. I lost my balance but I was up in an instant, kicking at the ribs until they fell apart from the rest of the skeleton. When all the bones were scattered in the grass, I ran after Fanie.

With one quick look at what I was doing, he had passed on. I took my place beside Rebecca, guiding the sled over the stones.

The left side of her body was covered by scars the colour of fresh liver, the claw marks of the lion. Where her arm had been chewed the flesh had twisted in its regrowth, knobs at which she tore because of the healing itch. I had to keep her hands still and as I bent over her I marvelled even yet that she lived. Maggots had crawled from her wounds no matter how often we washed them, her skin had shrivelled with a burning fever, but still her fragile breath continued. Looking into those dark eyes, as fathomless as the night sky, I wondered why God had let her live, and then remembering Fanie's love for her, I was glad.

Doctor Besil had warned us to feed her often for she was getting little nourishment from the weak pap we made out of the kaffir corn, fed to her drop by drop. Every hour or so Fanie would draw the donkey into the shade and I would feed her by soaking a piece of my petticoat in the watery pap.

'We will stop at the first kraal we come to,' said Fanie. 'Milk is what she needs. The Kaffirs will be kind to us because they know I helped Doctor Besil.'

'Pray God Paul Du Plessis doesn't find us.'

Once Fanie said to me while we were marching, 'You could have gone to Plessisburg with your nonnie but you came with me. I love you more now than ever I did.'

'Who would have guided the sled and nursed the old nuisance if I had not come with you?'

The way grew soft underfoot as we came to the gently rolling mountains and we saw again the wide basin of thorn and the forests.

On the third day, we saw a horseman riding towards us; and I was reminded of a youth riding to meet his beloved one Christmas time long ago.

'Plessis,' said Fanie, a shudder rolling over his body.

'Now let me speak, Fanie, for if he knows she is with Doctor Besil he will shoot us down and go after them. I have a plan.'

When he came up with us, he sprang from his horse, shouting, 'Mittee. Where is Mittee?'

I stood between him and Fanie. 'Baas, she was in the waggon when it was swept away by the river over a high krantz. There was nothing left, basie, nothing. We had got out of the waggon to make camp but she was lying down resting when the river came down.'

Now he will kill us, I thought, watching his eyes flash and darken and flash again as though a storm were raging behind them.

'Show me the place.'

Fanie shook his head. 'We can't go back. My mother is dying from want of food.'

Paul slid his rifle from its sling. 'Show me the place, bastard.'

'Let me draw a map for you . . .'

For answer, Paul sent a shot across the sled. Fanie cowered over Rebecca, his eyes as ferocious as Paul's. Paul mounted his horse and with the rifle across his knees, drove us before him into the mountains, moving his hand on the gun if we spoke one word.

He would not let us stop to feed Rebecca, he would not let us rest for more than an hour at a time, though Fanie and I went on our knees for Rebecca's sake. We travelled even in the darkness and then he would speak, though not to us, to himself or to an unseen person.

'I came as soon as I could. I had to stay with my men to the last. The Tommies are all over the valley, they'll be living in our house now . . . Why did she leave her rings, she was still my wife. Hi, Mittee, if I had only come sooner.'

When I had fallen twice, he left me behind with the sled and pressed on, Fanie running at the stirrup. I rested in the shade beside Rebecca after I had fed her but when the sun began to turn and still they had not come back, I drove the donkey on again, afraid that night would find us there with no shelter. I passed the cave without seeing them and made my way painfully to the river.

Fanie was on his knees, hewing a cross from a tree trunk with his knife, while Paul sat unmoving, a figure as menacing as I had pictured him on the night we set out from the valley. The sun had fallen behind the farthest ridge and a chill wind, with a taste of mist in it, whispered through the trees.

The wind seemed to ripple through Rebecca's body and pass through her throat in a long, faint sound. I tried to feed her from my own mouth but her lips turned cold beneath mine. I threw myself upon her like a lover to warm her but not a tremor came from her wasted body.

Fanie had set the cross on the edge of the krantz, piling stones round it to keep it secure, and now Paul was carving Mittee's name into the wood. As he cut each letter, he called upon her and the echoes laughed back at him. As though she had answered he reached out his hands to the delicate sound. 'Mittee, Mittee.'

I whispered to Fanie, 'Rebecca is dead,' and pointed to the rifle that lay in the grass behind Paul. Only Fanie and I know that he lies at the bottom of that terrible gorge.

Fanie tells me that the English soldiers who settled in the valley after the war still speak of Paul as the mad Boer General for he led his men in charge after hopeless charge long after the valley was overrun. It was only when he saw that the end had come that he went after Mittee, though he told nobody, not even old Gouws, so that it is believed to this day that he fell in the battle for the valley. The Du Plessises put up a tall monument over a body found on the ridge weeks after the battle, a grand sight to see, says Fanie, even if the wrong man lies beneath it.

The weathered cross stands stark against the sky, as a warning to travellers through the mountains. Only faintly can you see the letters of Mittee's name carved in the wood and the few who pass that way spell it out with difficulty, throwing the word to the laughing echoes, as Paul did when he cut it out of the wood.

For me the shine of the stars and the colour of the sky have grown dimmer. When I was twenty I would sometimes stand alone on a kopje and reach my hands to the sky or lay my heart against the veld for I saw God in all the world about me. I used to laugh so loudly then that Mittee would shake me to quieten me.

GLOSSARY

The following is a list of the majority of the Afrikaans words which appear in *Mittee*. The definitions are intended as a loose translation of the words as they occur in this Penguin edition.

aits!	look out! help! sorry!
assegai	spear
baas/basie	master/young master
biltong	air-dried salted strips of boneless meat
boermeal	brown wheat flour
buchu brandy	an infusion of buchu leaves in brandy, used medicinally
burgher	citizen
bywoner	tenant farmer
calabash	gourd
dassie	rock-rabbit
doek	headscarf or cloth, tied about the head in various ways
duiker	small species of antelope
hoera	hooray
hotnot	vulgarization of Hottentot, sometimes used as an exclamation
impi	a Zulu fighting force
inspan	to harness up oxen
jukskei	game of skill similar to horseshoe pitching, but played with yoke-pins
Kaffir	former, now pejorative, term for a black person
kaross	blanket of sewn animal skins
klipspringer	mountain antelope
koedoe	large species of antelope with curling horns
kopje	hillock
korhaan	bustard
kraal	enclosure for animals; tribal village
krantz	overhanging cliff-face or crag
laager	encampment of waggons
lappie	cloth or rag used for cleaning
mealie-meal	finely ground maize meal
morgen	measurement of land, a little over two acres
Nagmaal	sacrament of Holy Communion, celebrated quarterly in the Dutch Reformed Church
nonna/nonnie	mistress/little mistress
oubaas	old master
Outlander (uitlander)	foreigner (especially English)
outspan	to unyoke oxen; to break a journey
rand	ridge of hills or mountains
ringhals	ringnecked cobra
rondavel	circular house, usually one-roomed

sjambok	whip made from rhinoceros or hippopotamus hide
skei	yoke-pin
springbok	species of gazelle peculiar to South Africa
stoep	raised verandah running round a house
thornveld	thorn-covered plain
tickey	old threepenny piece
tickeydraai	traditional dance
tronk	prison
veld	grass-covered plain
veldschoens	handmade shoes of untanned hide
voetsak!	get lost!
voorloper	leader of a team of oxen
Voortrekker	Boer pioneer

Afterword by J. M. Coetzee

Daphne Rooke was born in 1914 in the Transvaal province of South Africa. Her mother came from a prominent Afrikaans family; her father, who was English-speaking, died in World War I. Educated in English-language schools, Daphne was also at home in the language and culture of the Afrikaner; an uncle, Leon Maré, still occupies a minor niche in Afrikaans literary history. Through spending part of her childhood in Zululand, she became familiar with the Zulu language and customs; her novel *Wizards' Country*, set in the Zulu kingdom of the 1870s, is one of the more thoroughgoing efforts of empathic identification by a white writer with a black world-view, albeit an imagined one.

In 1946 Daphne Rooke won a contest for new writers, for which the prize was publication of her manuscript (ironically by an Afrikaans publishing house – till the 1970s English-language publishing in South Africa tended to wait rather timidly for London's lead). Retitled *A Grove of Fever Trees*, her novel came out in 1950 in the United States, and then in Britain. It was soon followed by *Mittee* (1951), which was widely translated and brought Rooke her first taste of fame and fortune. During the next fifteen years she produced a series of successful novels (*Ratoons* 1953; *Wizards' Country* 1957; *A Lover for Estelle* 1961; *The Greyling* 1962; *Diamond Jo* 1965), as well as children's books. Though widely read, she was not regarded (and perhaps did not regard herself) as a serious writer: her romances of blood and passion set in bygone times or in incestuous settler communities – 'colonial Gothic', one critic called them – seemed to have little relevance to the great issues of the day.

Married in 1937 to an Australian, Irvin Rooke, Daphne Rooke left South Africa for Australia definitively in 1965. There she wrote *Boy on the Mountain* (1969), set in New Zealand, *Margaretha de la Porte* (1974), set in nineteenth-century South Africa, as well as more children's fiction.

Since 1987, when *Mittee* was republished in South Africa, there has been a rebirth of interest in Rooke in her native land. To a large extent this interest has been generated by feminist readers and critics of a literary tradition that has been shaped to an unusual extent by women writers. The originating South African novelist was Olive Schreiner (1855–1920); the 1920s and 1930s were dominated by Pauline Smith (1882–1959) and Sarah Gertrude Millin (1889–1968); the pre-eminent figure since the 1950s has been Nadine Gordimer

(b. 1923); while the formative period spent by Doris Lessing (b. 1919) in Southern Rhodesia and South Africa earns her a natural place in the tradition. The first question to ask, then, is whether Rooke belongs in the line of Schreiner, Smith, Gordimer and Lessing, writers engaged with moral and political issues of class, race and gender in South Africa, and with the deeper human problems of colonial and postcolonial southern Africa in general, or with Millin (say) and the exploitation for literary/commercial ends of the more spectacularly violent features of South African life, the more picturesque episodes of South African history.

'Sometimes she forgets I am a coloured girl and calls me Sister. I love her and I hate her.' The 'coloured girl' who speaks is Selina; the 'she' who sometimes calls her sister is her childhood playmate Mittee, to whom she is now bodyservant, confidante and sexual rival. In a more equal world would Mittee and Selina be true sisters, would there be love and no hatred between them? Sceptically one answers, No: the germ of sexual rivalry lies too deep. What makes Daphne Rooke's *Mittee* different, then, from any other story of two girls competing for the same man – a man who, in this case as so often, is worthy of neither of them?

The answer has to do with the racial caste-system of colonial South Africa (*Mittee* is set in the Old Transvaal, but the mores and prejudices of Paul Kruger's Republic, as Rooke presents them, are no different from those of the Cape Colony): Selina desires Mittee's beau, the villain Paul Du Plessis, *because* Mittee (in her milk-and-water way) desires him, *because* Mittee is the object of Selina's obsessive imitation in all affairs, *because* to Selina her own desires are by definition inauthentic, the desires of 'a coloured girl'. The stratifications that set white and black in worlds apart, and leave 'a coloured girl' wandering in no-girl's land between them, define the consciousness of Mittee and Selina and of everyone in their society – everyone except the missionary-doctor Basil Castledene who, formed not in the colonies but in England, will eventually open Mittee's eyes to the error of her ways and take her away to civilization. What makes Rooke's girl-rivals different, then, is that one of them, the disadvantaged one, acts as a sexual being not out of pride of the body, not to assert her own desire and desirability, but in order to enact the desires, and to have a far-off experience of the desirability, of the rival who obsesses her, yet whom she can no more *be* than the leopard can change its spots.

This is by no means the whole story, however. It is the story that Selina, as storyteller, allows to emerge. But we would not be attributing excessive subtlety to Daphne Rooke, behind Selina, to wonder whether there is not a degree of self-deception in Selina's story, perhaps even a degree of willed self-deception. For though Selina tells a story in which the desires of white girls are authentic and the desires of coloured girls mere pathetic imitations of them, the novel *Mittee* tells a story in which Selina is the passionate woman whom Paul, once he has had a taste of her, cannot leave alone, while Mittee, confined by propriety as much as by layer after layer of clothing, is barred from fulfilment, moving from the shock and disillusionment of the nuptial bed through a phase of embittered contraception to what one can only imagine as ethereal transports with Castledene. In other words, there is a second story looming behind the first, a story invisible to its teller, in which Selina, by virtue of her colour, is the child of nature to whom pleasure comes naturally, while Mittee remains a frustrated heir of civilization and its contempt of the body.

I doubt whether Rooke sees through, or even consciously recognizes that she is here invoking, a myth of the black man – and even more the black woman – as a creature of nature in instinctive touch with his/her own desires, a myth which the greater colonial enterprise had no difficulty in incorporating into its stock of received ideas, particularly since its obverse side is that the black (wo)man is *slave* of her/his desires, incapable of those sublimations from which higher cultures grow. I am not even sure whether, at this stage of her career, Rooke questions the folklore that the merest touch of 'black blood' makes one *in essence* black, a child of nature, wild.

There are two related episodes in *Mittee* that are clearly intended by Rooke to reflect on the question of wildness and civilization. In one episode, a half-tamed baboon is loosed from its chain and terrorizes the women of the farm till Castledene arrives to calm it and lead it away. The farmers are not there to protect their women because they are away fighting the British; the baboon stands for the wildness that conquest has penned up but that may erupt as soon as the iron colonial grip is relaxed. (Shortly before this episode two black men do indeed exploit the absence of the farmers to go on a rampage. To her credit, Rooke does not indulge in the *ne plus ultra* of colonial horror-fantasies, a scene in which white women are raped, though she does come close to it. As for the offenders, the colonial grip soon reasserts itself: they are tracked down to the mission station and summarily castrated.)

But there is a second captive ape in the novel, a female with a 'tragic' face that sits on its pole forever staring toward the mountains where 'its tribe lived its thrilling life'. Under Castledene's tutelage, Mittee sets this monkey free. 'It's the most wonderful thing I ever saw!' cries Mittee as it races away to freedom. Wonderful indeed;

but, in the context of Rooke's parables of captivity, what does it mean? What is Mittee learning should be unchained, and what is the admiring Selina (also half in love with Castledene, though too overwhelmed with awe to do anything about it), telling the story over Mittee's shoulder, learning too? And what of ourselves, Rooke's readers: what are we being told?

I will not pursue the answer to my question because it is at this point, more or less, that Rooke loses control of her tale. And not only in *Mittee*: in other novels as well (most damagingly in *A Lover for Estelle*) she has recourse, when the going gets tough, to whisking her characters off into the wilds, away from civilization and its nagging discontents, to face life-and-death adventures instead. It is this habit of evading the implications of her own fables, this rather easy way of bringing novels to an end, that most damagingly backs the charge that Rooke is a mere romancer, out of her depth with larger issues.

I have thus far written of Selina as playing out the myth of the half-caste (the *bastard*, in even blunter old-style racist terminology) as a divided self, yearning to be white and civilized, drawn back willy-nilly to the darkness of nature by her never wholly submerged blackness. In South African literature, this is a myth associated particularly with Sarah Gertrude Millin and with her widely read novel *God's Step-Children* (1924). God's step-children are, in Millin's words (from a preface she wrote to a reissue of the novel in 1951, the year in which *Mittee* appeared), 'the mixed breeds of South Africa, those . . . who *must* [my emphasis] always suffer.' 'Mixed blood' is, to Millin, the source of 'tragedy': *God's Step-Children* tracks, through generation after generation of a single family, the tragic workings of the taint of black blood in the lives of those unfortunate enough to bear it.

Sarah Gertrude Millin is not a lone figure in the annals of racist thinking. On the contrary, she inherited from European and American biology of the nineteenth century an entire pseudo-science of degeneration which associated race-mixing with the decline of civilizations. Political discourse in South Africa between the world wars is full of reference to this pseudo-science. While the atrocious extremes to which the prescriptions of racial eugenics were carried under Hitler had the effect of driving the science of degeneration underground, and perhaps even of killing it, in the West, the shadow of the Nuremberg trials passed over South Africa too lightly to drive the lesson home: the laws of *apartheid* passed after 1948 depended heavily on it for their justification.

In line with conventional wisdom about people of mixed race, then, Rooke portrays Selina as a divided self; furthermore, the question of what kind of self Selina's posterity will have is blocked by having her left sterile after the jealous Jansie's assault on her. But, one must add, there is no hint that Selina bears the fatal flaw of degeneracy (her experiment with home-made brandy does not mark the beginning of a slide into alcoholism, for instance), and indeed her end is by no means tragic: sundered from her beloved Mittee, she nevertheless achieves modest happiness with the dutiful, easily pleased Fanie, while the tyrant Paul meets with a well-deserved nasty end.

Rooke returned to the Mittee–Paul–Selina triangle twice more in her career, developing different aspects of it. In 1962 she published *The Greyling*, an altogether more sombre book written in the shadow of the notorious Immorality Act. A young coloured woman who bears her white lover's child is murdered by him as he desperately tries to protect himself from exposure. The murderer's parents, conventional Afrikaners and supporters of the government, undergo a catharsis of pity and terror, adopt the child, and leave the country. Like Alan Paton's *Too Late the Phalarope* (1953), *The Greyling* records the devastation wrought by a law that sought to police the most intimate acts (the South African censors struck back at once, banning it). It is Rooke's most overtly political novel, one in which she adopts, not without unease, the mode of naturalistic tragedy practised by Hardy and Dreiser. The tragedy she sees, however, is not Millin's tragedy of blood, in which misfortune proceeds inexorably from a taint in the blood, but the tragedy that results when a fragile and unequal sexual relationship is placed under threat of public censure and legal prosecution. The coloured woman in Rooke's story is friendless and socially isolated, the white boy has a streak of sadism (to say nothing of racism) in him: disaster is inevitable.

In 1974 Rooke re-explored the Mittee–Selina rivalry in a novel of failing power, *Margaretha de la Porte*. The wealthy heiress Margaretha has a Bushman servant and 'sister', a vulgar and irreverent shadow of herself, envied and punished for the satisfying, 'natural' sex-life she seems capable of leading. After some highly implausible machinery has been brought in to justify the move, Margaretha, in an act of mercy, strangles her mortally wounded shadow-sister with her bare hands; the book ends with an unhappy Margaretha, thwarted as an artist, baffled in her desires, facing the whispered censure of her community.

Thus far I have treated the tensions with which Rooke deals, and which structure her books, as racial in nature. But the murderous Paul in *Mittee* and Marten in *The Greyling* are not only whites exercising white power, they are men exercising male power in the crudest of ways. Rooke's novels are full of male violence. A farmer stifles his dying wife's newborn child, forcing his daughter to bring up her own illegitimate baby in its place (*Ratoons*). A German baron packs off his gifted but eccentric young bride to a bleak asylum to have the nonsense knocked out of her (*Margaretha de la Porte*). A teenage boy rapes and kills an insufficiently welcoming girl (*Boy on the Mountain*). An Indian husband rapes his eight-year-old bride (*Ratoons*). A miner rapes and casually disposes of a woman (*Diamond Jo*). An attractive, simple-minded boy turns out to be a murderous psychopath (*A Grove of Fever Trees*).

Male power in Rooke's world is not exercised at a remove (through money, for instance): women who look to men for love are as likely as not to find violence and oppression instead. This is the disillusioning truth Mittee discovers when she marries Paul. It is a truth Selina has already learned, though it does not stop her from returning to Paul again and again. What draws the two so obsessively together? To explain Paul's craving, Rooke seems to hark back to the folklore of the *luxe et volupté* of the half-caste woman, mixing savage abandon with European refinement of pleasure. Selina's own motivation is harder to understand or accept. Is she simply continuing to compete sexually with Mittee; or is Paul to be understood as one of those dark, forceful men whom, in the world of romance, women find irresistible; or is Selina, as a creature of romance too, seeking in Paul's embrace her own romantic doom? The retrospective first-person narrative mode makes deeper motives such as these difficult but not impossible to explore. As is often the case when she is in a fix, however, Rooke dodges the problem by shifting into a higher rhetorical gear: 'Would I live again those nights of terror and passion? Each time I said to him, I will never come here again. But when the moon was high and nothing stirred on the veld but the night wind, I would leave my mat in Auntie Lena's house and run down the path . . . to the great wild fig tree.'

The somewhat asexual Mittee is not typical of Rooke's heroines. For the most part they are frankly physical beings, in quest not only of love but of glamour and of sexual experience too. In the context of the high-minded but rather prim South African liberal novel, Rooke's world of pissing and farting, of menstruation and masturbation and orgasm (for which her code-word is 'his/her moment') is a welcome relief. It is a world seen through the eyes of children: not of the presexual children of Schreiner's *African Farm* but of vigorous late teenagers, typified by Andrina in *Mittee*, who stalks about in a sexual fever-heat, laughs 'low and sweet' in the bushes, allows 'a long, slender leg, bent in ecstasy' to stick out – desiring beings not yet trapped in the net of proprieties and obligations that has turned their parents into such hypocrites. In this respect Rooke brings together two commonplaces of Romantic primitivism: that savages and children are Man in unfallen state, that civilization is the great enemy (in an interview as late as 1956 she spoke of her fear that the Zulus would be spoiled by civilization; *Wizards' Country*, over which she laboured for three years, is a lament for the passing of the old Zulu world).

In fact, it can be argued that for Rooke the fundamental conflict is not between black and white, not between man and woman, but between young and old. The narrator-heroes and -heroines of her books are all young; even when they are nominally looking back on their youth from a distance (as in *Mittee*), this distancing device is purely nominal: the narrating, experiencing sensibility is young, indeed juvenile. *Boy on the Mountain* breaks down the book-trade distinction between juvenile and adult fiction in a disturbing way, weaving a trail of drug addiction, violence, sex and death through a story of public schools and masculine sports, of youthful camaraderie and gauche courtship. The crude comedy of *Mittee* (circus animals lifting their tails and spraying the well-dressed public, old men swallowing lizards' eggs thinking they are pills, runaway carriages that upset their drivers into patches of thorns) appeals to a child's sense of humour. Selina's consciousness may be intended to be a divided consciousness, a bastard consciousness, or something even more complicated, but it is above all a juvenile consciousness, unrefined, unsocialized, crude, eager.

Crude and eager too are the young Afrikaner men who surround Mittee: great laughers and jokers and pinchers of bottoms and players of pranks. With a difference, however: Rooke has an eagle eye for the sadism indulged by a male culture of pranks, and for the sinister latitude allowed to prank-players in a country where a white skin means invulnerability (the prank-players set an Arab's beard on fire and pass on, laughing at his anguish). In a telling comment on these same young men, now become fighters in a war against the British, she writes: 'Their eyes had grown watchful. Sometimes they spoke of the War; of the stealthy rides across the veld, of the blowing up of trains, as exciting as a vicious practical joke.' Practical jokes and sabotage: two sides of the same coin, the first a training-ground for the second, turning boisterous boys into hard men.

One of Rooke's more engaging features as a writer is a robust familiarity – or at least the appearance of such – with the wider world. She crashes boldly into such preserves of the male writer as public-school life, warfare, sport (even boxing!) and casual philandering. She seems to know all about the economics of sugar farming, the workings of land tenure, the tricks that traders use to cheat rural blacks. She handles colloquial Afrikaans, which she imitates in English to give the dialogue of books like *Mittee* a stylistic colouring, with a sure hand. (This practice explains such exclamations as 'All the world!' or 'Almighty!' which pepper the dialogue, as well as Mittee's odd-sounding and vulgar warning to Selina, 'Watch your mouth, you thunder, you lightning!' When Selina is spoken of, in her presence, as a 'creature', more of a racist jab is intended than may be apparent: *skepsel*, which 'creature' translates, is a common term of disparagement for a person of colour.)

On the other hand, Rooke's novels are no models of fictional composition. All too often she loses her narrative line in a welter of detail, in recountings of tangential events, parades of ephemeral characters with confusing names, writing with her nose so close to the page that she loses sight of the larger picture.

Like other novelists of her era, she thought of the last decades of the nineteenth century – the scramble for diamonds and gold, the Zulu Wars, the Anglo–Boer War – as the high point of South African history, a time when adventure and excitement at last broke into the country's long provincial slumber. These decades supply the materials for her historical romances. Reading Rooke today, we would probably find more sobering historical interest in a novel like *Ratoons*, set in her own day, which traces the ramifying tensions in the microenvironment of a white farming community as it loses land to more enterprising Indian competitors and begins to clamour for protective legislation ('Group Areas').

Rooke's position on black–white conflict is broadly liberal. In *Mittee* she sides with the missionaries as protectors of black interests against the rapacity of white farmers. In *Wizards' Country* she records the less-known aftermath of the pitched battles fought and lost by the Zulus against British armies: organized destruction of their homes and decimation of their herds by gangs of settlers. If her novels in general give a voice to the woman as underdog, and the child as double underdog, then *Mittee* in particular gives voice to the black woman child, trebly oppressed. (To cap it all, Selina is shunned by the Shangaans, her mother's people.)

Rooke's treatment of settler society – the society in which she grew up in Natal – varies from the genially satiric to the savagely accusatory: some of the malicious exchanges of gossip in *Ratoons* are worthy of Patrick White's Sydney suburbs. If she avoids adult protagonists, it is perhaps because she cannot imagine an older person who has not been deformed by the boredom, moralism, philistinism and prejudice of colonial life.

Parents in Rooke's world are capable of the vilest oppressions.

They extort emotional and sexual consolations from their children, they tell them the most fantastic lies (that they are feeble-minded, that they bear hereditary taints, that they are products of incestuous unions) and hint at the most fearful punishments (castration, sterilization) to keep them at home and prevent them from knowing love. Mittee has had the good fortune to lose both parents at the age of two. She promptly discards the name they gave her (Maria) and becomes her own person, Mittee – a baby-name, as Castledene observes, and one she has difficulty outgrowing.

The generative energy for Rooke's fictional project comes from a shadowy family ur-romance whose outline is only dimly discernible at the surface level. It includes siblings locked in murderous rivalries, revered but treacherous fathers, engulfing, devouring mothers. The family in Rooke's imagination is the site of a war of all against all; those who escape alive refrain, perhaps wisely, from reproducing it.

CLASSICS OF THE TWENTIETH CENTURY

The Age of Reason Jean-Paul Sartre

The first part of Sartre's *Roads to Freedom* trilogy, set in the volatile Paris summer of 1938, is in itself 'a dynamic, deeply disturbing novel' (Elizabeth Bowen) which tackles some of the major issues of our time.

Death of a Salesman Arthur Miller

One of the great American plays of the twentieth century, this classic study of failure brings to life an unforgettable character, Willy Loman, the shifting and inarticulate hero who is none the less a unique individual.

The Echoing Grove Rosamond Lehmann

'No English writer has told of the pains of women in love more truly or more movingly than Rosamond Lehmann' – Marghanita Laski. 'This novel is one of the most absorbing I have read for years' – Simon Raven in the *Listener*

Three Lives Gertrude Stein

A turning point in American literature, these portraits of three women – thin, worn Anna, patient, gentle Lena and the complicated, intelligent Melanctha – represented in 1909 one of the pioneering examples of modernist writing.

In the American Grain William Carlos Williams

'It's as if no poet except Williams had really seen America or heard its language' – Robert Lowell. 'Mr Williams tries to bring into his consciousness America itself ... the great continent, its bitterness, its brackish quality, its vast glamour, its strange cruelty. Find this, Americans, and get it into your bones' – D. H. Lawrence

Man's Estate André Malraux

Man's Estate (*La Condition humaine*) emerged from Malraux's experience of witnessing the doomed Communist rising in Shanghai in 1927. Against a background of violence, betrayal and massacre, his characters are driven to try to transcend the 'human condition'.